Also by Jim Brown

24/7

JIM BROWN

BLACK VALLEY

PAN BOOKS

FT
Pbk

First published in Great Britain 2003 by Pan Books
an imprint of Pan Macmillan Ltd
Pan Macmillan, 20 New Wharf Road, London N1 9RR
Basingstoke and Oxford
Associated companies throughout the world
www.panmacmillan.com

ISBN 0 330 41246 9

1 3 5 7 9 8 6 4 2

A CIP catalogue record for this book is available from
the British Library.

Typeset by SX Composing DTP, Rayleigh, Essex
Printed and bound in Great Britain by
Mackays of Chatham plc, Chatham, Kent

To Kenneth and Beverly Herr, whose wisdom, love, and guidance has helped me more than they will ever know.

And to Kathryn, who holds me at night when the dark things slip off the page.

acknowledgments

My deepest thanks to my agent, Mark David Ryan, of the New Brand Agency, whose instincts continue to amaze me. And to Joe Blades, Vice President, Executive Editor, Ballantine Books, whose sage advice continues to teach me.

Many people helped in the completion of this book without necessarily realizing it. I would like to thank a few of them starting with my parents, Franklin and JoAnne Brown, who have always encouraged and nurtured my imagination; Shane and Carrie Hawks, whose passion for life and art is contagious; Brian and Lynne Lamb, whose friendship is like a lighthouse whenever I lose my way; Colin and Alison Stanton, who have been like family over the years; and Lauren Herr, who always offers just the right encouragement at just the right time.

And a heartfelt thank you to my baby brother, Tim Brown, and his wife, Vickie, who shoulder far more than their fair share of family responsibilities.

There are countless others I haven't acknowledged yet, so I guess I'll just have to keep writing books.

THEN

1

WHITEY DOBBS GIGGLED as dirt struck the top of his coffin. Not a giggler by nature, he was surprised by his reaction but continued to snicker in reply to each flat, dull thump. The coffin shook at first, then settled in as the sound began to recede, dirt on wood, dirt on dirt, becoming fainter, farther, until – nothing.

Quiet as a grave.

He laughed aloud, shattering the new silence, the sound of his own voice rushing back to him, a reminder of his close confines. Whitey put his hands over his mouth to stifle a snicker, chiding himself for his lack of control.

Get a grip. Don't waste oxygen.

Tentatively, like a newborn, the teenager explored the parameters of his world. His head rested on a thin pillow; his bone-white hair touched one end of the coffin, his feet just two inches shy of the other. The sides, padded and laced, pressed against his shoulders. Add in the extras and there was barely enough room for a body . . . *his body.*

How did the dead tolerate it? Nicely, he supposed. No one had ever complained.

Maybe he should suggest that as a motto for Perkins Funeral Home: *Eight hundred buried – no complaints*. The laughter came like vomit, swelling in his throat, rising up and rushing out. He fought to hold it back but feared he would choke.

Get control, get control.

He blinked to see if his eyes were open. Nothing. It was the blackest dark he had ever seen. Could you see the dark? He touched the lid of the coffin. It was just inches from his face, yet completely invisible . . . so close, so oppressively close. *No, since I can't see it, it ain't there*, he decided. It's easy to fool yourself in the dark.

Or go crazy.

Snicker.

Get control.

Despite the restrictions he managed to work his right hand into the pocket of his jeans. His fingers touched the smooth wood exterior of the knife. With the touch came control. This wasn't so bad, not bad at all. He was only seventeen, but he had already seen real horror. He'd looked right into its bloodshot eyes, smelled the liquor on its fetid breath, and fed it to the blade.

Nah, this wasn't bad at all.

He eased the knife out of his pocket, his fingers caressing its contours like a man touching a woman's breast. In his mind he traced his movements, seeing the knife's cherry-wood handle, painted a glossy ruptured-blood-vessel red, balanced by chrome caps on each end. On one side was a small, flat button – *the switch*.

He pressed it.

Click.

Flip.

Click.

Flip.

Not the smartest thing to do when you're as blind as the dead and confined to a coffin, but he wasn't worried. He knew this blade.

Like a teenage boy knows his dick, his father would say. Only his father couldn't say that, seeing how he was dead and buried in a coffin all his own.

Snicker.

This switchblade was his friend, protector, collaborator. It would never hurt him. And maybe when this was all over, he would feed it, give it a special treat, a taste of a sassy, spoiled little rich kid. There was a prissy bitch down at the college; he'd had his eye on her for some time. Maybe she should be next? Yeah, definitely the next.

He giggled aloud.

Where were they now? He wondered. Where were his four new friends? Had they finished? No, it was a very deep hole, six feet under. They were still up there. He just couldn't hear them anymore. Must be working up quite a sweat, shoveling all that dirt. The thought of them – four strapping rich kids in expensive shoes and sporting five-dollar haircuts – actually breaking a sweat appealed to him.

And what was he doing while they worked, while they performed physical labor for perhaps the first time in their pampered little lives? Nothing.

Just lying here, me and the worms; as still and quiet as a dead man, while you boys . . . alive.

He couldn't hold it back; the laughter came in waves.

JOHN EVANS DUMPED the last shovelful of dirt on to the fresh grave, then patted it down with the back of the shovel. The other three watched silently. Even trading off among the four of them, they were bone tired. John took a handkerchief from his back pocket and wiped sweat out of his eyes as the last red fingers of sunlight clawed at a purpling sky.

His cousin Mason took a beer from the cooler and opened it. "Hell of a deal," he said, taking a long, deep drink. He belched. "Hell of a deal."

"Damn. I can't believe we did it," Clyde Watkins said. "We really, really did it." Thick locks of auburn hair fell across his forehead. He pushed them back with his fingers.

"We?" Mason snorted. "Fuck that. Me and John did most of the work."

"Hey, I helped," Clyde said, brushing dirt off his trousers.

"You couldn't do shit for bitching."

"So? I don't like rutting around in the dirt like a pig. Shoot me." He straightened up, smoothed his shirt with the back of his hand, and smiled. "I have to save myself for the ladies."

"Fuck you," Mason said. He looked at the grave and laughed nervously. "Fuck you."

Nathan Perkins sat on the tailgate of the truck, kneading his hands. His eyes, magnified by thick glasses, seemed tethered to the fresh mound of earth.

"You okay?" John asked.

Nathan nodded, then pushed his glasses up the slope of his nose. His hand shook.

"Did we have to . . . to – you know, bury him so deep?"

"Six feet. No more, no less," John said, rolling his shoulders and rubbing the back of his neck. His muscles ached and burned. At six two, with a chest that could be rented out as a billboard, John Evans was an imposing figure. Still, standing on the crown of Hawkins Hill, with the town of Black Valley, Oregon, spread out before him like ruined stars banished from heaven, he felt positively tiny.

John stomped on the grave, his heavy boots packing the dark brown earth.

"Jeez, I can't believe the son of a bitch is down there," Nathan said.

Mason Evans grinned, his teeth iridescent in the twilight. "He's down there, all right. You can bet your sweet ass on that." He cupped a hand to his mouth. "How's it going down there?" he yelled to the grave.

"Shhhh . . .," Nathan said, casting a cautionary glance at the mound of earth.

"What?" Mason challenged. "You think the son of a bitch can hear us?" Beer and saliva escaped with the words. "You worried big, bad Whitey Dobbs is going to dig his way out and get you?"

He laughed, then looked at the others to join him. But John was too tired, his thoughts coiled in a knot of confusion and anger. Clyde just shrugged and smiled.

John watched the encroaching night, the slow, subtle saturation of dark, the elongating of shadows and pools of indigo and purple expanding languidly.

"Maybe this isn't such a good idea," Nathan said, running his finger between the collar of his shirt and his neck. He licked his dry lips. "I mean, what good can come of it? What's the best we can hope for?"

"Hey, we talked about this, and you agreed," Mason said, pointing with his beer bottle for emphasis. "You agreed. We all did."

"I know, I know, it's just, well . . . if Dad finds out I'm the one who took the coffin, he'll kill me."

"He'll never know," Clyde assured him, speaking with a confidence that always gave added weight to whatever he said, even when it was bullshit. He put an arm around Nathan's shoulder. "Besides, if he does kill you, I bet he would do the embalming for free."

Mason laughed too loudly. Nathan simpered.

John Evans said nothing, crossing his pylonlike arms across his broad chest. There was little that worried John, less that scared him. Still . . . He looked around the crest of Hawkins Hill. The darkness beneath the Douglas firs was slowly but aggressively crawling toward them.

John took a beer from the cooler. He put the cold bottle on the back of his neck and rolled it with the palm of his hand, letting it cool his tired muscles. A fresh wind moaned in the night bringing an unexpected chill.

He shuddered. A chill? Why did it always seem colder on Hawkins Hill? Dean would have known.

He looked down on Black Valley. Not much of a town, John thought, but it suited him. He liked the sameness, the continuity. Besides, when outsiders came . . .

He looked at the mound of earth. Anger flashed anew. He closed his eyes to let it pass. He opened them and looked at the sky. Thick clouds bottled the ambient light, cicadas sang their one-note song, and Whitey Dobbs remained buried in the loamy earth on Hawkins Hill.

"Let's ride," John said, hazarding one final look at the grave.

John and Nathan climbed into the old primer-gray truck they had used to haul the coffin. Nathan slid into the driver's seat as Mason and Clyde piled into Mason's '65 Chevy. The engine turned over on the first try. John looked back at the crown of Hawkins Hill; it was circled by healthy Douglas firs, but nothing grew in the center except a few faded weeds. No one knew why. Some said the place was spoiled, just bad land; others said it was haunted, that spirits killed whatever was planted.

"Jesus," Nathan cried, standing on the brakes, truck and passengers pitching forward then rocking to a stop. In the spray of the headlights a black leather jacket hung suspended in the air.

It swayed in the breeze and John saw the thin tree limb.

"Dobbs hung it on a sapling before we put him in the ground," John said.

"It looked like it was floating, you know?" Nathan said, then laughed nervously.

John glanced back at the hill.

Spoiled land . . . haunted . . . spirits kill whatever is planted.

Well, Whitey Dobbs was planted there now.

DEAN TRUMAN CLEANED the tabletops with a damp cloth and thought of Judy Pinbrow. He refilled the napkin dispensers, restocked the straw boxes, checked the salt and pepper shakers, and thought of Judy Pinbrow. He collected two stacks of mud-brown plastic trays from the top of strategically placed trash cans, passed them over the counter to the manager of the diner, then bagged and carried out three sacks of garbage, and thought of Judy Pinbrow.

Seven forty-five P.M.

She would get off work in fifteen minutes, be here in sixteen. He threw the garbage into the Dumpster, then walked back to the restaurant. He paused before going inside and took a deep, deliberate breath. The night air was damp and invigorating. *Stay calm, stay focused*, he told himself. This time there would be no wimping out, no distractions, no excuses.

"Judy, would you like to go out with me sometime?" That's all he had to say. It was simple, easy, but time dependent.

In two weeks Dean Truman would graduate from high school; then it was goodbye, Hooterville and goodbye, Judy Pinbrow – unless he screwed up his courage to at least ask her for a date. Judy was the stepsister of his best friend, John Evans. He had known her all his life and loved her, to some degree, just as long.

But Dean had never said a word. Can't be rejected if you don't take a chance. Can't win either.

I can do this, he told himself. *I can do this.*

He went back inside. The lights flickered. A second later thunder shook the store. The cash register pinged.

"Damn," Mr. Dwyer, the shift manager, cursed. He slapped the cash register on the side, then looked sheepishly at his customer. "Damn thing's froze up again."

"It's the storm," said the customer in a voice too big

for his body. "Damn thing came out of nowhere."

Larry Pepperdine was a disc jockey at the local radio station and as close as you could get to a celebrity in Black Valley. Dean had met him through Clyde Watkins, who worked at the station on weekends.

The lights flickered again. The cash register pinged. "Doggone. Sorry, Larry, it's gong to take at least five minutes for this to unfreeze. You can wait or – hey, Dean. I got a Buster Burger with cheese, fries, large Coke, and an apple pie."

"What size fries?"

"Extra large."

"Comes to five dollars and forty-nine cents."

Mr. Dwyer gave Larry an is-that-okay? look.

Larry smiled. "Sounds good to me. I've got a twenty."

"Change is fourteen dollars and fifty-one cents," Dean said before being asked.

Mr. Dwyer paid the customer out of his pocket, then scratched a note to himself to ring up the order later.

"How does he do that?" Larry asked.

The manager beamed. "That's nothing: watch this. Dean, what time is it?"

Five minutes until Judy Pinbrow arrives.

"Seven fifty-six," he said.

Larry checked his watch. "Bingo. And he didn't look at a clock?"

The manager puffed out his chest as if the trick had

been his own. "Not even a glance." He sacked up the goods. "I've tested him, tried to trick him. Doesn't work. Dean Truman always knows what time it is. Always."

"Jeez, kid, are you psychic or something?" Larry asked. "Is it some kind of magic?"

The manager made a face. "Don't say that."

"Magic?" Dean said, his voice several decibels higher. "Magic? There is no magic."

"Now you've done it," the manager said, rolling his eyes.

"Magic is the sanctuary of the ignorant. Everything, I mean everything, can be explained with science – if not today, then tomorrow, but eventually and with certainty. This is the most superstitious little town I've ever seen."

"It comes from living beneath the Hill," Larry said.

"Hawkins Hill?"

"Here we go," the manager said, shaking his head and chuckling to himself.

"More poppycock. Ghost stories, designed to scare children, that have somehow wormed their way into our collective conscience. The Hill is a fraud, a joke, and we're fools to be intimidated by it."

"Told you," said the manager.

"Is he always like this?" Larry asked.

"Only about science and spooky stuff. A side effect of being a brain, I guess."

Dean looked down at his feet, suddenly self-conscious. He picked up a cloth and began wiping the counter. "Sorry. I get carried away sometimes."

Larry Pepperdine laughed. "Hey, I'm with you buddy. The only magic I believe in is the magic I make with the ladies. Know what I mean?"

He winked and Dean blushed.

The disc jockey took his sack and was about to leave but stopped. "Have you heard from Clyde Watkins and John Evans yet? I'm curious how it went."

"How what went?"

Larry frowned. "You don't know? I thought, since you were friends and all . . ." He shook his head. "Never mind. Catch you later."

Dean nodded and went back to cleaning the countertop.

Seven fifty-eight P.M.

Judy Pinbrow worked next door at Helen's Cards and Gifts, and her Saturday-night shift ended promptly at eight. In recent weeks it had become her custom to stop by the restaurant after work and order a strawberry sundae with extra nuts, then sit near the front counter swinging her legs and talking to whoever was in the store. Dean would always make idle chitchat – ask her about movies she had seen, books she had read – but nothing more.

He envied her stepbrother. John the fearless. Nothing scared John, nothing intimidated him. John Evans could do anything. Talk to a strange girl – no problem. Fix a busted clutch – give him a wrench and get out of his way. Set a broken bone – he had done it for himself. John could mend, cut, saw, hammer, paste, plaster or punch any problem into submission.

All Dean could do was math in his head and tell you what time it was without looking at his watch.

"Just ask her out," John had told him. "I know she likes you. Besides, what's the worst that could happen?"

She could laugh at me, call her friends over and have them laugh at me, put my picture on a light pole so everyone in town could laugh at me, and then, the worst of the worst, she could say no.

Nevertheless, the Saturday before last Dean had almost done it, had almost summoned his courage. But the words had hung on his tongue like dew on a flower petal: "Judy, would you like to go out with me some-time?"

Then Whitey Dobbs had entered the diner.

"How's it hanging, Jimmy Dean?" he had asked, then laughed, a sound that caused Dean's flesh to crawl.

The moment was gone, lost like a child's balloon released from a sticky grip.

How's it hanging, Jimmy Dean? Always the same inane joke. But Dean had laughed, as he always did. Whitey Dobbs was the kind of person you went along with and hoped would leave without hurting you.

Judy wasn't in school the following Monday or Tuesday. And when he saw her in the cafeteria on

Wednesday, she had been uncommonly quiet, avoiding eye contact. Now Dean had the sinking feeling that he had missed his best chance. Hopelessness caught him by the throat.

Last Saturday she hadn't shown up at all.

His best chance blown because of a distraction, because of Whitey Dobbs.

How's it hanging, Jimmy Dean?

Whitey Dobbs. It wasn't just the knife, or the rumors, or even the white hair. It was the way he walked, the way he carried himself, the way he looked at you with those dark, deep eyes, like twin tunnels to hell.

Scary.

He had been particularly scary that night, though Dean would be hard-pressed to pinpoint why.

How's it hanging, Jimmy Dean?

EIGHT P.M.

Judy's shift was over, Dean thought.

The cash register pinged.

"Aha," the manger cried in victory. "Working again."

Now that he thought about it, there was something else strange about that Saturday. Dobbs had hung around for a long time, almost to closing. When he left, Dean had spoken the customary farewell: "See you later, alligator."

But Dobbs hadn't replied with his usual "After a

while, crocodile." Instead his face split into a bone-numbing grin. He leaned across the counter, so close that Dean could smell alcohol on his breath, and in a whispered sneer replied, "Ninety-nine Einstein."

Ninety-nine Einstein?

What the hell did that mean?

Then Dobbs had laughed, that God-awful, high-pitched cackle that put Dean in mind of angry crows on a tombstone.

Ninety-nine Einstein?

Odd. Whitey Dobbs was still laughing when he walked out the door.

Three minutes after eight.

Judy was late. The heavens rumbled. The lights flickered, holding on to darkness a second longer than the time before. The cash register pinged. The manager cursed.

Dean Truman frowned.

Ninety-nine Einstein?

SUCK AIR.

In the box under the earth Whitey Dobbs inhaled from a stiff plastic mask. The air tank was a comfort and a burden, increasing the time he could safely spend buried, decreasing the space he had to spend in it. To make room for the tank, he had to double up his legs and change positions to keep the blood circulating.

What if the preppy boys were wrong about how

much oxygen he had? What if he ran out of air, or worse? Oxygen tanks were tricky things. Turn the knob too much, a spark, and – *kaboom* – he'd be applesauce.

In addition to the oxygen tank, Mason Evans had mounted a small transistor radio to the interior side of the coffin. The radio, as much as the oxygen tank, was Dobbs's lifeline, keeping him informed of the time, allowing him to calculate how long he had left. He had been underground for thirty-eight minutes.

Twenty-two minutes to go. Piece of cake.

With six feet of earth above him, Whitey was surprised the radio worked at all. Still, it could pick up only one station: KDLY – "All country . . . all the time." In some ways that was worse then being buried alive.

Buried alive.

"I can do this." Twenty-two minutes. Nothing to it. Nothing. Hell, was this the harshest thing they could come up with?

"We've seen you around. You're not like the rest of the wussies in this piss-ass town. You've got an edge. I like people with an edge," John Evans had told him. "We're sort of making our own fraternity, want to know if you're interested."

Ordinarily Whitey Dobbs couldn't care less what anyone thought. But John Evans was different. He was the only person in this butthole town who might actually hold his own in a fight, and as a result, the only person Dobbs really respected.

"So, what's the catch?" he had asked. Dobbs had never had friends before, and he was surprised how much the idea appealed to him.

"There's an initiation. We've got to know if you have the stones or not."

That had pissed Dobbs off. He had almost pulled his knife on the big guy, but something in John Evans's eyes caused him to pause, some innate animal sense that told him if they fought, one of them would die.

"Give it your best shot," Dobbs had answered.

John nodded, then in a flat, even voice asked, "Are you afraid of the dark?"

Suck air.

THE DOBBS FAMILY, or what was left of it, had moved to Black Valley eleven months ago, shortly after Whitey's father died.

For Whitey, Black Valley had one and only one attraction – Aunt Gerty, his mother's timeworn older sister. While working in the sawmill, her husband had sliced his arm off at the elbow and bled to death before his coworkers could get him to the hospital. It was his own fault – everybody said so, even Aunt Gerty. But the plant had paid up nicely, leaving Gerty set for life with enough left over to take care of the poor baby sister and her vagabond family.

Whitey's older sister, Mary Jean, the bitch, ran off with a trucker less than a month after they arrived. The last anyone had heard from her, she was living in sunny fucking Florida.

So long, loser.

Soon after that, Whitey's mother discovered the comfort contained in a quart of Jack Daniel's. She moved into the bottle, and Whitey Dobbs was on his own.

"Just the way I like it," he said, grinning in the dark.

If the hicks in this dinky-ass town had seen him in Baltimore, they wouldn't have known him. Back then everyone knew him by his real name: Melvin. He was just another teenager, with moss-brown hair, acne, wet dreams, and a father who occasionally mistook him for a punching bag.

A good beating will make you a man, his piece-of-shit father used to say. Apparently, he was also trying to make a man out of Whitey's mother; she wore black eyes like other women wore new dresses. But Mary Jean, *the bitch*, got off without a swat. No, that wasn't true, not entirely. Whitey had heard the sounds coming from her bedroom whenever his father declared it was time to "feed the snake."

And she had been doing just that since she was twelve years old.

But not Tandy. Whitey's ten-year-old sister had always been special: smart, attractive, self-confident – a fluke, a unique splash in the Dobbs family gene pool.

"When I grow up, you and me are going to move to California," she would say to Whitey.

"California? Why California?"

" 'Cause that's where all the magic lives. I've seen it on TV. They've got palm trees, the Pacific Ocean, and sunshine, always sunshine. It never rains in California. That's a fact – they even wrote a song about it."

You and me. You and me.

Poor, sweet little Tandy.

Seemed like she had been fighting off the old man's advances from the crib. As a result, it was Tandy who received the harshest beatings – worse than Mama, worse than Whitey.

Worse.

But she never gave in. Never.

Click.

Flip.

Click.

Flip.

Dobbs worked the switchblade in the dark. He had found the knife in an alley shortly before *it* happened. One motion and *zing,* the blade danced in the air, reflecting unseen light and feeling alive in his hand. It was his first real taste of power, his first friend, and two weeks later he gave it its first meal.

The old man had beaten him badly that night, breaking his nose and a couple of ribs. Whitey's eyes were so swollen he could hardly see. Turned out he would rather have been blind.

They were all at home when it happened: Mama huddled in a corner, semiconscious, face red from

21

the beating; Mary Jean on the couch crying, watching.

That was when Daddy started on Tandy, right there in the living room. Whitey had tried to stop him. All he got for his efforts was a sound thrashing that left him whimpering on the floor, seeing through almost closed and mostly blurred eyes, almost blind, but not blind enough, lying there worried, worthless, and watching.

Don't remember. Don't remember. Tandy fought, fought hard – too hard.

Then his father screamed.

It was the sound of time screeching to a halt. That was followed by a quieter, subtle sound, just a snap, like a bug crushed beneath a boot, a twig snapped by a transgressor – the sound of Tandy's neck breaking.

Then the true silence, the pure and evil silence – his fiery baby sister a dead thing, a rag doll on the floor.

As the reality of what he was seeing clawed into Whitey's denying brain, it got worse.

That was when Whitey Dobbs went crazy.

2

"KDLY TIME IS TEN MINUTES *on the flip side of mine. I'm Larry Pepperdine and this is Hank Williams Jr. . . .*"

How much longer?

Suck air.

Fifteen minutes. The twangy country music filled the box like cold, wet mud. Whitey Dobbs rubbed the handle of his knife; he tentatively touched the blade. It felt warm. What if they forgot?

Suck air.

No, don't think about it; this is a piece of cake. He wasn't afraid of the coffin, or even of being buried, it was just that with all that time in the dark, alone with nothing but memories, scenes began to play across his useless eyes without invitation.

Suck air.

The police said it was self-defense. His sister's dead body and Whitey's own beaten face left little doubt. But there were still questions. He overheard a policeman talking with a nurse outside his hospital room.

". . . like something out of a nightmare, the big guy

23

filleted and gutted like a prize fish. And the blood, God Almighty, it looked like the kid had bathed in it . . . hell, looked like the whole damn room had been painted with it. Twenty-two years on the beat and I ain't ever seen nothing like it. And," the cop concluded with incredulity, "he's only fifteen years old."

"What about his hair?" the nurse asked.

"Brown, until yesterday. Now it's as white as cotton. Every hair, down to the root, white as a ghost."

Four months later, after the investigation had been closed and the newspapers had grown weary of the story, the Dobbs family left Baltimore for Oregon. Amazingly, the police returned the knife. Whitey vowed it would never leave his side again. Never.

Suck air.

"KDLY weather, it's fifty-eight degrees outside, and your local news is next . . ."

Black Valley wasn't Baltimore, but that was okay because he wasn't Melvin anymore; by then everyone, including his mother, had taken to calling him Whitey.

Despite his hatred of the old man, Whitey had inherited his father's violent streak – and his urges.

Feeding the snake, his father called it.

Whitey Dobbs had lost his virginity behind the high school band room on a Friday afternoon. The girl had been resistant.

Click.

Flip.

The knife had been persuasive.

It had been less then six hours since he had murdered his aunt. And it was the memory of smothering her with a pillow that kept him excited.

The police said his aunt died in her sleep. There was a small inheritance plus the house, which meant his mother could pretty much go to drinking full-time, leaving Whitey to his own devices.

Pocket money and most of his fun came from night jobs. Every few weeks or so Whitey would pick a house, sometimes in Black Valley, most often in other towns, then slip in when the residents were away or asleep, taking just those items that he could fence in Eugene. Sometimes he would pick out a woman, too, if she lived alone or her father or husband was away. There had been eight by his reckoning since that day behind the band room, eight different women and not one report. The knife could be very persuasive.

"For service, dependability and friendly financial help, come to the Farmers and Timber Bank, serving Black Valley for thirty-five years," the radio crackled.

Not much longer.

Suck air.

The giggles returned. If this was the toughest thing they could think of, they really were wimps.

So what if they buried him alive on the crown of the Hill. Hell, they left him with an air tank and a radio, for God's sake. *Easier than a ten-dollar hooker on a twenty-dollar date.*

Hawkins Hill.

Was that supposed to scare him?

He had heard the stories. High above the city, encrusted with trees, save a bald crown where only pale grass grew, Hawkins Hill was the source of rumor and legend. *Spoiled land, spirits dancing, haunted hill.*

Yeah, right.

On the radio Larry Pepperdine was giving the local news, something about a city council meeting, then some accident out in the country.

Suck air.

Hawkins Hill.

Something cold touched his leg. Whitey Dobbs yelped into his air mask.

What the hell? His mind raved, his cool forgotten. Rats? Snakes? Worse? Could something have gotten into the closed coffin? Using his left hand, he felt his leg. Water, just a few drops. He felt along the seal of the lid – wet. The coffin was leaking!

"Got to remember to complain to Perkins Funeral Home." He laughed, the momentary panic forgotten. "It must be raining like a mother for water to soak down to here." Funny, the radio hadn't said anything about rain. The news was over; Dolly Parton was singing a song that was far too perky for words.

What if the coffin continued to leak? What if it began to fill with water?

Suck air.

He closed the blade, then sprang it open again.

Click.

Flip.

The feel and the sound reassured him.

No, there was nothing to worry about. His time was almost up, and besides, he had air. Even if the stupid coffin filled with water, he could still breathe. He had an oxygen tank.

Whitey giggled into the mask.

On the radio the music stopped.

"This is Larry Pepperdine with a KDLY news update. There is new information now on that River Road accident. . . ."

Time's almost up. I can take it.

"Oregon State Police now confirm that four people are dead after their car was hit by a train at Junction Crossing, west of the city. . . ."

Suck air.

"The dead have been identified as . . ."

Suck air.

". . . Mason Evans, . . ."

The muscles in his arms began to twitch.

". . . Clyde Watkins, . . ."

A sharp, jagged shiver carved its way up his spine.

". . . Nathan Perkins, . . ."

He caught his breath in quick, hysterical jerks.

". . . and John Evans. . . ."

His heart froze between beats.

"All four were pronounced dead at the scene. Police say the accident appears to have occurred after the boys ignored the train-crossing lights. . . ."

The radio continued, but Whitey was no longer listening.

The only people who knew where he was, the only people who could free him, were dead.

His brain seemed to shrivel. Logic was gone, understanding was gone, control was gone. The world had been reduced to a single, all-consuming focal point: the lid.

He dropped the knife. He pushed against the top of the coffin with both hands, pushing with every ounce of strength in his body, pushing till his arms throbbed and the joints felt read to burst.

The lid remained steady.

Suck air.

There's an initiation, John Evans had said. *We've got to know if you have the stones or not.*

And now John was dead, Mason Evans was dead, Clyde Watkins was dead, Nathan Perkins was dead. No one knew where Whitey Dobbs was. No one knew he had been buried alive on top of Hawkins Hill.

And soon Whitey Dobbs would be dead.

THE BLOOD CAME with the speed and fury of a storm. Gena Lynn Blackmoore put her hand to her nose in a futile attempt to stop the tempest. Her hand filled to overflowing with crimson.

"A bad one, a very bad one," she whispered. She fetched a roll of paper towels from the pantry. "A very bad one," she repeated. Hadn't been like this since . . . ?

"The fire in sixty-eight," she muttered, her words as soft and fragile as a butterfly's wing.

The Black Valley Elementary School had gone up in a bright flash of red and yellow. Seventy-two kids died. The cause was never determined.

"All the same, it's a God-blessed miracle that more didn't die," her father had said, hugging her tightly.

Gena was only in the third grade at the time, but she knew it wasn't a miracle; it was the blood.

It had come that day, as it did now, gushing from her nose without warning, without stopping . . . and . . .

And what?

And she had known. When the blood came, so, too, did the feeling, she ran out of the class, rushed to the bathroom. When she was alone in the hall, the sensation grew stronger. She stood still, listening to the blood, her face drained white, as her dress and hands turned scarlet.

Then, with bloody fingers, she pulled the fire alarm.

In the aftermath no one realized that the alarm had sounded a good three minutes before the fire began. But once it was ignited, the blaze was so fast that three minutes was of little help. Not all of the classes made it out.

But hers did.

How many more would have died if not for . . .?

"The blood."

She never told a soul. Who would believe it? Born

29

and raised in the shadow of Hawkins Hill, she was already considered a little weird, even at that age. Sometimes even she didn't believe it. Perhaps it was a dream, a childish fantasy, wishful thinking – rearranging her memories to put herself in the heroine's role, a way of dealing with the trauma. But deep down she knew the truth.

So long ago, so very long.

The blood was just a dream – a faraway nightmare – nothing more . . . until now.

The sky roared; the rain fell harder.

Something bad was happening.

"What?" she asked.

This time, the blood was silent.

WHITEY DOBBS WOKE. He had passed out, exhaustion and fear casting him into a pit of mental darkness every bit as black as the grave.

How long had it been? How much air was left?

He grabbed the now silent radio and jacked the volume; nothing happened. The batteries had died.

"And so will I."

Suck air.

He could feel wetness; was the coffin still leaking? No, this was too warm to be rain. Putting a hand on his crotch, he realized he had peed in his pants. It didn't matter. A lot of things didn't matter when you were going to die. His heart shut like a fist around a wrench of rage and terror.

He began to pound the coffin lid, screaming with each blow.

The knife?

Click.

Flip.

He stabbed the top of the coffin, the blade sinking deep into the wood. Almost too deep; adrenalized muscles pulled it free. He stabbed again and again and again. Each time the knife bit into the lid, slashing the lacy canopy, gouging at the rigid ceiling. The blade sank deep, deep.

Then it was stuck. He pulled with both hands.

Snap.

The handle pulled free, the blade still buried in the wood – broken.

"No, no, *no*," Dobbs screamed, pounding the lid, striking with bare hands. All his might behind each blow, flesh to wood, flesh to wood.

Something warm cascaded down his arm. Blood. He was beating his hands into a bloody pulp, but the lid held firm.

"I could kill them all, I could kill them all!" Warm blood splattered his face as he battered the coffin lid, each blow sending a sword of pain down the length of his arm. He didn't care. Pain meant he was still alive.

If he could have seen in the dark, he would not have recognized his own reflection. His eyes saucer wide, patterned in red veins, his hands bloodied and mauled, rivulets of red racing down both arms, scarlet droplets covering his face, his teeth, his death-white hair.

The pain was eternal. His arms stopped moving, no longer strong enough to respond to his mental demands.

Silence.

A quiet a thousand times louder than the greatest sound the world had ever heard. The sound of nothing, of the end, of death.

Then . . .

3

She wasn't there. Her shift had ended more then twenty minutes ago, but so far Judy Pinbrow had failed to show. Was she angry? Had the weekend before last really been Dean's only chance, his only *real* chance? And now that he had blown it, was she lost forever? Was he doomed to a life of incompleteness? He could not imagine a future without her.

Where was she?

The fry machine issued a brain-numbing, elongated note. He drained the basket and dumped the fries with Pavlovian indifference. A baby cried. A mother shushed it with a pacifier. A man with long brown hair, beard, and mustache sat in a back booth, pumping a straw up and down through the plastic lid of his large soda, producing a disconcerting squeal.

And still – she wasn't there.

The door opened. Dean looked up expectantly.

In walked John Evans, Mason Evans, Clyde Watkins, and Nathan Perkins. The gang. They had been together since elementary school. Dean knew each of them, their moods, their likes and dislikes, as well as he knew his own. And that experience told him something was wrong.

Nathan's face was sallow, Mason and Clyde appeared positively delighted with themselves, while John had a sphinxlike expression.

They shook off the rain, then took a table not far from the counter – their usual. Clyde bought a round of Cokes, including one for Dean.

"Okay if I take my break, Mr. Dwyer?" Dean asked his manager.

"Sure, sure. Business is as dead as a graveyard."

A look passed between Clyde and Mason. They bowed their heads and snickered.

Dean slid a plastic chair up to the table, then turned to John. "Larry Pepperdine came in earlier. He asked if I knew how it went?"

John nodded, a slight movement like a mailbox in a stiff breeze.

"He seemed surprised that I didn't know what he was talking about," Dean continued.

"Uh-huh."

Clyde and Mason passed out the drinks, their faces flagged with smiles. Nathan tried to mirror their enthusiasm but failed miserably, looking instead like someone enduring a hidden pain.

"Okay, what the hell is going on?" Dean asked.

Clyde and Mason chortled. Nathan made a small bleating sound.

"Tell me right now or—"

"Or what?" Mason challenged. "What? You going to make me?"

"Hey – hey easy, guys," Nathan interjected. "Come on, keep your voices down. Stay cool. No fighting in the group. We're a team – Flash Five, remember?"

Flash Five. Dean smiled.

Ask any member of the group what it meant, and you would get a different answer. Clyde, the best looking, said it was because they were so photogenic. (They weren't.) Mason, the car nut, said it was because they drove fast and lived faster. (They didn't.) While Nathan, the meekest, said it was because they had rescued a group of cheerleaders from one of the mysterious flash fires that tended to plague Black Valley. (They wished!)

Whether the others chose to remember it or not, Dean knew the truth. And the name never failed to make him smile.

"Nathan's right," Clyde said. He held up his hand and spread his fingers. "Flash five, stay alive. Flash Four, group no more."

Dean relaxed. "You're starting to sound like Whitey Dobbs."

Clyde's smile slackened. Nathan shifted nervously in his seat. John Evans stared at nothing, then said, "Funny you should mention Dobbs."

Whitey Dobbs?

Ninety-nine Einstein.

"We buried him on top of the Hill tonight," John said evenly.

Mr. Dwyer lowered a basket of raw potatoes into a vat of hot oil; it hissed like a thousand coiled snakes.

GENA BLACKMOORE WAS DYING, a fact as cold and hard as the floor she was lying on, as sure as the falling rain. The blood wouldn't stop. She had tried to call for help, but the phones were out. The *storm*. Perhaps the neighbors? She had made it to the front door before collapsing in the archway. Rain splashed in through the screen. She could see the sky, see veins of lightning throb across black, muscular clouds.

The storm and the blood and the bad thing. All connected. Somehow.

Bleeding to death in my own home – goodness, won't Joel be shocked? Her husband was working the night shift and wouldn't be home until midnight. *How large will the puddle of blood be by then?* She wondered.

Her thoughts were becoming more disjointed, broken.

"Mommy?" The small, sweet voice focused her consciousness. She tried to turn her head but couldn't.

"Piper?" She said, not sure if she had actually spoken or only imagined she did. Piper. Her four-year-old daughter was supposed to be in bed, sleeping the sleep of the innocent.

"Mommy, what's wrong?"

Piper.

Gena's face flashed white from a spike of lightning and the heavens roared like a wounded beast. Something touched the back of her head, tiny fingers caressing her hair.

"Mommy hurt."

"Piper. No, honey, go back to bed." She gagged, choking on her own blood.

"Mommy, get up."

"It's all right, honey, go back to sleep. Mommy is just resting."

"I'm scared."

"Just a storm . . . ," she struggled, the words clotting in her throat. "Don't be afraid."

"Not scared of the thorm," said the child, stepping between her fallen mother and the open door. Lightning flashed. Gena saw her daughter in strobing silhouettes.

"Scared of the bad thing," Piper said, turning to face her mother. A small trickle of blood was running from her nose.

"Piper?"

The skies erupted.

The mother of all lightning – a prolonged, sustained flash that was brighter than the sun but void of warmth. And in the doorway? Behind her child. A man. A man?

Joel? No, not her husband. Long hair, a beard. She opened her mouth to speak, to ask for help. Blood bubbled in her throat, cutting off the words, the air. Then darkness. The flash was gone.

"Mommy? Mommy, the bad thing?" she could hear her daughter cry, so small, so fragile next to drumming thunder.

"Mommy . . . *Mommy* . . . *Mommy* . . ."

LIGHTNING – blinding, impossibly harsh – shredded the night. Mason Evans hit the brakes. The Chevy slid on the rain-sheathed road, turning sideways. The lightning held. Dean could see an open field: fence posts garnished with barbed wire, cattle with their heads up and their eyes wide in fear – a tableau painted in electric white.

The lightning held.

Impossible, Dean thought, his mental clock marking the time. A bolt of eternal light?

He could see the gray, drumming rain; tall, thick weeds undulating in the wind; a crow in hurried flight.

And still the lightning held.

Thunder exploded, shaking the car, shaking the road, shaking the world.

Darkness rushed back like the ocean into a fresh concave.

"What the fuck was that?" Mason asked.

Dean felt his heart beating in the back of his throat. *More than half a minute. The lightning bolt filled the sky for more than half a minute. Not possible. Not possible.*

Mason shook his head, blinking like a child pulled from slumber. "Jesus! Did you guys see that?"

"The blind could see that," John answered from the

backseat. "Unless you want Nathan and Clyde to plow into us with the mortuary truck, I suggest we get going."

Mason Evans gunned the engine and straightened the car. "What the hell was that? How can lightning last that long?"

How? Science. Everything could be explained with science. There were no secrets in the universe, Dean thought, only equations not yet solved.

"It can't," he answered. "It must have been a series of continual flashes spaced so close together that it gave the impression of one contiguous burst."

Mason sped up, still watching the sky, flinching with each new flash.

Dean had done something he had never done before: he left work early. His manager had been understanding, but Dean was still troubled about abandoning his post. Or was it missing a chance to see Judy that really bothered him? The memory of Judy's smile played in the back of his mind like a continual song. Her capricious, winter-blue eyes, her delicate cheeks and pert nose, all framed in a cloud of sun-blond hair.

Dean pushed the thought of Judy Pinbrow out of his mind, focusing instead on their conversation, on what John had told him about Whitey Dobbs's initiation ceremony.

"A tape? That's what you owe Larry for? He made a tape?" Dean asked. The stars and moon had vanished. Lightning revealed massive, roiling clouds. Their air was restless and rich with the scent of ozone.

"Yeah, then I gutted the insides of an old radio and installed the tape player. Pretty slick, huh?" Mason said, his timidity quickly evaporating. He drove with fresh abandon, taking curves with quick, tight jerks of the wheel. Twin beams splashed across the blacktop and vanished into the night.

"Sick is what it is."

Mason ignored the jab, reveling in his own creativity and craftsmanship. "You should hear it. Larry did a whole hour-long radio show – songs, commercials, the whole shebang."

"Including the news," Dean finished. Mason grinned. In the glow of the dashboard light his teeth seemed phosphorescent, jagged by shadows. Big John Evans sat in the backseat, arms stretched out, silent and stoic.

"And his news story," Mason continued, "says there's been an automobile accident and that John, Clyde, Nathan, and me are dead. We're fucking dead, man."

Mason cheered, releasing the wheel and slapping his meaty hands together in a single note of applause. "That motherfucker is buried alive, and he thinks the only ones who know where he is are dead. Whoo-*ha*! Brilliant, ain't it?"

Dean Truman felt a thorny stroke of apprehension,

as if something with a barbed tongue were licking his spine.

The road began to rise, crawling up the side of Hawkins Hill.

Anger, like lava under pressure, pushed against his self-restraint. He closed his eyes and tried to pinch off his emotions. When he spoke, it was with measured restraint. "Why? Just tell me why, John? I thought it was weird that you guys were hanging around with a creep like Dobbs. But Jesus, he's dangerous. Seriously. He is not someone you want to be screwing around with.

"And this." Dean held out his hand. "All you've done is piss him off."

Drops of rain, silver in the wash of the headlights, slammed into the windshield. Dean shook his head. "Why would you do something so . . . stupid . . . so vicious?"

"Because we couldn't kill him," John whispered from the backseat.

Lightning bathed the sky, revealing John's face. He was serious.

Dean shuddered from a sudden chill. Something terrible had happened.

"I don't understand you, John, and I don't understand any of this. Nobody deserves this kind of treatment."

"Tell that to Judy." John's words were a whisper, but Dean heard the name as a shout.

"Judy?"

"Tell him, man," Mason urged.

Judy.

Dean felt the dimming fog of distress growing around his peripheral vision. A strange, unearthly sense of foreboding throbbed with each beat of his heart. He wanted to stop John Evans from saying what he was about to say.

"That bastard raped her. Whitey Dobbs raped my sister. He raped Judy."

Judy.

Dean Truman's vision narrowed, the world consumed by shifting gray static. He bit his lip until he drew blood, the salty copper taste lost in the general disarray of his senses.

The rain fell harder and faster.

In the darkness John Evans told the story. He had first noticed something was wrong the Sunday before last, when Judy's ever flowing smile suddenly seemed to dry up. He thought she was melancholy about the end of school. She liked school. Maybe she was a little sad that Dean was going off to college. But then on Monday she didn't go to class, same thing on Tuesday. Until that point Judy Pinbrow had maintained a perfect attendance record.

Even though she was his stepsister, John had always been close to Judy. Opposites in body and mind, but identical in their devotion. She was usually the one who pulled him from the pit of depression, made him talk about what was troubling him, and more times than not, made the world a place worth living in. But now it was John's turn.

He confronted her. She feigned sickness, then distraction, but her efforts to smile were feeble. The truth came with tears.

"It happened two Saturdays ago," John said. "After she left you at the restaurant. She was parked behind the flower shop next door. And that's where Dobbs was waiting."

Dean closed his eyes. His mouth was dry, his throat scoured. He listened even though he didn't want to hear.

John explained how Dobbs had grabbed Judy from behind, his hand over her mouth, clotting her screams. How she had heard a small, chilling sound, barely audible over the drumming of her heart.

Click.

Followed by the touch of something cold and biting, dimpling her neck. Whitey said the knife had a name: Switch. It was his best friend, and unless she did just what he said, he was going to let Switch see what the inside of a pretty little girl looked like. He then dragged her behind the store to the trash bin; there, on top of empty boxes and dead flowers, he took her.

"Why didn't you tell me or Dad, or the police, for God's sake?" John had asked his sister.

"Because you would try to kill him, but you can't," she said without qualification. John exploded with anger, but Judy calmed him with tears. If he wanted to help, he had to stay in control. And then she made him promise that neither he nor any of his friends would lay a finger on Whitey Dobbs, that they would never physically harm him in any way.

"You can't hurt him, nobody can. He will kill if you try. You, me, Mom and Dad – everyone."

"Bullshit! But if you really believe that, let's at least go to the police."

"No. He's not human, and the police can't stop something that's not human."

Then her voice broke. And between choking sobs she explained how she had arrived home that night, locked all the doors and windows, then stood in a scalding shower wondering if she would ever truly be clean again. She told him how she had put on her pajamas but couldn't stop trembling. How, less than twenty minutes after being raped by Whitey Dobbs, she had heard a small sound in the darkness of her bedroom.

Click.

Whitey Dobbs had raped her again.

THE RAIN INTENSIFIED. Lightning shattered the heavens, followed quickly by a cannonade of thunder. The searing flash revealed a low ceiling of black-gray clouds, the texture of dirty snow, clumped together in a series of inverted moguls and plastered to the nighttime sky. Water-gray trees swayed in a harsh wind; twigs and leaves scampered across the roadway.

"Why would Dobbs agree to be buried alive by the brother of the girl he raped?" Dean asked.

It was the first anyone had spoken since John had finished the story.

"We have different last names, John Evans and Judy Pinbrow. He doesn't realize she's my stepsister, and he doesn't have any friends to tell him otherwise."

Dean took a deep, slow breath. A new thought occurred to him. "When did he rape her?"

"Saturday, two weeks ago."

Ninety-nine Einstein.

"Two weeks ago?" Dean suddenly felt light-headed. "And it happened after she left the restaurant? I was working that night."

"You couldn't have stopped it. You couldn't have known that bastard was waiting for her. Right there behind the flower shop. Probably saw her leave and hid in the shadows until she reached her car." John's voice was steady and even but carried an edge every bit as sharp as a razor. "Don't blame yourself."

"It's not that, it's . . ." Dean felt as if his brain had been replaced with helium and at any moment his head would float up out of his shirt collar and bounce against the Chevy's ceiling. "He couldn't have done it. He couldn't have been waiting for her."

"What the hell are you talking about?" Mason demanded.

Dean felt his throat constrict as the truth became

suffocatingly apparent. "He was still in the restaurant."

"What?"

"He didn't leave until an hour after Judy left."

"You're wrong," John said.

Ninety-nine Einstein.

"No. No, I'm not."

"Then?" John's question dangled in the air like a hangman's noose.

"Then Whitey Dobbs couldn't have raped Judy."

THEY GOT OUT of the car. A cold rain pelted their hair and clothes. The mortuary truck rumbled to a halt behind them. John and Mason grabbed shovels and quickly went to work.

Dirt had turned to mud, adding several pounds to each shovelful of earth. They worked in silence, steady and focused, keeping a constant pace.

A pair of Coleman lanterns cast a cold, yellow light, revealing an ever growing hole as the skies tried to fill the void with rain.

After twenty minutes they had barely dented the grave. The five were bone tired.

Then the rain stopped.

Like a sprinkler that had been turned off, it ceased to fall, and just as quickly the clouds dissipated. A canopy of stars and a bright moon took their place.

The boys returned to the task with renewed vigor. Dean and Nathan were resting when John, Mason, and Clyde hit the coffin. Not waiting to lift it out of the grave, John shoved away the black earth and water, his thick fingers feeling for and finding the clasp that held the lid in place.

Dean and Nathan were sitting on the tailgate of the truck, wet, cold, and filthy. They couldn't see the coffin but they could smell it, the air becoming suddenly ripe with the odour of sweat and urine.

"Oh, my God," John cried.

"Oh, Jesus, is he dead?" Nathan asked, rushing to the grave. Dean followed.

"Worse," John said.

The lid was open. The inside was revealed in lantern light and starlight. The lace box was soiled with dirt, urine, and blood. But the coffin was empty.

NOW:

Twenty-two years later

4

"WHAT IS IT?" she asked.

The server, who was wearing a body apron, hair net, and scowl, poked the item in question with a spatula. The indentation stayed for a moment, then the meat slowly returned to its original form.

"Salisbury steak," he said.

Piper Blackmoore frowned. "It doesn't look like Salisbury steak."

A protracted sigh leaked from the student's listless face. "You want it or not?"

"It's shaped like a triangle."

"It's a wedge."

"A wedge? Since when does meat come in a wedge?"

"I said it was Salisbury steak; I didn't say it was meat."

Piper laughed, then realized the lethargic student hadn't intended to make a joke.

"And what's with the gravy? It's got a" – Piper squinted for clarification – "a yellow tint to it."

The student slid the spatula under a wedge of pseudomeat. "Want it or not?"

"What the hell. You only live once, right?"

No answer.

"Give me two. I'm getting a plate for a friend."

"Must not be much of a friend."

He slapped two wedges of meat on to two separate plates and handed them over the sneeze guard without further comment. Piper had the unprofessional urge to put her thumbs in her ears, wiggle her fingers, and shout, "buggah-buggah-buggah," just to see if she could elicit a response.

The other servers were slightly more communicative than the boy with the mystery meat, but only slightly. Piper finished the plates with whipped potatoes and, in deference to her lunch date, carrots in lieu of tapioca pudding. Expertly lifting the two trays from the travel bars, she stepped around two others in line and headed for the cash register.

A *chill* both cold and hot, electrifying and numbing, surged through her small, tight body. She shuddered. The plates trembled on the trays.

Cold-hot.

Her vision dimmed. The world tilted. Tiny pinwheels of light spun at the outer reaches of her peripheral vision.

Cold.

"Miss? Miss?"

Piper blinked. She was breathing hard, heart throbbing.

"Miss?"

She dropped the trays on the chrome slide-rails by the cash register. Too hard. The carrot sticks jumped. The wedges of meat covered with yellow gravy remained steady.

"Card, please," said the cashier.

Her vision cleared. Piper blinked again and focused on the face in front of her. Young. Another student. Hair net, apron, but this one was smiling, with large, fish-belly-white teeth.

"What?" she asked, more to herself than to the cashier.

"Your lunch card. I need to punch it."

Piper fumbled in her pocket. Her fingers felt swollen, blunt, void of their usual fluidity. She found the card and presented it.

The smiling student took it and punched twice. "You okay?"

Piper forced a smile and shrugged. "Just got the heebie-jeebies, that's all. Silly."

"Somebody walked over your grave."

"What?"

"Your grave. You know, where you're going to be buried. That's what my grandma used to say whenever anybody got the shivers. She'd say, 'Somebody's walking on your grave.'"

He returned her card. His incredibly wide smile widened further.

Walking on your grave.

Piper Blackmoore shuddered.

*

53

THE CLASSROOM WAS PAINTED faint green, with waist-high, dark brown molding, the same color as the expanding concentric circle of water damage tattooed on the acoustic-tile ceiling. A chair with a missing leg was propped in the east corner like a disciplined child. A spider worked a web on the west side.

There were no clocks in the room. He didn't own one. Dr. Dean T. Truman always knew what time it was. Nevertheless, he imagined he could hear ticking, the steady marking of time, each beat pushing them closer to the end, closer to the death of Black Valley.

Unless . . .

Dean chewed his lower lip and looked down at the letter in his hands. It had been folded in thirds and worn thin at the creases from excessive handling. Three phrases seemed to blaze on the paper: FINAL OFFER, STATE-OF-THE-ART, HAWKINS HILL.

Tick, tick, tick.

It's up to you, Dean, Nathan Perkins had told him. *You're our only hope, our only chance.*

Dean Truman wiped his face and looked around the room. It was an old room, in an old building worn by time and use. The blackboard was actually black and bore the pale residue of many an erasing. The floor, once beige, was now faded yellow. Wires like hordes of black snakes crawled from behind twelve arcane computers sitting atop six scored tables.

The letter felt heavy in his hands. He laid it on the

desk and smoothed it with his palm. What to do? What to do? He took a deep, slow breath; the air was redolent with the scent of ozone and chalk dust.

The south wall held a paper-laden bulletin board, four sheets deep, and looked like someone had taken the contents of a trash basket and pinned them to the corkboard. The north wall was dominated by multi-framed windows fringed in dirt and dust. Dean looked out the window; less than ten yards from the classroom the ground began to rise, climbing steadily to 2,215 feet: Hawkins Hill.

Tick, tick, tick.

Wasn't life supposed to get easier with success? When had winning a Nobel Prize become a drawback?

"How many job offers have you turned down?" Nathan had asked. "Ten, twenty, more? How much money?"

"I don't care about money," Dean said.

"Obviously. So you don't want to leave Black Valley. That's fine—"

"I *can't* leave Black Valley."

"Okay, whatever. As the mayor and as your friend, I'm delighted you want to stay, but just between you and me, if we don't do something soon, there isn't going to be a Black Valley. NxTech is that something. They're laying it at your feet, at our feet. All you have to do is say yes."

Yes. If only it were that simple.

In Black Valley timber was king. But thanks to the

Endangered Species Act and poor management, the king was dead. Without the logging there were no sawmills; without sawmills there were no jobs; without jobs there were no customers. Fourteen businesses had closed or gone bankrupt in the last year alone. With more expected, unless . . .

The deal had been brokered by Clyde Watkins, now a congressman, and on the surface it looked perfect.

"They're bringing the mountain to Muhammad. You say yes, and NxTech will build their next research facility here in Black Valley. You don't have to leave. You get a new job and a state-of-the-art facility to continue your almighty research, and we get a new company and close to three hundred jobs."

"NxTech is a bad company. Their environmental record—"

"So? If they locate here, they will have to follow our guidelines. They've already made a bid for the land on the Hill and have agreed to abide by our building codes, saving as many trees as possible and preserving the integrity of the butte."

"But other places . . ."

"What? They made some unwise choices? Harmed the environment in some third-world country. So what if they did? What's past is past. How can your saying no to this change any of that?"

Nathan was seized with a new thought. "But if you say yes, then you're on the inside. And with your clout you'll be able to make sure they never harm the environment again. Besides, if you don't, Black Valley is dead."

Tick, tick, tick.

Dean folded the letter and put it back in his blazer pocket. He had to make a decision. Nathan and Clyde were expecting an answer this afternoon.

"HEY, what's up, Doc?"

Dean raised his eyes. Doubt forgotten, guilt shoved aside, angst evaporated, the world was put on hold by the presence of Piper Blackmoore.

She stood in the doorway holding a pair of lunch trays, from which emanated the fragrance of recently reheated meat.

"Pop quiz and no peeking," she said. "What time is it?"

He smiled.

"Twelve oh-two," he said with complete confidence. "Of course, the bell rang a few minutes ago, so it's hardly a fair test."

"Good point." She held up the trays. "You forgot to eat – again."

"No."

"No?" She cocked her head to the right, looking at him from the corner of her eye, dimples kissing her sanguine cheeks. "You've eaten?"

Dean stood, sweeping the air with his hand, beckoning her to enter. "As a matter of fact, I have not eaten, but not because I forgot."

She entered the room in a bounding stride that he had come to associate with excited children, puppies – and Piper Blackmoore. He cleared a place on his desk and pulled up a second chair.

"It was all part of my sinister plan. My machinations to get you to serve me."

She laughed, an unencumbered sound. Dean was certain that if the Fountain of Youth were ever discovered, the bubbling waters would sound like this.

"You horndog. You're such a flirt, Dr. Truman."

He chortled at the commonalities of the description, its inclusiveness. Piper Blackmoore was one of the few individuals who treated him as a regular person and not as the poster child for technogeeks, and by doing so, insinuated he actually had a life beyond these four walls.

He growled, trying to sound lascivious and failing miserably.

She was clearly amused at the attempt.

At five foot two inches, she was a small woman but nonetheless shapely. Her legs were sculpted and contoured by a morning regimen of calisthenics and a six-mile run. Her small, heart-shaped face was accented with deep, shadow-brown eyes flecked with gold. Her short black hair was so vibrant it looked wet. *Not like any history professor I ever had in school*, Dean thought. But then, there was nothing common about Piper Blackmoore.

They were diametric opposites; by all rights they

should have been at each other's throat. She was thirteen years his junior, young, flirty, full of life and not afraid to show it. He was older, quieter, a genuine nerd who had never outgrown the awkward stage. He was grounded firmly in science, while Piper never met a crazy theory she didn't embrace.

"Coye Cheevers saw a ghost," she said, as if to highlight his thoughts.

"Cheevers is not the most reputable of sources," Dean said as he carefully opened his paper carton of milk.

"He's a cop."

"Uh-huh."

"A deputy sheriff."

"Yes he is."

"A man of the law." She snapped off a bite of carrot.

"He's the sheriff's second cousin," Dean said. His milk carton open, he moved on to the meat.

"You're friends with the sheriff?"

"Yep, John Evans and I go way back." He speared the Salisbury steak with a plastic fork.

"Sheriff Evans hired him." She swallowed her carrot and then scooped a spoonful of whipped potatoes.

"So?"

"So, doesn't that say something about Cheevers's credibility?"

"Yeah, it says he is very credible as the sheriff's second cousin." Dean sawed the meat with a plastic knife. For a moment the wedge seemed unaffected, then finally, reluctantly, it gave in.

"There is more to the world than computers and numbers, Dr. Dean T. Truman." She pointed with her spoonful of potatoes for emphasis. "A lot more."

"Never said there wasn't, but it can all be explained by science."

"Bullshit."

"Waste product produced by a male bovine. See, science."

She laughed, her eyes echoing her throat.

"Where at?" he asked as he sawed another piece of meat, a process he would continue until the entire wedge was divided into individual, bite-size portions. Then and only then he begin to eat.

"Where at *what*?" Piper teased, biting off her own slice of steak. She didn't share his methodical culinary style, moving freely among meat, carrot, and potatoes with no discernible pattern or reason.

"Where did he see the ghost?" Dean speared a bite of Salisbury steak, put it in his mouth, and chewed.

"He was at the school crossing – you know, getting ready for the morning traffic."

"He saw a ghost at the school crossing?"

Piper swallowed her meat, then sipped her milk. "No. He was at the crossing. It was in the sky."

"In the sky?"

"Flying."

"Flying?"

"Is there an echo?" She smiled and swallowed something: meat, potato, carrot – he had lost track.

One bite of steak finished, Dean started on a second. All things in time, all things in order. "So, Coye Cheevers saw a flying ghost."

She nodded and bit her carrot, chewed, swallowed, then snagged a piece of meat. He winced at the juxtaposition. She noticed and smiled coyly.

He sipped his milk. "Was it a male or a female?"

"What?" she asked, her young face dimpling.

"The ghost."

"I thought you didn't believe in ghosts."

"I don't. But for argument's sake, was this *supposed* ghost a man or a woman?"

"Neither." She went back to the potatoes.

Dean frowned, perplexed. Piper Blackmoore smiled with obvious delight.

"You know, as arguments go, this is not your best," he challenged.

"It's not mine. It's his." Back to the meat.

"Okay, let's review: yesterday morning – at approximately, what? Six forty-five? – Deputy Cheevers was at the elementary school crossing when he saw an androgynous ghost flying over the city. Is that about it?"

She nodded again. Commas of rich black hair bounced against her forehead. "That's it – except it wasn't an androgynous ghost."

"It wasn't? Then, what was it?"

"It was a machine." She drank her milk and studied him over the top of the paper container, taking delight in his surprise.

Aware of this, Dean tried to limit his expression. She enjoyed shocking him, whether it was about the supernatural world, which she openly endorsed, or whether it was flirting, wearing her sexuality like an evening gown.

"A machine?"

She cupped her hand to her mouth. "Echo, echo, echo . . . ," she repeated with diminishing volume. "Maybe I should yodel. Would you repeat that, too?"

"Yodel?" he said before he could stop himself, then winced.

Piper clapped her hands in pure, childlike delight.

Dean laughed at himself, amazed at how quickly and easily she could touch the child in him. "Okay, okay. So tell me, how can a machine be a ghost?"

She shrugged. "He said it appeared out of nowhere, then disappeared – just like a ghost."

A thought occurred to Dean. "That would make it a UFO."

She shook her head. "It was *not* an unidentified flying object."

Dean held up the palm of his hand. "Thank you."

"Because it was identified."

"So it was a plane?"

"No. It was a truck."

"A truck?"

"A ghost truck."

Dean laughed out loud.

"A flaming ghost truck," Piper finished, laughing with him. Then, raising her right hand, added, "I kid you not. That's his story."

"Is this official school business?" he teased.

"Yes, it is." She had finished her carrots and now reached across the table and speared one of his. "Part of my job as junior member of the history department is to embarrass any Nobel Prize-winning colleagues as much as possible."

Finishing his meat, Dean moved on to his potatoes.

"Truth is, I don't put much stock in Cheevers's sighting," Piper said.

Dean clutched his heart. "Quick, call the papers. Piper Blackmoore found a crazy idea she didn't embrace."

She threw the carrot stick at him. But her brown eyes continued to smile. To *flirt*. No, he was too old and she was too pretty. He thought of Mavis Connetti, a local businesswoman he had been dating, sort of, then he thought of his Judy. A cold snake of guilt climbed up his spine. How long had it been since his wife's death?

Sometimes it seemed like forever, other times it seemed like yesterday.

No, don't think that way. Remember what John said: "Judy would have wanted you to get on with your life."

He felt his throat constrict.

"Hey, Doc, you okay?" Piper asked.

He swallowed and smiled. "Yeah, I'm fine, just fine."

She turned her head and looked at him out of the corner of her eye. "Now you're just bragging."

He laughed. In many ways it was Piper and her effervescent personality that had brought him back from hopelessness and depression following Judy's death.

Because of some placement procedure that Dean was never able to figure out, her classroom was just across the hall from his. She had started teaching at Westcroft College last year. Since then, she frequently took her lunch with Dean. He wasn't sure why; he suspected pity but refused to let himself dwell on it for fear of diluting the magic.

Piper challenged him, shocked him, intrigued him.

"Penny for your thoughts," she said, wiping her mouth with a napkin.

He felt his face redden.

Her smile expanded. "You horndog. You were thinking about sex."

The reddening became a fire. He felt flushed.

She saved him from self-immolation. "I turned in the report to Mayor Perkins. You know, detailing the history of Black Valley. I don't think he's too happy with it."

"Why not?"

She shrugged. "It wasn't what he expected. In fact, it was pretty weird. He asked about you, though, asked if you had made a decision yet. Have you?"

"NxTech."

"NxTech."

He shook his head. "Not yet. It's just—"

Suddenly her face slackened. She stood up quickly, biting her lower lip.

"What is it? Piper?"

Her teeth dimpled her lip, the healthy, warm pink turning white.

"Piper?"

"Somebody's watching us."

He looked out the row of windows. A wind teased the brush and wild grass that grew just beyond the campus grounds, on Hawkins Hill.

"There's no one out there," Dean said, purposely striking the tones of teacher to pupil.

"It's just . . ." Her eyes narrowed. The grasses waved. "Just one of my . . . *feelings.*"

"Ah." Dean sat.

"Ah? What do you mean, 'ah'?" Piper challenged, glaring at him.

He took a spoonful of potatoes. "Nothing."

"I don't think so. That was definitely something. You mean 'ah' as in 'Ah, just another one of Piper's silly, superstitious reactions.' "

"I only made a sound," Dean defended. He ate his potatoes. They were cold. "It's not even a word."

"Close enough. I know what—" her eyes widened. "There, there by the oak. A man. He's moving."

Dean stood. He caught a flash of something. Dark cloth. A cape?

"He went behind the tree." She slapped her hands excitedly. "Aha!"

"Aha?" Dean frowned.

"Yes, I see your 'ah' and raise you a 'ha.' I told you someone was watching us. I knew it."

Dean moved to the far north corner of the room, where he could see behind the tree.

"I could *feel* it," Piper said. Her voice softened. "In fact, I've been feeling strange all day long."

"Piper," he called.

"But I told you someone was watching us. Now do you believe me? Now do you see that some things are bigger than science?"

"Piper, come here."

She hurried to where he stood. "What? Can you see him from there? Who is he? Do you know him?" She reached the corner and stopped, the truth revealed.

"There's no one there," Dean said.

"But I just saw him. You saw him."

"No, I saw a flash of something. A towel blown off someone's line, a tree limb, something, but not a man."

"He was there. He was looking at us. Right at us."

Dean returned to his seat. "Your potatoes are getting cold."

66

She remained in the corner of the room, looking, searching.

Searching for leprechauns and fairies, Dean thought. It wasn't her fault. She came from a superstitious family. Orphaned at the age of four, she had been raised by her father, just the two of them alone in that big, old house on the other side of Hawkins Hill. Piper Blackmoore possessed the mind of a scholar but the heart of a child. Open to all the possibilities – and impossibilities – of the world.

Dean had known her mother, not personally but by reputation. She had considered herself a psychic, picking up pocket change by reading fortunes in tea leaves and outstretched hands.

Piper had heard the stories. This, he suspected, was the true source of her belief in the unbelievable, as if by embracing the supernatural, she was somehow embracing her mother.

Piper returned to her seat. Her smile had vanished. It was as if a great cloud had suddenly blocked the sun.

He wanted to reassure her. Instead all he could do was offer her his analytical assessment of what had just occurred. "You have excellent peripheral vision. I'm sure you glimpsed something without realizing it."

She looked at him, the fluorescent lights flickering in her soft, brown eyes. She tried to smile, but her gaze returned to the window. Outside, the sky was clear except for the northern horizon, where a thin line of charcoal clouds lingered. Stark, bare limbs reached towards the sky like skeletal hands grasping for salvation.

"He was watching us. I'm sure of it."

The trees shook in the cold, stiff wind.

IT TOOK DEAN a disproportionate amount of time to get his mind off the young history professor and on to his work. His internal clock said he had less than ten minutes before his class started, less than an hour and a half before he was due to meet Nathan Perkins and Clyde Watkins downtown with an answer.

Something.

The hair rose on his arm.

The air seemed suddenly cold and impossibly thick. He looked out the window at the foot of Hawkins Hill. The wind had picked up. Tree branches reeled, sending a flurry of rustling leaves tumbling through the air. Tall, dry grass swayed.

Something?

The windowpane exploded.

Glass sprayed across the tabletops, floor, and wall. A small projectile flew so close to Dean that he felt the air rip. The glass struck the wall like a cannon shot. The object burst through the Sheetrock wall.

He stumbled, his heart flash-frozen between beats. He looked at the wall. He forced himself to swallow, then to breathe. He could hear movement in the hall. Hell, he could see movement in the hall. The object had created a jagged hole roughly the size of a softball.

Dean stumbled out of the door. Piper's class had spilled into the hallway. A mass of students gathered around something on the far wall.

He caught Piper's eye. "What the hell was that?" she asked.

"I don't know. It just . . ." His words dried up. His mouth felt thick with cotton.

He shooed the students away. Piper hurried to his side.

The object, a burned, crimson-brown, was embedded deep in the wall; a faint contrail of dust rose in the air. Dean moved closer.

"What is it?" Piper asked.

"A brick. I think it's just a brick. But—"

Piper finished his thought. "How do you throw a brick through a window, then a wall?"

A subtle odor caught Dean's attention. The contrail. Not dust, but *smoke?*

He reached out and touched the brick. His hand jerked back. The pads of his fingers burned. Hot! The clamor of the students was like the roar of a distant surf. He recognized questions, but by their inflection, not their content. His thoughts were elsewhere.

A brick?

He stumbled back into his classroom and stared at the ruined window. Outside, a cold breeze continued to ruffle the leaves. But that was all. Nothing else moved. A brick? Dean had been looking out the window when it happened. Certainly the brick had been traveling fast, and yet there was no one out there.

5

METAL JOINTS SQUEALED as the traffic light swayed in the teasing wind. A four-cylinder Honda Civic grumbled impatiently, held in place by a single red glow, while cars graced by the emerald shine were granted immediate passage. An old Cadillac in excellent repair purred by. A Ford Explorer with a dent in the rear fender followed, chased by a battered Dodge truck with a bad muffler and congested engine.

But he could still hear the light.

Squeak, squeak, squeak.

Main Street was a stereotypical carpet of black asphalt that stretched down a six-block hall of posed buildings before unraveling into frayed, wandering threads. The tallest building was five stories and stood three blocks to the east, but the skyline was dominated by the green behemoth that rose regally to the north.

The name, Hawkins Hill, was a misnomer; at 2,215 feet, it was actually a butte, not quite a mountain but certainly more than a hill. Behind it grew the Cascade

Mountains, but their grandiose topography was blocked by the city's proximity to the closer Hawkins Hill.

Hawkins Hill.

Construction on the butte was strictly regulated. Roads and homes were carefully inserted, built beneath the dominating Douglas firs so that, from ground level, Hawkins Hill appeared to be an untouched mound of pristine greenery.

Squeak, squeak, squeak.

The arc of the swaying traffic light had increased.

The wind brushed his cheeks, faint like a whisper. Though the sky remained predominately blue, the treetops swaggered, the first to feel the coming bluster. A cold wind, he knew. An unusually cold wind. Hot air rises, cold air falls. Usually.

Usually.

The green light turned amber, indifferent to the weather.

Squeak, squeak – zzzzzzz.

The traffic light blinked once, twice. A jagged streak of flash-white electricity arced from the traffic light to the securing power line. Sparks exploded, spewing a plume of electric flares into the air.

The light flashed once more, then went black, dark, *dead*.

Traffic stopped. Drivers were startled, paused by indecision.

The dead light rocked.

Squeak, squeak, squeak.
It was coming.
Coming.

MAYOR NATHAN PERKINS LOOKED OUT at the city, his city, and smiled. It was a good town, an honest town, but unless Dean Truman said yes to NxTech, it would soon be a ghost town. No, Dean would come through. He had to. The last four years had been hell, pure hell, watching as the city died, as businesses dried up like blood on the sidewalk, as people left, abandoning their generational homes in search of greener pastures.

Then Dr. Dean T. Truman won the Nobel Prize in physics.

That had certainly shaken things up. Suddenly the whole world was looking at Black Valley. He could almost hear the stuffed shirts in their fancy schools, with their ten-word titles and their smarter-than-thou attitude, gasping with surprise. Before the prize, no one had ever heard of Dean Truman or Westcroft College or Black Valley, Oregon. But they had now.

And the fact that Dean had developed his theories without funds or equipment, using nothing but his brain and his uncanny ability to reason, made the story even more amazing. Nathan had tried to read Dean's groundbreaking paper when it first appeared in the scientific journal, but he couldn't get past the title: "The Multifunctionality of Quantum Physics and Superstring Mechanics: A Study of Duality and Energy Reproduction."

But he had read the stories in the mainstream press. *Newsweek* had referred to Dean as "the Johnny Cochran of science, bending the laws of physics to the point of breaking."

The job offers had been incredible, and Nathan still didn't understand why Dean had turned them down. Truth was, Nathan had been too busy pining over the death of his city to notice. Then came NxTech. And with it the answer to Black Valley's problem.

It wasn't just the jobs the new plant would bring; it was also the support businesses. Nathan had done the research. In every place NxTech built, dozens of support businesses followed. This deal could transform Black Valley from a dying timber town to a booming high-tech hub.

Nathan reclined in his wing-backed leather chair, head hammocked in his hands, enjoying the faint scent of lemon furniture polish. If Dean accepted the NxTech offer, what would Black Valley be like in five years? In ten? NxTech was just the beginning. Nathan could envision an onslaught of growth and expansion as the city became a harbor for technology, a place you went to, as opposed to a place you drove through. A budding city that retained small-town sensibilities.

The thought was as warming as a well-stoked fire.

On his obsessively neat gunmetal desk lay the tax assessor's projected tax bill for NxTech's first year.

Even with incentive breaks it came to $1.2 million.

Put that in your pipe and smoke it, Portland, Eugene, and Salem.

He knew what the rest of the state thought of Black Valley: weirdo world. Strange things happened in that little burg sandwiched between the Willamette River and Hawkins Hill.

Freaky things.

And historically, they were right.

When NxTech first expressed interest in locating here, Nathan had commissioned a complete historical profile. He hoped to use the city's rich history as further incentive for other support businesses. Piper Blackmoore, a young history teacher at Westcroft College, had taken quickly to the task. He had received her report this morning. It was fascinating reading, but completely worthless for his purposes. He could never show it to any prospective business partner. Never.

Freaky things.

At least two other settlements had been started here and failed. One, by Native Americans in the 1700s; the other, years later, by stragglers from the Oregon Trail. Both had been destroyed. The first, by a devastating wildfire that burned the valley to the ground and gave birth to its name: Black Valley. The second was abandoned after the settlement was pummeled by "stones falling from the sky."

Raining rocks.

The third settlement, started eight years later, was the one that founded the city. Still, unusual events continued to occur. How else could you explain a small-town teacher at a nickel-and-dime college winning the Nobel Prize in physics?

Odd? You bet, and I'm damn proud of it, Nathan thought.

From his perch on the third floor of City Hall he could see most of downtown. The stores, made of wood or brick, were mostly one or two stories; several were boarded up. Traffic was steady but not brisk. The sidewalks were remarkably clean, gutters freshly swept, leaves collected. A pair of old oaks stood vigil on the courthouse lawn, swaying back and forth in a growing breeze like a pair of aging beauty queens waving to the masses.

The traffic parted as a screaming fire truck raced down Main Street.

Fire truck?

His secretary was at the door before he could buzz her.

"It's just a field fire out on Douglas Road," she said, anticipating his question. "Nothing to worry about. Sheriff Evans is at the scene. He says it will be easy to contain, but he might be late for the meeting with you, Dr. Truman, and Congressman Watkins at the Triple-D."

He thanked her and sat back down in his chair. His earlier euphoria gone. His thoughts hijacked.

Two settlements. The first destroyed by fire. The second by stones.

Fire and stones.

THE BRICK WAS SEVEN INCHES LONG and three inches wide, charred but otherwise totally and mundanely normal – that is, if you disregarded the fact that it had just traveled through a window, through a wall, and partially through a second wall.

Dean Truman reviewed the facts as he pedaled his ten-speed fourteen blocks from the school to downtown Black Valley. The thin, tight bicycle tires sang on the cool asphalt. The bike was Dean's principal form of transportation and would continue to be so until winter ice and snow made two-wheeled travel inadvisable.

Seven inches long, three inches wide, charred?

The bicycle was a statement about the environment, or so he told everyone. "Saving the earth with every pump of the pedal." The truth was more selfish; it was his chance to think, to daydream, to wonder.

A window, a wall, a second wall?

The school had called the sheriff's department to report the vandalism. But a small fire in the county had tied up officers.

Seven inches long.

After examining the brick and finding it devoid of uniqueness, Dean had turned his attention to the damage.

"What do you hope to find by looking at a hole in the wall?" Piper had challenged. She was putting on a brave front, but she hugged herself while she talked and complained about a chill only she could detect.

One of her special feelings? Dean wondered.

He measured the distance from the shattered window to the floor, the distance from the hole in the wall to the floor, then the distance from where the brick had stopped to the floor. "By calculating the angle of descent, while compensating for the friction of the glass, wood, and Sheetrock, then figuring in the size and weight of the object, I should be able to estimate a relative velocity. Then, by extrapolation, a point of origin."

"In other words, find out where it came from," Piper said, succinctly cutting to the heart of the matter.

"Exactly," he confessed.

"So who can throw a brick that fast?" Her brown eyes had a faraway look, the pupils constricted to pinpoints as she answered herself. "Obviously no one. So the question is *what* can throw a brick that hard?"

What?

Perhaps it was because he knew Piper's predilection for such things, but the way she said that one word made him uncomfortable. It made him think of fictional monsters that crawl from under a child's bed and into an adult's psyche, making that one word far more sinister than any four letters had a right to be.

What?

As he pedaled the bike on to Main Street he ordered his mind to evaluate the question from the proper perspective, the scientific perspective.

All things can be explained by science. All things.

Maybe not today, maybe not tomorrow, but eventually. *All things. Even "what."*

Could the brick have been hurled from an explosion? That would explain the charring, but no one had heard a blast, and a preliminary investigation of the campus turned up nothing to suggest there had been one.

But what? A machine? Perhaps one of those tennis cannons that fired yellow balls at weekend athletes? No. He doubted such a thing could provide the necessary lift to propel a brick, much less at such a high speed.

Then, what?

How about a baseball pitching machine? Certainly it would have more oomph, but the question of mass still troubled him. The brick was heavy. Too heavy. Perhaps if the machine was modified?

He chewed on this idea and decided it had the best flavor so far. A baseball pitching machine, or something like it, perhaps something used in construction that he wasn't aware of, or even something created just for that purpose.

Still . . .

An unwanted thought lingered in his mind like a bitter aftertaste. He had been looking out the window when the brick burst into the room. And the brick seemed to have come from *nowhere*. The question repeated, this time in Piper's voice.

What?

Dean parked his ten-speed in the bike rack, stretched, and took a deep breath. He could detect the faint scent of wet pine mingled with the contradicting odor of smoke. On the horizon what had been a thin line of clouds was growing, thickening; deep bruise-colored cumulus squirmed and rolled like a nest of angry, writhing snakes. A breeze, light but edged in ice, slid into town like an advance scout for a weather-borne army that was amassed and waiting just beyond the hill.

What?

MAVIS CONNETTI RANG UP the customer, thanked him for stopping in, then closed the till. It was late, too late for lunch, too early for dinner, but the Triple-D was more than half-full. Laughter rose in puffs, like dust being beaten from an ancient rug, while the moderate clatter of silverware on ceramic plates provided a continuous, almost restful background noise. The air was thick with the smell of cooked meat: burgers, steaks, and ham and the overlying scent of baking bread.

The tarnished bell over the front door tingled. Mavis looked up and smiled.

Dean.

Tall and excessively lean, Dr. Dean Truman moved with a graceless yet effective long-legged stride. His eyes were squinted, his thoughts elsewhere. His hair was mussed from riding his bike without a helmet, she noted. He tried to smooth his hair with the palm of his hand as he took his usual table by the large front window. He sat down; his cowlick popped up.

A waitress pulled her pad from her apron and took a step toward Dean's table. Mavis waved her off. The waitress grinned.

Officially the restaurant was named the Downtown Daily Diner, but everyone in town knew it as the Triple-D, a name that had more to do with Mavis's spectacular breasts than any alliteration. She didn't mind. She had long since come to terms with her own anatomy, choosing not to take offense at the proffered sexual innuendo, but deal with it instead with good humor and leniency. And she had become quite efficient at giving as good as she got, frequently skewering anyone who was naive enough to think her bra size and IQ were in inverse order.

She picked up her own pad and headed for Dean's booth.

She had returned to Black Valley twelve years ago, giving up a promising career with a brokerage firm in New York City after her father suffered a debilitating stroke. Taking over the family business was a temporary fix. When her father died, it became permanent. She had, somehow, managed to stay in business despite the dwindling economy. But now, like every-one else, she was at the end of her fiscal rope. She could keep the diner open another month, maybe two, but no longer. Unless Dean Truman said yes to NxTech.

It bothered her that both her professional and personal life centered on Dr. Dean T. Truman.

She licked her lips and squared her shoulders, unconsciously touching her hair and straightening her blouse. She felt nervous and uncomfortable, like a schoolgirl at the spring mixer.

Mavis and Dean had dated off and on for more than three years. Everyone thought of them as a couple; everyone thought they would marry. But the relation-ship had become stagnant, threatening to collapse from its own weight. Eight weeks ago she had laid down the law. "Either we take our relationship to the next level, or it's over."

He had been surprised and distraught. But not enough to propose.

Since their breakup Mavis had had plenty of time to reevaluate, to study how the relationship had gone wrong. Her conclusions were disturbing. It wasn't just the lack of a proposal; it was a lack of depth. Despite three years of dating, their relationship remained shallow. A fact underscored in fluorescent yellow by his refusal to let her even enter his house.

His house?

What was it about that hovel? What was he hiding?

"If you're afraid I'll be bothered by the mess, don't

be. I know how bachelors live," she had reassured him.

"It's not that, it's just . . ." But he never finished the sentence, never offered an explanation. And never let her inside.

The sad truth was, in some ways, he was still in love with his first wife – still pining for Judy. Was that why he wouldn't let her inside his home? Their home? Maybe, but Judy had been dead for twenty-one years. What sort of secret could you keep that long?

DEAN HAD JUST SAT DOWN when the bell over the door announced the arrival of Mayor Nathan Perkins. Time had been good to him, adding a little weight to his frame, while brush strokes of gray gave him a more dignified look. His glasses were still as thick as a beer bottle, and at times his magnified eyes made him look like a character from a Disney cartoon.

"Sorry I'm late," Nathan said, sliding into the booth.

"Just got here myself. But John may not make it."

"Yeah, I heard. Fire out on Douglas Road."

Mavis Connetti brought over two glasses of water and smiled. "Evening, Dean, Mayor. What will it be? Full deal, or sit and sip." She was a tall woman – *statuesque* was the word that came to Dean's mind – with long, raven hair and a round, friendly face. She also had, to quote Clyde Watkins, the "nicest rack in western Oregon, if not the whole state."

"Just coffee for me," Dean said.

"I haven't had lunch," Nathan said. "Give me the Number Four; no mustard and extra fries and a cup of coffee." Then, grinning like a seventh grader with a secret, he added: "So why is it that when I, your beloved mayor and humble civil servant, come in by myself, I never get waited on by the owner?"

"What can I say?" Mavis said, sticking her pencil behind her ear. "I've just got a thing for guys with really big . . ." She stopped.

Dean felt a pause in the air.

". . . brains," she finished. Then, wearing a mischievous grin, she leaned down and kissed Dean gently on the cheek. Her breast caressed his arm. She knew it, as well as the effect it was having on him. A small smile of victory brushed her face as the professor's cheeks burned red.

Both men watched her go, appreciating the view. "She's a looker, Dean. Something special. You two still dating?"

Dean shrugged. "Sort of."

Nathan shook his head, then pushed his glasses back up the bridge of his nose, as much from habit as from need. "Sort of? A woman like that you don't just leave waiting. Somebody is bound to snap her up."

"It's too soon," Dean said. He traced circles with his finger on the Formica-topped table.

"Too soon? It's been, what? Twenty-one years?" Nathan reached out and put his hand on Dean's.

"Look, as your friend, I'm telling you, it's time to move on."

Someone laughed. They both looked across the room to where four men sat in a corner booth. All but one were cackling. Dean smiled. It was a safe guess that the fourth man had made a lewd remark and Mavis Connetti had deftly and effectively cut him off at the knees.

Nathan was right, she was something special. But . . .

"Sure your work is important, but so is living. Judy knew that. And when she was with you, you knew that, too."

Twenty-one years? Had it really been that long? It seemed like only yesterday that Judy had suffered her first heart attack. Then three weeks later his wife, his friend, his soul mate, was gone. Reduced to a memory. A bioelectric spark; existing only in the electro-chemical exchange between synapses in his brain.

After her death Dean had spent three months locked in the cold, whitewashed clapboard house that had been their home. When friends tried to visit, he shooed them away. Only John Evans and Nathan Perkins had been allowed through the sacred door-way, and even they were carefully restricted to the small, cluttered den.

"Jesus, Dean, you act like you're hiding some-thing," John had remarked. It was their last visit. After that no one was allowed in – no one.

Dean occupied himself with tears and self-pity and, finally, with the search for a family heirloom, a locket – a gift to Judy on her thirteenth birthday from her grandmother. She was never without it. Silver and heart-shaped, the locket was embossed with delicate roses on the front and back. It opened with a simple spring lock. After they were married, Judy had placed a photograph of Dean on one side and herself on the other.

If he could just rub his fingers across the surface of that locket . . . Somehow he felt that modest gesture would bring atonement, closure. But the locket was nowhere to be found. Like Judy, it seemed to have vanished from the world.

Westcroft College was a simple school with a small faculty and nominal enrollment. But Dean had come to love it. When he returned to school, he threw himself into his work. And, as a result, later, won the Nobel Prize in physics.

But in truth he would rather have had the locket.

Three years ago Mavis Connetti had asked him out. Despite himself, he had enjoyed her companionship. She was very different from Judy, and that dissimilarity helped.

They had necked in the car like a couple of high school kids, but when she proposed spending the night with him, he faltered. He could tell she was hurt and embarrassed. He yearned to reassure her, to tell her it wasn't her fault.

"Why won't you invite me in?" she had finally asked.

Because I can't, he longed to say. *The same reason I can't let anyone in.*

Since then their relationship had cooled. The flirting continued, but so far Dean was stuck in neutral.

"How's Ava?" Dean asked, hoping to change their conversation and his thoughts.

Mention of Nathan's young bride brought a smile to his lips. "Great, absolutely great." He pulled a napkin from a chrome dispenser and wiped away a smudge on the Formica.

"If someone had told me twenty years ago that someday I'd have a woman like Ava, I wouldn't have believed them. I mean, jeez, a guy like me married to a girl like that?" Nathan shook his head. "I tell you, I must be the luckiest son of a bitch in the world."

Nathan and Ava had been married less than a year, their union still a mystery to many, but Dean understood it. In appearance they were opposites. She was flashy, young, a bit gaudy but attractive, drawn to bright colors and grandiose ideas; he was conservative, detail oriented, and no-nonsense. Yet Dean could honestly say he had never seen a happier couple.

"Jenkins Jones and Meredith Gamble came to see me about Ava's painting in the city council room," Nathan said.

Ava was an aspiring painter whose work looked more like an artist's drop cloth than art. Recently she had taken to "sprucing up City Hall" by donating several of her brighter, more eye-numbing pieces.

"And?"

"Meredith said the colors clashed with the decor. Jenkins was a little more to the point. He described it as, quote, 'butt-ugly – in fact, perhaps the most butt-ugly painting ever produced in the entire butt-ugly world.' "

Both men laughed.

"So, what are you going to do?" Dean asked.

Nathan shrugged and pushed up his glasses. "What can I do? Jenkins Jones is chairman of the city council, Meredith Gamble his second, but Ava's my wife."

"So?"

"So I'm siding with the one who keeps me warm at night."

"Jenkins."

Nathan made a face, but his smile never diminished. "I took the painting down and hid it in my office. Ava almost never goes into the city council chamber, and when I know she's going to, I'll just slip in first and hang it up."

Dean laughed so hard he choked.

"It's worth it, let me tell you. Which is why I say you should not let a woman like Mavis get away." Mavis brought their food and drink then left with a smile. Dean wasn't sure if she had heard Nathan's comment or not.

Dean shifted uneasily in his seat just as the bell over the door rang. "Look who finally showed up," he said.

Congressman Clyde Watkins entered the Triple-D. Greeted by a flutter of handshakes and backslapping, he slowly made his way toward Dean and Nathan.

"Hey, hey, guys." He held his hand up, fingers spread. "Flash Five, stay alive . . ."

"Flash Four, group no more," Nathan replied. "You need new material."

"Sorry I'm late, got waylaid glad-handing in Eugene. God, those people love to debate. There were protestors outside the assembly hall decrying the destruction of the old-growth forest, using signs made out of" – he paused for effect – "paper. Hello, can anyone say 'hypocrisy'?"

Dean chuckled.

Nathan shook his head. "I thought you were for the environment."

Clyde took a seat, then took a sip of Nathan's coffee. "I am, as long as it doesn't piss off the timber barons."

"Now, that's hypocritical," Nathan proclaimed. "And ew, gross, you've ruined my coffee."

"Come on, Nathan, you're a politician. You know how it works. Money makes the wheels go round. No money, no campaign; no campaign, no reelection; no reelection, no way to help anybody. Politics. And what do you mean, 'gross'? My germs aren't good enough for you?"

"It's not your germs I'm afraid of catching. It's your ethics."

"Don't worry; it'll never happen." Clyde stole a french fry, then added in a hush, "I don't have any ethics."

Dean laughed out loud.

Even Nathan chortled. "I may be the mayor, but I refuse to think of myself as a politician. I care about this place. I want to make a difference."

Clyde waved off a waitress approaching with a menu, then helped himself to Dean's untouched glass of water. "I want to make a difference, serve a cause, fight the good fight. All that happy horseshit, but I can't do it from home. You have to get in there and mix it up with the other fat cats in Washington. Then and only then can you accomplish something."

They talked, about politics, the economy, Clyde's eighteen-month-old daughter. And through it all Clyde and Nathan jabbed at each other like an old married couple. Dean allowed himself a moment of satisfaction. Pleased as always that his old friend, and new congressman, Clyde Watkins felt comfortable enough to be candid and clear with them.

Whenever Clyde was in town, the old gang tried to get together. The fire kept Sheriff John Evans away, and his cousin Mason had long since moved to Portland. But even with just the three of them, it was an enjoyable visit. No matter how brief.

The congressman checked his watch, then looked at

Dean. "So, what's it going to be? Can I tell our friends at NxTech that it's a go? You'll work for them?" Then to Nathan, "I think they want to break ground within the month."

"Great," Nathan said.

Dean was silent.

"What?" Clyde asked. "You're not still having doubts, are you?"

"I – I don't know. NxTech makes me uneasy."

"If this is about their environmental record, we've already discussed that. You can do more good inside the company than out," Nathan said.

"No. It's not just that. It's, well, I've been looking into the company. And, well, they have one division that deals with nothing but weapons research."

Nathan looked at Clyde. The congressman smiled. "So? You won't be in that division."

"Yeah, but it's the same company. They share information."

Clyde shook his head, his smile remained steady. "Come on, Dean. Your research is on what? The dualities of quantum Silly String, or something like that."

" 'The Multifunctionality of Quantum Physics and Superstring Mechanics,' " Dean said.

"So does it have anything to do with weapons?"

"No, but—"

"Do you see any weapons-related application?"

"No."

Clyde held up his hand. The smile widened. "So

what's the problem?" He didn't wait for an answer. "Well, I'm off. Got to get to Salem."

"Big fund-raiser?" Nathan chided. "Smoky back-room dealings with the timber boys?"

"Nah, strictly K.A.S."

Dean arched a brow. "K.A.S.?"

"Kiss Ass and Smile."

Clyde Watkins left as he came, working the room – smiling, laughing, shaking hands, slapping backs. Forever the politician.

Nathan went to get a fresh cup of coffee.

DEAN TRUMAN LOOKED OUT the window. The band of gray clouds continued to grow on the horizon. A terse wind teased the almost bare trees on the courthouse lawn. A sheet of newspaper capered across the grass like a flightless bird, past a light pole, past a fire hydrant, colliding with the leg of a man sitting on the courthouse bench.

Dean frowned.

The stranger sat as if he were sleeping, hands folded, head down. He wore a burned-brown cowboy hat pulled low across his forehead, the floppy brim masking his face. He was dressed for inclement weather even though the forecast called for clear skies and sunshine. The long, army-green raincoat was dirty and frayed.

The wind picked up; the edges of his coat flapped like the moldy wings of a long-dead raven.

As Dean watched, the stranger raised his head, revealing long brown hair, a beard, and a mustache.

Dean didn't recognize him. The man ignored the newspaper flapping at his leg. Instead he stared straight ahead, looking at—

At me?

The distance was too far to be sure, but to Dean it felt as if the stranger was looking at him. No, *watching* him. Dean flinched, looking away as if caught ogling a friend's wife. He stared at the tabletop. But the stranger stayed on his mind. He seemed so . . . so out of place.

Dean looked back out the window.

The stranger was gone.

Dean checked the panoramic view of the city. The man in the coat was nowhere to be seen.

The stranger couldn't have left that quickly. Could he?

UNITED STATES CONGRESSMAN CLYDE WATKINS vigorously dried his hair with a rough hotel-room towel and marveled at his own sexual prowess. He had lied to his wife, lied to his staff, and lied to two of his oldest friends, although technically he had done a lot of ass-kissing and smiling.

"Bang-shang-a-lang," he said to his reflection in the hotel mirror.

To Clyde's way of thinking, his prevarication was his friends' fault. If they could only understand the need, his overwhelming got-to-get-me-some-of-that need, then he would have been truthful.

Excuse me, friends, he would say, *I have to go shag the monkey.*

But he couldn't tell the truth, not to a couple of prudes like Nathan and Dean. About politics, yes; about sex, never.

He knew what they would say. *What about your wife, what about your daughter? What about them?* Clyde loved them very much. His sexual urges were insatiable, a fact that Dean would no doubt attribute to some deep-seated insecurity, so he dealt with those needs discreetly, lying to his family and friends to protect them.

He had been seeing the young, enthusiastic, and incredibly flexible staff worker on and off for more than a year now. Usually their trysts were reserved for Washington, D.C. but she had been in town visiting family, and well, the temptation was too great. So were the odds of getting caught. *Don't pee in the pool,* his father used to say. In other words, don't dally with the dolly in your hometown.

But sometimes he just couldn't say no.

Clyde lowered the towel. His hair stuck out in a hundred different directions. Still, there was a twinkle in his eyes, a curl to his lips. "You are one fine-looking piece of manhood," he told himself.

His reflection smiled back.

Sure, it had been dangerous, foolish even, but that had only added to the excitement. "Kept me pumping," he said, winking to himself.

The hotel-room door opened, squeaking like a yawning mouse. In the bathroom Clyde paused. *She's back.*

His athletic partner had returned for thirds. Miffed but titillated, Clyde yelled out, "Now, honey, we talked about this. I've got to hit the road." He stepped out of the bathroom, towel around his shoulders, pushing his hair back with his right hand and reflexively sucking in his gut. "Besides, baby, that last time left me as sore as a—"

Disbelief cleaved his words. His mind stumbled. His mouth was dry, face slack, his eyes widened in terror. His heart, his breath, his soul, went into lock-down.

The other man grinned.

Then United States Congressman Clyde Watkins got really scared.

6

PIPER BLACKMOORE put two bags of groceries on the floorboard and one on the passenger seat, then slammed the door. The black Ford Ranger shot out of the Shop-Lo parking lot and on to Davis Street like a thoroughbred out of the starting gate. Piper turned on to Asher Drive. The groceries rocked. She frowned, then begrudgingly eased off the accelerator, taking the next corner with a slow turn rather than her usual tire-squealing jerk.

She worked her way through the back streets, heading steadily north, sketching a jagged course on her journey home. She knew dozens of ways to go home but was always exploring new avenues. When you were born and raised in Black Valley, Oregon, you took your fun where you could find it.

She liked to go fast. In college she had dated a guy who was into motorcycles. And although the relationship never went anywhere, she had enjoyed the arousing sensation of shooting down the highway on a brightly colored, two-wheeled bullet. The relationship ended when she realized she was more attracted to the bike than the rider.

This latest route had come to her over breakfast, and although it was taking a temporary jaunt to the northeast, she hoped the absence of traffic lights would compensate for the more indirect course. She turned on to Maple Drive, then took a quick left on to Percy and was abruptly brought to a halt by a dreaded orange-and-black, diamond-shaped sign advising CONSTRUCTION AHEAD.

"Damn," she cursed. Percy Street was being expanded into four lanes, a process that left it all but impassable. She examined her options, then pulled into the rear parking lot of the Daybreak Hotel. The building faced Emerald Street. If she could wiggle through the car-clustered back lot and around to the front, she could slip back on to a main road and skirt around the inconvenient construction zone.

Again she was thwarted, this time by a large semi bearing the hotel logo that was being unloaded by three men in blue-and-gray jumpsuits. "Damn, damn, double damn."

So much for hurrying.

She sat for a moment trying to calm herself, a little startled by her disproportionate anger. Why was she so frustrated? On edge? It was just a game. There was no real hurry to get home. Nothing waiting but memories and ghosts. She rubbed her arms. She felt as if someone were scratching on a blackboard, clawing at the surface with dry, chipped nails.

She shuddered.

Goose bumps rippled her arms. She felt . . . ?

Like someone was walking on her grave.

The Ford Ranger droned impatiently. Piper Blackmoore shook her hands, flexing her fingers. Why did she feel so . . .? What?

The sun caught the windshield of a parked car; a burst of reflected light flashed in her face, causing her to squint. She held a hand up to shield her eyes. The rear of the Daybreak Hotel was industrial beige and brown with setback service doors and a triple row of windows, twelve long.

The window.

Something caught her eye. Face shielded from the splintered sunlight, she could clearly see into the window of a hotel room, just in front of her and one floor up. Two men appeared to be . . .?

My God.

As she watched, one man dropped to his knees, arms flailing; the other stood over him, hands around the fallen man's neck.

Choking him.

NATHAN PERKINS LOOKED out the window of the Downtown Daily Diner and chewed on the last of his fries. Dean Truman tracked his gaze. "As much as I love the idea of NxTech coming in here," Nathan said, "I still wish they had decided to put the darn thing somewhere other than Hawkins Hill. That place gives me the willies."

"Superstitious bunk," Dean snapped. "Completely unsubstantiated poppycock."

Nathan sipped his coffee. The warmth of the brew formed a fog of condensation on his glasses. He didn't seem to notice. "Always the scientist. Even after . . ."

The statement went unfinished.

The subject taboo.

"Well, gift horses and all that. I suppose I should just be grateful that we have such an outstanding citizen as yourself. Even if we don't understand that scientific voodoo you do, everybody respects you."

"Well, not everybody," Dean said. He sipped his coffee, then told Nathan about the brick through the window.

Alarm spread across his old friend's face. "You've got to tell John."

"The school reported it."

"This is serious, Dean. It could have taken your head off."

"At least then I wouldn't have to make a decision about NxTech."

Nathan tapped the table with his knuckles. "I'm not kidding. If not you, someone could have been hurt."

Dean sipped his coffee, holding the cup to his lips a moment longer, the rich aroma filling his nostrils. "Probably just kids. Or maybe protestors. You know, like they get down in Eugene."

Nathan nodded. "A few shortsighted people are always against the expansion."

Dean pointed with his index finger. "Exactly. Kids."

"Violent kids," Nathan added. "A bullet doesn't have an age limit. Remember what happened in Springfield."

Springfield, Oregon, May 21, 1998. Four dead, twenty-five injured. A fifteen-year-old boy charged with walking into the school cafeteria and gunning down his classmates.

"It wasn't a bullet. It was a brick."

"Still applies. Violence breeds violence."

Dean was quiet.

The brick.

It had appeared from nowhere.

He scanned his mind for an explanation. Maybe his eyes were getting bad? He should have them examined. If he was nearsighted, that might explain why he hadn't seen the originating point of the brick. Or perhaps it was launched from a natural blind spot, a position Dean couldn't see?

Somebody's watching us, Piper Blackmoore had said. Than a swish of – what? He had seen something. Cloth. A cape? Yeah, right. He was being stalked by Batman. Still, it was shortly after that the brick was thrown.

And what about the velocity? Through the window, through the wall. No one could throw a brick that fast. Then *what?*

A massive hand landed on his shoulder and Dean jumped. He looked up into the face of Black Valley County Sheriff John Evans.

"Clyde gone?" John asked, taking a seat at their table. He was holding a fresh cup of coffee.

"Just missed him," Dean said.

Nathan wasted no time. "John, glad you're here. Tell him, Dean."

"Is this about the thing at the school?" John asked. "You okay?" The sheriff turned his substantial gaze on Dean, his stoic face reflecting a subtle glint of worry. Since Judy's death John had been increasingly protective of Dean, almost as close as brothers.

"I'm fine."

John frowned. "Probably just kids."

"See?" Dean cried triumphantly.

"Still, I'd best look into it. Can't be too careful with our number-one citizen."

"See, right back at you," Nathan crowed.

Someone laughed on the other side of the diner. Dean looked up and caught Mavis's eye. She winked. He smiled and looked away shyly.

"Looks like rain," John said.

Outside, the thin line of gray clouds had expanded, like oil on water, filling a quarter of the sky.

"Forecast says sunshine all weekend," Nathan complained.

John shrugged. "Still looks like rain. Smells like it, too."

Ozone? That's what Dean had thought of a moment ago and then forgotten. There had been a strong scent of ozone just before the brick smashed through the glass. Or was he imagining that?

"You riding your bicycle?" John asked.

"Saving the environment with every pump of the pedal." The deepening gray clouds were clustering like conspirators near the top of Hawkins Hill.

John took a deep drink from his cup, then set it down on the table. "Come on. We'll throw your bike in the back of my Jeep. I want to swing by the school and take a look at that brick."

"There's nothing to see. I'm telling you, you're over-reacting."

"Maybe. But I'd rather be too careful—"

"Than not careful enough," Dean and Nathan said in unison.

An unusual smile, like a curl of wood from a whittler's knife, creased John's face. "Guess I've said that before."

"About a billion times," Nathan replied. "Make that a billion and one."

Ozone? Dean pondered.

THE DESK CLERK WAS A HUSKY MAN with a young boy's face. He was talking on the phone when Piper ran into the lobby.

"He's trying to kill him!" she shouted. "In the room. You've got to stop him."

The clerk held up a portly finger, then uh-huhed someone on the phone.

"He's killing him!" Piper shouted.

"Excuse me, please." The clerk put a hand over the mouthpiece. "I'll be with you in a moment."

Emboldened by fear and adrenaline, she reached across the desk, jerked the receiver from the clerk's frankfurter fingers, and slammed it into the cradle.

"Hey, what do you think you're doing?"

"There's a man being murdered in one of your hotel rooms."

The clerk blinked as if a flashbulb had just gone off in his face. "Murdered? What do you mean, 'murdered'?"

"As in no longer living, you idiot. For God's sake, give me the passkey and dial nine-one-one."

That got his attention. "Betty, call the sheriff," he said to a woman pushing a cart of soiled linens. He pulled a key ring from a hook under the desk. "Which room?"

"Second floor. I'm not sure. I saw it from the parking lot."

They took the stairs two at a time. The stairwell emptied into the middle of the hallway. Twelve rooms facing the rear parking lot – six on the right, six on the left.

"Which way?" the clerk asked.

"Left."

Despite his girth he moved quickly, rushing down the hall, Piper at his heels. "Which room?"

Piper ran her hand through her hair. Her skin felt

galvanized. The tips of her fingers cold. "I don't know, I don't know. I didn't count. I just looked up and there they were. Start knocking on doors."

The clerk went to the closest door and started pounding with the soft side of his fist. "Hotel manager. Open up!"

When there was no response, he used the key, disappeared, then reemerged shaking his head. "It's empty."

Piper had moved past him, past the next door and the one after that. A thunderstorm was raging beneath her skin. Her blood had been replaced with Freon, chilling her body as it rushed through her system. *No, no*, she silently said at each door. Then she stopped.

"Here. They're in here," she screamed, then began hammering on the door.

"How do you know?" The clerk raced to join her, passkey held in front of him like a protective sword.

"I just do. Open up." She beat the door with rapid fire. "Open up."

The clerk pushed her aside. His breathing was labored; a fine mist of sweat had already formed on his oval face. He put the key in the lock. It clicked. The knob turned freely. He pushed. The door shook, moved a fraction of an inch, then stopped.

"What?" The clerk was momentarily baffled, then realized what had happened. "The slide lock. Someone must have engaged the slide bolt from the inside."

Piper Blackmoore shook her arms and flexed her

fingers, like a gunfighter getting ready for a show-down. *In that room, in that room, whatever it is, it's in that room.*

"He's dying," she whispered.

"Stand back." The clerk retreated to the opposite wall, then, running slammed into the door with the full force of his body. Wood splintered. The door swung open. Unable to stop his momentum, the clerk tumbled forward, landing hard on the industrial green carpet.

The room was open before her. A bed, nightstand, bathroom (door open), a shelf with a bar for clothing, complete with hangers dangling from it. A TV mounted on the wall.

The bed. Bare feet. Someone was lying on his back on the other side of the bed. Driven by some internal scream of urgency, Piper stepped over the fallen desk clerk and rushed into the room.

On the floor lay a naked man, hair still wet from the shower, face the color of typing paper, mouth agape, eyes wide, tongue swollen. Choking.

And around his bruised-purple neck, clutching the skin in a pincer grip, a hand and nothing else.

7

NATHAN PERKINS STOPPED HIM in the hall outside the intensive care unit. "He's alive, Dean, barely, but alive."

Dean Truman nodded, his pulse surging, his breathing shallow. "We were at the school – the brick, John wanted to see it – when we got the call. What happened? The desk nurse said he choked."

Nathan Perkins shifted nervously. He wiped the edges of his mouth with his hand, then said, "He was strangled."

"Strangled? What do you mean? Strangled? How? Who?"

"I don't know. They called me at the office. I don't know anything else. It doesn't make any sense."

A page summoned Dr. Pompaous to the third floor. An orderly pushed a medical wagon with a wobbly left wheel down the green-and-beige-tiled hallway. The errant wheel squeaked like a rusted shutter hinge in a windstorm. *Squeak, squeal, squeak, squeal*.

"And there's something else going on," Nathan said. "I don't know what, but there is definitely something else. John's talking to Piper now."

"Piper? Piper Blackmoore? What's she doing here?"

"She's the one who found Clyde. They say she saved his life. Gave him CPR right there in the hotel room."

An old woman in a flannel nightgown inched her way down the hall with the aid of a chrome walker.

"What were Clyde and Piper doing in a hotel?" Dean asked. The answer flashed across his mind. Clyde had always been a ladies' man, and Piper Blackmoore was certainly attractive. Clyde and Piper? No.

"She wasn't with him. At least, I don't think she was. Sounds like she saw him through a window or something." Nathan shook his head and studied his faint reflection in the polished floor. "I don't understand any of this. I'm waiting on Clyde's wife to get here. And the baby, my God, she's just eighteen months old."

John Evans came out of a room two doors down. A disheveled Piper Blackmoore was two steps behind. Guilt for his earlier thought squeezed Dean's heart. Next to the sheriff, she looked like a small, frightened child. She pushed her black hair behind her ears, then hugged herself.

Dean wanted to go to her, to comfort her, to hold her. But he didn't. "You okay?" was all he could muster.

Her brown eyes were moist and red. A feeble smile, like a static charge, flicked across her soft, gentle face. "Been better."

John took off his flat-brimmed hat. "Doctors say Clyde's in a coma. By all rights he should be dead. He's in a critical but stable condition."

Dean could hear the labored breathing of the ancient heating system trying to hold winter at arm's length. Somewhere a monitor beeped. The orderly stopped the cart he was pushing, pulled out a tray, and entered a room four doors down.

"He was strangled? How? I mean, was it an accident?"

A look passed between the sheriff and the young history professor – a look that chilled Dean.

"It wasn't an accident," John said. Dean noticed his friend for the first time. Sleepless nights had left black troughs under his red eyes. His face was tense. Eyes squinted. Preoccupied.

"There's something else," Dean stated. "What aren't you telling me?"

The sheriff looked down the hall. The old woman had reached the nurses' station. Their whispered conversation indecipherable, rustling like leaves in a rain gutter.

The orderly returned to the cart, pushing it. *Squeak, squeal, squeak, squeal.*

"Come with me," John said.

SHE RAN with the wind at her back, pushing, shoving, encouraging her up Hawkins Hill. Arms pumping in sync with her legs, heart pumping in sync with her arms, condensed air puffing in controlled bursts like a steam locomotive from a time long past, climbing, climbing. The sun was already perched on the western horizon. A low ceiling of clouds made the night seem impatient.

But she would finish her run. Whether it was working on the city council, running her own business, or raising a family, Meredith Gamble never did anything halfway. And one of the things she did was run. Every day, seven days a week. In the morning if she could; in the evening if she had to. After joining the city council, jogging had been a way of releasing pent-up frustration. That it helped her drop twenty pounds and develop an athlete's frame was a pleasant bonus. Now it was as much a part of her life as her husband or her children.

Hawkins Hill rose before her. She followed the trail up, up, up.

Keep running.

Her route changed from time to time; when winter finally established its frigid grip on Black Valley, she would confine her jogs to the valley floor, doubling the length to compensate for the lesser grade. Usually, it was well into December before she made the change. But this year, with clouds as dark and ominous as a gun barrel and taking a marksman's aim on the earth, this year she knew she couldn't wait that long. In fact, if the weather continued to deteriorate, this would be her last chance to circle the base of Hawkins Hill.

Something stung her face. A sharp pain. She shook her head. A *bee?* Too cold. She slipped the glove off her right hand and touched her cheek. A shard of glass no larger than a dime was embedded in her skin. She pulled it out, the point red with blood. She touched her face. Her fingertips came away crimson.

Damn.

She pulled a tissue from her fanny pack – her utility belt, her husband called it – and applied it to her cheek.

She kept running.

Glass?

She must have stepped on something in the near gloom, flinging the chip into her face. Too dark, too cold. Below, in the valley, where the houses huddled like kittens around a mother's belly, streetlights stood sentry over the sidewalks, looking warm and inviting. This was definitely her last run around the hill.

Something struck her chest. One, two, three . . .

What the—

Glass? Three more shards. They struck her jogging suit but didn't penetrate the thick layer of clothing she wore. She plucked them out. Two like the first, one the size of a fifty-cent piece. Big enough to hurt. This was getting dangerous.

She thought of stopping, of searching for the source. No. She never stopped. Not unless it was completely unavoidable. Someone had been here before her and shattered a bottle on the trail, that was all. Surely she was out of the field of glass by now?

Nevertheless, she scanned the ground ahead of her as best she could. The trail appeared free of debris.

Something bit her leg. Two more fragments hit her right arm and shoulder. She bent to pull the glass from the top of her leg. Tiny shards struck her scalp, like sharp, hard pellets. She stumbled as a larger fragment of glass struck her in the right side. Hard. Fast. She felt the impact before she felt the jabbing pain.

Stabbed.

She had been stabbed. The glass cut through her clothing and deep into her flesh. A dark, burgundy bloom spread across her jogging suit. Feeling light-headed, she stumbled again, yet somehow, miraculously, she stayed on her feet. Her steps, however, were short and faltered.

White pinwheels materialized in the corners of her vision. She suddenly felt flushed. What was happening? Where was the glass coming from?

She raised her head, looking down the long, narrow trail. And then she saw it. At first it looked like a curtain of rain, only it wasn't. Crimson fingers of light from a decaying sun reached out, refracted and reflecting. Not rain.

Glass.

A shower, a storm of glass, hurtling straight for her – straight for her.

Meredith Gamble opened her mouth to scream. Then hundreds, thousands, of vulgar shards hurtling at impossible speeds hit her body with an unyielding force. One shard pierced her leg to the bone. A sheet of glass the size of a shingle hit her neck, severing the jugular. Hot blood spewed into the air, a liquid imitation of the setting sun. Glass struck her again and again and again.

Her body jerked like a doll on a string in the hands of a clumsy puppeteer, held upright by a continuous, endless storm of rending glass.

DEAN TRUMAN JERKED BACKWARD. They were standing by a tall table with a small chrome tray in the center. A white cloth had been pulled back, revealing a human hand. "What the hell? Is that for real?"

John nodded. "Miss Blackmoore and the clerk say, when they found Clyde, this was around his throat, strangling him."

They were in the morgue, where their conversation was underscored by the constant drone of the refrigeration units. At the back of the room one of the fluorescent lights flickered but stayed on.

"Strangling him. That's impossible."

The hand was pinkish gray, like meat left out too long. Lying palm up, the hand's fingers were slightly curled. Dean's initial alarm faded. Panic ebbed, replaced by the tide of a new emotion: curiosity. "Do we know who it belongs to?"

John pressed his left fist into his right hand, cracking the knuckles, a frequent gesture when he was frustrated. "No missing hands have been reported at lost and found."

Strangling him?

Dean exhaled. "Let's take a step back. Any idea what Clyde was doing at a hotel?"

"A woman, most likely. You know Clyde. So far, we haven't found her. You were one of the last to see him. Anything unusual happen? Did he seem distracted? Impatient?"

"He was in a hurry, like always, but nothing unusual." Dean thought of the stranger, the man with the long, dark coat and tattered hat, the man watching but not watching – there, then gone. It was an errant thought. No connection, the scientist decided. Besides, the stranger had had two hands.

"So, what do you think? You're the county coroner."

"Don't remind me." When all three doctors at the small city hospital had turned down the job, John and Nathan had turned to Dean, double-teaming him until he took the position. They argued that, as a scientist, his analytical mind would allow him to detach himself from the more grisly aspects of the job.

To his disappointment, they were right. But that didn't mean he had to like it.

"Have you checked for splatters and blood droplets – outside as well as inside the room, in the hallway, and in the stairwell?"

"My best deputy, Jerry Niles, is down there right

now, but so far nothing." John swiped a hand through his bristlelike hair. "No weapon, nothing. If someone was choking Clyde, and Clyde cut his attacker's hand off in self-defense, then the attacker took the weapon with him and left his hand. Another thing: the blood – there isn't enough of it."

John laid his hat on a countertop, took a handkerchief from his pocket, and wiped his forehead. "Any thoughts?"

"I usually have a little more to work with than this," Dean replied.

A smile actually crossed John's face. Dean imagined the sound of plaster cracking. "Give it your best shot."

Dean bent down, his face only inches from the appendage. A small pool of blood had collected on the tray just below the wrist. "It's a recent cut, very recent. Based on the slight degradation." He took a pen from his pocket and pushed the pad of the index finger. "And by the degree of rigor mortis, I would say it was cut off less than an hour ago."

He stood, walked to the end of the table, and bent again, studying the hand from a different angle. "It was definitely cut off. There is no sign of tearing or rending. Whatever was used was one hell of a sharp instrument."

He strode back to where he had started, picked up the tray, and turned into the light to see the wound better. "The bone is sliced. I'm not sure, but it appears to have been done with one stroke. There's no sign of sawing or repeated cutting."

"One stroke?" John asked incredulously. "What the hell could do that? An axe?"

"No, an axe cuts at an angle; this is completely straight." Dean used the pen to lift a flap of flesh. "See, it's severed cleanly. Amazingly so. There's no serration. Bone is porous but thick; you can't slice through it like cutting through a birthday cake."

Dean set the tray down and returned his pen to his pocket. "And I can also tell you, this is not the hand that choked Clyde Watkins. If he was strangled by a hand at all."

"I've seen the bruising. It's consistent with someone using his hands."

"Well, it wasn't *this* hand."

"How do you know?"

"For one thing, it takes a hell of a lot of strength to strangle someone – almost impossible to do with one hand." He nodded toward the tray. "Again, I'm no medical doctor, but the ligaments here don't look particularly well defined. This is not someone who does physical work for a living. Besides, it's an impossible scenario."

John put the handkerchief back in his pocket, but the pensive look remained. "The whole damn thing is an impossible scenario. Miss Blackmoore says she saw two men through the hotel window, one choking the other. When she and the desk clerk arrived, they found the door locked from the inside. They had to break it down. Clyde was the only one inside. They didn't leave the room until the paramedics arrived, about the same time Jerry and I got there. It's a single room with a bath. There's not even a closet, just a pole under a shelf to hang your clothes on. So, if there was no one else in that room, who locked the door?"

"Someone who went out the window?"

"Nailed shut. The owner put in air-conditioning about three years ago and didn't want guests leaving them open. Believe me, no one went out the window."

The fluorescent light at the back of the room flickered again. The strobing effect of light and shadows made the fingers of the severed hand appear to move. The high-pitched hiss of the faltering light now competed with the refrigeration drone.

Dean clutched his hands and steepled his index fingers, then gently tapped his lips. "Locked from inside: what kind of lock?"

"Slide and catch. Simple design. The main component is mounted on the door. You then lift the lever and slide the small pin into the metal receptacle mounted to the door frame."

The light flickered again, then returned to normal. The hissing stopped.

John put on his hat, moved it once to secure its placement, then ran his thumb and forefinger across the brim. "Like I said, the whole damn thing is impossible."

8

"THEY WERE STUNNED," Nathan Perkins said, slipping the green, Japanese-silk pajama bottoms over his dead-fish-white legs.

"So they really liked it?" Ava asked, her bat-wing-size eyelashes fluttering with excitement.

"They really liked it." He hated lying but hated hurting Ava even more.

She squealed with delight, hugging him against her sizable, and almost-paid-for, chest. "What did that old stuffed shirt Jenkins Jones say – exactly?"

The most butt-ugly painting ever produced in the entire butt-ugly world.

"I don't remember," he lied again, part of him amazed by how quick and easy the words came.

She frowned. "But you said they liked it?"

"They did, baby, they did. They were bowled over. Even that old fart, Jenkins Jones. It's just there were so many wonderful comments that I can't really remember who said what. That's all."

Ava giggled and clapped her hands. Like a child, Nathan thought. It was a frequent observation. She was fifteen years his junior. Not a child in any chronological sense, yet she maintained a youthful zest and temperament. So what if she was moody and flashy, with taste that ran toward the extreme?

They had met in Portland. She was a clerk at the Hertz car rental booth, but she handled herself as if she were a queen. That was her way. "You are as you act," she was fond of saying. And Ava acted as if the world was her plaything. Six months after meeting, they were married and Nathan had become her favorite toy.

It was the most impulsive thing he had ever done, and eyebrows in Black Valley were raised high. But most of the criticism could be dismissed as envy. Nathan had never before been the subject of envy, and it was an experience he liked.

Ava invigorated him.

"I'm really glad they liked it, but I hope they understand what I'm trying to say," she said as she lowered her legs beneath the silk sheets of their king-size bed. Nathan did the same but with greater caution. Silk pajamas on silk sheets made him nervous. Any sudden moves and he would shoot right off the bed.

"Nathan, are you listening to me?"

"Yeah, sure, honey."

"Is something wrong? You seem distracted."

Nathan took off his glasses and set them carefully on the nightstand. He rubbed the sore spot on the bridge of his nose. One of these days he would get contacts – if they ever made contacts with the consistency of ashtrays.

He had purposely not told her about Clyde. He knew she would become distraught. Better to wait until morning than upset her now and have them both lose seep.

"It's Dean," he said, then realized it was, in part.

"Dr. Truman?"

"Yeah, we had lunch together. And well, someone threw a brick through his classroom window."

"How awful. Was he hurt?"

"No. In fact, he didn't seem worried about it, which worried me. So I made him tell John."

"Good for you."

"John went up to the school with him." He turned on his side, carefully. Elbow on his pillow, head in his hand so he could see her, watch her, breathe her. She favored him with a smile that sent electric shivers through his groin.

"Is he still seeing Mavis? He needs a good woman, and she's the best."

"No, she's the second best," he said. "I got number one." She giggled and Nathan realized it was the first truthful statement he had made all night. "But no, they're not really dating right now."

"Why not?" Ava asked, genuinely concerned.

"He says it's Judy." Nathan paused. He heard the living-room clock chime. "I talked to Mavis afterward.

She said he stopped seeing her after she tried to visit him at home."

"His house? Why does he still live in that dilapidated place? He can certainly afford better. Especially now."

"I know. But he's always been weird about that house. Almost protective."

"He's a bachelor. Maybe he just didn't want her to see the mess it was in."

"The few times I've been there it's been immaculate. Everything neat, concise, orderly. Just like Dean. No. There's something else. I just don't know what it is."

"Back to my art," Ava said, slipping off her pajama bottoms. "Tell me everything they said, every word they uttered about the painting. And I'll listen quietly because it's not polite to talk with your mouth full."

She slipped under the covers, and Nathan Perkins began to lie.

PIPER BLACKMOORE SHOOK HER HANDS and flexed her fingers. The empty hall of the second floor of the Daybreak Hotel stretched out before her like a long, narrow question. Twelve rooms, six doors to a side. The flat, worn carpet was gray and burgundy in a series of triangles. She hadn't noticed that before. Four doors down, at the next to the last room, multiple strips of yellow-and-black crime scene tape crisscrossed the broken entrance.

"You okay?" Dean asked.

She dry-swallowed and smiled as she pushed her hair behind her ears. "Yeah, I'm fine."

Sheriff John Evans carefully peeled back the tape. He motioned for Dean and Piper to join him.

Piper's eyes were as open as the door, drawn to the room like light sucked into a black hole. She could see the bed. Was there a body outline on the other side?

The clerk who had broken down the door was so distraught that he had to be medicated. That left Piper. She had agreed to retrace her steps after the sheriff told her that Dr. Truman had a theory.

"I'm glad somebody does," she had whispered.

Dean touched her arm. She took comfort in the gesture, dry-swallowed once more, then recounted her story.

The whole thing took less than five minutes. Part of the time Dean seemed as focused as a laser; at other times, distracted and distant.

When she finished, all eyes turned to Dean. The professor didn't seem to notice. He spent four minutes staring at the back of the broken door. He steepled his fingers and tapped his lips. His eyes moved rapidly, shifting from spot to spot, calculating as if reading unseen numbers, deciphering invisible words.

"Got a passkey?" Dean asked.

John held it up. "Got it from the relief clerk."

"Good. Let's go to the next room and I'll show you what happened."

*

PORTLAND, OREGON, WAS DOMED with a clear, purpling sky. Light gray ribbons of interstates crisscrossed the lazy Willamette River, disappearing into a city of multicolored brick, glass, and steel; a new city with an old-world charm. Seattle Lite, one travel guide described it. But Mason Evans knew better. It wasn't what Portland had that made the difference, but rather what it *didn't* have: the tourists and the aggressive commercialism. It was, at least for now, the undiscovered country, as beautiful as the land of Oz and almost as magical.

It was Mason Evans's birthday, and in a rare glimmer of mercy the vile woman who had once been his wife had allowed the kids to spend the day with their father. Or maybe it was just that the kids were getting too old for the Wicked Witch of the Northwest to sway them.

The big man smiled. He was grayer, heavier, but still a formidable fellow with an imposing posture. He worked out daily, priding himself on his physique. He no longer worked on the construction sites, but when you owned a construction company, it helped to look like you could still hammer a nail with the best of them.

"Jeffrey Hill's daddy bought them a Jet Ski," Donald announced without prerequisite. The fresh-faced fourteen-year-old smiled as he gnawed on a slice of pizza.

"Well, since it's my birthday, maybe you should buy me a Jet Ski?"

Donald wobbled his head, chewing with his mouth open; he paused for a moment, as if considering the idea. "Sure. Just bump up my allowance a hundred thousand dollars and I'll buy you two Jet Skis."

"Eat your pizza, smart guy. You already make more than some of the fellows that work for me." His birthday – Mason couldn't remember the last time he had enjoyed it so much. Professionally he was a success. M. C. Evans Construction was one of the largest, fastest-growing companies in the state, but personally he just couldn't seem to get the hang of things. His first marriage lasted only three years and had produced nothing but pain and alimony. His second lasted twice that long, but ended just as badly – with more alimony and, this time, child support.

But the kids made it worthwhile. Tina had been born right away, Donald five years later. They were the only thing in his private life he had ever gotten right.

"Tina, the pizza's getting cold," he called upstairs.

"Down in a minute, Daddy."

He saw Donald every other weekend and whenever the Blazers were having a home game that wasn't on a school night. But Tina – his time with her was precious and rare. And now that she was going to college, living in a dorm at the University of Oregon two hours away, it was even rarer.

Seeing her bounce down the stairs, ponytail bobbing behind her, Mason was overwhelmed with a sense of nostalgia – remembering her as a Barbieloving, cartoon-watching, lap-sitting Daddy's girl.

"I'll just grab a slice of 'za for the road," she said, removing a triangle of Canadian-bacon-and-pineapple from the box, and leaving a contrail of cheese, which she broke with her finger and looped on top.

"I'll just grab a slice of 'za for the road," Donald said, mimicking his older sister.

She slapped the back of his head, as much by reflex as annoyance. "Why don't you grow up, worm?"

"Why don't you throw up?"

"Oh, that's good. Snappy comeback."

"Snappy comeback," Donald echoed.

"Donald."

The fourteen-year-old smiled, unfettered. "I'll take a slice of 'za. Why can't she talk normal?" He looked at his sister as she bit off the point of her slice. "It's pizza, *peeee*-tzah. Not, 'za. Whatcha do when you order a hamburger? Say, 'Give me some 'urgers to go'?"

She slapped the back of his head again with her left hand, pizza wedge perfectly balanced in her right. "Jerk," she muttered.

"Jerkette," he replied, then flinched, expecting retaliation. But she ignored him, concentrating instead on finishing her food.

Mason noticed her overnight bag at the foot of the stairs. "You're leaving? Already?"

"Daddy, I have a term paper due next week."

"But there's no school on Monday. It's an in-service day. That gives you three days."

"But I've got a two-hour drive." She abandoned the crust in favor of a fresh piece. "Oh, gross – onions." She flicked the offending vegetables into the box lid.

"You like onions," Mason said.

"Not anymore."

"Since when?"

"Since she fell in loooove," Donald crooned.

"Shut up, jerk."

"A new boyfriend?" Mason asked.

"It's no big deal, Daddy. Nothing to wrinkle about."

"That's not what she told Deirdre on the phone this morning," Donald said, then affecting a falsetto voice, reenacted the conversation. " 'Oh, Dee – he's just the best, a real hunk. I've never met anyone like him in my entire life – he's so different.' "

"Die, dweeb!" She flicked an onion bit at him. It struck his cheek, then dripped down on to his white T-shirt.

"Daaaad," Donald wailed.

"Jerk," she snapped.

"Kids," Mason barked – saying that one word, that one way, that they both knew meant *Stop this before I get mad and you get into trouble*.

Mumbling and whining, Donald left to wipe his face and change his shirt. Tina wasn't the only one who was becoming image conscious, Mason noted with a measure of sadness.

Alone with Tina, he pushed the subject. "Now, about this boy . . ."

"Daddy."

"I'm just curious."

"For one thing, he's not a boy. He's a man."

Mason shuddered despite himself. "Does he go to the U. of O.?"

"Yeah, but he's about to graduate. He's really nice, Daddy, and so cool."

Donald returned sans onion but still wearing the same shirt, a photograph in his hand. He stared at the picture as if trying to decipher some alien language. "He doesn't look so special to me."

"Ahhhh – give me that, you creep." She moved fast, snatching the photograph from his hands and slapping the back of his head in what, to Mason, looked like one smooth stroke.

"I'd love to stay and play games, but I've really got to go." Then to her brother: "If for no other reason than to get away from you."

He smiled. "Thank you very much."

She smiled back. "You're not very welcome." She checked her watch. "Oh, God, I'm late."

"Late? How can you be late?" Mason asked. "Classes don't start until Tuesday."

"She must have a date," Donald deduced. "A date with Mr. Wonderful."

Tina glowered, retrieved her bag from the foot of the stairs, then returned to Mason, her small, delicate hand landing on his shoulder like a sparrow on an I-beam. "Next time, Daddy, I promise, you can give me the third degree. But I really do need to get on the road."

He laid his hand on hers, covering it two times over. She gave him a soft kiss on the cheek. "Happy birthday, old man. I love you."

"Love you, too, honey." He kissed her hand, then reluctantly let go.

"Bye, creep," she said to Donald as she hurried for the door.

"Bye, dork," he answered.

At the doorway she stopped. "Where are my keys?"

"On the table by the phone," Mason answered on a hunch.

"Yeah, here they are. Thanks, Daddy. I'll call soon, promise." And she was gone.

THAT NIGHT, after he returned Donald to the clutches of his ex-wife, the house seemed a vacuum, as cold and lonely as the dark side of the moon. The place was really too big for just him, but he kept it anyway. It was too full of memories, too infused with the feel of the children, for him to sell it.

He dropped a pair of ice cubes into a pebbled glass. They rattled like transparent dice, then hissed with joy at the first splash of Scotch. Minutes later he repeated the process but without the ice.

When the phone rang, he half expected it to be one of the children saying they had left this or that. They always did. He was disappointed when it turned out to be business.

"Mason?" It was his chief foreman. "We got that load of lumber in from Oakridge today. You want me to take it over to the Hamptons' site in the morning?" The man had been with Mason for more than ten years. He was a quiet, cautious fellow who wouldn't take his shirt off without running it through channels. Not the most vibrant employee, but the one least likely to pick the company's pockets.

"That's what we bought it for, ain't it?"

"Just checking." The phone line crackled. "You okay?"

"Sure, I'm okay. Why the hell wouldn't I be?" Mason barked.

"No reason. You just, well, you sound half-drunk."

"That's right. Only half-drunk – and I'll finish the job when I get off the damn phone." Somewhere in the cavernous house a grandfather clock chimed. Mason was aware of the chimes, but couldn't follow the count.

"Alrighty, then. Just asking. And happy birthday."

Mason sighed, struggling to control his misplaced hostility. "Thanks."

He hung up without saying goodbye and reached unconsciously for his Scotch. He drained it in one turn.

Something caught his eye. A photograph. The one of Tina and her new boyfriend? A fellow who was so totally cool. *I'll have to send it to her*, Mason told himself.

She must have left it on the end table when she was looking for her keys.

The picture.

He's not a boy. He's a man. The statement played in his head like an unnerving echo.

Mason put down his empty glass, went into the foyer, and picked up the picture. Tina, dressed in a bright-yellow-and-green University of Oregon jersey, was smiling like the morning sun, and with her – with his arms around her . . .

He's not a boy. He's a man.

In the picture with his daughter . . .

I've never met anyone like him in my entire life – he's so different.

The room began to spin. His mind lost all mooring with reality. He struggled to maintain consciousness.

Mason Evans had felt this way only one other time in his life: the night they had opened the coffin and found it empty.

He began to scream.

DESPITE HER ASSURANCES, Dean was concerned for Piper Blackmoore. Even as he worked – calculating, evaluating, and postulating – he kept a close eye on the young history professor, watchful for the first hint, the first indication, of *shock*. She had been put in a horrifying situation and had responded remarkably well, had even saved Clyde's life. But now, as the surging tides of adrenaline began to subside, the mental, emotional, and physical effects of the event would surface. And returning to the scene of the crime could only make things worse.

The room was identical to the one in which Clyde had been found. Same carpet, curtains, bedspread. Same layout: a single room, one bed, one nightstand, wall-mounted television, no closet, and a simple bathroom with a shower, sink, and mirror. He checked the windows. John was right; they were nailed shut.

He took a quick look at Piper. She was chewing on a fingernail. Her complexion was a shade paler than normal.

The door to the hotel room contained the same interior lock as the other. He inspected the slide bolt. It was old, like the hotel. He slipped the small, knobbed handle up, out of the retaining notch. It held. He smiled and looked over his shoulder. The others watched as if he were Siegfried and Roy and a pride of white tigers all rolled into one. He found the attention uncomfortable.

Dean reached into the sleeve of his raincoat.

Nothing up my sleeve, he was tempted to say. He pulled a single black thread approximately fourteen inches long from the frayed lining. "Piper, you stay in here. John, why don't you step into the hall so you can see what I do?"

He waited until John was in the hall. The bolt knob remained outside of the notch. Dean looped the thread around it, stepped into the hall trailing the string behind him, then gently closed the door so as not to cause the knob to fall back into the notch. He pulled carefully, felt the thread grow taut, pulled harder, then heard the faint *click*. He then smiled.

"Try the door," he told the sheriff.

John turned the handle. The master lock turned easily, but the slide bolt was now engaged, effectively locking the door from the inside. "Well, I'll be damned."

"Thread. He used a thread?" Piper's voice carried through the door.

Dean knocked. "You can let us in now."

She did, her eyes wide with surprise.

"So the person who tried to kill Mr. Watkins locked the door from the inside by pulling the bolt into the holder with a thread?" Piper repeated.

Dean held up a cautionary finger. "Possibly. It's just one of the many ways the same circumstances could have been created."

"Many ways?"

"Yes. I stopped reading locked-room murder mysteries when I was thirteen because the answers were all too apparent. And frequently I could figure out easier, better ways to do the same thing."

"I'll have my deputies check the room for fiber evidence," John said.

"Thread?" Piper said again.

"Everything can be explained by science," Dean said. His oft-used refrain.

"What about the hand?" Piper challenged.

Her color had returned. She really was a remarkable woman. "Applied after Clyde was choked. Still—" A thought hung just out of reach.

"Whose hand is it?" John interrupted. "And if the wound is as fresh as it appears—"

"Then the victim would have to be nearby."

Squawlk. John's radio bleated. *"Base to one-oh-one, base to one-oh-one – Sheriff, you there?"*

John keyed the mike. "Go ahead, Maggie."

"Better get over over to Hawkins Trail . . ." Static swallowed the next two words, but Dean could make out the final phase, *". . . a ten thirty-two."*

As country coroner, he knew what a 10-32 meant. "A body," he moaned.

John's already stern face became granite. "I think we just found the victim."

9

THE SUN WAS GONE, as were the stars and moon. In the moment between shutting off the car and turning on the flashlight, Dean Truman had the unnerving sense that the world had disappeared, as if God had snatched it away.

John's police-issued flashlight cast a cone of yellow-ivory light. "Sure you want to do this?" he asked.

"Yeah, I'm sure," Dean replied as they headed up the trail. "This close to the school, it may be someone I know. Besides, I'm the county coroner. I have to."

The path, worn into the side of the butte by continual use, circled Hawkins Hill at a slight, steady incline before dropping back sharply and depositing the traveler at the beginning of the trail. In the summer it was frequented by many serious joggers. Even in the fall, when all the leaves were gone, Dean could occasionally see bobbing forms in bright Lycra huffing their way around the circumference. Not so much in the winter. And this early cold spell had already shooed away most visitors.

They turned the bend and spied an island of harsh,

blue-white light emanating from a pair of powerful halogen lamps. The lamps, on sturdy metal stands, operating on independent power supplies, were staged on opposite sides of the path.

Dean had the discombobulating sensation of watching a movie: an archaeological dig revealing ancient secrets newly discovered, or clandestine government agents stealing away the remains of some extraterrestrial spacecraft that had smashed into the side of the hill.

Spacecraft? Where had that come from? Dean shook his head, attempting to slough off his uneasiness. What was wrong with him? He was a scientist. Spooky sensations and flinching at bumps in the night were the purview of the uneducated. His was a trained mind, trained almost from birth to seek, examine, and comprehend.

Yet the sense of foreboding remained.

Something crunched beneath their feet. John shone the light on the ground. The earth glittered.

Glass?

Dean's steps faltered. His legs seemed tentative. The sheriff continued. Dean scrambled to keep up. He recognized John's deputies, Jerry Niles and Coye Cheevers. The latter shifted his weight from foot to foot, shoulders hunched, wringing his hands, nervous as a death-row inmate. Cheevers was not a strong man. His position with the sheriff's department was the only solid evidence that big, bad Sheriff John Evans had a tender, albeit small, heart at his center. The deputy wiped his mouth with the back of his hand, then stepped into the shadows.

Dean could hear him retching – the sound of dry heaves, of a man who had already purged.

The path, and much of the surrounding ground, sparkled as resplendent light was caught, refracted, and splintered into a thousand pieces. And in the center? Dean forced himself to look and immediately understood his uneasiness.

A thing. A *thing*. That's what it was. The pretense of humanity was minimal, its similarity to a person like that of a shadow to its caster. Dean recognized dark hair, flashes of pink flesh. A mound of shredded, slashed fabric and flesh – white, blue, black, and red. Lots of red. A crimson, dirty red. The color of blood stained with sin and secrets.

Subconsciously he must have recognized the fabric and, by extrapolation, the victim. Meredith Gamble. She was on the city council. He had seen her just yesterday. She was a jogger. Hardcore. She would be on the trail when all others had called it quits for the season.

Dean stopped just outside the cone of light. John continued on, talking to his crew, the ground crunching beneath his feet.

"Meredith Gamble." Dean realized he must have said the name out loud. Conversation stopped. The sheriff and his deputy looked back at him.

"You sure?" John asked, though the words were more statement than question. John Evans had always placed his highest confidence in Dean. Even before the awards and accolades, it was John, more than anybody, who had treated Dean with professional respect.

"I can't be sure without a closer look, but the clothes . . ." He stepped into the light. The ground crunched beneath him. He squatted. Thousands and thousands of shards of glass – some no larger than a BB, others the size of a fist, at least four pieces the length and shape of a license plate.

Glass?

The thing on the ground, the thing he believed to be Meredith Gamble, had been shredded and slashed, but by thousands of shards of jagged glass, hundreds of which protruded from her body like bloodstained quills. There were entrance and exit wounds where thousands of splinters had slashed completely through the body, leaving ragged holes in cloth and skin.

"What is this, Sheriff? What happened?" Deputy Jerry Niles asked his superior. He was a young man with serious, hard eyes.

But the sheriff had no ready answer. Though he maintained his trademark expression of stoic control, his jawline revealed a silent clenching and unclenching of teeth, the only hint of frayed nerves.

"Nothing around for thousands of yards," Jerry continued. "Closest building is the school. Cheevers checked and said there was no broken glass, except for one windowpane."

John looked at Dean, both realizing it was his window, shattered by a brick that very afternoon. But that one pane could not account for all the glass on the ground, the bushes, and the flesh of Meredith Gamble.

How had it gotten here? How could it have been hurled with such force?

"An airplane?" John asked. "Could it have come from an aircraft?"

"A plane." Dean warmed to the idea. "Possibly. That would certainly explain the lack of obvious origin, as well as apparent velocity."

"I can check with the FAA," Jerry said.

Dean stepped closer, squatting near the body. He was greeted with the dreadful smell of raw flesh and blood. *Meredith*. He fought his gag reflex by summoning the scientist. He studied the body with a practiced detachment. "Whatever the origin, it hit her body with tremendous force."

Dean chewed on a new thought. "Point of impact was face on." Dean looked up and out into the darkness, out to where he knew the trail continued to climb.

"She would have had to be lying on the ground to be hit in the face from falling debris." He stood and took several steps back, then squatted again. "Can I see your flashlight?"

John tossed him the large plastic instrument. Using

the pen he had used earlier to examine the hand, Dean turned over several shards of glass. He knew he was breaking regulations, contaminating a crime scene, and dozens of other rules, but John made no effort to stop him.

"John, Jerry, you may want to bag this," he said, using lingo garnered from movies and novels. He pointed to a row of glass. "The shards show remnants of blood and cloth, like they passed through the body."

"Through?" Jerry questioned. "That's five feet away. Then—"

"Then she would have had to be standing, meaning the glass came at her head-on – meaning it couldn't have fallen from a plane."

"Then from where?"

The night hung in silence.

"There's another problem," John said. "She's still got both her hands."

Somewhere in the dark Deputy Cheevers retched again.

HIS PASSKEY GAVE HIM ENTRANCE into the building. He flicked a switch; a single row of lights winked to life, shoving shadows to one side. He used a different key to unlock his classroom. Inside, Dean Truman paused before turning on the lights. Out his window he could just make out the glow from the large police lights.

The image of Meredith Gamble flashed involuntarily

in his mind. Hacked to death by *what*? Where had all that glass come from? How had it been delivered with such force?

He flipped three switches. Multiple rows of light hummed to life. The classroom woke.

Dr. Dean Truman was a scientist. Logic was his constant companion. A man accustomed to deciphering the undecipherable. His curiosity and determination had provided the propulsion that drove his career. There was always an answer – always. It was that kind of determination that had won him the Nobel Prize.

Dean retrieved his briefcase from the only closet in the room. A piece of cardboard had been taped over the shattered pane. He checked to make sure all the windows were locked, gave the room a final once-over, turned out the lights, and left, securing the door behind him.

He was fumbling with his keys, searching for the building key in the subtle shine of the single row of lights, when he heard a sound.

A strange yet vaguely familiar sound: scratching, squealing.

He stopped, holding the keys quietly. The hair on the back of his neck rose like a porcupine's quills.

Scratch, scratch, scratch . . .

His arms and legs tingled with the prick of a thousand pins.

Scratch, scratch, scratch . . .

He listened, trying to locate the point of origin.

Familiar and – coming from the classroom? Dean turned and stared at the freshly locked door, his eyes wide with incredulity.

Inside?

Scratch, scratch . . .

The sound stopped. His heart drummed in his ears. The hum of the lights suddenly seemed ominous, dastardly, like the whine of a thousand blood-lusting insects moving through the rafters.

Insects?

Scratch . . .

His hand moved on its own, smoothly and seamlessly from hundreds of mornings of practice, his fingers dexterously selecting and inserting the proper key. Hand on the knob, turning. He pushed the door open but remained in the archway, peering from the semilit hallway into the total darkness of his classroom.

Nothing moved. No sound. Even the air seemed paused.

It was the scientist who stepped forward, the scientist who noted the absurdity of his situation. A grown man shivering in the hall because of – what? A noise? A sound? An unidentified scraping from an empty room?

"Ridiculous," he said aloud to underscore his personal disgust. But even this irrational fear could be explained by rational thought. Just minutes earlier he had been standing inches from the shredded corpse of a woman – a friend. His nerves were raw, his emotions exposed. The sparks of irrationality were completely and utterly understandable – but to a scientist, not acceptable.

And he was a scientist.

With that, Dean's hand went to the wall, fingers flicking the three switches simultaneously. Once more the fluorescence revealed – nothing.

An empty room.

The same room he had left just moments before. And the sound? The scratching? Rats, perhaps. Although he had seen none of the telltale signs, no chewed papers or tiny, hard, black rat turds, still it was possible – hell, even likely. It was an old school.

Only – what?

It hadn't sounded like rats. The noise had been faint and – *familiar*.

His mind finally settled on a definition. The blackboard. The scratching sound of chalk – *not chalk, something* – on a blackboard.

He turned to confront the board.

Instantly his mouth was dry, his throat clouted with disbelieve.

He stared and blinked and stared some more.

Cut into the milky blackness of the board, where just seconds before there had been nothing more than the wisp of chalk dust, were five simple words.

Impossible words.

How's it hanging, Jimmy Dean?

10

PIPER BLACKMOORE WOKE with a jolt. She was sweating. Her pajamas stuck to her skin. Yet she was shivering – and panting like a runner. A mild electric current licked her body, causing the fine hairs on her arms and neck to stand on end. She clicked on the light, chasing away the shadows. Her extremities tingled, and for a moment, the heartbeat of a hummingbird, she was afraid she wasn't there, sure that if she looked at her hands, she would see – nothing.

Nothing.

The faint electric hum of the clock radio lured her back to reality. The time was 12:11 A.M. Her sleep had been erratic, though she could not pinpoint why. Thunder? She remembered hearing thunder deep in the night. Thunder in October?

Climbing out of bed, she parted the tieback curtains. A dirty gray, diffused light oozed in through rain-starred windows. Outside, the earth was being scrubbed by a hard, pounding rain. Droplets the size of a man's thumb whacked the ground, sending little pellets of dirt and water several inches into the air. A dome of bulky, foreboding clouds lurched over the crest of Hawkins Hill.

The large, open-faced thermometer mounted on the back porch put the temperature at thirty-four degrees. Almost freezing. Too cold for thunder. Down twenty degrees from last night.

Cold.

Trembling, Piper hugged herself. What was it that student had said in the cafeteria line? *Somebody walked over your grave?*

She went to the bathroom, turned the shower on full, and let the room fill with steam. She peeled off her sweat-soaked pajamas and gave herself to the hot, vigorous embrace of the shower.

Water pounded her skin, helping to allay the uneasiness. But not entirely. It couldn't wash away what stirred beneath the epidermis. Piper Blackmoore was accustomed to strange feelings – they were old friends. Even the scary ones. She couldn't remember a time in her life when she didn't feel things others could not.

But this was different.

She laid her head deep into the spray, letting the warm, pulsating water knead her scalp. *Different?*

With her heart rhythm under control, her breathing measured, she could examine the sensation from a better perspective. Scientifically, Dr. Truman would say. Dean. She laughed, warmed by the sound of her own voice as much as by the water. He was a singularly fascinating and frustrating man. As focused as a laser, as precise as a calculator, yet, at the same time, it wasn't beyond him to be frivolous, to occasionally poke his head up from the abstract world of physics and notice the scent of a flower, an old decorative brooch, or even a new pair of Nikes she had bought on an indulgent whim because she liked the pretty neon-green swoosh.

Piper let the thought warm her further.

Dean Truman. They were polar opposites. He the scientist, she the – *what was she?* Open-minded? Aware? Able to accept and believe things that couldn't be qualified and measured. Yet they enjoyed a rich relationship. She was drawn to him despite the thirteen-year age difference.

She shut off the shower and dried herself with a large, fluffy towel. She vigorously raked her fingers through her short black hair and shook her head. Sleep was no longer an option.

She padded across the hardwood floor to her closet. She dressed in jeans, a white blouse, and a rust-and-white Westcroft College jersey.

In the kitchen she fixed herself a poached egg and toast and began heating a kettle of water for coffee. She had lived in the old farmhouse all her life. She had been born here; her mother had died here. It was a house of barbed memories.

Somebody walked over your grave.

When the teakettle whistled, she jumped.

The uneasiness that had seized her in her sleep still clung to her waking mind. She brushed the hair back from her face and sipped her instant coffee from a Mickey Mouse-embossed mug.

"You're being foolish," she chided herself. "Like a spooky old woman."

The room answered with silence. *Thunder*. In her mind she remembered that much. The roiling thunder. Only there wasn't any thunder. Not in October. Not today, with the temperature plunging toward freezing.

A jolt.

At first she thought she had stepped on an electrical wire. A surging, sense-numbing jolt. Gooseflesh rose on her arms.

Something was happening.

She had to go.

Where?

She wasn't sure, but she would know when she got there.

DEAN TRUMAN JERKED.

Nothing.

He pulled harder – putting his back into it, as his dad used to say. The wooden board remained defiant, intact. Hammered into place more than twenty-one years ago, it still prevailed, barring admittance to the small, sublevel basement; there was no other way in.

It hadn't come from here. No, not from here.

His hands hurt. The imprint of the boards left deep

crevices in the skin. He brushed his palms together, then pushed the bookcase back in place, once more hiding the barred entrance from view. He went to the kitchen and warmed his hands under a stream of hot water. The skin slowly reverted to normal. Would that his mind were so easily changed. But fear and confusion clung to him like the odor of the dead.

God, what a morbid thought. Where the hell had that come from?

From tonight, his mind answered. *A slaughtered woman, a severed hand.* More than adequate reasons for jittery nerves, only that wasn't the force that drove him. That wasn't what had his mind spinning at an unprecedented speed.

How's it hanging, Jimmy Dean?

Dean opened three cabinets, searching until he found what he wanted – what he needed. The bottle of Canadian Mist whiskey had been a gift the Christmas before. He was not a drinker by nature, so the bottle had remained unopened. He broke the seal, poured two fingers' full into a juice glass, added twice that amount of Diet Coke, then drank the concoction in one turn.

His system responded quickly. The alcohol seared his nerves, rushing to his extremities.

The blackboard would be gone tomorrow. He had seen to that by calling and leaving a message for janitorial services. With his newfound celebrity status, Dean knew he could pretty much get anything he wanted. He had never abused his power – until tonight.

Vandals, he had reported. The same vandals who had earlier shattered his classroom window with a brick.

Only, he no longer believed that to be true.

This was no random act. This was too specific. Too exact. Cutting him to the heart like a surgeon's scalpel. The phrase. How had they known? Only a handful of people knew of that particular little taunt. A handful, and they were all accounted for or – dead.

Dean took the bottle by the neck and dragged it to the dining-room table. He poured himself another drink, but with less Coke.

Judy.

It had been, what – twenty, twenty-one years now? Had it really been that long? Sometimes it seemed twice that; other times, he half expected her to come padding out of the bedroom wearing those big, mock-puppy slippers and a long, crimson cotton robe with a fluffy white collar.

"It makes you look like a ten-year-old," he would kid her.

"I am a ten-year-old," she would answer. "At least, I wish I were."

Wish I were.

Forget the Nobel – marrying Judy Pinbrow had been the highlight of his life. He had loved her for as long as he could recall. First puppy love, then teen lust, finally developing into the mature affection that lasted through the years and beyond the grave.

But the Judy that Dean had married was not the same Judy he had pined for. She was changed, different. "Damaged goods," she claimed.

How's it hanging, Jimmy Dean?

They had never spoken of the rape or of that night – but in some ways it was responsible for all that came after. Despite his love for her, Judy's head had always been in the clouds, her eyes on faraway places, adventure, and challenge.

Until the rape.

She was never the same. Instead of adventure, she craved security. Instead of challenge, she sought routine. Dean Truman was tailor-made for the role of husband-protector-provider.

Though simple, theirs had been a happy life until the baby. No – that wasn't true. He had been happy, but not Judy; her eyes never seemed as focused as before . . .

Before Whitey Dobbs.

But it wasn't Dobbs. That was the hell of it. Dean Truman had been with Dobbs at the exact moment the sinful act had supposedly taken place, and despite his disdain for the arrogant bully, he knew Dobbs was innocent of the crime that John and the others had so creatively punished him for.

If not Dobbs, who?

Something had happened; that became undeniable

when, in the following weeks, Judy Pinbrow was clearly pregnant.

Dean had done the gentlemanly thing. He offered to marry her; she accepted. The hasty union meant sacrifice. He could no longer entertain ideas of going to an Ivy League school, even with the academic scholarships. Money that had been saved for his education now went for doctor's visits, rent, groceries. He would never forget the look of disappointment on his father's face when he first told him.

But eventually they had come around, when they saw Dean's determination to still make something of himself, despite the self-inflicted academic exile, and when they saw his unequivocal love for his young bride.

Dean looked around the aging clapboard house. God, he hated this house.

"So why did you buy the damn place?" Nathan had asked. "It's bad enough that you were renting it, but to buy it? Jeez. Move. Get out of that two-story ghost house."

But he couldn't.

Baby bones.

It was shabby then, worse now, despite thousands of dollars of restoration attempts.

"I could build you a new home – hell, a great home – for half of what you're spending just to keep that old place barely livable," Mason Evans had harangued.

Dean dreamed of a new house. He had even toyed

with the idea of buying a second home but keeping this one – leaving it empty. But he couldn't.

Baby bones.

There was always the chance that someone, kids on a dare, bums looking for a dry place, would stumble inside. Would discover . . .

Dean finished his second drink. A tepid, fuzzy-eyed feeling overcame him. It was not a pleasant sensation. It meant a lack of control, and that was unacceptable – unacceptable. He looked at the bookcase that hid the small basement door.

"Ridiculous," he said, calling for the scientist in him to return. His reaction was completely out of proportion with events. The vandalism indicated someone with a shared knowledge of his past.

How's it hanging, Jimmy Dean?

That did not, however, mean the vandal knew the full story, and it was an even greater assumption to believe he knew about the basement.

Buried him alive for a crime he didn't commit. Never found the body.

The sealed basement door mocked him.

Baby bones.

Shortly after they were married, Dean had used a portion of his college fund to rent this house near the Westcroft College campus. It was old and musty, but affordable. Temporary. Judy was well into her pregnancy, and Dean treated her as a knight would a lady fair.

The pregnancy was difficult, and Judy spent much of the time confined to bed. Then one night . . . It was cold, he remembered that, unbearably cold; the roads were closed, the pass to the north was sealed. The snowplows stayed busy trying to keep the main road and the Willamette Bridge clear. Without the bridge or the pass, Black Valley, Oregon would literally be severed from the rest of the world.

Dean was working two jobs as well as going to school. One of those was in the pharmacy. People needed their medicine, and since most couldn't get to the store, the store had to get to them. Using the company four-wheel drive, Dean ventured deep into the foothills, twice becoming stuck and having to shovel his way out.

It was close to midnight before he got home. The first thing he noticed was the *cold*. It was almost as cold inside as out. No, that wasn't right. Later he had been able to run water; the pipes hadn't frozen, it had just seemed that cold. Cold but different. He called her name. No answer. He looked for a note, thinking something had happened to the furnace, forcing her to take solace with a friend.

"Dean?"

A fragile voice whispered as if his name were made of glass.

"Dean?"

Judy. He found her in the bedroom.

Baby bones.

On their bed. The blood – oh God, the blood. The bed was covered, the sheets saturated. Judy was exposed, naked, and the source of all the gore. *Gore*. She had given birth. While he was off taking care of others, his wife had had the baby, alone, in this cold, cold house.

Her face was a shade of white he had never seen before and hoped never to see again – white and bloodless.

He still had the four-wheel drive and used it to rush her to the hospital. All the way there, until she passed out from exhaustion or lack of blood or both, he kept asking, "Where's the baby? What happened to the baby?"

She had answered only once. Her words colder than the worst winter wind. "The devil gave me the child, and the Lord took him away."

After reassuring himself that Judy was in the hands of those most likely to help her, Dean had returned to the house in search of the child.

Nothing.

Blood, afterbirth, but no baby. No baby.

A thin blood trail led from the bedroom to the basement door. The overhead light didn't work. Dean found a flashlight, then went down the short flight of stairs. It was a basement in only the loosest sense of the word, little more than a crouch-high crawl space with a hard, dirt floor. A dirt floor in Oregon was like a swimming pool in Alaska.

Dean remained on the stairs, letting the cyclopic beam of the flashlight drag across the dank, dark earth. The night was so silent he imagined he could hear earthworms squirming in the ground. His breath came in short, desperate gasps. The shadows seemed to have weight and mass, physically recoiling from the cone of yellow-white light but ever present, pushing forward.

If the child was here, it was under the black, soppy ground. It wasn't alive. A vision of Judy flashed in his mind. Judy in the bed, lying in a pool of her own blood. Could she really have dragged herself down here?

Stillborn.

That must be it. The child had been stillborn, and Judy, fueled by grief, had buried the remains, here in the basement. Stillborn. At least, he hoped it was, prayed it was, had to believe it was. The alternative was unbearable.

Dean retched, gagging in the dark.

He pulled himself up the stairs. He found the two-by-fours and nails in the garage. Then, finding the studs buried in the wall, he hammered the boards in place, forever sealing the basement and the secrets it bore. He shoved a heavy bookcase in front of the door, then stepped back to survey his work.

Baby bones?

Somewhere, in his mind, a child cried.

Stillborn. Had to have been.

Where's the baby?

The devil gave me the child and the Lord took him away.

There were questions, lots of questions. But the loss of blood had left Judy weak, debilitated. She never left the hospital. One week later she was dead. Myocardial infarction, triggered by severe trauma and stress. It was rare in a girl that young, but it happened, or so the doctor said. In deference to Judy's family, the baby was listed as stillborn.

Then Dean Truman was alone. Alone in a house he hated but could never leave. He couldn't. There was a secret in the basement.

Baby bones.

11

MASON EVANS DROVE like a madman, pushing the imposing motor of the Delta 88 to its limit. In the back of his mind, buried behind a torrent of emotions, a thought vied for attention. It cried out for him to slow down, warning of the dangers of driving too fast, reminding him of the time he would lose if he was pulled over by the Oregon State Police.

To hell with it! He pressed the pedal to the floorboard.

The sun was pulling itself up on the eastern horizon, turning the cloud-filled sky a deep orange-purple, the color of rotting fruit.

His telephone conversation with Tina's roommate raged in his mind like a wildfire.

"Let me speak with Tina," he had demanded to the groggy girl, jerking her from slumber.

"Mr. Evans?" The roommate's voice revealed confusion. "What time is it?"

What time is it? How could she be so blasé when the world was coming to an end?

"Two, three A.M. I don't know. I just need to speak with Tina. Now."

Pause. He could hear her breathing, detect the faint sound of movement, the squeak of the bed, the rustling of sheets. "She's, uh, she's not here right now."

"What? She left Portland almost six hours ago. Where the hell is she?"

"I – I'm not sure." She was lying. But she was Mason's only hope. He fought the urge to scream, to howl like a burning timber. Instead he searched his mind for her name – Debbie . . . Demi . . . Denise . . .

"Deirdre, listen to me. I know you girls stick together, and I can appreciate that. But listen to me. This is important, Deirdre – a matter of life or death. I swear on my mother's grave."

"I – I don't know, Mr. E."

"If you're worried about her getting into trouble, don't. This isn't about breaking rules. I'm trying to save my daughter's life."

A moan of indecision came across the phone line. "She won't be back until Tuesday."

"Tuesday? Where is she?" He realized he was being too belligerent and silently scolded himself.

"She's out with that new guy, her new boyfriend."

Mason's hands began to shake. White points of light danced in the corners of his vision. *Don't lose it, old man. Don't fucking lose it*, he screamed in his head.

"Where?" His voice was hoarse with sudden terror.

"I don't know for sure."

"Deirdre. *Please!*" He had never begged for anything in his entire life, but it didn't matter. When it came to his daughter, he could beg with the best of them. All he wanted was for his daughter to be safe.

"She said something about a house in Lane County. It was his, I think, or maybe his parents', but it's empty."

"Where? What part of Lane County?"

The line was quiet. "I'm not sure."

Try, Deirdre. For God's sake, please try."

"Mr. Evans, are you all right? Are you sure Tina's not going to get into trouble?"

"*What fucking city?*" he screamed.

The girl on the other end of the phone began to cry.

"I'm sorry, honey, I'm so sorry." He tried to catch his breath. "Please, Deirdre, please . . ."

"They're not in Portland or Eugene. They went to Berry, Blanchly – it was something like that."

"Black Valley? They went to Black Valley?"

"That's it."

He left the house.

"Mr. E – Mr. E., are you there? Is everything all right? Mr. E., you aren't having a heart attack, are you? Mr. E. . . . ."

Her words sounded in an empty room. Mason Evans was driving to Black Valley.

HE STOOD by the corner, leering down the hall. The green-and-white-tiled floor gleamed as if wet. The fetid odour of industrial-strength disinfectant, ammonia, and fresh wax irritated his nasal lining. From his vantage point, in an alcove with a pair of vending machines, he could see the nurses' station on the right and the four intensive care units on the left. Each room was fronted by a large, plate-glass window and identified with numbers, eleven inches tall, one through four.

Clyde Watkins was in room number one.

There were two nurses: a thin girl with a nervous nature who fluttered from room to room like a pollinating bee, and an older, heavier woman who sat in command behind a waist-high counter.

Squinting, he could make out the prone form of a man in room one – centered in a nest of technology. Tubes, wires, machines, bags, and poles crowded round him like gaunt, wary spectators. Multiple devices produced a faint but irritating cacophony of tones and beeps.

He waited. He watched. He fidgeted.

Click.

Flip.

Click.

Flip.

When the thin girl entered the farthest room and the charge nurse went into the office behind the counter, he moved – quickly, as was his nature; quietly, as was his gift. He reached the room in less than a heart-beat.

PIPER BLACKMOORE HAD NEVER broken the law. Not so much as a traffic ticket. So it came as a great surprise when she found herself breaking into the county morgue. She had tried to resist an urge that she couldn't quite explain. But something was happening; something was dancing on her nerves, causing the hair on the back of her neck to rise, causing her flesh to repeatedly pebble, causing tiny bolts of God's own lightning to shoot up the length of her arm and bounce around inside her chest, her head, her heart.

Something odd was happening. That was how she felt. No wonder people in town thought she was four pancakes shy of a stack.

It had started yesterday. No, before that. But only in bits and spurts. It had actually been going on for a while, but now – now it was happening more often, lasting longer. Waking her from her sleep. And she would be damned if she knew what "it" was. But the electrical current that had taken up residence just beneath her skin told her the answer was here – in the morgue.

News of poor Meredith Gamble had been the talk of the town this morning. Word was, it was an accident, but someone had started a rumor that it was more than that.

Mrs. Humelory over at the Perk Up coffee kiosk thought there was a madman at large. "One of them slashers, like Jack the Ripper," she declared as the machine hissed and fussed and oozed out Piper's morning cappuccino. "A serial killer. Like you see on the TV, only this one is here."

"Mrs. Humelory, I strongly doubt anyone in Black Valley is a serial killer," Piper had argued, waiting for her coffee and wanting desperately for the conversation to end. The rain hadn't let up, and despite the little awning over the drive-up window, cold droplets of water and a harsh, icy wind found their way into Piper's truck.

Mrs. Humelory didn't seem to notice or mind. "Of course, it's not anybody in town. It's one of them strangers. A drifter. Most likely from Portland or Eugene. Yes, definitely Eugene, they're all half-crazy there anyway."

Like Piper.

No, she wasn't half-crazy. She was completely crazy – breaking into the county morgue like some ghoul.

Her criminal career almost ended before it started. She had slipped past the hospital staff without trouble. She thought she was home free, when she turned the corner and almost ran into the sheriff's deputy sitting at the little utilitarian desk outside the morgue entrance.

Pulse thundering, she jumped back behind the wall.

A guard. They were guarding the morgue. Why? She waited, breathing silently, half expecting the deputy to jump up and grab her, slam her face against the wall, and read her her rights. But nothing happened. After a couple of minutes she ventured a look.

The deputy was leafing through a copy of *Hunting*

and Fishing. She recognized him. Cheevers. Not the sharpest crayon in the box. That was good. As her mind raced over possible scenarios, the deputy solved the problem for her, abandoning his post for a visit to the men's room.

The morgue was unguarded.

Why was there a guard in the first place? she wondered again. Chain of evidence, perhaps. Hadn't there been a controversy about that in the O. J. Simpson trial? The presence of a guard added unexpected weight to Mrs. Humelory's assertions.

It also meant the body of Meredith Gamble was inside.

Piper hesitated, stalling for the tug of sensibleness, her rational mind, to reassert itself and stop her from going through those doors. But the static. Was that what it was? The static was greater here. The lightning storm that raged beneath her skin had intensified.

Something on her face. She put her had to her nose. Her fingers came away red. *Bleeding.* She took a tissue from her pocket and wiped away the blood. She crossed the room quickly. Maybe it was locked? The knob turned easily. Piper Blackmoore entered the county morgue.

DEAN TRUMAN ARRIVED at Westcroft College early Saturday morning, just as the maintenance men were about to haul the ruined blackboard out of the room. "Could you cut out this section for me?" he asked.

Raphael, the older of the two, pushed his NO FEAR cap back with his thumb and considered the request. "The graffiti? You want to save the graffiti?"

"Examine it, actually. Under a microscope."

"If you say so, Doc." Producing a thin-blade saw from a bottomless tool kit, Raphael began cutting.

Scratch, scratch, scratch . . .

A malignant fear clawed up Dean's spine. He took a step back and wiped his face. The fear extended its reach, embracing his chest, raking his heart with dirty, jagged nails.

Scratch, scratch, scratch . . .

The sound wasn't the same. But close. The fear continued to climb, reaching the base of his neck, gripping his shoulders, and hoisting itself up, striding his head, muffling his ears, scratching at the corners of his eyes.

". . . idea who did this?" The words were faint and seemed to come from some place faraway.

"Doc?"

Dean blinked. An idea darted across his mind, then was gone.

"You okay?" Raphael stopped sawing.

Dean grasped for the idea but found nothing. He shook his shoulders and straightened his back, as if to shake off the childish, irrational fear. "Fine – distracted, that's all."

This appeased the handyman. He returned to his task. "I said, any idea who did this?"

At the front of the room the younger man triggered an electric drill. The frantic whine was a welcome reprieve from the incessant sawing.

Raphael kicked the ruined board and pulled a three-foot-square section free. "There you go, Doc. Knock yourself out."

Outside, the gaunt limbs of a naked oak tree rapped on the window. The rain had started shortly after midnight and was still falling, propelled by a cold, driving wind, cutting across the gray sky in harsh, diagonal slashes.

Raphael stood up, rolled his shoulders, and gave the weather an appraising look. "Getting ugly out there. Weatherman didn't say nothing about no rain. Least not like this. The skies look mean. Damn mean."

Mean.

Something in the distance caught Dean's eye. Up on the side of Hawkins Hill. A flicker. A dot of color. The lashing remains of the crime scene tape pulled free on one end and flapping like a yellow flag, marking the spot where Meredith Gamble had been slaughtered.

The fear reclaimed its shoulder perch, leaned over, looked Dean in the eyes, then licked his face with a cold, rough tongue. Dean shuddered with revulsion. He looked down at the message slashed into the blackboard, then back at the roiling black-gray clouds.

Mean.

*

MAMA?

The chamber reeked of formaldehyde and alcohol. Three rows of five-foot fluorescent lights illuminated the stark gray room. The last row of lights was malfunctioning, one pole completely dark, its companion dying. The bad bulb whined and flickered, flared and dimmed. Shadows slashed across the cold concrete floor.

Mama? Why would she think of her mother? In here of all places, why her mother?

Piper Blackmoore's head had been spinning ever since she entered the room. The spurting, dying light didn't help. *A buzz?* No, a gray zone, like a deep, circling fog, surrounded the memories she held of her mother. Meager memories, swathed in cotton, unseeable, unknowable. She had been only four when her mother bled to death on the living-room floor. They said Piper was with her, holding her head – crying – covered in her mother's blood.

Something bad is coming. The memory was insistent. She heard the words in her mother's voice.

Not words, warning.

Something bad is coming.

It was what her mother had said the night she died. And now that memory reasserted itself with such clarity and intensity that Piper felt as if her mother were in the room with her, standing just beyond the row of gurneys, tucked away in a shadowed corner, appearing and disappearing in opposite accord with the flickering light.

Something was going on beneath the Douglas firs of Black Valley, Oregon. Something bad was coming.

Coming home!

The thought came to her with shocking clarity. Whatever it was, it was returning.

Something bad.

A tingling numbness in her extremities, like experiencing a mild electrical shock, brought her to full alert.

The hand. She found it in a tray in a small refrigeration unit – bagged, tagged, and waiting for the crime lab to pick it up. Slowly she took it out of the wrappings.

Pain . . . great pain . . . cold and hot. The hand had been removed from a conscious person; the owner had watched it happen. The pain was unbearable, but the terror was worse.

Fear.

Of what? Of losing a hand, of dying?

No.

Fear of not dying. Of living in a world where . . .

Sweat spilled from Piper's pores. Her brow was knitted.

What was the hand afraid of?

A blinding flash of light, but not white, not any color . . . dark . . . a flash of dark light . . . and pain.

. . . of living in a world where such things could exist.

Then the hospital alarm screamed.

12

THE CLOSER HE GOT to Black Valley, the worse the weather was. Fitting. As he crossed the Willamette Bridge into the city limits, the rain was falling like millions of air-driven nails shot from heaven. Even the roar of the big Delta 88 engine was muffled by the pounding rain. He was driving more on instinct than vision.

The same instinct that had caused him to steal three sticks of dynamite from one of his construction sites and lock it in the trunk.

How am I going to find her?

Black Valley wasn't a large community, but it was big enough to make it impractical, if not impossible, to knock on every door. Besides, even if he could, what would he say? "Excuse me, my name is Mason Evans; I'm a contractor from Portland and I'm looking for my daughter, Tina. Perhaps you've seen her? She's five three, one hundred and ten pounds, with long, dark hair. Always smiling, always happy, and traveling with . . . an abomination to God, truth, and life itself – traveling with the devil or the devil's stepchild."

They would think him crazy. And maybe . . . maybe they were right. It made no sense. Emotionally, physically, and mentally drained to the limit, he knew that he couldn't handle this alone. His only chance of finding Tina was his cousin John. As for making sense of all this? They hadn't spoken in years. Never got along that well to begin with. No reason to think that he would be the least inclined to do Mason a favor. Still, the only one, the only conceivable person who could understand the impossible, was Dean.

He needed Dean Truman.

THE FIRE ALARM SCREAMED, wiping out the bleating of countless machines demanding attention, demanding action.

Fire.

The hospital staff moved in jerks like old, stop-action animation, not sure where to go. All practice, all mandatory instruction, was gone, worthless, forgotten in the blaring panic, fanned by the shrieking alarm.

On the second floor both nurses ran from the intensive care unit, hurrying down the hall to the main station, looking for guidance. After all, the patients in ICU could not easily be moved. At least one was alive at the discretion of the machines; to disconnect him, to move him, would be to kill him.

Alone, the man who had pulled the alarm slipped into ICU room number one.

Click.
Flip.

FEAR LASHED HER BODY like a wet leather strap. Piper Blackmoore wasn't sure what was happening. She left the morgue at a full run. She slid to a stop. Her face just inches from Deputy Cheevers'. She paused. For a brief second she thought he was the cause of the alarm. That he had seen her enter the morgue, and even now his backup was screaming its way toward the Black Valley Hospital. She half expected him to cuff her.

You have the right to remain silent . . .

But his eyes were too wide, too white. He was scared or confused or both. If he had seen her exiting the morgue, it hadn't registered. They exchanged a look of mutual panic and disbelief, then he zigged and she zagged and they were both moving again.

Stupid, superstitious woman, Piper chastised herself. *I get the willies, and what do I do? I break into the county morgue. Oh, good thinking, Piper. Nothing calms a girl down like communing with the dead and playing with severed body parts.*

Her Nike track shoes squealed, but held, as she rounded a corner and headed for the exit. She reached the door to freedom, to the outside world, at the exact moment that the alarm stopped.

She stopped, hand on the door.

Something.

She let go of the door.

The sound of running feet reverberated off the sterile walls.

Something.

She crossed her arms, fingernails digging into her flesh. The sensation she had felt outside the hotel was back, stronger than ever.

Something.

Her fear was inextinguishable. Yet . . .

Without knowing why, or consciously deciding to do so, Piper Blackmoore turned and went up the stairs. She was headed for the second floor.

DAMN RAIN, *damn Weather Channel, damn bunions*. The ground was loose and malleable, sucking on his feet like a newborn pup on its mother's teat. He marched through puddles four, five, six inches deep. Water found its way over the tops of this boots and up his pant legs, making him wet and miserable despite the expensive, water-repellent rain gear.

Damn rain gear.

Just a little hunting, that was all he asked. Just a little time alone in the woods. His gun in his hands, his sights on his prey, the sound of the shot, the smell of gunpowder. Hell, even the danger of hunting out of season hadn't stopped him, but now a little rain was threatening to do what the law could not – and that made Kirby Boray mad.

Damn mad.

He had given up after three hours – three hours of pure hell. Forget the Bible. Hades wasn't a lake of fire – it was just a lake, miles and miles of water. Water up your nose and down your boots, water on your head and under your shirt. He had wasted a Saturday for this?

Damn bad luck.

He was nearing the truck, or at least where he thought the truck was, when the ground gave way. Kirby hit the mud and leaves and shot down the incline like a puck on ice. Sliding, twisting, rolling, turning.

Cursing. Or at least trying to curse. Leaves and mud and twigs got in his mouth and his beard, his eyes. His hood came off and rain played a drum solo on his balding scalp, then found entrance to the few dry, warm places that still remained on his body.

He held on to his gun. There was that, at least. And he hadn't blown his hands off, which was a distinct possibility, since the weapon was loaded and ready. When he came to rest at the foot of the hill, Kirby Boray looked like the very ground he had walked on. Mud, leaves, briars, and branches – they all clung to his legs and back and face and arms.

There was mud in the gun barrel.

"Not my rifle! Shit fire and fart snowballs!"

Damn mud. Damn leaves. Damn briars.

Kirby raised himself up on his elbows, brushing mud out of his eyes. He saw something he didn't believe, so he shut his eyes and opened them again. But it was still there.

A body. A human body.

"Damn," he said. And the body said nothing.

DEAN MADE NOTES in the three-by-five-inch spiral notebook he always carried with him. The figures looked like rat scratches in Sheetrock. All the information he had gathered from the dissected sheet of spoiled blackboard, dutifully logged and represented on the scored paper.

As he told his students, science was 45 percent collecting information, 40 percent interpreting that information, 10 percent inspiration, and 5 percent sheer, dumb, blind luck. Although sometimes, he confessed, the percentages were exactly reversed.

Dean closed the notebook and put it in his breast pocket. The collection of data had shooed away the illogical fear that had been crouched on his shoulders since the night before. Facts and figures. The sincerity of science. His bastion. His salvation.

Dean stood and straightened his coat. He ran a hand through his dark hair, pushing it more or less in place. The air was filled with the scent of sawdust. He looked out the window, at Hawkins Hill, where Meredith Gamble had been sliced to death.

The crime lab would determine where the glass was from. As for velocity? An aircraft remained the most logical possibility. He wondered if John had heard back from the FAA. Although there had been no plane crash, that didn't mean an aircraft hadn't been damaged.

And the angle?

Straight ahead. How could glass fall horizontally? It must have been caught in a powerful gust of wind. Looking out his window, watching the rain lashing the earth, he could believe it. Except he wind had not been that strong last night.

The phone rang, snapping him from his thoughts.

"Dean?" the phone line crackled and popped.

"John? Is that you?"

"Dean? Can you hear me?"

"Barely. The phones are acting up."

"Yeah . . ." His next words were garbled. ". . . way all day . . . phone company . . ."

"John?"

"Dean?" the line was suddenly clear.

"Yeah, I can hear you now, but talk fast before we lose the connection."

"Cheevers is on his way to pick you up. I need you at the hospital." His voice sounded heavy, as if his words had actual weight. "It's Clyde. He's dead."

13

RAIN TURNED TO SLEET, hard pellets of ice that shattered into thousands of shards as they slammed against the wet, black asphalt. The north wind had intensified. Leafless trees shook and shuddered. Power lines swayed in frighteningly wild arcs. On Hawkins Hill tree limbs, suddenly heavy with ice, moaned and creaked.

Then the snow came. Gauzy and brisk, it filled the natural gashes and depressions of the landscape, evening out the roughness of nature, covering the city in a shroud of deathly white.

And still the forecast called for clear skies and moderate temperatures.

NATHAN PERKINS FOUND AVA WAITING in a black teddy – an index finger in her mouth, one leg arched and rocking back and forth, giggling at the expression of raw lust that consumed her husband.

Ava took the lead in their lovemaking – always the insightful, inventive lover.

Nathan was still breathing hard and sweating

when he answered the phone. A trucker who had barely made it over the pass had contacted the Oregon State Police, who had then contacted the sheriff's department, who in turn called the mayor. The storm was worsening. The pass was closed. And the only connection between Black Valley and the rest of the world was the thin concrete bridge spanning the wind-frenzied Willamette River. He had to get the snow-plows out and the sand-trucks moving, had to make sure that bridge stayed clear. He thumbed his glasses up the bridge of his nose and told his wife, "I have to go."

Ava flapped her artificially extended eyelashes, brushed her chemically goldened hair behind her ears, and thrust out her scientifically enhanced breasts. "No. Stay."

Lust and love were powerful forces. She embraced him for a full minute, the fate of his city balanced against his desire for his wife. As if sensing his struggle and knowing she had won, Ava Perkins mercifully released him.

"Go," she said through pouty lips. "Go. Take care of your precious city, but make sure you don't forget to come home."

Forget to come home? Nathan Perkins was more likely to forget to eat.

"She's so fake," his mother had complained upon first meeting Ava. "All phony: chemicals, silicone, hair weaves, makeup – a completely artificial woman."

"If she's artificial," his father had said, "then give me the ingredients so I can make one for myself."

Nathan smiled at the memory and at his wife. His muscles burned warmly in the afterglow of their vigorous lovemaking, aching slightly as he dressed for the deteriorating weather conditions.

"Don't forget your scarf," she reminded him, then wrapped the scarf she had made for him, a heinous thing of neon-yellow and red strips, around his neck. She kissed him once, quickly on the lips, then covered the lower portion of his face with the cloth.

AT FIRST Nathan felt silly, leaving his expensive home on Brentway Drive dressed like an Arctic explorer, but thirty seconds of exposure to the freezing wind obliterated such thoughts. How had it gotten so cold so fast? Where had this storm come from? There had been nothing about it on the Weather Channel.

He tried to reassure himself. So what if there was a little snow, a little rain? This was Oregon, and Oregonians were not easily scared off by the weather.

Not easily scared at all.

Outside, the snow continued to level the terrain.

WHEN DEAN ARRIVED at the hospital, Piper was waiting with John Evans outside of intensive care unit number one – Clyde Watkins's room.

"Are you all right?" Dean asked her.

She looked up at him, eyes widened with helpless

misery. Then she hugged him, burying her face in his chest and sobbing.

". . . could have stopped it, could have stopped it," she mumbled.

"Could have stopped who?" he asked.

"Not who – what," she muttered. *"It."* The words clogged her throat. He held her closer.

Could have stopped what? It?

"Is there somewhere my friend and I can talk?" Dean asked the nurse.

"There's a small office behind the station," she answered tentatively, looking to the sheriff for approval.

John nodded.

"Give us a minute," Dean said to John.

The room contained a brown metal desk, two filing cabinets, and a bookshelf bursting with binders, folders, and medical texts. They sat on the edge of the desk. He held her, stroking her hair. As she cried he comforted her, then slowly, gently, he asked the questions he had to ask. After ten minutes the nurse entered. She mindfully, tenderly, pried Piper's arms from around Dean's neck. "Come on, dear, let's get you that cup of tea."

Piper started to leave, then stopped, turned back to Dean. "I could have stopped it. Could have. But I wasn't fast enough. I just wasn't fast enough."

The nurse shushed her, enveloping the smaller woman in a large, securing embrace.

*

JOHN AND DEAN STOOD OUTSIDE ICU room number one and waited until Piper was gone. "She knows things," John said. "This place was a mess. Someone pulled the fire alarm, and despite their training, the staff didn't know what the hell to do. Still, the nurses say, they had been away from the unit less than five minutes when Piper came running out of the stairwell screaming that Clyde Watkins was in danger."

Dean squinted as John took a step closer to him.

"How did she know? How the hell did she know?" John asked. "First the hotel, now this?" His flat-brimmed hat hovered at Dean's forehead. "I know she's a friend of yours, but she's either a suspect or . . ." He paused. The hospital sounds seemed faint and faraway. "Or she really is psychic."

Dean rubbed his fingers across his lips. He inhaled slowly. The air smelled worse than usual – acidic, suffocating. "She's neither. Piper Blackmoore is intuitive. Exceptionally so, but intuitive and that's all. She subconsciously collects and processes information, everything from body language to circumstances, making subconscious deductions that then float to her consciousness. To her, it's like getting the answer to a math problem without doing the work. She doesn't know how she does it."

"But you do."

"Yes, I believe so. Piper was in the hospital when the alarm went off. In the morgue."

John took a step back. A rare look of surprise flashed across his face. "The morgue?"

"She says she felt compelled to look at the severed hand. Says it brought back old memories, buried memories, detailed images of the night her mother died."

John pushed his left hand into the palm of his right and methodically began cracking his knuckles. The lines on his face were now etched into a scowl. "How does a severed hand relate to her mother?"

"It doesn't, at least not directly. The common denominator is trauma. It's not unusual for one traumatic event to trigger memories of another."

"But how did she know about Clyde?"

"The fire alarm. Remember, she saw someone trying to kill him in the hotel. When the alarm went off, some part of her realized the odds were pretty good that it was a distraction. But on a conscious level all she knew was that Clyde was in danger."

"All right, I can see that." John took a deep breath and held it for a moment, then led Dean into the room where their old friend's body remained. He pointed to the bed. "But how do you explain this?"

Clyde Watkins's eyes were closed, his lips slightly parted, his face bloodless. A thin trail of gore ran from his forehead to the right of his nose, down his cheek to his chin and then on to the bed.

Flash Five stay alive. Flash Four group no more.

The pool of blood on the sheet was smaller than

a fifty-cent piece, meaning Clyde had died quickly; the bleeding had stopped when his heart stopped beating.

But the wound?

"I've never seen anything like it," John confessed.

The blood originated from a hole, a small, three-quarter-inch gash, pierced just above the center of his eyes. "It looks like a knife wound."

"Yeah, that's what I thought, too." John pulled the flashlight from his belt and aimed the beam into the gash. "But look how deep it is."

Dean took the flashlight and leaned down for a closer look. The stench of death was heavy, cloying. John was right. The wound was deep, too deep. One blow.

"That's bone, Dean. That's straight through the skull. No knife can do that. A bullet, yeah; but a knife, no way. No way."

AVA PERKINS STOOD by the door watching as a thin film of ice grew inward from the edges of the beveled glass. The snow crystals were jagged and irregular. Beautiful and unpredictable. She wondered if such a thing could be duplicated with oil and brush. Perhaps her next painting? *Ode to a Frosted Glass*.

She giggled at the idea, then hurried into the den, where a gas fire appeared to burn artificial logs in the brick-lined fireplace. It was much colder now, a fact accentuated by her skimpy attire. But she kind of liked it – liked the way the frigid breeze licked her nipples, making them hard and excited.

She touched herself between her legs. A shudder of exhilaration rippled through her. Her fingertips rubbed the thin fabric between her legs. She shuddered. Even after vigorous lovemaking she sometimes liked to masturbate. A fine meal deserves a fine dessert.

Thump.

She stopped

The fire hissed.

A cold wind stroked the windows.

Thump, thump.

Ava Perkins cocked her head. A loose shutter?

Thump, thump.

No, the sound seemed to be coming from inside the house.

With no thought of danger, no sense of uneasiness, clad only in a will-o'-the-wisp nightgown, Ava marched confidently into the hall, tracking the noise. The long, picture-laden hallway ran the full length of the house. Rooms off to either side offered a variety of choices, from the kitchen to the guest bath to the – master bedroom?

Thump, thump, thump . . .

It was coming from the bedroom.

Away from the fire Ava felt the cold reassert itself. The icy air wrapped around her legs and thighs; a faint, chilled breeze sighed, dimpling her flesh. She stood still.

"Ava."

A whisper. Nothing more. The sound of the wind sighing through the eaves?

"Aaavaaaa . . ."

No, not the wind. A sharp, distinct bolt of fear arched across her thoughts.

"Who's there?" she demanded, her voice as thin as her nightgown.

"Nathan?" she begged as much as asked. Had her husband returned to surprise her? She almost giggled, warmed by the thought.

"Aaaavaaaa . . . come play with me."

The fear returned. That wasn't Nathan's voice. That wasn't . . . anyone's voice.

Ava Perkins felt naked, more naked than she had ever been in her entire life. She turned, no hesitation this time, and took one step toward the den.

And in a flash it happened: a powerful arm hooked her neck, an icy hand covered her mouth.

Cold, so cold.

How had he gotten here so quickly? From the bedroom to the end of the hall in a blink.

"Aaavaaaa . . ."

The voice. She could feel contrasting hot and cold breath on her neck, close enough to lift her hair as he spoke. She willed herself to break free, but the grip, the godforsaken icy grip, held like frozen steel clamps.

"Don't fight, Ava. It's time to play."

14

THE BLACK VALLEY SHERIFF'S DEPARTMENT was located next to the four-story, L-shaped hospital. The latter was tall and elegant, with trim lines and a stylish portico. The former was short and weathered, with red brick and faded brush, fronted by long, plate-glass windows. Mason Evans pulled into a slot marked VISITORS, shut off the engine, and studied the building.

The blinds were up. The lights were on. The facility was electric with activity. It was obvious something was going on.

Tina?

The thought struck like a shark – unseen, unexpected, unstoppable. Had something happened to his child? Was he too late? Was that the reason for all this activity?

Mason got out of the car, not bothering with an umbrella. Snow, sleet, and rain pecked his head like starving crows devouring a dead man's eyes.

Inside, the action was even more intense – with people hurrying from place to place, communicating in shouts.

"The phones are in and out," a woman yelled. "Any word from the phone company?"

"They say they'll fix it but can't find the problem," a deputy answered.

Mason recognized a short fireplug of a woman as Maggie Dane, John's assistant. "It's not just the phones. The radio is acting screwy, too."

"Mrs. Dane?"

She looked up. A pair of glasses hung from her neck like a bird feeder. "You from the phone company?"

"No. I'm John's cousin Mason—"

"Mason. Mason Evans, right. I'm sorry, Mr. Evans, things are sort of crazy right now." She checked her watch, then rapped it several times with two fingers. "Damn thing is stopped again."

She checked the wall clock. "You made great time. Must have been in the area, huh? Well, make yourself comfortable. It will be a while before they finish processing the body."

The body. The two words skewered his soul like a double-bladed sword. He felt the blood leave his face, felt his equilibrium fade, his vision constrict.

". . . all right? Mr. Evans, are you all right?"

"My daughter," he croaked, like a creature of stone uttering its first words. "Tina."

Maggie Dane frowned. "Tina? I don't know a Tina. Is she coming? If so, she's not here yet. Do you want coffee or something?"

"Not here? The body."

Maggie paused. Mason detected a faint shudder of her lower lip. "Yes, poor Mr. Watkins. He was a good man."

"Watkins? Clyde Watkins?" Mason suddenly felt better and worse at the same time.

She reached out and took his hands. She was a sweet woman who smelled of Jean Naté and hair spray. "Don't you worry. John will get him. John will find the bastard who murdered your friend."

"Murdered?"

Concern molded Maggie Dane's face. "Wait a minute. You didn't know that Clyde Watkins was murdered this morning?"

"Tonight? No. I'm here for my daughter. I'm looking for my daughter."

"Ah, dear Lord, look at what I've done. You didn't know. Mr. Evans, I am so sorry. I never would have blurted it out like that if I knew. It's just, your timing and all. It made sense."

"Clyde was murdered, how?"

Maggie Dane took a tentative swallow. "I really can't say any more."

"John—"

"Yes, I'll tell him you're here," she said, turning to go.

He grabbed her by the arm, his grip tight enough to dimple the fabric of her dress. "Tell him I know who did it."

*

THE STRANGER DRIFTED DOWN the frozen-food aisle, navigating around the pyramid of creamed corn, stopped briefly at the canned peaches, and in general acted very much like a typical customer. But Jenkins Jones knew better. You didn't last twenty-two years in the grocery business, and almost as long on the city council, without learning a thing or two – no sirree, Bob. As the stranger moved about, Jenkins watched him travel from monitor to monitor, tracking him, thanks to a series of security cameras mounted throughout the store.

Jenkins prided himself on being alert, aware. Always on the lookout for anything out of the ordinary: shoplifters, food-sneakers, drugged-up hippie freaks looking to steal his hard-earned money, then throw him in the back room, locking him in with all the female cashiers and forcing him (at gunpoint) to make madman monkey-love to Virginia Haulsy, his newest checker, an eighteen-year-old with auburn hair, full lips, and breasts that could be used as beach umbrellas.

"It could happen," he muttered in the small, empty, paper-strewn room that was his office. "It could happen, uh-huh."

At his advanced age, with the good years not so good and the remaining years not so plentiful, Jenkins thought about it a lot. Obsessed about it, some would say. He had never been robbed, but he kept a .45-caliber revolver in the bottom drawer of his desk just in case; failing that, there was also an extra-lube, natural-feeling condom ribbed for her pleasure.

Just in case.

The stranger wore a long, dingy, dark green rain-coat, faded jeans, work boots, and a floppy-brimmed, dark brown cowboy hat. The hat hung low over his face. Jenkins got the impression of a beard and could see shafts of long, russet-brown hair hanging over the man's collar as he disappeared from one monitor, then reappeared in another.

Long hair? Like a hippie. But a cowboy hat? "Never heard of no cowboy hippies – no sirree, Bob," he muttered, then cringed, knowing his wife would chastise him. *Only crazy people talk to themselves*, his wife always said.

"I ain't crazy," he told the empty room.

The stranger stopped and put two cans of pork and beans in his cart. *Do drugged-up cowboy hippie freaks looking to rob a place and force the owner to do the nasty with throbbing young girls eat pork and beans?*

Jenkins licked his suddenly dry lips. The stranger's cart filled slowly. Canned goods, TV dinners, junk food. Other than his attire, there was nothing exceptionally peculiar about the man. Yet he made Jenkins as nervous as a toad on the interstate.

"Yes sirree, Bob," muttered, then grimaced for having spoken aloud.

The stranger moved to aisle seven, chips and bread. He stopped and studied a bag of rippled barbecue potato chips, dropped them in his cart, then—

For no apparent reason the stranger looked up. His big, brown, floppy cowboy hat rose slowly, like a radar dish. Jenkins could see a beard, definitely a beard, thin mouth, a moustache, small nose and eyes. His eyes? The iridescent glow of the humming fluorescent lights reflected vigorously off the stranger's black-peril eyes.

The eyes shifted. The stranger was now looking at the camera, into the camera directly into the lens, directly at—

Jenkins backed away from the monitor. "Son of a bitch is looking at me," he sputtered.

Old fool, he heard his wife saying. *Only an idiot would talk to himself and then think a stranger could see him through a video camera.*

Jenkins straightened his shirt and leaned back over the monitors. The stranger was still there, still looking at the camera. Bottomless black eyes seeming to see right through the screen and right into Jenkins's soul.

"Old fool," Jenkins muttered.

Then the stranger raised his right hand and . . . he waved.

Jenkins Jones staggered back, knocking a stack of papers off his desk. He bent over, picking the papers up off the floor, shuffling them in no particular order. Flustered, scared. He took a moment to catch his breath. Anger welled up inside him.

"To hell with this," he muttered, dropping the papers. They fell back to the floor in a flap of chaos.

"And to hell with worrying about muttering," he muttered. "It's my damn store, I'll mutter if I want to. And I'll be damned if I'll let some cowboy hippie freak make me nervous in my own damn store. No sir. No sirree, Bob."

Jenkins stepped back to the monitors; he glared at one screen, then another, then another, then another. And saw – nothing.

The stranger was gone.

"What the hell!" He scanned all the monitors: fresh foods, chips, soft drinks, frozen foods, beer and wine, soups, medicines, hygiene products, greeting cards, bakery goods, checkout, front entrance, back entrance.

The stranger had been at the rear of the store. The back entrance was locked. Even at a full run he couldn't have made it completely out of the building without Jenkins seeing him. No way.

"No way. No fucking way?"

Gone?

DEAN TRUMAN INSISTED on driving Piper Blackmoore home. He took her truck while Deputy Jerry Niles followed behind in the sheriff's department's Jeep Cherokee. At her door, beneath the shelter of a small porch, Dean had an overwhelming urge to kiss her. Arrested by guilt, he gave her a firm hug instead. She kissed him on the cheek. Her breath was fresh, with the slight hint of herbal tea. Nice.

The urge to kiss her was almost unbearable.

*

THE POLICE RADIO CRACKLED like burning wood, static consuming every third word. *". . . erry, is Dean . . . skkrrkk . . . you . . ."* Dean recognized the deep baritone of Sheriff John Evans.

"Radio's been acting up all morning. Getting worse by the minute. Phones aren't much better." Jerry Niles leaned forward, looking at the sky between swipes of the windshield wipers. "Must be this storm."

"That shouldn't affect the phones," Dean said. "The cables are underground."

Out the passenger's window the falling snow obscured the world in a white frenzy much like static on a television, an illusion that meshed well with the snarling radio. *". . . skkrrkk . . . is Dean with you?"* John asked.

Jerry took the microphone from its cradle and pressed the curved button on the side. "Yeah, I'm taking him home."

"Nix that . . . skkrrkk . . . ack here . . . skkrrkk . . ."

"Come again, Sheriff? You're breaking up," Jerry said.

The static ebbed. *"I said, bring Dean to the station house . . . skkrrkk."*

Dean held his breath. Jerry spoke his thoughts. "Ah shit, what's happened now?" He handed Dean the microphone.

"John, this is Dean. What is it?"

The radio growled.

"It's Mason Evans . . . skkrrkk . . ." Static ate the words. *". . . skkrrkk . . . okay, but . . ."*

Skkrrkk.

The signal cleared just enough for Dean to make out the two last words: *". . . Whitey Dobbs."*

JOHN EVANS RUBBED THE STUBBLE on his face with the knuckles of his left hand. His eyes were hammocked by dark circles, his brow ridged with deep troughs. "Mason is in my office," he told Dean. "Let's go to the break room."

Dean nodded and followed. A relatively small room situated at the back of the station house, the break room consisted of an oval table with four chairs, a deep, chrome double sink, a soda machine, a snack machine, and an old Kenmore refrigerator that rumbled like an idling 747. A white, industrial-size coffeemaker sat on the chipped Formica counter flanked by brown coffee rings.

"First Clyde, now Mason," John said. He took a cup from the dishdrainer, filled it with the tar-looking coffee, and offered it to Dean.

"Uh, no thanks. What about Mason? Is he hurt?" The image of Clyde's dead, blood-striped face flashed in his mind. Bile rose in the back of his throat.

"No. He's fine, at least physically." John took a sip of the dark coffee, then made a face like a kid trying to swallow nasty medicine. "But mentally he's a mess."

John leaned back, resting his elbows on the counter-top. Dean could hear the old Formica creak under the weight. The coffeepot gurgled, happily creating more of the thick, black ooze for mass consumption. John dropped his head, studying the yellow tile floor that had once been white. "The thing is" – he shook his head – "God, you're going to think he's crazy. I mean, he's my cousin, for Christ's sake."

Dean pulled out a chair and sat. "After today nothing could surprise me."

John raised his head to meet Dean's gaze. "Okay, how about this? Mason is completely convinced that his daughter is dating . . ." He took a breath. With anyone else Dean would have thought it was for effect, but with John the gesture spoke to just how hard it was to say what he had to say. "He's positive his daughter is dating Whitey Dobbs."

Dobbs. The name sent a bolt of fear through Dean's nervous system.

"That's" – he started to say "impossible" but censored himself – "improbable. His daughter's name is Tina, isn't it? She's what – eighteen? Dobbs would be at least thirty-nine by now."

John stroked his chin and sighed. The coffeepot babbled. The Kenmore rumbled. "This is where it gets weird."

This is where it gets weird? Dean thought.

"He says she is dating a seventeen-year-old Whitey Dobbs. The same Whitey Dobbs we buried twenty-two years ago on Hawkins Hill. Unchanged and unaged, and he says he's got a picture to prove it."

"Seventeen? That's absurd."

"Bingo."

Dean rubbed his temples, attempting to dissuade the budding headache he knew lay just below the surface. *Crazy* was a word that was often tossed around with humor, but if John had assessed the situation correctly, there was nothing humorous about Mason Evans's condition.

"Now you see why I called," John said. He sounded tired, lightning strikes of red laced the whites of his eyes. "The best I've been able to piece together is that Tina is off with some guy named" – he took a notebook from his breast pocket and flipped a couple of pages – "David Levin, twenty-four-year-old graduate student. Comes from money. His parents have a cabin up on Creed Lake. Maggie's trying to get the address now."

How's it hanging, Jimmy Dean? The memory of the ruined blackboard flashed full in his mind. He hadn't told John about this latest vandalism. He wasn't sure why. "Have you seen the picture?"

"Yeah, it's a fuzzy Polaroid, but this guy's got dark hair and a dark complexion. He doesn't even resemble Dobbs."

IT HAD BEEN OVER A YEAR since Dean Truman had seen Mason Evans and longer since they had spoken. A chasm had developed between them shortly after the burying of Whitey Dobbs, a gulf that had never fully been breached. Mason had taken good care of himself. His form was still firm and athletic. But his face was the color of flour and his eyes were wide with fear.

"Hello, Mason." Dean offered his hand.

Mason ignored the hand, instead embracing Dean in a deep bear hug. "Dean, thank God, thank God. If anybody can figure this out, it's you. You've got to help me. Help Tina. You've got to."

"I'm going to check on the search," John said, leaving them alone in his office. Dean sat on the corner of the desk. He motioned for Mason to take a seat in one of the two padded chairs.

"Did he tell you?" Mason asked. "Did he tell you who's back?" He didn't wait for an answer. "Whitey Dobbs, that's who – Whitey fucking Dobbs, and he's got my daughter. He's got my Tina."

Mason dropped his head into his hands. A mournful wail escaped his lips. His shoulders shook.

"I know it sounds crazy," Mason said, talking through his hands, not looking up, as if the concern on his mind was so heavy he could no longer lift his head. "I don't pretend to understand it. But it's true. That motherfucking, white-haired bastard is back. He's back and he's got my daughter." He moaned in pure, undiluted agony, his pain so raw, so visceral, that Dean felt his own eyes moisten.

As sympathetic as he was, Dean had to ask himself: How could anyone believe that Whitey Dobbs was back and still seventeen years old?

How's it hanging, Jimmy Dean?

Dean suppressed a shiver.

Then, in soothing, pacifying words, they talked. After assuring Mason that his daughter would be found, that Sheriff John Evans would not stop until she was found, Dean expanded the conversation.

They talked about Mason's company, his two failed marriages, the pressure, the loneliness, the kids, and finally the guilt. And all the while Mason clutched his hands and cried. Then he listened as Dean explained that the boy in the picture was a young man named David Levin, that his parents lived in Salem but owned a house on Creed Lake. And that John was calling the parents at that very moment to find out just where the house was.

"But the pictures – it's Whitey Dobbs!" The photograph lay face up on John's desk. Mason watched it like a camper would a snake.

"No," Dean said as he leaned back and studied the photo. The young man with Tina Evans had dark hair and tanned skin with an almost feminine face; he bore no resemblance to Whitey Dobbs. "The pictures is of David Levin. But – but you saw Whitey Dobbs?"

Mason looked up at his old friend with questioning eyes. "Then you believe me?"

"I believe you saw something, but it wasn't what's in this picture, so that means it was from your mind."

Mason trembled.

"It's caused by guilt and stress and a thousand

other little things that build and grow until, like an earthquake, something gives."

"But it looks so real," Mason protested. The large electric clock mounted on the west wall hummed in poised silence. Behind Mason the wood-paneled wall was dappled with plaques, certificates, and awards. Dean's reflection was caught, distorted, and blurred in multiple strips of brass.

"I know it felt real. That's what makes it so frightening." Dean reached over and slid the photograph to the corner of the desk. Mason recoiled, drawing back in his chair, turning his body so as not to see the picture, even in his peripheral vision.

Dean pointed. "Look at it."

Mason laced his thick arms across his massive chest. His lips were a line in the sand, his eyes squinted. Dean smiled. This was the Mason he knew – stubborn, bullheaded, uncompromising.

"Look at it," Dean repeated, more sternly this time. Then added: "Unless you're afraid."

Anger flashed in Mason's dark eyes. The big man turned back to the desk, paused to take a deep breath. Then, like a man plunging naked into an icy lake, he leaned forward to look at the picture.

The moment hung as if suspended from a single silver thread of a spider's web. The clock hummed. Movement was audible outside the door. But in the office, in the room where Mason was staring at the photograph, time hesitated.

Mason looked up, his eyes as wide and open as French doors, pupils overwhelming the brown-green of his irises. "He's gone. It's not him."

He looked back at the photograph, no longer trusting his own senses. "It's not him. It's some kid. Some normal-looking kid. But . . ."

The wrinkles in his leathery, sun-washed face collected like storm clouds and he began to weep – this time with relief. "It's not him. It's not Whitey Dobbs," he mumbled.

THIRTY SECONDS LATER the door opened. It was John Evans. "We found her, Mason. We found Tina, and she's all right. One of my deputies is bringing her in right now."

After thanking Dean and John profusely, Mason rushed out to wait for his daughter. John followed.

Alone in the sheriff's office, Dean sighed, the tension headache he had been fighting had taken hold. Looking down at John's desk, he saw the photograph Mason had been carrying like a totem. He had left it behind.

Dean smiled. That was a good sign. The photo had become the crux of Mason's delusions; relinquishing it meant he was truly on the road to recovery.

Dean picked up the photograph and drew it close for a detailed look. He was more tired than he thought. The photograph seemed fuzzy and undefined. He closed his eyes for a second, letting them rest behind the lids, then opened them, blinked several times, and again looked at the picture.

Whitey Dobbs looked back.

His heart shrank away in fear and terror. A cold pall settled over his mind. His breath was short and choppy.

Calm down, he told himself. *Don't hyperventilate.* Stress and guilt – wasn't that what he had told Mason?

It's just a hallucination. But even the thought of hallucinating was disconcerting to a scientist, and as Mason had said, it looked so real. He closed his eyes, but the image clung to his retinas like the red tinge of a bright flash. He could see Tina, her hair pulled back and tied into a ponytail. She was wearing a yellow-and-green school jersey and jeans. *And beside her?*

The image of the dark-headed David Levin was gone. In its place stood Whitey Dobbs, his arm around the schoolgirl's tiny waist, his smile askew and vulgar. It was the same Whitey Dobbs who had been buried alive twenty-two years ago. The exact same . . . to the day . . . not a moment older.

"No," he said aloud. "Dobbs is not in this picture." His words lacked that ring of certainty. Yet he knew the statement was true.

In defiance of his fear Dean opened his eyes and stared at the picture again.

The ivory-headed teen looked back. Then Whitey Dobbs . . . winked!

15

PIPER TOOK HER SECOND HOT SHOWER of the day. She ran the water as hot as she could take it, standing under the spray until her skin turned pink and warm. She dried, slipped on a pair of sweats and a T-shirt, then lay across her bed. Sleep took her like a thief in the night.

She dreamed of severed hands and dying men, and somewhere in the haze of dreams, events became surprisingly clear. All the fragments of her life suddenly made sense. For the first time she knew exactly what she had to do and how to do it.

But when she woke, confused and disoriented, two hours later, the revelation was gone. All that remained was the screaming urgency of her mother's long-ago warning.

Something bad is coming.

THE KITCHEN CLOCK SAID it was five minutes till eleven. John took three pieces of cold chicken from the refrigerator, ate them over a paper plate, and washed them down with a beer. The image of Clyde

Watkins dead, a hole stabbed impossibly through his skull, clung to John's mind like dried cereal to a porcelain bowl.

It had fallen to him to tell Clyde's wife. The woman, still in shock from news of her husband's attack, had been too numb to cry. The couple's eighteen-month-old child had squirmed and whimpered in her mother's arms.

John had waited until family members arrived. Even then the wife, the *widow*, did not cry. The look of total confusion so dominated her features that it was impossible to visualize her any other way.

Most of the incidents he dealt with as sheriff were pretty straightforward – domestic disputes, trespassing, vandalism, and the occasional dumb city boy playing Daniel Boone and getting himself lost in the mountains.

Simple.

But a severed hand? A mutilated woman? A stab wound through the skull?

Hell, that wasn't normal for anywhere – even Portland, even fucking-crazy Los Angeles.

In the last three years his job had become increasingly difficult. As the big mills closed down, new problems opened up. Many proud, confused, suddenly unemployed men with no income but plenty of bills and time began to drink and then turn ugly.

The new plant promised new jobs, new hope. Things should be getting better, not worse.

When Dean Truman won that whatever-the-hell-it-was award, John Evans was not surprised. By his way of thinking, Dean was the smartest man in the state. Maybe even the world. He had always known that. Some folks, like Mason, resented Dean, and he guessed he could understand that, too. But John was never bothered by his friend's brilliance. In fact, he respected it – used it.

They had been together since the first grade, an unlikely pair. Dean was thin and large-jointed like a praying mantis. John, always big for his age, was muscular, stocky, and strong like a beetle.

"Brains and brawn," John's father would joke.

Dean would always defend him. "John's a smart guy. Don't underestimate him."

But John didn't mind. He was a practical fellow.

In school, teachers repeatedly offered to allow Dean to skip ahead several grades. But Dean's parents would have none of it. "His social skills are as important as his academic skills," they had said. And John had felt himself fill with deep pride because as Dean's best friend, he was part of those social skills.

They each had their strengths and often traded services. It was a good relationship.

Or was it?

John had been married twice, but never anything serious. Odd way of putting it, but true. After Judy died, the two old bachelors had begun to spend more and more time together. Maybe too much time. Maybe using each other as a crutch, an excuse not to have to go at it out in the real world.

He would have to think about that.

Sex helped. As sheriff, John was always running into some lonely young thing looking for a quick romp in the sack. No emotions required.

Dean, however, was not so inclined.

If there was anything John envied about Dean, it was Mavis Connetti over at the Triple-D. She and John had gone out a few times. But she only had eyes for Dean, and the poor fool was letting all that potential affection go to waste.

John took out another beer, found a bag of half-stale chips and returned to the table.

After the award Westcroft College, and by default Black Valley, received national attention. The new NxTech plant could be just the beginning, a facility that would help Dean push his science further, as well as offer a tremendous training ground for young high-tech engineers. Sony Disc Manufacturing, which already operated a plant in Springfield, was said to be expressing interest in Black Valley. Things were finally looking up. Black Valley seemed ready to turn the corner.

Then it all went loony.

John finished his beer, then went to the bathroom. He caught sight of himself in the full-length mirror.

He turned to check out his form. He was still a big man – imposing, strong, but heavier than . . .

Than when we buried Whitey Dobbs in the cold, dark ground.

Dobbs? He was starting to sound like Mason.

John went back to the kitchen and broke his own rule by having a third beer. Thinking about Dobbs, about Mason, was stupid – and John Evans was anything but stupid. He was a practical man with a practical man's mind – and he had dismissed Dobbs the day after it happened.

Unlike Dean.

The scientist had obsessed on it. Only, he wasn't a scientist then – just another kid, albeit a bright kid. But he changed after Dobbs. They all had. The odd thing was, in some ways life had seemed to get better.

And what about Whitey Dobbs?

John's practical mind told him that someone had obviously dug him up. *But wasn't there a storm?* Maybe someone dug him up before the storm?

Sheriff Deats, the law back then, had almost shit a brick when a couple of hunters found the grave. But he wasn't able to connect it with the boys. It was nothing more than a strange hole in the ground, another mystery to add to the legend of Hawkins Hill. Funny, back in the old days everyone seemed to have some story about that place.

AN ICY WIND FLUTED through the trees. Mouth-size snowflakes plastered his hair to his head like cold, wet kisses. Nathan Perkins grinned behind the bright wool wrap around his face. He was relatively warm, thanks to his scarf.

Gloved hands fumbled with the keys as he poked at the lock, stabbing repeatedly until he found the hole. He turned the key. *Click.* The lock hadn't frozen, thank God. He twisted the doorknob and pushed. The door opened one inch, then stopped.

What? He examined the frame and saw the culprit. The chin lock was in place. For once, Ava had actually heeded his advice. Good for her, bad for him. He called her name through the crack in the door. Warm air rushed past his face like hyperactive children eager to play in the snow.

"Ava?" The house was quiet.

"Ava?" No television. No radio.

"Damn."

He rang the bell. A brisk wind broke over the porch banisters, licking him with a wet, icy tongue.

The house remained silent.

Turning up the collar of his Gore-Tex jacket, he hunkered down and stomped back out into the storm. His steps left deep imprints in the snow, which quickly began to fill even as he walked.

The back porch was a two-step concrete platform. There was no awning. He unlocked the door with the same key, turned the knob, and pushed – *thunk*.

The back door was chained as well.

"Shit!" He pounded on the door and called her name. He felt a *new* cold, this one internal, starting at his heart and radiating outward. "Ava?" Infinitely colder than the harshest Arctic wind.

"Ava?" This time a whisper.

Something was wrong. Her car was in the garage. The power was still on, so there was no need to abandon the house. Besides, she wouldn't have gone out on a night like this.

He had a brief image of how she had been dressed when he last saw her. How simple and helpless she had been. "Ava?"

Nathan Perkins was a slight man. Thin as a rail, all bones; his skin sprayed on like metallic paint. A hundred forty pounds, if you counted his clothes. But when he hit the door, striking with his gaunt right shoulder, it was with the force of a man twice his size, and on the second try the doorframe splintered, ripping the chain lock from its berth.

The inside of the house was just as he had left it – only different.

Nathan walked through the kitchen, then the den. The *TV Guide* lay open on the arm of the couch. A half glass of Diet Coke sat unfinished on a silver coaster. The artificial fire burned brightly, flames dancing, encouraged into a tribal frenzy by the hustling air.

Atop the handcrafted mantel laced with detailed molding stood a pair of red, unused candles in glass holders, their wicks virgin white. Next to that, a wedding picture. Ava smiling and Nathan, who looked like a little boy playing dress-up in the stiff, black tuxedo.

But it was the center of the mantel that drew his attention – the centerpiece that held his eyes and stalled his breath. An anniversary clock, a glass-ensconced face with visible workings, a trio of brass balls turning slowly beneath it, designed to mark time, tick by tick by tick. The hands on the clock face were spinning, while beneath them the three brass balls revolved like a cyclone. Tiny, hair-thin, blue sparks snapped between the brass and clockwork.

Sparks?

What was happening here?

He called her name, again and again, his voice rising an octave with each cry.

The spinning clock mirroring his thoughts. *Spinning, spinning, spinning.*

Leaving the den, he went into the hallway.

The door to the master bedroom stood open like an invitation. Suddenly, Nathan Perkins wasn't in such a hurry. Maybe he didn't want to see what was in that room?

Maybe?

His watch, a Casio Data Bank Telememo 150, inexplicably began to flash. The alarms intended to mark appointments began to beep. Thin hairs of blue electricity, like the sparks in the anniversary clock, flickered and pricked his skin.

Nathan rushed into the bedroom. Only one light was on – a small, shaded lamp that cast a hoop of yellow, leaving the rest of the room in shadows. And in the center – his wife's shredded nightgown.

Shredded.

Ava.

His watch beeped incessantly.

Somewhere in the dark, refuged in the shadows, something moved. A muffled cry drew his attention. In the corner, against the wall, he saw her – shadow on shadow. Her body covered by another, a man.

"Ava!" he screamed.

The man turned, then yelped in surprise and pain. Ava had bitten the hand that covered her mouth.

"Nathan!" she shrieked.

In the silence of the dark Nathan Perkins cocked the pistol.

The man-shadow moved quickly, too quickly. The lamp suddenly hurled across the room. Nathan ducked in the new darkness as it struck the doorway, showering him with ceramic shrapnel.

He recovered quickly, muscles fueled by fear. He slapped the wall, found the light switch, and flicked it on. Ava lay naked on the floor, blinking in the new, blinding light, eyes wide with fear but miraculously unhurt and—

Alone?

The man-shadow – her attacker – was gone, leaving Nathan with a single, vague impression of white hair.

White hair.

16

DEAN TRUMAN DID SOMETHING he had never done before. He took down a bottle of Valium from his medicine chest, threw two pills in his mouth, and chewed them like candy. Twenty minutes later he took two more, planning to continue the process until he slept or overdosed.

Even with the pills, sleep was slow in coming – but deep and hard when it arrived. *"How's it hanging, Jimmy Dean?"* Whitey Dobbs was alive and grinning in his dreams.

"Ninety-nine Einstein," He waved, then reached out from the Polaroid, his arm expanding in distorted proportions, becoming normal size. Grabbing Dean by the collar. Gripping the fabric in his fist. *"Ninety-nine Einstein, ninety-nine Einstein, ninety-nine Einstein,"* he repeated. Then he laughed. The sound of a thousand baby bones being dropped into a giant metal pail.

Ninety-nine Einstein.

Dean woke gasping for air, his face veiled in sweat. He opened his eyes, trying to climb from sleep. The room was dark and still and – being visited.

Someone was in the room.

The thought was primal – undeniable. He wanted to call out, to scream, but his mouth wouldn't work. The Valium held his muscles. His mind was thick and slow. Was he dreaming? Another hallucination? His eyes adjusted to the dark; he could just make out a figure, a shape, an outline. He strained, almost able to see a face . . . *almost*.

IT WAS AS IF someone had slapped him, and slapped him hard. Dean was fully awake, brought around by the harsh realization that he was not alone, not fantasizng. Someone was in the house. His house. Did the intruder know?

Baby bones.

Not just in the house, in the room. Someone was in his room. A figure . . . in the dark . . . at the foot of the bed. Adrenaline rushed through his body, obliterating the effects of the Valium. He snatched the heavy, windup Big Ben clock from the nightstand and heaved it with all his might.

"Jesus . . .," cursed the dark figure, ducking the ballistic timepiece.

How can anyone move that fast? Dean asked himself. *No, they aren't moving fast, I'm moving slow.*

"Calm down, just calm down," said the shadow in the dark. "I didn't mean to frighten you."

"Dobbs?" Dean asked, his voice raspy, dry, the sound of sandpaper on a hard-wood floor.

"Who?"

"I've got a phone," he yelled at the shadow-figure.

"Good, we can order pizza."

Pizza?

"Turn on the light, Doc."

Pizza? Dean awkwardly reached out for the lamp. His thick fingers found the neck and traced it to the switch. He turned it on. The white glow doused the room, revealing his visitor. "Piper?"

She was wearing a ratty leather jacket, corduroys, and black Doc Martens. A black-and-navy stocking cap covered her head. Her eyes were too wide, her cheeks too pale.

"Sorry to scare you, Doc. But you didn't answer the doorbell." She was fidgeting, wringing her gloved hands, glancing over her shoulder. "I was only half kidding about that pizza. Too bad nobody is delivering in this weather." She checked her watch. "Or at this time of night."

"I've got leftovers in the kitchen."

"Good, I'm starving. I haven't eaten since this morning."

Dean got out of bed, forgetting he was wearing only his nightshirt and boxers.

He snatched a robe off the back of a chair, but not before Piper saw enough to make her grin.

"GIVE IT TO ME AGAIN," Dean said, running his fingers through his thick, brown hair.

Piper had been hungry. She had already consumed half a portion of sweet-and-sour chicken and a plate of rice, and was now working on a can of Campbell's Chunky Vegetable Beef.

"See, I knew you would think I'm crazy. Got any crackers?"

He got up, took a pack of saltines from the box, and placed them by her bowl.

"Thanks. You should be the last person I go to – I mean, you being Mr. Science and all. But maybe that's why I came."

She split open the pack of saltines, removed three, and crushed them in her hand, dusting the remains into her bowl. "Maybe I want you to tell me I'm crazy. No, to prove to me it's all in my head."

Dean was silent.

Over the sink hung a black-and-white Felix the Cat clock, bought by Judy when she and Dean were first married. The tail swung like a pendulum while the eyes ticked right to left, left to right.

"It reminds me of you," Judy had said, mounting the cartoon clock on the kitchen wall. He suspected it was just a ploy to win his approval of the silly thing. "Back and forth, back and forth, always trying to look at both sides."

Back and forth.

Was that what he was doing now? Was that why he had not summarily dismissed Piper's assertions out of hand? *That and an impossible, moving photograph. That*

*and a message carved into a chalkboard by a seven-inch
blade, the exact length of Whitey Dobbs's beloved switchblade.*

"How did you get in?"

"Back door."

"It was locked."

"I unlocked it."

Dean frowned. His eyes involuntarily looked to the
living room, where the bookcase hid the basement
door. *Baby bones.* He didn't like company. Even Piper's
company. Not here. Not in his house. Not this close to
the basement.

"Doc? I am crazy, right?"

"You want to be?" He meant it as a joke, but she
held the question and studied it.

"It's better than living in a world where someone
can cut off a person's hand while they're still alive,
where bricks fly through walls, and people can be
slashed to pieces by an impossible storm of flying
glass."

They were quiet for a moment. Piper's spoon
remained resting in the bowl of soup.

"Something's wrong with me, Doc. I feel like I have
spiders crawling on the inside of my skin. And it's getting worse." She shook her head. She had removed the
stocking cap, but her short, dark hair remained plastered to her skull, except for a few defiant sprouts. "If
I'm not crazy, then something really weird is going on.
Something bad. Don't ask me how I know. I just do."

She reached out and grabbed his arm. Her hands were still cold despite the gloves she had been wearing. He met her eyes. They were beautiful eyes, sensuous eyes. If it were possible to see the impossible, it would be with these eyes.

Crazy. Was she? Was he?

"No." He laid a hand atop hers. "No. You're not crazy."

"Then?" The word trembled.

"Listen to me." Dean said. "It's not just you. Okay? Other people are seeing things . . ." Steam rose from his coffee cup. "*I've* seen things."

Her dark eyes brightened. "You?"

"Things I can't explain." *How's it hanging, Jimmy Dean?* He closed his eyes. "Things I can't explain – yet."

Something moved across the irises of Piper's eyes. Something blue, almost *electric*. Dean involuntarily drew back in his chair. Piper seemed unaware of the phenomenon. Or had it merely been a trick of light, a random reflection?

"It's in your coat pocket, isn't it?" she said more than asked.

Dean watched her eyes. Her words were distant, lost to his curiosity. *Electric?*

"Dean?"

He blinked, realized he was staring, and smiled self-consciously.

"I know I'm beautiful," she ran her fingers through

her hair. "Especially with this wet-dog look working for me, but—"

"No. It's just . . ." He shook his head. "Never mind. You were saying."

Over the sink Felix the Cat kept time, his eyes shifting from Dean to Piper, Piper to Dean, his molded plastic smile giving the appearance of great interest and amusement.

"Your coat," she repeated, pointing towards his jacket, hanging on a peg by the door. "The thing you saw. The thing you can't explain. It's in your coat?"

"How could you . . .?"

She smiled. Felix the Cat smiled, his tail flicking away the seconds. "I feel it."

For a moment Dean was made of stone. Despite his assertion that science could answer all, despite his belief in the no-nonsense physics of life, he found he had absolutely no interest in seeing the Polaroid again. Ever again.

Then why bring it home if not to study it?

Tired of waiting, Piper got up and went over to the coat. She fished the picture from the correct pocket without searching, without hesitation.

"How did you know?"

She shrugged, looking at the picture.

"What do you see?" he asked.

"A young girl and boy. They look like a couple. A happy couple."

Now for the $64,000 question.

"The boy. What does he look like? What color is his hair?"

Piper touched the photograph. She frowned. "Brown. His hair is brown. But—"

Her body stiffened.

Did I see that?

She was trembling.

"Piper?" Dean went to her. Even through her coat he could feel the *cold*. "Piper, what is it?"

A trickle of blood crawled from her nostril.

"Something's coming." Sharp blue, undeniable sparks flashed across her eyes. "Something very big is coming."

17

AN ICY WIND SCOURED THE STREET with
enough strength to physically shake the Ford Ranger.
"Where are we going?" Dean asked again.

"I don't know."

Wipers beat back fat, insistent snowflakes. Dean
could just make out the shape of houses and the
orange-yellow shine of the sodium-vapor streetlamps
through the ice-encrusted window. But the road itself
remained a nebulous thing.

Only a fool would be out on a night like this.

"Piper, I really think we should turn back—"

"Shhhh." She leaned over the steering wheel,
staring out the windshield. Her eyes sparked. In the
dark cab of the little black truck there was no mistaking
it. *Her eyes are literally sparking. How is such a thing
possible? And what does it mean?*

The truck turned left on Friedman, then right
on to Willamette, the main highway. The heater
huffed mightily, blasting them with hot, dry air
but failing to counter the soul-numbing effects of the
cold.

The streetlamps became fewer. They were heading out of town.

"Piper, I really think—"

"Shhhh, it's close, very close." She pressed the accelerator. The truck sped up, indifferent to the weather. Dean felt his heart climb up his throat. He didn't know what frightened him more, her driving or her eyes.

The town fell behind them and the world was reduced to the dual cone glare of the truck's headlights. It was a white, swirling, foreboding world. And it was rushing by much too quickly.

"Piper—"

"There, over there . . . ," she said, pointing out the window into the ambiguous white. She hit the brakes. The Ranger didn't stop. Instead it became a large black sled, skidding, sliding, swerving to the right, finally coming to rest horizontally across the highway. Dead center, as far as Dean could tell. If another car came—

"Get out."

"What?"

She opened her door. The interior was flooded with light. A swirling breeze rushed in and stole all the warmth from the air. The headlights revealed an empty field. Where were they? Piper had disappeared into the dark.

"Dean, hurry," her voice cut through the swoosh of the frigid wind. Dean stepped into the storm. For a terrifying second he was blinded, flakes batted his eyes and exposed his face. "Where are you?"

"Over here. Follow the sound of my voice."

His breath swirled in front of him, adding to the visual confusion.

"Over here," she repeated, acting as his auditory beacon.

Dean found her twenty feet from the truck. She was behind a tree, taking refuge from the harsh winds. Dean thought he knew where they were. He could just make out what appeared to be a bridge, and deep below it would be the dark, rushing waters of the Willamette River.

"There," Piper repeated, this time pointing to the sky.

Dean looked up. A star? No, it was moving. Meteor? No, brighter, bigger and growing by the second. Bright enough to be seen despite the storm. Flames. It was on fire. Whatever it was, it was impossibly big, burning and flying through the cold night air.

"Jesus."

Piper shivered. He put an arm around her. As they watched, the flaming object grew larger. "Mother of God, it's coming this way."

He tried to leave, but Piper remained stoically. She turned her gaze to him. "No, it's not going to hit us."

Blue sparks in night-black eyes.

Dean could hear it now, the whistle of something

rushing through the air, the flap of whipping flames. She was right. It was going to miss them, but it was going to be very close.

He could make out a shape now. Sort of. "It looks like . . ."

What?

"A truck," Piper said. "A semi."

Dean nodded in the dark. She was right. He could see it now. It was a big diesel Peterbilt with a tanker attached. He could just make out the wheels, dark in the surf of yellow-orange flames.

As they watched, the burning diesel truck smashed into the Willamette Bridge. The cargo, whatever was contained in that long silver tank, exploded. For a moment the entire southern valley was bright, illuminated by the blaze of a new sun. The noise shattered the snowy silence.

A wave of hot air struck their faces, whistling in the dark.

"Get down," Dean screamed, pushing her to the ground, covering her body with his as shards of concrete and asphalt rained down on them. Embers shot out in a thousand different directions.

A slab the size of a baseball struck Dean in the small of his back, knocking the air from his lungs.

"Dean?"

Pebbles and firefly embers peppered the snow around them.

"Dean?" Piper repeated.

"I'm – I'm fine," he lied, sucking burning-cold air into his empty lungs. He rolled off her. "You?"

"Okay. Good Lord!" she said, rising to her elbows.

Below them the road was still lit by a raging fire, casting flames and shadows in a thousand directions. The fire emanated not from the bridge, but from somewhere far below – down near the river. There was just enough light for them to see that the Willamette Bridge was no longer there.

Destroyed.

With the pass closed and the bridge gone, the city of Black Valley, Oregon, was truly and totally alone.

18

TICKTOCK, *ticktock, ticktock*.

Sheriff John Evans could hear his grandfather's pocket watch ticking. He knew it was impossible. The watch, a family heirloom, was safely buried deep in the pocket of his uniform, which was covered by his thick, insulated, outer coat. But he could hear it. Hear it marking the seconds, keeping time – no, not keeping time, counting down.

Counting down. Down to what?

Though Ava was physically unharmed by the attempted rape, doctors were keeping her hospitalized overnight. She was sedated and sleeping soundly. In many ways she was doing better than her husband. Nathan was frantic. He had been given something for his nerves but was still wired.

John wiped his face with his hand. It came away damp, sweaty. He contemplated it as if seeing blood instead of perspiration. *Sweatin' in the snow, hell of a deal*.

Nathan's words still rang in his head. "He had white hair, John. That's all I saw was white hair. Ava saw it, too. The color of bleached bones. You know who had hair like that, don't you?"

Whitey Dobbs.

Ticktock, ticktock, ticktock.

"He was in the room with me, John. I never saw him, but I could feel him. I could hear him. And" – Nathan talked between gasps of air and debilitating tears – "I never saw him leave, he was just gone."

Ticktock, ticktock, ticktock.

The phones were shit. Radios not much better. John had managed to talk to the Oregon State Police, but only for a minute, just long enough to tell them that all hell was breaking loose. The storm had come from nowhere, they told him.

Never seen anything like it. The closest anyone could recall was a tornado or microburst, back in 1974, that sprang from nothing, took the top clean off a grain silo, and vanished. It was so powerful, they never found the debris. It was obliterated. In a state that averaged no more than one tornado a year, the storm was a complete surprise. But even that was isolated, confined.

Nothing like this, nothing.

Even now, as snow piled on Black Valley, the weather wizards down at the Eugene television stations were still saying it was impossible. Should not be happening. A little rain, but that was all.

The storm had come from nowhere.

Ticktock, ticktock, ticktock.

*

DEAN AND PIPER ENTERED the Black Valley Sheriff's Department with the storm snapping at their heels. John wasn't in his office or in the main work-room. They found him in the break area, sitting alone at the small oval table, an untouched cup of coffee in front of him.

He didn't look up.

"The bridge is out," Dean said.

"Ava was attacked," John replied.

"What?" The refrigerator hummed roughly. "By who?"

John raised his head. "Good question. What about the bridge?"

Dean opened his mouth but made no sound; questions clogged his throat.

Piper answered for him. "A truck, a big fucking flaming truck. Struck the bridge and exploded. *Kaboom!* Just like Coye Cheevers said he saw two days ago. Except this one landed."

John was silent.

"You don't understand," Piper said. "It *hit* the bridge. But not from the road, from the sky."

John nodded.

"You hear what I'm saying? A burning semi fell out of the fucking sky and slammed into the Willamette Bridge, blasting the hell out of it." Piper's voice was strained and high, nearing hysteria. "It fell out of the sky. And – and I knew it was going to happen."

The vulnerability in her voice jerked Dean from his haze of confusion.

John accepted the news as if such things were commonplace. A new panic flared in Dean's mind. *Come on, John, we need you. Don't go crazy on us. Not now, not now.*

"What about Ava?" Dean asked, hoping to make the lawman focus.

John met his eyes. His jaw tightened. "Recovering. Sleeping. But Nathan's a basket case. He says her attacker was a man with white hair."

Silence filled the room.

The sheriff looked at Dean. "We're cut off. The pass is snowed under. Bridge is gone." He motioned toward the blinded windows. "Helicopter can't fly in this. You tried the phones?"

Dean shook his head.

"Gone to shit. Not just the phone line. Cellular, two-way, all of it. You can make out a word here or there, but otherwise static."

"We're on our own," Dean said, suddenly understanding the sheriff's mood. Might as well look for answers in the blackness of a cup of coffee as anywhere else.

"There's more." John's voice was as still as the night was frantic.

Dean pulled out a plastic-backed chair and sat heavily. *More* was not the word he wanted to hear.

"I haven't told the others yet. A hunter found a

body up on the north side of Hawkins Hill. Been there awhile, at least ten years, maybe longer. Not much to go on, but enough to tell the poor son of a bitch had been mutilated."

"Mutilated," Dean repeated.

"Missing his right hand."

"Ten years?" Dean muttered.

"Ten years? What does that mean?" Piper asked.

"It means he's done it before," John said with a steady voice.

"Before?" Piper repeated. Dappled in the light and shadows of the break room, she looked like a little girl.

"Serial killer?" Dean ventured. "Someone repeating a pattern."

John nodded. "The ten-year gap could be due to prison time or, worse, could mean a drifter who kills and keeps moving."

"Different jurisdictions, different states. A roving serial killer is hard to identify, let alone catch. And without phones there's no way to get any outside aid."

"Flaming trucks, showers of glass, serial killers?" Piper shook her head. "How can all this be happening?"

John returned his gaze to the motionless coffee. "Found a wallet on the corpse."

"A wallet?" Dean asked.

The sheriff looked up again. Even in the veiling darkness his cold, hard eyes seemed hazy, moist. "It's

Larry. Larry Pepperdine. Our old buddy, our old fucking DJ buddy, Larry Pepperdine."

Piper jerked. A shudder ran the length of her body.

Her eyes, her eyes, Dean thought. *Sparks of blue.*

"What the fuck?" John saw it, too.

"Something's coming," Piper whispered.

MAVIS CONNETTI PLAYED the message for a third time. The phone had awakened her from a deep sleep; the answering machine had caught the call before she was able to emerge from slumber.

She played the message again to make sure, absolutely sure, that she had heard right. It was Dean. His voice tinny, spilling from the machine.

"Mavis, . . . I need to talk to you . . . I need to see you. . . . I've been a fool. I need you. Please come over to my house. We need to talk – talk about us. Don't try to call me. I won't discuss it on the phone . . . Please come . . . I looove yoouu."

Dean.

She tried to call him back despite his instructions, but the phones were out.

Dean?

She was both thrilled and baffled. *He wants me,* she thought, a wave of excitement crashing over her body.

Please come over to my house.

His house. That had been part of the wall he had put up. The dividing line. How could their relationship flourish if she wasn't even allowed in his house? But now? The invitation was a sign that he was ready for a true relationship.

She dressed without making a conscious decision to do so. Outside, the night howled. A cold, nasty wind slammed against the storm windows. A horrible night to be out. But . . .?

Please come over to my house.

"Oh, Dean, are you really ready?" she asked the air. "I am."

19

DEPUTY JERRY NILES WAS OFF DUTY. It was late. He was tired and tense and looking forward to nothing more than putting his body in park, his mind in neutral, and watching the world go by on his twenty-one-inch Sony Trinitron television. It didn't matter what program was on. He would watch anything – sitcoms, dramas, PBS specials on the mating cycle of the Cajun moth, anything. Just as long as it made that requisite mind-numbing noise.

Cindy, his wife of three years, recognized the mood and accordingly gave him a wide berth. She did not ask why he was two hours late, again, or why he spoke in one-word sentences, his eyes never meeting hers.

His goal was obvious and simple – to sit in his old, plaid, saggy-bottomed chair and vegetate. The glow from the television lit his face as the buzzing voices dulled his senses. He pressed the remote. A TV family was having a TV-family crisis. One of the children needed a lesson in friendship. Part of his mind noticed that TV families never had to discuss things like severed body parts shoved down the throats of beautiful women. He shooed away the thought. He tried to find comfort in the canned laughter as the TV child learned that true friends were the best friends of all.

Knock, knock, knock.

Jerry frowned and studied the screen, willing himself to ignore the knocking at the back door. He tried to lose himself in the pixels on the screen, tried to mute the frantic exchange between his wife and the visitor.

He didn't even look up when his wife apologetically led the visitor into the den, then stepped in front of the television. He tried not to listen as the kid spewed out his story, all the while nervously kneading his box-boy apron.

To his credit, Jerry hung on to the illusion that he was off duty – despite the frantic nature of the boy's plea, despite the fact that his wife was physically blocking his view of the television – until he heard: ". . . we were doing stock when he came in. Guess we forgot to lock the door. You said to let you know if anything unusual happened. Well, this fellow, this stranger, is pretty unusual. He's still at the store. Mr. Jones is trying to delay him till you can get there. He figured it would be quicker to tell you than to call into town, what with you living so close and all."

The stranger!

"Mr. Jones says it's the same guy he saw before. Fellow wearing a green coat and a big – uh – floppy hat."

Jerry almost heard the click; the sound of that switch in his head flipping from off to on, bringing his senses to full and instant alert, the switch that made him a cop.

Jones's market was just two doors over. Jenkins Jones had reported seeing the stranger once before. John had told them all to be on the lookout for anyone, anyone out of the ordinary.

His wife knew the moment when his mind went back on duty. *Maybe she heard the click?* Not successfully masking the concern on her face, she dutifully and gingerly handed him his gun belt.

For just a second, the time it took to take the belt and wrap it around his waist, Jerry wondered how she did it. How she tolerated the hours, the moods, the uncertainty. And for the first time he wondered how long before she would burn out – give up and leave him – or before duty won and Jerry didn't come home.

He kissed her.

It was quick but heartfelt. He kissed her on the lips, in the living room, in front of the box boy, trying to convey all his emotions, regrets, and desires in that instant – with that one move and no words.

Then he was gone.

After he left, Cindy Niles stood quietly in her living room, her fingers on her lips, tracing the touch of his lips – trying to overcome her surprise.

She cried.

He had never done that before, never been that

passionate, that concerned, and it scared the hell out of her.

THE SKY WAS BLACK and the ground was white, as if someone had taken a negative picture of the world and pasted it to the windshield of Mavis Connetti's Jeep Cherokee. Ordinarily, nothing short of a fire could get her out on a night like this. But Dean. Dr. Dean. That was different.

His house was dark when she arrived.

The doctor's not in.

The storm, it must be the storm. His power was out. That meant candles and a fireplace, all very romantic. The wind clawed at her like a hungry horde as she hurried up the walkway and climbed the steps to the porch.

She pressed the doorbell, the wind preventing her from hearing its peal. No response. Maybe he wasn't home? No, if his power was off, then the doorbell wouldn't be working. She knocked instead.

Creak.

The door opened. Just a bit. A crack of dark about two inches wide.

"Dean?" her heart sprinted. "Dean, are you there?"

No answer.

She eyed the small gap, the strip of dark, searching for evidence that he was home. "Dean, it's me, Mavis."

No answer.

A tree limb cracked, sounding like a gunshot. The door opened wider, silently now – and Mavis felt an irrational wave of fear.

"Dean?"

The opening was now almost six inches wide. The streetlight leaked in slightly, hinting of depth and definition – a world beyond the black.

Had it been the wind? A strong gust perhaps, one strong enough to force the door open?

Creak.

A foot wide now. She could see the first trappings of furniture, the light colors of a sofa.

"Dean, is that you?"

Silence.

Like a helium balloon being jerked by a child, Mavis felt her emotions pulling her – jerking her toward the safety of the Jeep. She turned to leave.

"Maaviss . . ." It was the sound of wind rustling through a heavily leafed tree. Had she imagined it? Wished herself into hearing it?

She stopped, turned back to the door. "Is that you, Dean?"

No answer.

"Dean, I don't like this."

"Mavis . . . ," said the voice, this time with greater clarity, as if her attention had given it definition. It was Dean. Wasn't it?

She took a step closer and pushed the door open. The scream of fear from her child's brain was almost deafening, triggering the memory of the message on her answering machine.

Something was wrong here. She had to get away.

"Mavis . . ."

Leave! shrieked her irrational mind.

As if sensing that thought, the voice said, "Mavis . . . I huuurt . . ."

The Klaxon wail of the child's warning was pushed aside, discarded like soiled clothing. "Oh, Dean," she cried.

And then she entered the house.

20

THE STRANGER WAS BROUGHT IN the back
way. His hands cuffed behind his back; Jerry Niles at
his side; Coye Cheevers by the door, gun in hand. The
stranger was taken directly to a holding cell, a no-
nonsense room of gray block and black bars in the
basement. Jerry pushed him inside, where the sheriff
sat waiting on the thin, flat bed.

The stranger's raincoat, hat, belt, and boots had
been removed. He wore jeans and a short-sleeved
black T-shirt. His socks were thick, dark gray wool. It
was as if he couldn't decide whether to dress for warm
or cold weather.

"Who the hell are you?" John demanded, anger
cutting deeply into his stubbled face.

The stranger smiled. The beard and long brown
hair had given the impression of age, but his eyes, gas-
flame-blue, made him look surprisingly young.

"He says his name is Elijah," Jerry said. He
remained behind the suspect, holding him by the cuffs.
"That's it. Won't give a last name."

"Elijah!" John spit the name as if he had just bitten

into something foul. "No last name? That's a bit odd, don't you think?"

"I find the truth to be the greatest conundrum of all," said the stranger. His voice was softer than John expected and, like his eyes, hinting at a young, vigorous mind and body.

John rolled his shoulders, suddenly uncomfortable. Troubled. Alert. Unnerved by the fact that this man was not what he appeared to be.

"He talks like that all the time. Son of a bitch wouldn't shut up on the ride over here. But it's all crazy talk."

The stranger smiled. "You think I'm insane, don't you? In fact, you want me to be insane. My insanity makes the rest of the world sane."

Jerry wrinkled his nose. "Yeah, yeah, it does. Means you're the sorry bastard that's been killing folks."

John nodded, a barely perceptible move.

Jerry responded by tightening the cuffs. Elijah winced but didn't complain.

"Now, perhaps you would like to tell us your real name," John said.

"I did, I do, and I will again," the man said.

Jerry clicked the cuffs another notch. The metal bit into the already puckered skin. The prisoner gritted his teeth. Then offered another smile.

"Mr." – John paused – "*Elijah*, Deputy Niles tells me you had a forty-five Magnum tucked in the waistband of your pants. You mind telling me what that was for?"

"What can I say? It makes me feel pretty."

Another click of the cuffs. The prisoner groaned. A thin line of blood appeared on the back of the man's left wrist.

John ignored the comment. "He also tells me that you don't have a license for it. Possession of a concealed weapon. That's our holding charge."

Coye Cheevers remained outside the cell, shifting his weight from foot to foot.

"Now, you can save us all a lot of trouble by cooperating."

"Just like it says over the urinal, 'I aim to please, so please aim.' "

Outside the cell Cheevers chuckled. John silenced him with a look.

"Where's the victim?"

"You're looking at him."

John was four inches taller than the stranger, but he loomed over him as if he were twice that size. His bearing was imposing. He took a step closer, so close that a breeze would have to turn sideways to squeeze between them. He looked down on the stranger, breathing so hard that each time he exhaled, the long, loose hair on the suspect's head fluttered. John held steady, letting the discomfort of the moment linger like the stench of fear.

"You cut off a man's hand on Friday. The doctors

tell me the victim was alive when the amputation took place. Now I want to know where that victim is."

The stranger bit his lower lip, chewed on it a moment. "Aw, I gotcha. I know what you're talking about."

John took a step back but remained tense, shoulders up, alert. "I don't know where *that* victim is because that's not why I'm here."

John and Jerry exchanged a look.

Jerry raised an eyebrow. "It's not?"

"No, sir."

John crossed his arms; they looked like two pylons forming the letter x. "In that case, mind telling us why you are here?"

The stranger grinned, a flat, long smile that curled at each end like a wood shaving. "I'm here for Dr. Dean T. Truman."

JERRY DUMPED THE CONTENTS of a Jones Grocery envelope on to the table. Yellow and crumpled, the newspaper clippings fluttered down to the top of the table. "I found these in his pocket."

"Twenty-two in all. Each one from the *Black Valley Register*. All detailing some tragedy, accidental death, missing persons case, odd weather pattern. Weird stuff. I can't make out a pattern yet."

The sheriff fingered a clipping about the small tornado in '74. The fact that he had just been thinking about it made him decidedly uneasy. They had moved up to John's office after the stranger's pronouncement, ostensibly to look at the evidence but also to regain control. John wasn't sure he could have contained his anger much longer.

I'm here for Dr. Dean T. Truman.

Was that some kind of a threat? Or just more gibberish?

The sheriff sifted through the clippings, isolating a small obituary. Under the picture was the name Judy Truman, beloved wife of Dean Truman. John felt the anger building in him, a hot river of emotion suddenly put under massive pressure. But there was something else, too.

Fear. John was worried. Was this one man behind it all? And if he was, how? And if he was responsible for all that was happening, could John and a few cell bars actually stop him?

"About Dr. Truman," Jerry said. "Elijah mentioned something like that on the way over here."

The sheriff took a deep breath. A wrinkle formed between his eyes. "What? That he wanted to see Dean?"

Jerry shook his head. "That's just it. It was odd. He didn't say he wanted to see Dr. Truman. He said he wanted Dr. Truman to see him."

DEAN WALKED DOWN the narrow hallway leading to the holding cells like a man walking the final ten yards to the electric chair. His throat was dry and his fingers itched. *How do you scratch your fingers?*

"Sure you're up for this?" John asked.

Dean dry-swallowed, gave a moment's thought to how nice a cup of hot tea would be, then nodded. "Yeah, I'm fine. Just fine."

Dean and Piper had waited at John's request while he questioned the suspect. By the time the sheriff returned, Piper had become increasingly agitated. Her eyes remained normal, but her nerves seemed stripped raw. She said she had a severe headache and went to lie down on the couch in the waiting area.

The holding room was a utilitarian facility. Two small cells occupied the left side. The floor was concrete and painted gray; the walls, cinder block and dirty beige. There were no windows in either cell, only a wire-framed cot and a stainless-steel toilet.

The stranger, Elijah, was in the second cell, sitting on the edge of the thin cot, arms resting on his legs, humming.

Humming?

Dean had prepared himself for many things. Humming, however, had not been one of them. And what was the tune? Almost recognizable.

Seeing them, Elijah jumped to his feet. Literally jumped. He was spry and younger than he looked. *He's not what he seems*, John had said. He had an athlete's body. Strong. Strong enough to cut a person to pieces?

"Dr. Dean T. Truman. It is most definitely an honor to see you again."

John cocked his head, a questioning look. Dean shrugged. There was no recognition on his part. "I'm sorry, have we met?"

The prisoner smiled, revealing a row of even, ivory teeth surrounded by a scruffy and spiky beard. *Like a keyboard in a brier bush*, Dean thought.

"Once," Elijah said, the smile growing. "Well, almost."

Dean frowned.

The stranger in the cell seemed practically jubilant. Was this some kind of game for him? Some twisted, perverted contest?

Elijah turned his head and studied Dean from the corner of his eye. "How much do you know?"

"Pardon?"

"I said, how much do you know?"

Dean anxiously gummed his lower lip. "About what?"

The stranger's shoulders slumped; the keyboard smile vanished. "Not much, huh?"

"Who are you?"

"Elijah, I've already told Johnny here."

Out of the corner of his eye Dean could see the sheriff visibly stiffen. Dean held a hand out to dissuade his old friend from acting. Then to Elijah: "Why did you want to see me?"

"No, no. Not see you. Been there, done that. I wanted you to see me."

"I'm sorry. I don't understand." Beside him Dean

could hear John breathing heavily, his frustrations and anxieties building toward eruption.

Elijah held up a finger. "Okay, first things first. Number one, you're not crazy."

That makes one of us.

"And number two: Pay attention to everything. That's important, Doc. Pay attention to everything that happens to you, around you, and near you. It's all important. Sometimes the little things are really the big things, know what I mean?"

Dean opened his mouth to say he didn't, but stopped when the stranger snapped up straight and hooped his hands on his hips. The keyboard smile was back. "Hey, Doc, watch this."

The stranger stood up perfectly straight and began to hum. Then he jumped a half foot to the left, hummed a bit more, and took a step back to the right.

Dean stared, speechless.

Elijah then put his hands on his hips and squatted, humming all the time.

John leaned over to Dean. "What's he doing?"

"I think he's dancing?"

He finished with a series of energetic pelvic thrusts, then smiled and asked, "Get it?"

Dean shrugged.

Elijah shook his head, looking mildly miffed, like a parent with a frustrating child. "Here, I'll do it again." He repeated the process.

"I think he's crazy," John said.

Dean nodded in agreement. If this was their killer, then he was doing a great job of laying the groundwork for an insanity defense.

"Let's get out of here," John said.

"Get it, Doc? Get it?"

They turned to leave, but the stranger was fast. He was at the cell door in two steps. He reached through the bars, grabbing Dean by the coat sleeve. John was almost as fast, turning around and knocking his hand away with a powerful blow.

Elijah yelped. He pulled his arm back through the bars and cradled it like a baby. "Damn, that hurt. Forgot what a tough motherfucker you are, Sheriff."

John's hand went to his sidearm. The stranger appeared not to notice; his attention remained on Dean. "You have to get it, Doc. You have to 'cause – well, damn. I can't tell you why. It doesn't work that way."

John took Dean, who had remained motionless through the whole thing, by the shoulder and led him down the hall to the door.

"Just pay attention, Doc," called the stranger. "Everything and anything. Everything and any—"

The door closed, clipping his words.

A DEEP FATIGUE SETTLED over Dean. Any effects of his earlier medication had long since been burned off. But now weariness hurried in to fill the cavity left by the ebb of excitement.

Questions, questions, questions – usually the scientist's divining rod, each leading to a new line of reasoning, each answer standing like a signpost to make his passage and subsequently guide others who may follow in his path. But so far it had been all questions and no *solid* answers.

Was it just coincidence that Mason had a hallucination about Whitey Dobbs on the day after someone carved Dobbs's old taunt in the dust-laden blackboard? Or that Nathan said his wife was attacked by a man with white hair? Or that Dean himself had hallucinated, seeing Dobbs not only in a photograph, but winking?

No. The odds were mathematically staggering.

But so far a reasonable solution had eluded him. Showers of glass, severed hands, flaming trucks falling from the sky. Too many questions.

It was impossible – hell, all of it was impossible. Where had the damn truck come from in the first place? No. Dean refused to give into that sort of thinking. Unusual, yes; unprecedented, certainly; but impossible – no. He had seen it happen. Now he had to understand how it had happened.

And how Piper had known it was going to.

Could she be part of some elaborate plot? No. There had to be another answer. She had claimed to have had an equally powerful feeling less than an hour ago in the sheriff's department, but nothing had come of that.

"Too much," she had said. "Too much is happening. It's suddenly all a jumble in my head."

Was he to believe that Piper Blackmoore possessed some power, some *supersense* that allowed her to predict the future? His own words came back to haunt him. *Magic is just science we haven't discovered yet.* Twenty-five years ago the thought of flipping open a palm-size box and talking on it like a telephone was science fiction – total *Star Trek*. Beam me up, Scotty. Now it was commonplace. Twenty years ago computers were the size of rooms; now you could carry them like notebooks. His multifunctional geek watch contained more sheer computing power than those first massive machines.

Magic. The devil's work. Or even the hand of God.

"You don't believe any of this, do you?" Piper asked, breaking the silence between them.

As if she read my mind. No, she read my face. He looked out the window as her truck crunched through frozen, snow-thick roads.

"I can tell you what I know. I know a woman was shredded in a shower of glass. I know Clyde was murdered. And someone tried to make it look like a severed hand was the murder weapon."

He took a breath. The truck's powerful heater roared. The engine ticked. "I also know a flaming truck fell out of the sky and destroyed the Willamette Bridge, and I know that somehow . . ." he rubbed his hand across his mouth, as if looking for a way to pull the words from his throat. "I know somehow you knew it was going to happen. Another thing. You're not the only one."

"What do you mean?"

"Remember what you told me about Coye Cheevers? What he said he had seen in the sky a couple of mornings ago? Only his didn't hit anything. Appeared and vanished, just like that."

Piper carefully turned into Flint Street. She was driving slowly; nonetheless, the big machine shuddered, the rear end slid to the left. She patiently regained control.

"But you don't believe it can happen." Her eyes were pinched. From the headache or her own search for words, he couldn't tell. "Even though you've seen it yourself, you still don't believe. You don't really believe what I feel."

The truck tried to slide again. She manhandled it back in line.

"I believe you believe. The mind is—"

She threw her hands in the air, temporarily freeing the truck to pursue its own course and causing Dean's heart to miss a beat.

"Here we go again," she said. "It's all a hallucination. The product of a powerful imagination in connection with an inquisitive, intuitive mind. I know, I know. You've said it all before."

She reclaimed the steering wheel. The engine groaned like a circus cat caught sneaking from its pen.

243

"But that truck. The bodies. Those things are real. Those things are not products of my imagination. Do you still believe it's science?"

Dean was silent.

They turned on to Beaker Street, leading to his house. The streetlamps cast yellow rings on the virgin-white snow.

"Can I ask you something?" Piper glanced in his direction. "Is it true that you, the sheriff, and the mayor used to be in a gang?"

"A gang?" Dean asked, genuinely surprised, then his face softened. "Ah, you mean Flash Five. Who told you about that?"

"Nathan. He's quite proud of it."

Dean laughed out loud. "Well, don't let him fool you. We weren't in the hood or anything. I mean, this is Black Valley. The only hoods here are on the front of cars. We were just a group of friends. Flash Five was just sort of our nickname."

"Odd nickname," she pressed. "What's it mean?"

His smile broadened. "Depends on who you ask. Everyone's got a different story."

"And yours is?"

"Embarrassing. But the truth."

She grinned. "Those are the best kind."

"We were just kids, really – eleven or twelve – and the high-school football team was having its best season ever. In fact, they were only one game from the state finals. But that one game was with Oakridge."

"Oakridge," Piper said solemnly. "Our archrivals."

"Exactly. Anyway, someone came up with the bright idea that it would be really funny if we waited down by the Willamette Bridge and – when we saw the Oakridge bus – turned our backs and dropped our pants."

Piper put a hand to her mouth and snickered. "Oh, God, you mooned the Oakridge football team?"

"No. We tried to moon the Oakridge football team. As I recall, Nathan was our lookout . . ."

"Him? With his thick glasses?"

"Bingo. So, he gives the word, we turn, drop our pants, and are laughing like fools with our little white butts hanging out in the air. Then the bus passes and I see written on the back BLACK VALLEY FIRST BAPTIST CHURCH."

"Oh, no."

"Oh, yes. We flashed the choir. I can still see Mrs. Abercromby's face, pressed against the glass, eyes wide, jaw somewhere around the floor."

"The organist?" Piper gasped.

"The seventy-two-year-old organist," he added. "It was the preacher who first called us Flash Five."

Tears welled up in her eyes as she laughed.

After a moment Dean's smile faded. "Flash Five, stay alive. Flash Four, group no more," he muttered.

"Dean?"

"Something Clyde used to say, and now . . ."

They sat in silence.

"So, do you think the stranger's behind all this?" Piper asked.

"Elijah? He's certainly crazy enough."

"Why did he want to see you? What did he say?"

Dean smiled.

"What?" she demanded. She had noted his smile.

Intuition, that's how she does it, Dean assured himself. Piper was in tune to the world around her, extraordinarily observant, albeit on a subconscious level, to even the slightest changes.

"Spill it, Doc. What did he say?"

Dean shrugged. "Nothing really. Just that I should pay attention. That I wasn't crazy—"

"Jury's still out on that one," she said with a snicker.

"And then he, well . . ."

She turned and looked at him, her face alight with a child's anticipation. "What?"

"Then he, well, he . . . sort of did a little dance."

Her gaze hung on him for a disturbingly long time. The truck appeared to be on autopilot. A smile creased her face, then she exploded in laughter.

"A dance – he did a little dance?" she asked, gasping for breath. "What kind of dance?"

The laughter was infectious. Dean tried unsuccessfully to keep the merriment out of his voice. "I don't know. A sort of two-step. The hokeypokey, something silly like that."

This only fueled her spasmodic laughter. It was a

cleansing laugh. After a day and night of piano-wire tension, it was the laugh of relief.

"Remember that movie, *Dr. Dolittle*?" she asked, catching her breath.

"With Rex Harrison?"

"No, the other one, with Eddie Murphy. The one with the guinea pig." She let go of the steering wheel and churned her hands as if stirring a giant pot, then, in a dead-on impression of the gravelly-voiced Christ Rock, she sang, "Get down tonight."

Dean cackled with delight.

The truck pulled up to Dean's house and glided to a halt like a lapping wave.

"Home, Doc. So, going to invite me in for a nightcap?" The glow of the dashlights brushed the left side of her face, high-lighting her apple-round cheeks and pert nose.

Dean wanted to kiss her. It was an urge so potent and overwhelming, it overcame his concern over their age difference and his usual guilt at the thought of wanting anyone other than Judy. A simple gesture would somehow convey all his thoughts and hopes, his needs and fears.

The world waited.

"Doc?" she cocked her head, favoring him with her right eye, the dashlights now sketching a soft emerald line across her jaw.

"Hello, Doc? Anybody home?"

Invite her in? He never invited anyone in.

He looked at the simple clapboard house.

A dagger of fear stabbed his heart.

"Doc?"

"A light's on." His voice dropped to a whisper, his words as cold, as vicious, as the north wind. "Someone's in the house."

21

SNOW MANTLED THE STEPS, creating an ivory altar leading to a long, dark porch. A fringe of icicles hung from the roof like a row of vulgar, jagged teeth. The house waited, dark, cold, empty, save for a small, flickering light from the upstairs window.

"Could you have left it on?" Piper whispered.

Dean shook his head. The corners of his mouth pulled down in distress. "It's not a lamp. It's a candle. And I'm sure I didn't light a candle."

"Maybe we should call the sheriff?"

"No time. It could be a fire. Wait here." Dean opened the truck door. The cold snapped at his cheeks.

"I'm coming with you."

"No, you're not. You're staying here." He stepped into the storm.

The coarse breeze scrubbed his cheeks. The snow was four inches deep. He sank to his ankles, each step crunching, the sound of breaking bones – tiny, fragile *baby bones*.

He mounted the steps carefully, slowly pulling his keys from his coat pocket. His hands were shaking; he looked at them as if they belonged to someone else, and touched the key to the lock. The door swung open.

Unlocked?

Muscles tensed in the back of his neck. His hand went to the light switch. Nothing happened. He tried again and again, as if repetition alone would cause the lights to flame.

Dark.

The acidic taste of bile rose in the back of his throat. No electricity. His breath was ragged, alarmingly irregular. He sucked cold air between his teeth and tried not to pant. Two steps in. The dark seemed to swallow him. He could barely make out shapes, guided more by memory than the feeble light leaking from a streetlamp. The house, the place that had been his home for more than twenty years, suddenly felt sinister.

A palpable sense of dread settled over him.

"Dean."

He jumped and turned, blood rushing to his temples. Piper stood behind him. "Jesus, you scared the hell out of me. I told you to stay in the car."

"I thought you might need this." She held up a gun. "I keep it in the dash."

"I don't know how to use a gun," he whispered.

"I do." She was looking around him, peering into the unnaturally oily blackness. "No lights."

"Not down here."

They had left the door open. Ice crystals skiffed in

on puffs of frigid air. The door moved. Hinges moaned. Dean inched forward, Piper at his back.

Somewhere in the sturdy darkness a radio exploded to life.

They jerked to a stop.

"What the hell is that?" Dean asked.

Piper cocked her head. "The radio? I know that song. It's 'Rock on,' by David Essex, only . . . different somehow. A remix? It's coming from upstairs."

"There is no radio upstairs," Dean muttered. "Not even a tape player."

"There is now. Either that or David Essex just broke into your house and launched into an impromptu concert. Where are the stairs?"

Dean moved forward. The music continued, loud and distant at the same time – the notes echoing as if played in a house ten times as large. He and Piper mounted the stairs slowly.

"Maybe I should lead?" Piper suggested. "I'm the one with the gun."

"No." His hands trembled, the start of a mutiny by his body. But the music held him.

Something about the music?

"You're right. It's the same, only it's not."

He continued up the stairs, the music growing louder with each step, becoming a physical presence in the dense darkness.

He gasped, his body betraying what the mind wanted to hide. His heart beat so hard, he feared his chest would explode. His memory reached the chorus a nanosecond before the song.

He reached the top of the stairs as the song reached the dreadful phrase.

"*Jimmy Dean* . . . thump, thump, thump . . . *Jimmy Dean* . . . thump, thump, thump . . .*"*

"The song's been edited. It's repeating the same line," she said. "Someone inserted the sound of a heartbeat."

Currents of fear sparked and sizzled in the deep chambers of his heart. His forehead was bathed in a clammy vapor.

"Dean?" Piper asked him, her voice coming from somewhere far away and possibly underwater.

"*Jimmy Dean* . . . thump, thump, thump . . . *Jimmy Dean* . . . thump, thump, thump . . .*"*

Dean tried to swallow. His throat was as dry as a desert bed.

"Why would someone edit the song?"

"Why?"

Why? Because only one person ever called him that. Because that person disappeared twenty-two years ago. Because someone was pushing Dean toward insanity, to a mental breach beyond which all reason was lost and thoughts were doomed to plunge down, forever dropping in a bottomless cavern of despair.

"*Jimmy Dean* . . . thump, thump, thump . . . *Jimmy Dean* . . . thump, thump, thump . . .*"*

The music had risen in volume. The heartbeats

throbbed in his head, shaking his very body, his mind, his soul.

There was a quarter-inch gap between the closed door and the carpet. The gap was illuminated by a thin, pulsing band of light. The bedroom. It was coming from the bedroom.

Piper moved around him and headed for the door.

"Don't," he called after her. She wasn't stopping. Her body became a shadow, dark on dark. Dean had the irrational feeling that a stiff breeze would whisk her away.

"*Jimmy Dean* . . . thump, thump, thump . . . *Jimmy Dean* . . . thump, thump, thump . . ."

He rushed after her. She reached the door. Gun in her right hand, she turned the knob with her left. Slowly, slowly. The door moved in silence or was perhaps overwhelmed by the drumming beat of the song.

She entered the room.

The candle sat on a table near the window. A small, thumb-size flame, flickering yellow and orange, fluttering in an imperceptible draft, casting a feeble cone of light. Piper started toward it. Dean stopped her, pulled her back, and took the lead. Fire shadows flashed like black lightning. The room seemed alive, writhing with the flame. Dean saw strobing snapshots of the bed, the end table, a desk.

The air seemed even colder here. If he could see, Dean was sure he would witness his breath crystallizing before him. The music was louder as well. But the flame offered too little light for the source to be found. A sustained shudder ran through his body.

Tentatively he stepped into the flickering tableau. Something touched his face . . . something cold and malleable.

Fear hit him with a lumberjack's fist. He reeled back, brushing against Piper. They both collided into the wall.

"*Jimmy Dean* . . . thump, thump, thump . . . *Jimmy Dean* . . . thump, thump, thump . . ."

His hands found the dresser. The dresser. There was a flashlight in the top-right drawer. His throat was tight and tasted of acid. Fatigue was gone, shrugged off and replaced by dread.

"Jesus, what was that?" Piper asked.

His fingers found the knob and pulled it open. The drawer squeaked. He found the light and thumbed the switch.

Flick.

A fan of harsh white spilled into the bedroom. Momentarily blinded, he nonetheless caught the glimpse of an image.

Something . . . dangling . . .

He blinked for vision.

. . . dangling . . . turning . . .

His eyes cleared.

Piper screamed. Dean tried to scream, but his throat was sealed by disbelief.

The body hung from the ceiling beam, a short, tight

noose around the victim's neck. The rope was obscured by the awkward fall of her head, hanging unnaturally to the side, an impossible position – unless the neck was broken.

When he had touched it, he had set the body swinging, twisting slowly at the end of the rope. It moved in and out of the flashlight's beam. Dean knew the face even before it turned into view. Still, he watched as the back of her head gave way to a profile, then her cheek, her eyes. . . .

Mavis Connetti hung from the rafters – neck broken. On her face was an unforgettable look of pure, unfiltered horror.

"*Jimmy Dean* . . . thump, thump, thump . . . *Jimmy Dean* . . . thump, thump, thump . . ."

Pinned to her breast was a large, awkward cardboard sign. Dean read the message before he could stop himself.

The note said: HOW'S IT HANGING, JIMMY DEAN?

"*Jimmy Dean* . . . thump, thump, thump . . . *Jimmy Dean* . . . thump, thump, thump . . ."

22

DUB PELTS KNEW CHICKENS. He knew them like other men knew their hunting rifle, fishing pole, or car engine. He knew their likes, dislikes, attitudes, and even their moods. Most people didn't even know chickens had moods, but Dub did. He knew how to look for the tiny but significant signs. Too much running and too little pecking meant something was a foot – unseen eyes of a predator were watching. Too much time at the water bucket could be the first hint of sickness.

Dub raised chickens because he had nothing better to do. He had retired four years earlier when the sawmill shut down. His wife was dead, his children grown and busy making messes of their own lives.

He raised the chickens as a hobby. Truth was, the girls, as he called them, were his only form of entertainment. It was like his own personal soap opera, except it was live and enclosed in chicken wire.

All that watching and all that studying was how he had come to know the chickens and their moods so well. "You watch, and if you have half a brain, you learn," he often said. No one heard but the chickens, and indications were they didn't listen.

But he always did, and this morning something was happening.

The mood in the coop was different – erratic. The snow had forced the birds inside. That, in itself, was enough to make them jittery, but there was something else. He could tell. There was something else entirely. Maybe a possum, a raccoon, or even a bobcat watching from the woods. Something was bothering the girls.

Most folks thought of chickens as dumb. And maybe they were, but they were smart, too, at least in an instinctual way. They could sense things other creatures couldn't. Maybe it was the good Lord's way of compensating them for a lack of brainpower. Whatever the case, Dub knew enough to take the shift in mood seriously.

Putting on his winter gear – a dark green, hooded poncho and calf-high rubber boots – he started out the back door toward the chicken coop, thought a second, then went back inside and returned with his double-barreled shotgun.

Chickens knew stuff.

There were bears in this part of the county. You didn't see them often, but you did see them. He loaded shells into both barrels, snapped the barrels back in place, then stepped out into the yard.

His boots sank in the deep snow as he plodded toward the coop.

He rubbed his thumb against the cold-metal side of the shotgun. He heard something a whistling, shooshing sound – and looked up. Snow found its way into his poncho. Cold beads melted, pooling in the nape of his neck. Others crawled beneath his flannel shirt, leaving a frigid trail in their wake. But Dub Pelts couldn't feel the cold. His eyes were held by the object in the sky, an object growing bigger and bigger and bigger.

He brought the double-barrel up without thinking, moving out of fear for himself and his girls. He fired until the gun dry-clicked. He didn't drop it. He couldn't move.

Ice on ice.

His heart froze in his chest. His breath ceased to move.

He was immobilized, stunned as he watched the flaming object score the sky.

THE SHERIFF'S DEPARTMENT HAD had its share of prisoners. Mostly just the drunk and disorderly, mostly overnight, and a few vagrants. And once, the Bendez brothers, who had gone on some cattle-shooting jag that ended when they turned on each other. It wasn't often, but it was enough for there to be a routine, a ritual.

Each morning Coye Cheevers would go across the street to the IHOP and get a breakfast for their visitor. He preferred the term *visitor* to *inmate*. Visitors weren't as scary. The breakfast was always the same: butter-milk pancakes, scrambled eggs, hash browns, and orange juice. But this morning was different. This morning the visitor was a killer, a real cut-'em-to-pieces, honest-to-goodness serial killer, just like in the movies. Just like Sir Anthony Hopkins in *The Silence of the Lambs*. Just like that.

What does a man who slices people to pieces eat for breakfast? Fava beans?

This quandary consumed several minutes. Finally, he decided on sausage links and eggs, poached not scrambled. Blueberry pancakes – no reason, it just felt right – and both milk and orange juice. Better to be safe than sorry.

Coye was feeling pretty good about his selection when he returned to the station and bounded down the stairs leading to the holding area. But doubt was never far away. What if the visitor didn't like eggs? What if he didn't like pancakes? He could be allergic to blue-berries. He hadn't thought of that. And the sausage links? What if he took it the wrong way? Coye's mouth was dry, his steps slowed by the morass of indecision. What if . . .?

"No, don't matter," he said aloud, to make it so. "Don't matter at all. This is what I got him and this is what he can eat, like it or not. He's the prisoner and I'm the police. Simple as that."

He reached out and touched the metal doorknob. *Skknapp* – a thin, jagged spark of blue electricity flared

259

from the knob to his finger. He jerked his hand away, almost dropping the tray. "Lord God!"

Static electricity. He must have been dragging his feet on the thick, new carpet the sheriff had put in last summer. He tried the knob again, slower this time. It didn't bite. He sighed with relief, opened the door, and went inside.

"Breakfast time. Now look, I got you sausage links, poached eggs, blueberry pancakes, and . . ."

Coye dropped the tray. His knees wobbled.

Holding cell number two was empty.

"Lord God!"

"TWO BABBLING MADMEN in two days," Jerry mumbled to himself. "Got to be a record." He pulled the squad car into a vacant spot outside of Macky's Bar. A brisk wind skimmed crystals of snow off the ground. Jerry hugged himself and shivered as he hurried into the bar.

He was standing in the foyer, stomping snow off his boots, when something caught his attention. A shadow. A vague impression of white hair. Someone outside. Standing. Just standing. On the other side of the street watching the bar. *On a day like this?* Jerry pressed his face against the cold, ice-encrusted window. His breath immediately fogged the glass. He used the sleeve of his coat to wipe it clean.

The man, the shadow, was gone. If he had ever been there. Was insanity contagious?

Jerry chortled to himself. "Getting jumpy, Deputy."

There were only two people in the bar: Leonard, the bartender who lived in the back, and Dub Pelts. The latter sat at the end of the bar, sucking on the long neck of a bottle of Heineken. Based on his posture, it wasn't his first.

It was Leonard who had called Jerry. The bartender met him as he walked in. "Been like that for the past half hour. Took me twenty minutes and almost as many drinks to get him to calm down."

Jerry pushed his hat back with his thumb. "Give it to me again. What did he say happened?"

Leonard wiped his hands on the ever-present apron. His voice was crusty, with a low, husky, mucus rattle, the consequence of spending too much time in smoke-thick rooms. "He was waiting outside when I got up, begging to come in. Eyes as wide as hubcaps. Started babbling, I mean crazy talk. Says his chicken coop was destroyed."

"His chicken coop?"

Leonard checked the old man at the end of the bar. "Yeah, completely destroyed."

"By what?"

"Fire."

Jerry sighed, a little relieved. That wasn't so bad.

Leonard squashed the relief. "Wait till you hear what started the fire."

"Fire?" At the end of the bar Dub Pelts raised his

head. It wobbled like a buoy on a choppy sea. "Fire. Gone. Completely gone."

He squinted as if attempting to hold his eyes steady. He found Jerry. "That you, Sheriff?"

"No, Dub. It's Niles, Deputy Jerry Niles." He headed toward the end of the bar before the old man could get up and attempt some perilous feat such as walking. "Sorry to hear about your chickens."

The wizened head nodded. His eyes closed, first the right one, then the left. For a second Jerry thought he had nodded off. Then his right eye opened again, the left following suit, but slowly, like a man swimming in mud.

"What about the fire, Dub? What caused it?"

The change was extraordinary. The old man sat up. His slackened face tightened. His eyelids were suddenly weightless. "The spaceship, that's what."

Jerry looked at Leonard, searching for a translation. The bartender shrugged, no explanation available.

"Spaceship?"

Dub nodded. White, frothy spittle collected at the corners of his mouth. "UFO. A fucking unidentified flying fucking object. That's what done it. I shot it down. Shot the hell out of it. But it crashed. Crashed right smack-dab in the middle of my chicken coop, burned up my babies, my poor, sweet babies."

His spine became pliable. He slumped forward. The face slackened. Jowls hanging like saddlebags quivered as the man cried in silence.

For a moment Jerry wasn't sure what to do. He had known Dub all his life. Knew him to be a bit peculiar, especially after his wife died, but this was way past peculiar.

"Don't believe me," the old man said, skewering him with his right eye. "Go up there and see for your fucking self."

Something new traversed the old man's face. His ruddy complexion turned to wax. Fear, a very real fear, burned behind bloodshot eyes. "Go see for yourself, but I'll tell you this, I ain't ever going up there again. *Ever*."

PIPER WOKE UP ALONE. It was a quarter to twelve. The sun was out. The bright, warm light reflected off the snow and spewed through the garden window. She sat up and rubbed the back of her neck. The fire in the fireplace was down to embers. It was the chill that had awakened her.

Alone.

Dean had been with her when she fell asleep on the couch. She had been holding him. Comforting him, rocking him, as he cried in gentle silence.

It was after two A.M. when the sheriff had sent them home. "Can you put him up for the night?" the lawman had asked. "I don't think he should be alone. You, either, for that matter. I can take your statements in the morning."

"I've got a guest room." But they never made it that

far. She fixed them something to eat while he made a fire.

They had sat on the couch, sipping wine and watching the flames dance like a spastic chorus line. Embers popping, the faint curl of blue-gray smoke rising slowly up the chimney. They tried to talk but didn't get far. Emotional burnout, she guessed. They were both completely exhausted.

At some point he had started to cry, and she had taken him in her arms to comfort him – stroking his hair, kissing his temples, holding him. And she cried, too. They had fallen asleep on the couch, locked in a spoon embrace.

Now he was gone. And she was, well, disappointed. *A woman's dead, and you're worried because your sleepover buddy left early. Shame on you.*

Piper stood and stretched. She was still wearing the clothes from the night before and felt grimy and worn, in need of a shower.

In the kitchen she found a note:

Got an idea. Gone to the lab. Borrowed truck. Back soon. Love, Dean

THE SHERIFF COMBED his hair with his hand, then placed his saucer hat just so on his head. He wrinkled his nose. He hated hospitals. Morgues most of all. Not the dead people. He could handle that. It was the smell. That god-awful smell that seemed to get in your clothes and hair.

He replaced the sheet over the face of Mavis Connetti, then slid the tray back into the chrome locker.

All filled up. *If anyone else dies, I'll have to start stacking 'em like cordwood.*

After processing Mavis – *process*, the word sounded so cold – John had spent another two hours grilling the stranger. Elijah. He gritted his teeth, his temples throbbing from a lack of seep. The stranger had only smiled. When he did speak, it was unintelligible, idiotic babble. John had lost his temper, and his professionalism. He had beaten the guy pretty good – busted his lip, left him with a shiner.

The man was definitely insane, no doubt about it. But there was also no doubt that he could not have killed Mavis Connetti. He had the best alibi of all: he was in jail at the time.

So, what did that mean? Two killers? Tandem murderers?

"Sheriff." The morgue door swung open so hard that it struck the doorstop and shot back, hitting Coye sternly in the nose. The deputy stumbled backward, blinking. John followed.

"You okay?"

Coye was holding his nose. "I tank I brawk my nozuh."

John pulled his hand away. The nose was red, swelling. "You didn't break your nose. It's not even bleeding. But you *are* going to break your neck if you keep running around like this."

"It just flew back an' hit me."

"Yeah, I was there, remember? Now, what's so damn important that you would run into a door trying to tell me?"

"It wan into me."

"Whatever."

The deputy's eyes crossed as he tried to look at his nose. Over the loudspeaker a nurse called an orderly to ward one.

"Cheevers," John snapped.

That got his attention. He looked up, his eyes wide. "The stranger has eshaped."

"What?"

"Eshaped," Coye repeated, wiggling his nose between his thumb and forefinger. "The stwanger."

"The stranger? Elijah?"

Coye nodded. "He eshaped. Gawn. Disappeared. Poof."

John ran for the door.

"It wasn't my fault, Shurrf. I bwawt him pancakes."

THE SNOW HAD STOPPED, John noted, as he dashed twenty feet between the hospital and the sheriff's department. But what was on the ground was staying. This morning the thermometer had dropped to eighteen degrees, but that wasn't right. John had been in eighteen-degree weather before, and this – whatever it was – this was a hell of a lot colder.

The warm air of the office hit him, but he didn't slow down.

"Phones are back up," Maggie Dane called, one hand over the mouthpiece. "OSP's on the line. They've closed the road on their side of the bridge and want to know if we've done the same."

John grimaced but didn't stop. "Tell them we're too fucking dumb to think of that. In fact, tell them we purposely left it open just to see how many folks it takes to fill up the gorge."

"Sheriff says that's an affirmative, Officer," Maggie said professionally into the phone. "The road is closed."

He almost smiled as he took the stairs. "Tell 'em to send a chopper; we need to get these bodies to the crime lab." He didn't bother looking back to see if Maggie had heard him. She always heard him.

The holding cells were built into the municipal building's basement. There was only one way in and one way out, a fact that had caused multiple clashes with the state fire marshal. Regardless, it meant that even if Elijah had exited his cell, he would still have had to go up these stairs and out that door, then through the middle of the office, to make it outside. John, who had had less than three hours' sleep, knew there had been someone here all night long, because more than half the time that someone had been him.

So how the hell could he escape?

Behind him came the hurried footsteps of Coye

Cheevers. John opened the door and stepped into the holding area. The stranger, Elijah, looked up from his bed and smiled. A bit of pancake suspended from a plastic fork. A Styrofoam plate balanced in his lap.

"Morning, Sheriff."

Coye caught the door before it closed, and hurried in behind his boss. He came to an abrupt stop – his nose, still red from the collision, suddenly forgotten. His eyes were on the man in the cell.

"No way. No way. I swear to God, Sheriff. I swear to God, he wasn't here two minutes ago. Nowhere." The bed was a small, wire-framed cot. He couldn't have hidden under it without being seen. There were no windows to crawl out of.

"Problem, Sheriff?" Elijah asked, smiling.

John didn't answer. He grabbed the cell door and rattled it. Locked.

"Sheriff, I ain't kiddin'. He wasn't here. I swear it. That cell was empty."

"Oh, by the way, thanks for the apple pancakes, Deputy Cheevers," Elijah said.

The start of a smile flickered on the lawman's long, thin face, then died in midbloom. "Hey, I didn't get you apple. I got you blueberry, and I dropped the . . ."

He looked at the floor, his face turning a shade of white John had never seen on a living being before. On the floor lay a spilled tray of pancakes, sausage links, and poached eggs.

"See? See, that's where I dropped it when I saw there was no one in the cell."

"It's true, Sheriff. He did drop the tray," Elijah agreed.

"See," Coye said, then frowned with mistrust. "Hey, how would you know? You weren't even here."

"That's when the deputy kindly went back and got a second order. Thank you again." He popped the wedge of pancake in his mouth and chewed on it with great satisfaction.

"Sheriff, I didn't—"

John held up his hand. "That's enough. Get something and clean up this mess."

"But, Sheriff?"

"Upstairs, now!" His voice left no room for negotiation.

The deputy slunk away, mumbling as he went. "Apple pancakes. Didn't get no apple pancakes. Got blueberry. He wasn't here anyway, so how would he know . . ."

Alone, John turned to face the stranger. The man who called himself Elijah. The man he believed was responsible for one, if not three, murders in the past forty-eight hours. The man most likely behind all the weird shit that was going on. Elijah speared another wedge of pancake and put it in his mouth.

The phones were working. That meant the computers were back up. That meant John could E-mail Elijah's mug to that state police. He had already completed the 189 questions that made up the fifteen-page VICAP Crime Analysis Report. That report could now be fed into the FBI's Violent Criminal Apprehension Program database, which would look for a matching MO. A man didn't just start cutting people up. He would have had to build up to it. And that meant other murders in other states.

Elijah.

Soon John would know his real name and who or what the hell he was dealing with.

Elijah smiled and smacked on his breakfast.

"Yeah, you go ahead and enjoy yourself," John said. "The party is about to be over. The phones are working. The Oregon State Police have a chopper on the way. Maybe I'll let them take you back. See how you like the less accommodating conditions down at the Lane County Jail."

He had said it just to get a reaction. Just to shake the smile off the smug bastard's face. The effect was greater than anticipated.

Elijah jumped to his feet, the plate of pancakes tossed to the side, forgotten. He rushed the bars, grabbing them and pressing his face in the space in between. The cockiness was gone, the snide mirth completely wiped from his blue eyes.

"Listen to me, Sheriff. Listen! You've got to tell them to turn around and head back to Eugene. You can't let that helicopter enter Black Valley."

"I don't have to do anything," John said, his

curiosity piqued by the abrupt change in the man. "Give me a reason."

"I can't." He studied the floor, then looked up. "You just have to, that's all."

John thought for a moment, watching his face. *His face? That was it. That was what had struck him as odd. The face that John had pummeled last night. It was unmarked. No busted lip. No black eye. No bruises.*

How the hell?

"Sheriff, please. I'm begging you. Tell the state police to turn around. It's almost here. Do you understand?"

"When you start giving me serious answers, I'll start giving your request serious consideration. But right now what you're telling me is, you're scared shitless of the OSP, which tells me you've got a record, most likely a long record, and that means your ass is grass."

Elijah let go of the bars. His arms dropped; his shoulders slumped.

Defeated, John thought. *I've got him. Smug bastad.* John turned to leave. When he reached the door, he paused to look back at the man in the cell. Elijah had returned to his bunk. He was sitting on the edge with his head in his hands, fingers gripping tufts of deep brown hair.

That was when John saw it. A dizzy whirl of confusion rose from somewhere in the back of his mind. For a moment something gray and flickering like static encroached on his vision, reducing it. The room seemed to spin. Confusion and exhaustion married, and the offspring was a debilitating sense of disbelief.

Elijah. The man in the cell had fresh mud on his pants.

23

THE COLD WAS DEEPER and more biting than Piper could ever remember. Thick, churning clouds, gun-barrel gray, hung over the community like a living canopy. The Ford Ranger once more shoved its way through the snow and on to the Chantilly-white roadways.

Dean had picked her up and gladly surrendered the driver's seat to her superior skills. Although he refused to tell her why he was smiling a lot. A bit of the old confidence, that spark she had noted when he was passionately teaching physics, flared once more in his deep brown eyes.

"Got an idea," his note had said. Had he figured it out? Could anyone? Was it even possible? If it was possible, then Dean was definitely the man who could do it. Piper found herself oddly reassured by that subtle upturn of his lips.

"Just a hint?" she pushed.

"I'll show you when we get there. John's meeting us at the hospital. I have to check something first."

*

PIPER AND JOHN WAITED in the hospital lounge while Dean conducted an examination of the bodies. An action that was strictly against the rules, but Piper had noted that when it came to Dean, the sheriff never hesitated to break the rules. His confidence in the scientist was unwavering.

As they waited, however, the sheriff seemed antsy, a condition that conflicted with his personality, his demeanor. Piper had never seen the sheriff antsy. Of course, there were a lot of things she had never seen before this week.

Dean returned from the morgue, removed a pair of surgical gloves, and deposited them in the white-and-orange, self-sealing canister marked BIOHAZARD.

"Well?" Piper asked.

"Step in here." Dean lead them into a wet lab, a facility used for the examination of body fluids. They followed him past the chrome refrigerators, past the centrifuge, test-tube racks, and waiting beakers, past the bulletin board cluttered with curled papers. They paused briefly for Dean to remove a photograph of someone in fishing bibs holding a large trout, then continued on to the rear of the laboratory, back to where the microscopes sat.

Dean slid the picture of the man and fish beneath the lens of the microscope, bent over, adjusted the focus, then invited them to look. John responded with silent compliance.

"What's this all about?" Piper wanted to know.

"Why do you want me to look at a magnified photograph of a man and a fish?"

"Just do it," Dean answered.

John stepped aside.

Piper placed her eye to the scope. Under the present magnification the photograph appeared as a series of smudged, multicolored dots. "Okay, I see it. I don't know what it is, but I see it."

"It's a normal photograph – that's what it is."

She raised up and Dean took her place, replacing the fish photograph with something else. "Now look."

Again Piper bent over and peered through the eyepiece. This time the effect was incredible. Instead of a flat plane of blurred, colored dots she saw a catacomb – a three-dimensional world of precise pixels, one before another in a random order in decreasing size.

"My God, it's beautiful."

John took his turn. "What is it?"

Dean's smile was wide now. A definite twinkle sparkled in his deep brown eyes. "Science, that's what it is," he said. "Pull it out."

John removed the second object from the slide tray. It was another photograph, this one of a young girl and boy.

"Tina," John said. "This is the photograph Mason had. The one he claimed to see Whitey Dobbs in."

Dean nodded.

"Whitey? Who's Whitey Dobbs?" Piper asked.

No one volunteered an answer.

"Now watch." Dean took the photograph, holding it between the thumb and forefinger of each hand, then moved so they could see over his shoulders.

Piper studied the photograph of the attractive young woman with brown hair pulled back into a long ponytail, sitting next to a young, clean-cut boy with close-cropped black hair. "What am I looking for?"

"Shhh," Dean admonished. "Just watch. Any second now."

The picture remained unchanged – a girl and a boy, sitting on a bench somewhere. Then . . .

"Jesus," John cried out.

Suddenly the boy was gone, replaced by someone else. Someone equally young but with *bone-white hair*. White hair? Whitey Dobbs?

Abruptly the boy in the picture came to life – *moving*. His slight grin bloomed into a full, teeth-baring smile. And then, to add wonder to wonder, he winked.

Both Piper and John took a step back. "How the hell?"

Piper looked at Dean, then at the sheriff. The former was smiling, but the latter looked as if he had just seen his own grave. "How—"

"Pure and simple science," Dean said brightly. "Well, maybe not simple, but certainly pure."

Dean held up the picture, waving it like a flag as he talked. "It looks like a normal photograph, but it's not. When it's magnified, you see layers upon layers of highly defined pixels. When you expose them to a mild electrical charge, they rearrange themselves, changing the image from David Levin to Whitey Dobbs."

"But it moved," Piper said. "It winked at me."

"Same process, just infinitely more intricate."

"So Mason isn't crazy," John said. "He did see Whitey Dobbs."

"Exactly, and so did I. That day in your office, but with a difference. With Mason it simply switched images from Levin to Dobbs, but with me it moved, like you just saw."

"How? I mean, I know you just explained all those dots on dots and electrical charges—"

"Particle realignment," Dean added.

"Yeah, but how? I've never seen or even heard of anything like that."

Dean sat on the corner of the brown table. He was in full tutorial mode now. "There are a lot of things you've never heard of that nonetheless exist. Television was out years before most people ever heard of it, let alone saw one. In 1958 no one had ever heard of a pop-top can. You had to use a can opener. Inventions we now take for granted were once wild flights of fancy. When they discovered the wreckage of the *Titanic*, you know what they didn't find?"

"Leonardo DiCaprio," Piper said.

"Besides him. Plastic. There was no plastic any-where on what was then considered to be a state-of-the-art mechanical engineering marvel."

"Because it hadn't been invented yet."

Dean's eyes sparkled. "Wrong. It had been, cooked up by a New York chemist named Leo Baekeland in 1907. The *Titanic* sank in 1912. Even though it existed, it hadn't come into common use."

John crossed his burly arms and nodded slowly. "So, you're saying the picture is just a trick. Science we've just never heard of. All right, I could see that for us, but what about you? Surely you've heard of it."

Dean grinned. "No, I've heard of things like it. Polymers that can change colors so a shirt that's red one day could be green the next. But nothing quite this advanced. I mean, we know photographs can be manipulated by computer. They even sell digital cameras that allow kids to add bunny ears and fangs to pictures of their friends."

He thumped the photograph with his ring finger. "This is what I call near-science – technology that is just over the horizon. Or at least I thought was just over the horizon."

A page called for the charge nurse to report to duty station 1. An orderly dropped a chrome bedpan that clanged like a gong. Piper could hear the faint squeak of white rubber soles on the hard tile floors.

"So why didn't the picture change for me?" John wondered. "And why didn't it wink for Mason?"

"That's the truly amazing part. Not only does the picture change, but the type of change is regulated by the person holding it. When you held it, nothing. When

Mason held it, Whitey Dobbs. When I held it, a moving image of Whitey Dobbs."

"Who's Whitey Dobbs?" Piper asked again.

The question hung unanswered.

"Somehow, perhaps it's body chemistry or fingerprint, but somehow the photograph determines who is holding it and responds accordingly. And there's more."

Dean pointed to a small, black box, roughly the shape of a lighter, with a clear, glass eye. "I found this sensor attached to the doorframe of my house. It's extremely advanced. That's what triggered the tape recorder we found upstairs, which then began to play the specifically edited version of 'Rock On.' "

"Science," Piper mumbled. "But why? Or more specifically, why you? Why not somebody else? Does it have something to do with this Whitey Dobbs character you both seem so intent on not telling me about?"

Dean and John swapped a look.

"I'll explain later," Dean promised. But his face said he was lying. Piper felt suddenly uneasy.

"The bodies," John said. "You wanted to see the bodies before the state police came."

Dean jumped up and pointed toward the second microscope in the room. "Yes, yes, the bodies." A slide was already waiting.

"Each time a knife or a blade is used to cut something, it leaves behind microscopic particles. Tiny bits of itself. I removed several particles from the hand and classroom and found a match."

"Your classroom." Piper felt anxiousness ripple through her body.

"The blackboard. John, I never reported it, but the night we found the body of Meredith Gamble someone broke into my classroom and carved a message into the blackboard. Whoever did it used the same knife or blade that severed the appendages. But the metal . . ."

He nodded toward the microscope. They both looked. John first, then Piper. What she saw was a small mass of something silver-blue and quivering. She looked to Dean for an explanation.

"It's a type of metal I've never seen before. But it might explain how a knife could stab through a skull."

"What about the flaming truck? And the glass storm that killed Meredith? How are those possible?" Piper asked.

"I don't know – yet. The truck must have been dropped from a cargo plane, something powerful and big enough to carry such things. As for the glass" – he shrugged – "I honestly don't know yet. But I will. And I do know it's not magic. It's not a phantom. It's simply—"

"Science," Piper finished. "Yeah, yeah, yeah, I've heard that song before. So how did I know something was about to happen? I mean with the truck?"

"You tell me."

Piper pushed her hair back behind her ears. "I don't

know. It was just a feeling." Suddenly she was aware that John was staring at her. She crossed her arms, emulating his own posture. Then she noticed Dean's penetrating glare.

"What? You don't think I'm involved in this, do you?"

"It would certainly make the most sense," the sheriff said, shifting his position. Piper noted he was blocking her only avenue of escape. It was a practical deduction, and John was nothing if not a practical man. Was he going to arrest her?

"Dean?" she pleaded.

The doctor seemed conflicted, as if his mind and his heart were at war.

"Dean?" she repeated.

The sheriff asked the same question with his eyes.

"John's right. It is the most likely scenario," Dean agreed.

Piper felt her heart flutter, literally flutter, as if suddenly sprouting wings and desperately trying to escape the confines of her chest.

"But not the only one," Dean continued. "And it wouldn't explain the sparks."

Sparks? What sparks? What is he talking about? Piper thought.

"Maybe you're sensitive to subtle changes in air pressure. Or maybe your body produces a higher than usual bioelectrical charge. Some people can't wear a watch because of it. It's rare, but it happens."

"I can't wear a watch," Piper said. "It always stops."

"There you go. That could also explain the sparks—"

"Sparks?" she asked.

"In your eyes." Dean frowned. "Oh, you didn't know about that?"

"Sparks in my eyes?" she asked, her voice rising, blooming with concern. "In my eyes?"

Dean made a gap with his thumb and forefinger. "Just little ones. But if you do produce a higher than normal bioelectrical charge, that would explain your sensitivity to such things. Particularly if some form of electromagnetic pulse is being used. That could also explain the trouble with the phones and the radios."

Once again John acquiesced to his old friend's wisdom. He relaxed his stance, but not entirely.

Piper was silent.

John scratched his face. "That takes me back to *why*. Why now? Why us? Why go to so much trouble?"

Dean shook his head.

It was Piper who answered. "Because of Dean."

To her surprise, John nodded in agreement. Dean, however, was confused.

In the small confines at the rear of the lab Piper began to pace. "Yeah, think about it. What have we got that no one else has? A Nobel Prize-winning scientist, that's what."

"I hardly think—"

She admonished him with a raised finger. "The person who killed Mavis left behind a tape recorder with a specially edited version of 'Rock On' and a candle to draw you in and freak you out. If what you say is true, and this is all *near*-science, then who has access to such technology?"

"A major company," said John. "Someone like NxTech."

"No, not NxTech. They've already got the best shot of getting Dean to work for them, but what about a competitor?" Piper reached the wall, turned on her heel, and retraced her steps. "Think about it. NxTech has bought Hawkins Hill and plans to build a multimillion-dollar facility in Black Valley just so they can have you working for them. They must believe your mind, your ideas, are worth billions. You mentioned the chemist who invented plastic. How much was that ultimately worth? Or the person who invented Scotch tape, nylon, Dacron, herbicides, transistors? How about the floppy disk, liquid crystal displays, Post-it notes? The value is unbelievable."

Dean sat back on the corner of the table, his earlier elation gone, guilt and fear flashing like lightning across his face.

"So you're saying it's all about money?" John asked. "All of this – this insanity – in the name of capitalism? Just to keep a competitor from getting the upper hand?"

Piper shrugged. "It wouldn't be the first time

unfathomable acts were committed in the name of greed."

"So why not kill him?" John said in his no-nonsense, practical voice that made even the extra-ordinary seem downright reasonable. "If what you say is true, we know they, whoever *they* are, are not deterred by the prospect of murder, so why not just kill Dean and be done with it? Problem solved."

Piper chewed on this suggestion. "Maybe it's more than that. Maybe they need him. Figure they can steal him from NxTech."

John squinted. "Or maybe they have a problem they want him to solve."

Dean frowned. "What do you mean?"

The sheriff sawed his lips back and forth, thinking. "It's like this. See, I know you. Sometimes if I need your help on something, or just want a different take, I sort of, well, bait you."

"Bait me?"

"Rather than just going to you with a problem, I dangle something in front of you, entice you a little – and away you go."

"Like with the hand."

"I ain't proud of it, but, yeah, like with the hand."

Dean stood up again. His face was red and puffy. "Mavis, Clyde, Meredith, all dead because of me. Toying with me. Even dredging up a trauma from the past, Whitey Dobbs. And how do they even know about that?"

John chewed on his lower lip and then said, "Mary Jean Wentfrow."

"Who?" Dean asked.

"Formerly Mary Jean Dobbs – Whitey Dobbs's older sister. I looked her up about fifteen years ago, wanted to see if Whitey had made contact with her. Just curious. She lives in California, been married and divorced three times. Looks like the poster child for white trash. For the right money, hell, for any money, I could see her getting involved."

Dean was wringing his hands. "So, they don't want to kill me, just drive me crazy."

Dean ran his hands through his hair. Tufts of brown stood on end. "They want to drive me crazy."

John shook his head. "That makes no sense. If you're crazy, you can't help them. And if you can't help them, then it's easier just to kill you."

"Maybe they just want to test you? See how far they can push before you crack?"

"No," John said. "It's nuts. Who would want to push a man toward insanity? And who has the technology to do what's being done?"

"I think I know." Deputy Jerry Niles had entered without them noticing. He still wore his heavy coat and gloves. Snow clung to his boots in bright white clumps. "I just came from Dub Pelt's place. He claims to have shot down a spaceship, and I think he may be right."

24

THE GIANT, orange-and-white Coast Guard Sikorsky lifted off from the helipad and soared regally into the sky. The air was as smooth as a pane of glass, and visibility was outstanding. In addition to the pilot there were two investigators from the Oregon State Police on board. The Sikorsky was on loan from the Coast Guard. It may have been a bit of overkill, but after talking with the dispatcher in Black Valley, Martin Ludlow, the chief investigator, wasn't taking chances. Four bodies in three days – unprecedented in a town the size of Black Valley.

Something was happening, something strange and dangerous. The Sikorsky, named for the man who invented helicopters, was a hale and hardy machine. And despite the baby-blue skies and weather service assurances, Ludlow felt safer having made a sturdier choice.

Twenty-one minutes into the flight he was proved right.

"Lieutenant, you may want to look at this," the pilot said.

Ludlow had been working on his laptop, trying to stay ahead of the paperwork curve. When he looked up, he was shocked by what he saw. A cloud – no, a cluster of clouds. But even that wasn't right. The word *cloud* was too feeble for the thing that hung in the sky above the tiny town.

It looked like a creature, a living, breathing, undulating beast coughed up from the bowels of hell and lurking over the unsuspecting community like an animal looming over its prey.

"What the devil is that?" he asked the pilot.

"Nothing on the official radar. It just sort of popped up."

"That? How could something that big just pop up?"

The pilot shrugged. A bead of sweat escaped his pores and slithered down his face. "If I didn't know better, I'd say we're looking at one hell of a thunderstorm. But it's too cold for that."

"They had an impromptu blizzard last night. That wasn't on the radar either. Just sort of happened."

The rampart of roiling black-gray continued to writhe, growing ever larger as the helicopter drew near.

"Can we fly through it?" Ludlow asked.

"Don't see any rain or snow yet. Probably looks worse than it is."

Ludlow nodded, hoping the pilot was right. His stomach began to twist along with the thick black clouds.

*

THEY PULLED INTO the macadam driveway. Two cars – John, Dean, and Piper in the first; Jerry Niles and Coye Cheevers in the second. A column of thick, ghost-white smoke rose from somewhere behind the ranch-style farmhouse.

John removed a shotgun from the rack and carefully loaded it. "You two stay here," he ordered, getting out of the car.

Dean watched through the now dusty windshield as John approached the house, cautiously flanked by the pair of deputies.

Only a few slivers of sun had slipped through the brewing clouds. Despite the time of day, the world had the look of perpetual twilight.

"Oh, my sweet Lord," Coye muttered, standing by the corner of the house. It was just a whisper, but in the still, purple haze of premature twilight everyone heard.

Dean leaned forward for a better look through the window of the squad car. Then he shot a glance at Piper, who was in the backseat. Her body was trembling, but not with fear.

She's feeling it again, Dean thought. *But feeling what?*

"Dean," called the sheriff, "come over here."

Dean got out and opened the back door for Piper. "Are you all right?"

She remained silent, her eyes, although not sparking, had the look of someone watching a dream or maybe a nightmare.

The chicken coop was completely destroyed. Columns of white smoke wafted into the air. And in the center was the object that had destroyed the coop – the massive ruins of a fire-scorched machine. The actual size was difficult to determine. It appeared slightly larger than a minivan, but the force of impact implied part of it was buried in the earth. Originally gray, it was now covered in scorch marks.

"God almighty, it *is* a spaceship," Cheevers whispered.

"I don't believe in spaceships," Piper said. "Or little green men, or any of that science-fiction stuff."

Dean turned.

She had shaken off her earlier gloom and appeared to be herself again. But her statement surprised Dean almost as much as the object that was smashed into the coop. "Wait a minute," he said. "You believe in ghosts, spirits, things that go bump in the night – but you don't believe in aliens?"

"At least my ghosts are from this planet."

"I don't know what to believe," said John, tipping his hat back with the flat of his thumb.

"Whatever it is, it's hollow," Jerry said.

"You touched it?" John asked.

"No, of course not. Damn thing's too hot. Besides, I was worried about radiation." He bent down and picked up a golf-ball-size rock and heaved it at the device. It struck with a definite *clulang*. "Hollow, see?"

Coye covered his face with his arms and grimaced.

"Don't be doing that. What if there's something inside? You don't want to be giving no aliens a headache or nothing."

"How do you know it even has a head?" Jerry challenged.

Dean titled his head to the side. There was something about the shape.

"Whatcha think, Doc?" Jerry asked. "I know it seems crazy, but Jesus, look at it. Dub says he shot it out of the sky. Those burn marks – I figure they are from entering Earth's atmosphere."

Dean walked toward the ruined machine, his head still tilted to the right.

"Hey, Doc, whatcha doing?" Jerry asked.

"Be careful, Doc," Coye advised.

"Dean?" Piper asked.

John was quiet, his trust in the scientist unflappable.

Dean stooped, picked up a rock about the size of a softball, and heaved it at the machine. It struck with a louder but definitely hollow *thung*.

"Doc, you ought not be doing that now," Coye moaned. "No, sir. Ought not do it."

Dean started walking again.

"Maybe you should stay back," Piper urged.

"Thought you didn't believe in aliens," he said over his shoulder.

"I don't believe in a lot of things, but that's no reason to be foolish."

290

Dean was within four feet of the object now. He could feel the heat rising from it, smell the burned wood and scorched metal. The wind shifted, wafting smoke in the opposite direction. For a just a moment he could see . . .

"Dean? Dean, you really shouldn't go any farther." Piper's words were lost to a new sound. A humming in his head. The resonating sound of an idea being born. He pulled out a white handkerchief and covered his mouth and nose, then stepped around the wreckage into the smoke. The stench was powerful, the atmosphere acidic. But he was on to something. His mind was calculating, figuring, reasoning.

He stopped.

Something in the wreckage was moving.

PIPER FELT HER HEART climb up her throat. Dean was gone. Swallowed by the white smoke like Jonah by the whale. "Dean, Dean?"

Her appeals went unanswered. The day was quiet. Dead calm. Piper realized she had not seen or heard so much as a bird since they arrived. The only sound was the faint *tick, tick, tick* of cooling metal. What was it Jerry had said about radiation? What if it was radioactive?

She didn't know. But she did know that looking at it, being near it, caused her senses to buzz, the fine white hairs on her arms and neck to rise.

Something touched the back of her hand. She jerked

as if bitten, swatting at it. Ash. A quarter-size flake of gray-white ash. That's all. What was she expecting? E.T.? Hadn't she told Dean she didn't believe in spaceships?

Well, he doesn't believe in ghosts, but that doesn't mean they're not real.

She was about to dismiss the concept as ridiculous when something in the smoke – the wreckage – *moved*.

And it wasn't Dean.

"John?"

"I see it." John brought the shotgun up, the butt pressing against his shoulder. "Boys."

She could hear the crisp snap of holster straps being undone, the scuff of metal on leather as weapons were pulled free. Jerry held his gun in a firm, two-handed grip. Coye held his in the same grip but with less security. The barrel wavered. Maybe the thing in the smoke wasn't the only threat?

"Dean?" she called again, her voice rife with a new urgency. "Dean, get out of there."

Bang, bang, ka-chow.

Her first thought was of a gunshot; someone was shooting at them. Then she realized the sound was too metallic. It was the noise of metal pulling free. The wind shifted; the entire front of the machine was revealed.

Ka-chow, ka-chow.

For the first time Piper noticed a small, rectangular door turned on its side like a downward-angled coffin.

Ka-chow.

The sound was coming from that door. Something – *something* was coming out.

The door popped open with a jerk. A chicken flew out. Then, through the haze, she saw him – Dean was crawling through the opening.

Dean?

He was coughing, his handkerchief covering his mouth. Soot and ash dusted his hair and face. His eyes were red and stinging. He waved away the smoke, then bent at the waist, hands on his knees, and coughed for several seconds.

When he was able to speak, he straightened up. "The whole left side is open. This is just part of it."

More things moved in the smoke. Chickens, she now realized.

"Part of what?" the sheriff asked.

Dean gestured with his handkerchief. "Look at it."

"Is it a spaceship?" Coye asked. "Lord God, it is, ain't it?"

"Look at it upside down," Dean suggested, then succumbed to another coughing jag.

Piper and the two deputies cocked their heads to the right, as Dean had done earlier.

"Yep, it's a spaceship, all right. An honest-to-goodness flying saucer, 'cept it ain't flying no more."

"Keep looking."

"Well, I'll be damned," Jerry whispered. "Sheriff, do you realize what this is?"

"What?" Piper demanded. "I don't get it. Is it a spaceship?"

"Not unless it was made in Kansas," Dean said.

John, who had remained stoic, nodded. "It's a silo, or at least half of one. A common grain silo."

Dean nodded. "See the smoke? Notice the color? White. That means something humid is burning, hay or feed. That's why I knew it was safe."

"A silo? But where did it come from?" Piper asked.

"The same place as the truck."

"You still think someone is flying around Black Valley setting things on fire and dropping them out of a cargo plane?" John asked.

"Possibly. They could have flown above the storm."

"But that's crazy," Coye said.

"Oh, and a spaceship isn't?" Jerry countered.

"Go on, Doc. Finish your thought."

Piper could tell that Dean wasn't sure that he could. Like someone playing chess in his head, Dean was deep in concentration but had come across a particularly difficult problem. "You said *possibly*. You don't sound convinced."

"I couldn't examine the truck wreckage, but if it's like this – I don't know." Dean chewed on his lower lip. "Even if a plane could have flown high enough not to be caught in the storm, the thing is, both the truck and the silo were burning."

"And?" Piper prompted.

"There's no pour pattern. Nothing to indicate an accelerant was used. This is something else. This wasn't a normal fire."

John's radio squawked. He answered, then nodded to the group. "Let's get back to the station. The chopper's coming in."

25

DEAN SPENT THE NEXT FIVE MINUTES making measurements and taking notes. Afterward he asked to be dropped off at the school. Piper rode back to the station with John; her truck was in the hospital parking lot. John studied the short brunette out of the corner of his eye. She was one to watch, a coiled spring that could go off at any minute.

John had decided there was only one way she could have known about the burning truck; she was involved somehow. And for all his logic, Dean couldn't figure it out, couldn't see past his penis. John had seen how the two looked at each other, like a couple of hungry dogs at a thick slice of T-bone.

John grimaced.

"You okay?" Piper asked.

He felt color rising in his face, as if he had just been caught playing with himself. "Headache."

When they arrived at the sheriff's department, the Sikorsky helicopter was the size of a quarter on the horizon. Jerry and Coye went to alert the hospital staff and to help prep the bodies for transport. John waited beside his squad car, hat in hand so as not to have it knocked off his head by the helicopter's tornadic wash.

Piper went inside the station to use the facilities, leaving John temporarily alone in the parking lot with his thoughts and the incoming helicopter. The hospital parking lot was the only place large enough to accommodate the big machine. Luckily the lot wasn't very full.

Course not. Most of those inside are dead.

No. That wasn't true. Nathan was in there, somewhere. Half out of his mind with worry. He had still managed to issue a proclamation apprising the citizenry of Black Valley that "due to an unfortunate accident to the south and inclement weather to the north, the town is temporarily cut off from the rest of the world." The notice went on to assure residents that there was nothing to be concerned about, this was only a temporary situation, the pass would be open soon. Meanwhile, the U.S. Army Corps of Engineers were feverishly working on a temporary substitute for the destroyed Willamette Bridge.

The last part was an out-and-out lie but a nice touch. A reassuring touch.

The Sikorsky was now the size of a child's wagon. Its gyrating blades and hearty engine reverberated in the cold, still air. With a backdrop of churning ink-black clouds, the brightly colored machine looked like a special effect, a dab of color inserted in an otherwise black-and-white TV commercial.

Listen to me, Sheriff! Listen! You've got to tell them to turn around.

The stranger's words thundered in John's head. It was the only time the man had seemed rational. John shifted his weight from foot to foot, then sat back on the still-warm hood of the police cruiser.

Tell the state police to turn around. It's almost here.

What? John wondered as the massive machine filled a quarter of the sky. *What is almost here?*

PIPER DOUBLED OVER. Her hands and feet tingled – no, burned – with the sting of 1,001 red-hot straight pins. A woman was beside her. John's assistant, Maggie Dane.

"You okay, dear?" she asked.

It had hit Piper without warning. She had been returning from the ladies' room when it happened. That feeling. *A billion dead souls dancing on my grave.*

Piper forced herself to straighten; her lips were unbelievably dry. Yet her eyes were blurred with tears. She looked around the room with her water-hazed vision.

"Dear?"

"She okay?" another person asked.

Piper blinked away the blur. Her eyes locked on the row of tall windows that covered most of the north side of the building. "It's coming."

"What, dear? Are you about to throw up?"

"It's coming. It's coming," she began to shout with

increasing volume. "It's coming. It's coming. Everybody get down. Now. Everybody on the floor."

Piper dropped to the carpet. Several others began to squat. "Down!" she screamed.

"What's she talking about?" a man asked.

Piper grabbed Maggie Dane by the arm and pulled the woman to the floor. "Down. Now—"

The man opened his mouth to ask a question.

The windows exploded.

A thousand daggers of broken glass struck his body, which jerked like a marionette with a knotted string. His mouth was still open. Blood bubbled from his lips.

Chairs toppled. Lamps went flying. Computer monitors exploded, then flipped on their sides. The building shook as a hot, searing wind charged into the room.

IT HAPPENED WITHOUT A PREAMBLE. No wavering, no fluctuation. It just happened. Somewhere in the back of his mind John was aware of glass shattering, screams, the tortured sound of rampant destruction, but his mind couldn't get past the helicopter. One moment it was hovering in the air, an impressive machine, a bright-orange-and-white testament to the technology of man – and the next?

The hulking machine slammed into the earth with impossible speed. The ground exploded with dirt and metal and fire. John wobbled on his feet, the building protecting him from whatever force had smashed the Sikorsky and was shattering the north face. Asphalt and machine parts surged into the sky, then tumbled back to earth.

Embers struck John's shoulders and head. He brushed away burning bits without acknowledgement. His eyes still locked on the crumpled corpse of the once magnificent machine.

The screams came as an afterthought, like thunder trying to catch lightning.

John ran toward the building. He knew without checking that no one could have survived the violent crash.

Entering the sheriff's department was like entering the ruins of a battlefield. Nothing higher than a desktop remained standing. Glass crunched beneath. Long green-brown pine needles covered much of the surface area.

Pine needles? Where did they come from?

Piper was bleeding from a cut to her forehead. Maggie appeared unscathed. Jerry stood over the bloody body of a copy-machine repairman screaming for a doctor. Coye stood beside him, fingers in his mouth, crying.

Before John could bark an order, a doctor and two orderlies entered the room and rushed to the man's side. *He's dead*, John started to say, then realized he couldn't know that for sure. Yet he did. Why?

Because you've seen it before.

300

The image of Meredith Gamble rose from his subconscious.

"Check the rest of the building," John barked. Jerry gladly relinquished his charge to the medical professionals. "Cheevers, get your hands out of your mouth and find out what happened. How many buildings are damaged? How many people hurt?"

The deputy nodded and ran out the back door, his footsteps crunching.

"Maggie, you okay?"

"Yeah, thanks to her," she said, nodding to Piper. "I'll call in the National Guard and contact OSP. What about you?"

It's almost here. It's almost here.

"I'm going downstairs to find out what hit us and how that bastard Elijah knew it was going to happen."

SHOCK FADED, replaced by anger and unflinching fury. John had been mad before but never like this. He tried to settle his temper. Sometimes, *sometimes*, when it got going . . . it was like a wildfire, a massive, out-of-control burn that charred and chewed anything and anyone that got in his way. Sometimes, when his blood was hot and he could physically feel it pounding in his veins, he would get "the urge."

Judy had seen it. It had been impossible to keep it from his younger sister. But she had never felt it, never been a victim of its fury, thank God. His little hissy fits, as she called them, frightened her – a silly name for a serious problem. But he had been able to hide one thing from her.

The intensity.

She never knew how oppressive and controlling the urge could be. *Sometimes . . . he just wanted to pound something – or better still, somebody – to jelly*. It was that uncontrollable side, that wild spot, that made John Evans embrace the philosophy of practicality with such zest. Only a practical man could hold the fire at bay.

But as he opened the door and entered the narrow hall between the holding cells, John Evans was not a practical man. His hands were clenched into fists, teeth grinding, face flushed from the fury of the internal burn.

It's almost here.

The stranger, Elijah, had known, somehow he had known, and now he was going to tell John how or he was going to die. John grabbed the bars and shoved the keys to the holding cell into the lock.

But his anger was swatted down as quickly as the Sikorsky from the sky. The holding cell was empty.

Elijah was gone.

26

SOMETHING ABOUT THE BURN MARKS. Dean sprinted down the white-and-brown-tiled hall, fumbled with his keys, then hurriedly let himself into his classroom laboratory. A Compaq Presario with a seventeen-inch monitor sat on his desk, courtesy of NxTech, part of their courtship of him. *Thank you, NxTech.*

He played the keyboard like a concert pianist. Within minutes he had found the program he wanted and began to enter data.

His clothes reeked of smoke, but there was no time to shower or even change. He had to follow this line of thought while it was fresh. Judy had once described Dean as a scientific bird dog chasing down the scent of an idea. But if something happened to break that process, to interrupt the hunt, he would lose his way and often his quarry – until he crossed the scent again.

His notes safely transcribed from paper to machine, he sat back in a plush, new Herman Miller swivel chair – *thank you, NxTech* – and let the idea settle.

The burns, the burns. If only he could get a look at that truck.

Dean steepled his fingers, began humming some tune from a rock opera, and slowly tapped his lips. There was no pour pattern, he knew that much. When a fire was started by an accelerant there were always certain areas that burned hotter than others. In arson fires, for example, the splash patterns of, say, gasoline can be traced by how deeply wood is charred. But there was nothing like that on the silo.

Dean pulled his worn wire notebook from his breast pocket and thumbed rapidly through it until he reached the crude drawing he had made of the wreckage. Cone shape, just the top quarter of the silo cut off diagonally at about a thirty-five-degree angle. He had shaded in the scorching with a pencil. A dozen or so elongated, almost perfectly straight, burn marks radiated out from bottom to top.

Burn marks.

"On the outside," Dean said, surprising himself. "It wasn't an internal fire, at least not solely. The metal was scorched from an external source."

He returned to the keyboard, playing the measurements in different variations. The pattern was simple – straight but of varying lengths. What did that mean?

"Burn marks, burn marks." He stood and began to pace. It was a trait he shared with Piper. Thinking of the smart young woman almost broke his concentration, but he forced his thoughts back in line. He held his hands behind his back and studied the floor as he walked. There was a visible trail between Dean's desk and the lab tables where the scientist repeatedly traipsed back and forth, back and forth, lost in a maze of facts, figures, and abstract conception.

Something about the burns. "I've seen those patterns before. Somewhere . . ."

He stopped, mentally thumbing through the thick files of his memory. *Patterns.* That was the key. He resumed pacing.

"Patterns," he said aloud. "It's not burn marks – at least, not *just* burn marks."

He laced his hands, leaving the index fingers extended, and tapped his lips, marking time like a metronome. A spark of static electricity shot from his fingertip to his lip, pricking him like a pin. He jerked in surprise, shook it off, locked his hands once again behind his back, and paced.

"It's a blast pattern," he said suddenly, his voice nearly shouting. Dean felt his blood surging through his veins. The world around him seemed to fade as his mind seized upon the idea. "Not from a fire but from an explosion. That's why the metal is scored on the outside. The silo was blown into that yard."

The brick. That's where he had seen similar scorch marks before, on the brick that had shot through his classroom.

Something else. Something that had plagued him since first seeing Meredith Gamble's shredded body.

305

Velocity. The shards of glass that killed Meredith had been traveling at tremendous speed. Speed that, until now, he couldn't identify. Now.

"The velocity of the glass is consistent with the force of an explosion." It raised more questions than it answered, but at least it was a start. He smiled, allowing himself a rare moment of pride.

He stopped pacing and held his hands out to the empty room, as if addressing a grand council. "Science. As I've always said, everything can be explained by science."

Click.

The doorknob to the utility closet at the back of the room turned. The hinges squealed as the door was slowly opened.

Dean's heart forgot how to beat; his lungs, how to breathe. At the back of the classroom a man leaned out of the darkness of the utility closet and into the doorway. A man with white hair and a dark complexion. A man untouched by time.

"Then, how do you explain me?" asked Whitey Dobbs.

27

"OVER HERE – those with surface wounds should be on this side of the room." Piper gestured as if trying to land a 747 – a task, she guessed, that would have been much easier than her current one. The hospital was packed. She had been recruited to help prioritize.

"My shoulder, something cut my shoulder," whined a large man in an expensive Italian suit. Piper recognized his face but couldn't attach a name. She guessed he was a businessman, perhaps a lawyer.

She checked the cut. "It's just a surface wound. It's not even bleeding."

"But it hurts," he sniveled. Piper wondered if he was more upset about the cut or the fact that his suit was ruined.

"You'll be taken care of."

"I shouldn't have to wait. I'm hurt."

He was at least a foot taller than Piper and he used his height as a weapon, stepping close and looming over her, head down, eyes tight. The young history professor held her ground. "Its called triage, sir. The nurses are assessing the wounded and treating them in order of need. You're in no real danger."

Deep canals creased his face. His lips tightened. "Now, see here, I will not be treated like a—"

"What? Treated like what? A regular person?" Piper grabbed him by his uninjured arm. Blood from a gash to her forehead had dried and stained her face. Her short, dark hair was alternately spiked and matted. "Tell you what, see that woman over there? Her husband has a two-foot splinter of wood sticking through his abdomen. You go over there and tell her your boo-boo's worse than his, and maybe he'll get up and give you his place on the gurney."

His face slackened. "I didn't mean . . . I wasn't thinking."

"No, you weren't, so please shut up and wait your turn, okay?"

Piper brushed a lock of hair from her face, then winced at the stab of pain. The three-inch gash in her head had scabbed over but still needed stitches. She worked on instinct, helping the belabored medical staff sort and treat the injured, comforting those in shock and soothing those in tears.

Several inquired as to her own condition, but she ignored them, preoccupied in the immediacy of the task at hand. Or perhaps hiding in it. If she stayed busy, she wouldn't have to contemplate what had happened and how she had known it was going to happen. More importantly, she wouldn't have to worry about the nagging feeling like electrified fingernails being raked across her skin – a different feeling, one that no longer meant that something was coming, but rather that something was *here*.

Lord God, in her heart she knew something bad was already here.

RED-AND-WHITE STROBE LIGHTS whipped across the ruined building. All three of the city's fire trucks were in full use – one in the rear of the building, where the charred husk of the once mighty helicopter smoldered; the other two in front, where most of the structural damage had occurred.

John stood on the opposite side of High Street and stared at his department in disbelief. Every window on this side of the complex had been blown out. Even the double-glassed entryway was shattered. A lamppost leaned like a broken finger. A Geo Metro that had been parked by the curb was now flipped on its side and slammed against the brick facade. Gas and oil poured liberally from a dozen ruptures. Firefighters doused the car in a thick, frothy goo to prevent it from erupting. The driver, a nineteen-year-old college student, had been inside the building paying a parking ticket. She and dozens like her owed their lives to Piper's warning. One of those was John's personal assistant and good friend, Maggie Dane.

"She saved us, John. She knew and she saved us," Maggie had said.

But how?

John studied the building. It wasn't the destruction that held him in a state of incredulity, but rather the lack of destruction. Despite the severity, all of the damage had been limited to an area approximately three hundred feet wide and five hundred feet long. Anything beyond those dimensions on either side, farther back or in front, remained untouched.

What the hell happened?

A blast of some kind, but where had it started? There was no sign of an explosion, only the after effects. John pressed his left hand into the palm of his right and methodically began cracking his knuckles.

It had come from the north, manifesting itself at approximately John's location from the opposite side of High Street, dissipating a few hundred feet beyond the building. The old brick structure had provided a rampart, protecting John from the brunt of the blast. The airborne Sikorsky had not been so lucky.

Three men dead.

Another killed in the shredding storm of glass. All told, at least thirty-five people had been injured. Seven were in critical condition.

The small hospital was filled beyond capacity. Inside, medical staff and volunteers worked to sort the wounded. He was not surprised to see Maggie take part, but he was surprised by Piper. It was her warning that had saved so many lives. And now she was working desperately to save more.

Still, how had she known? What else did she know? And whose side was she really on? John didn't have the answer, but he knew who did. Whether he liked it or not, it was time for Dean to put his feelings aside and start answering the hard question.

John looked up. It started to snow again.

THE IMPOSSIBLE MAN STEPPED from the cloaking shadows of the utility closet and into the blue mist of the lights. He opened his arms, cocked his head, and offered Dean a smile. Curled lips pulled back, revealing a hammock of teeth bedded in healthy pink gums. His dark skin, a staggering contradiction to his ice-white hair, was smooth, line free, and ageless.

Unembraced by time, no hug, no touch, not even a kiss.

"Miss me?" asked the impossible man. "Been a while."

Dean's head throbbed from waves of increasing pressure. His breathing was labored, as if someone or something had sucked all the air from the room and replaced it with a thick, invisible stew. A heaviness fell over his body.

"Don't you have something to say to me? How are you? Where have you been? Sorry we killed you? You know, something along those lines."

Dean's forehead was hot, his extremities cold. Strange barbed tendrils wrapped around his skin and squeezed. His terror-bound voice refused to rise above a gasp, a whisper. "Who are you?"

Confusion, like the light of a fluttering candle, flickered across the man's face, then was gone. The smile widened. "You know me." He rapped his chest with a clenched fist. "We're buds, amigos. Hell, we've shared the same women."

He stepped closer, leaned forward. He was still several feet away, but Dean could have sworn he could feel his breath, a hot-cold mixture of death and pain and *onions*.

Onions?

"I got to tell you, the tits on that last one" – he shook his hand as if touching something hot – "yow-sir, Triple-D indeed. Know what I mean? Course you do. Hell, not even you would be fool enough to pass up a tour of those Grand Tetons. What was her name? Mary, Martha – no, Mavis. That's it, Mavis."

A finger of anger took root and began to climb Dean's spine, bringing with it the fortitude necessary to withstand the crashing tide of fear and disbelief.

"I'll ask you again: who the hell are you?"

The white-haired man stopped at the first lab table. He picked up a Bunsen burner and pointed it at Dean. "*Ka-pow.*" He put it back, opened a drawer, and rifled through the contents. Dean could hear the clack of pencils and pens, paper clips and notebooks. "No smokes? What's the use of having all these fancy-ass lighters if you don't have a fucking cigarette?"

He looked at Dean and arched an eyebrow. "You don't happened to have a cig, do you? Ha – what am I thinking? Of course you don't. Unless they're offering a merit badge in smoking."

He slammed the drawer shut. The report seemed impossibly loud in the room. He took a step closer.

The anger that had forestalled a paralyzing fear was faltering. Dean took a step back, his legs touching his desk. He wanted to turn and look, wanted to search for a weapon, wanted to do – *something*. But he couldn't. He couldn't take his eyes off the man with the white hair.

He dry-swallowed, took a half breath, and said, "Whitey Dobbs is dead."

"Now you're getting it." The man looked around the room, his eyes wide, excited. "Course I'm dead. Just like turbotits – what's-her-name, Mavis? Just like Larry Pepperdine and Clyde Watkins are dead."

Another step closer. Only two lab tables separated them. Again Dean imagined he could feel the other man's cold-hot breath.

"Just like Judy is dead."

A bolt of jag lightning stabbed Dean's chest.

"You remember Judy, don'tcha? John's little sister. Cute button nose, pouty lips, big blue eyes. Sweet piece of ass. Yes sir, mighty fine piece of ass. Now, that was a woman. Good fighter, better lay. Once you worked the mad out of her."

He made a pumping gesture with his hands and hips. "Know what I mean?"

Fury ignited. Dean stood straight. This time it was

he who took a step toward the other man. "Go to hell, you bastard."

"Been there, done that." He shrugged. "Hello, aren't you paying attention? How else do you explain the fact that I'm here now, as baby faced and beautiful as ever, while you're – well, Jesus, Jimmy Dean, you've gotten old. I mean, you were no stud to begin with, but would it kill you to do a sit-up once in a while?"

Dean forced himself to focus, to examine the face of the familiar stranger. "Plastic surgery – either to make you look younger, or to make a younger man look like Dobbs."

The white-haired man cawed. It was the same mocking, crowing-sounding laugh that had been unique to Whitey Dobbs.

"Surgery?" Another step closer. One table between them. "You ever heard of surgery this good? Huh?"

He turned his head to the right and then the left. "No lines, no scars, no surgery. Again, it's that dead thing. Turns out dying is very good for the skin. At least for me it was."

The static sound of fear rose in Dean's ears. Could it be? No. "Science has come a long way in the last few years."

Whitey Dobbs gritted his teeth. His hand moved so fast that sound came before recognition of movement. Bunsen burner, microscope, test-tube rack, all hurled off the desk. "Science? I can't believe you're singing that same old song. Haven't you learned anything?

314

Science is to the universe what snow is to Alaska, just a covering. There are some things stronger than science, some things unexplainable with science."

He had cut the distance to within five feet. His deep brown eyes burned from some internal fire. "And I'm one of them."

"I don't—"

"You don't know shit." His face was flushed, his eyebrows furrowed, his nostrils flared. For the first time Dean realized he was looking into the very real face of Whitey Dobbs.

Whitey Dobbs?

The moment hung. Dobbs took a deep breath and held it until his anger subsided. "Been a long time in coming, but payday is finally here, baby, and I've come to collect."

Click.

Flip.

Dean heard a sound he hadn't heard in twenty-two years but had never truly forgotten. He looked down to see the cherry-wood handle and shimmering steel blade of Whitey Dobbs's infamous switchblade.

The blade? It looked sharper, almost pulsing. Unlike any metal he had ever seen before.

Dobbs smiled again. Dean realized if a shark could show emotion, this was what it would look like. Dobbs held the blade up, turning it this way, then that. Tiny suns of light flared off the knife.

"You never did get it, did you?" Dobbs said. He was

315

speaking quietly now, almost like an aside. "Never figured it out. Never realized what she really needed."

"I loved Judy."

"Loved? Hell, you weren't even there when she died. What kind of husband are you? Going to school while your wife lies in intensive care, dying from a massive coronary."

Dean blinked, too surprised to feel the sting in his eyes. "No one saw a heart attack as even a possibility. I rushed to the hospital soon as I heard."

Dobbs made a looping gesture over his head like a cowboy with a lasso. "Big fucking deal. You rushed to the hospital, but you were too late, weren't you?"

Hot tears crawled down Dean's face. The hum of the lights sounded like a distant wail of mourners.

"You may not have been there, but I was." Dobbs lay his cupped left hand on the lab table, now just inches from Dean. "She may have died, but she didn't die alone."

"What? What do you mean?"

"Course, I ain't saying it was my fault altogether, but the shock of seeing me again did cause the needles to jump on that heart monitor of hers."

Anger, fear, disbelief – all collided in a cataclysmic rush of emotion. Dean felt the strength evaporate from his knees.

"Well, mustn't wear out my welcome just yet. Besides, I have a dinner date."

A flash of pure white lightning illuminated the

classroom, obliterating the shadows and fuzzy blue hue of the fluorescents. Moments later thunder roared. *Lightning?*

Dean looked at the window. Snow was falling again. *Lightning in a snowstorm?*

When he turned back, Whitey Dobbs was gone.

Dean waited, held in the pregnant pause. Some part of his mind was telling him all that had just transpired was a hallucination, a waking dream. Anything was better than accepting the other option. But when he looked down at the lab table, the one on which Dobbs had placed his cupped hand, he knew it was no dream, no hallucination.

Lying on the black, hard top of the lab table was Judy's missing locket.

28

THE ENTIRE BLACK VALLEY Sheriff's Department was there: two full-time deputies, Maggie Dane, three dispatchers, two part-time workers, and the sheriff himself. Yet the meeting room seemed empty. Always in the past this contingency of brown-shirted, badge-wearing, gun-carrying men and women had been more than enough to handle whatever situation arose. Today, however, they seemed frightfully small, while the problems before them seemed impossibly large – and growing.

Two nonmembers of the sheriff's department were in attendance: Mayor Nathan Perkins and history professor Piper Blackmoore, the latter at the insistence of Maggie. After what Piper had done earlier, no one questioned her presence. Some even took comfort in it.

Although dressed in his traditional coat and tie, Nathan still wore the frosty-eyed look of a man in shock.

They were meeting in the city conference room, a large, wide room with chairs, tables, and even a piano, available to the public and used for everything from city council work sessions to children's recitals. All the functioning, pertinent equipment – radios, computers, copier – had been moved there as well.

Still, the room seemed frighteningly empty.

Unlike at other meetings there was no joking, no gossip, no cookies or doughnuts. The room was as somber as a funeral parlor, and John's gaunt, sleepless face had the pallor of a corpse.

"Merciful God, Sheriff, what's going on?" Coye begged as much as asked, making no effort to hide the raw fear in his voice. "We're cut off. With the pass snowed under and the bridge out, we're completely cut off from everybody. Can't even fly in. Not in this weather. That helicopter, that was one of them big 'uns. If that can't make it, nothing can. And what about the stranger, Elijah? See, I told you he got out, Sheriff. I told you."

"That's enough, Cheevers." John's deep baritone had the tone of command but lacked its usual projection.

The deputy continued. "Now he's free, out there somewhere, waiting – and we're trapped here with a psycho serial killer."

"I said that's enough," the sheriff bellowed. The room became quiet. John knew he had stopped the conversation but not the thoughts. He could see it in their faces as each member of his team came to terms with the horrific reality of their situation.

"You've got it wrong, Cheevers," John said at last.

"You're wrong. We're not trapped here with a psycho. The psycho is trapped here with us. And we are going to catch the son of a bitch."

"What about the weather?" Nathan asked. "It's like Mother Nature has gone crazy. Anybody ever hear of wind like that?"

A moment rolled by like a silent caisson.

"I have." All eyes turned to Piper. She had washed the blood from her face and hair. The thin black line of stitches crisscrossed a cut on her forehead. "It happened in 1845 and again in 1932, as well as something similar in 1968. There was also the microburst in 1974."

"Micro-what?" Coye asked.

"*Burst* – superconcentrated downdrafts of air."

"Think that's what hit the station?" John asked.

"Possibly."

"Didn't seem very *micro* to me," Jerry said. A tinkle of nervous laughter rose from the group. John smiled. Grateful for the break in tension, aware the deputy had done so on purpose.

"It was either that or a small tornado," Piper said. "Anyone see a funnel cloud?"

Everyone shook their head. Piper continued. "According to folklore, in the early 1700s a strong, hot wind blew down half an acre of Douglas firs and set the ground on fire, wiping out the Native American tribe that had settled here."

"Fire. It was a hot wind, almost scorching," Jerry said.

"In the 1800s a settlement of pioneers were wiped out when a violent wind battered the valley into pulp."

Piper waited till the rustle of nervous chatter died down, then continued. "In 1968 survivors reported a similar hot wind just before the elementary school erupted in flames." Piper squinted in thought, then winced at the pain caused by pulling on the stitches.

"Whatever it was, it was blowing north to south," John said.

"That's right." Piper's eyes brightened. "I didn't put it together until now, but they all did. In all the accounts of strange winds survivors describe it as blowing north to south."

"Maybe it has something to do with the valley – you know, the terrain," Jerry suggested. "Maybe our geographical layout generates this phenomenon."

Someone coughed. The coffee machine, saved from the ruined break room, gurgled contentedly.

"But what about the lightning? Lightning in a snowstorm?" asked Coye. "This happened just a little while ago – lit up the whole sky and lasted forever."

"There have been similar accounts," Piper said. "Reports of odd, sustained lightning strikes lasting for several seconds, by one account up to a minute. The last time it happened was the night my mother died."

"But that's impossible," Coye said.

321

"No, it's not," said John. "I've seen it, too."

"I remember that night," Nathan said. He looked at John. "That was the night we buried Whitey Dobbs."

Maggie arched an eyebrow.

"That's the second time I've heard that name," Jerry said. "Who the hell is Whitey Dobbs?"

"You mean *what* the hell is Whitey Dobbs," Nathan whispered, then fell silent, his mind retreating to the gray weightlessness of a medicated world.

"All I know is we're trapped," Coye repeated. "We got a serial killer, freaky weather, and Lord God only knows what else – and we can't do nothing. Nothing."

"That's enough. We're cops. There is a killer out there, and it's our job to find him," John said.

"I hate to be a doomsayer," said Jerry. "But we don't have access to a crime lab, no way of examining the bodies. And no one has even mentioned the other stuff, like the glass storm that shredded Meredith Gamble – and what about the truck? Where the hell did it come from?"

John slammed his fist on to the tabletop. The sound of flesh hitting wood echoed like a gunshot.

A pall of silence returned.

When he was sure he had their attention, John began to speak. He was confident, self-assured. "You all know who Dr. Dean T. Truman is." Heads nodded around the room. "If the fine folks at *Newsweek* magazine are to be believed, Dean is one of the ten smartest men in the world. Even as we sit here squealing like a gaggle of frightened schoolgirls, Dean is up there at the college working in his lab, chasing down the answers to all your questions."

He paused to study their faces. No one seemed to breathe. They desperately wanted to believe, needed to believe.

He looked at his second-in-command. "You're right, Jerry. We don't have a crime lab and we do have a lot of weird fucking shit going on, but we also have something else. A genuine, honest-to-God genius. And if I were a betting man, I'd put Dean Truman's brain against the devil himself."

HE GAVE THEM ALL ASSIGNMENTS to collect as much information as they could. Exact measurements – where the windstorm had begun, where it had ended; the distance the debris had traveled; a list of all the debris, like pictures on Maggie's desk that seemed to have just vanished.

"Facts and figures, folks, facts and figures," he said. Duties assigned, he sent them to work with orders to meet again in one hour.

With the copier and a mug shot, flyers were made bearing the picture of Elijah. John wanted the flyers plastered all over town.

While his orders were being carried out, John made his way to the school to check on Dean's progress.

*

PIPER WAS LEAVING the dayroom when she picked up one of the hastily made WANTED posters for the mysterious Elijah. It occurred to her that she had never seen him and so would not be able to recognize him if she did.

She looked at the photograph.

The memory came like wind over water.

That face? It looked somehow familiar.

A ripple, then a wave, building to a tsunami. Suddenly, she was there again, back to the night of the storm, back to the night her mother died. Standing over her fallen parent watching the very life drain from her, not understanding, not knowing what to do.

"Mommy? Mommy, what's wrong?"

Her mother's face flashed white from a spike of lightning and the heavens roared like a wounded beast. Mommy was lying on the floor looking out at the storm. Lying in a pool of her own blood.

"With fingers awkward, stubby, and small, Piper reached out and touched her mother's hair.

"Mommy hurt."

"Piper. No, honey, go back to bed." She gagged, choking on her own blood.

"Mommy, get up."

"It's all right, honey, go back to sleep. Mommy is just resting."

"I'm scared."

"Just a storm . . . ," her mother said, struggling. "Don't be afraid."

"*Not scared of the thorm,*" Piper said, *stepping between her fallen mother and the open door.* "*Scared of the bad thing.*"

Piper turned to face her mother, a small trickle of blood beginning to run from her nose.

"*Piper?*"

Piper looked out the door. Lightning flashed, revealing a silhouette, a man standing in the doorway. A man? How could she have forgotten that?

"*It's okay, little girl. It's okay,*" *said the man, his voice as soft as a snowfall.*

Another flash, his face revealed. "*It's okay, you'll be all right. I promise.*" A face? A face she had never seen before and would never see again.

Piper looked down at the flyer in her hand. *Until now.*

The memory let go slowly, a python slackening its grip. Her mind snapped back to the present. My God, where had that come from? Her hands were trembling. She felt something on her face, she touched it. *Blood.* Her nose was bleeding.

DEAN HELD the small, heart-shaped locket in the palm of his hand.

Judy's locket.

He rubbed his thumb over the rose petal engravings, feeling the slight rise and fall of the metal. How long had he wanted to do this?

If I could just feel it again.

Then what? Everything would be all right? Wasn't that what he had thought? As if Judy's locket were a magic talisman that could somehow spirit away the pain.

And now—

Here it was, finally in his hands. But . . .

The grinning, jack-o'-lantern face of Whitey Dobbs flared in his mind.

Suddenly the locket felt heavy, hot, *ruined* – soiled by the touch of the impossible man, the ageless monster who made a mockery of Dean's very life.

Maybe seeing me prompted the heart attack.

Whitey Dobbs's words ran in his head like a perpetual Klaxon. All that searching and he could never find the locket. Now he knew why.

Whitey Dobbs had it.

But that was impossible. Impossible.

Hadn't aged a bit, not a nanosecond.

Impossible.

She didn't die alone.

Impossible.

Please, dear God, let it be impossible.

Running his finger along the edge of the locket, he found the locking mechanism. Then, using his thumbs, he found the seam and carefully opened the locket.

Inside on the right was a picture of Judy – sweet, wonderful Judy, exactly as he remembered her; on the left, where Judy had so lovingly placed his picture all those long, dead years ago, was a grinning, sneering image of Whitey Dobbs.

It means we'll be together forever.

THEY GATHERED BACK at the conference room exactly one hour after they had left. Everyone was there except for John and Dean. Coye sat outside in a small, brown folding chair waiting for them.

Piper rubbed her hands together, as if trying to start a fire, and found her mind drifting back to the stranger, Elijah Bones. The more she thought about it, the clearer the memory became. The man she'd seen that night was tall – of course, when you're a child, everyone is tall, but she remembered other things: he wore blue jeans, muddy boots, and a long army-green coat with a black T-shirt, and a floppy cowboy hat sat low on his head.

The same clothes Elijah had been wearing when Jerry arrested him. How was such a thing possible? What did it mean?

Piper looked at the clock. John should have been back by now, Dean in tow. What was taking so long? Even though he was the last person likely to believe her, she desperately wanted to see Dean.

Where were they?

COYE KNEW there was a problem the minute the severed head rolled in the door like a bloodied bowling ball. For one thing, as the head tumbled, skidded, and thumped against the conference room door, it left a skittery trail of blood and neck guts on the tan carpet. Sheriff Evans didn't like blood and neck guts on his carpet. For another thing, seeing the severed head was sure to make the deputy pass out, and Sheriff Evans didn't like his passing out.

But he couldn't help it, he thought, as the world faded to black.

THE THUMP at the door was firm and solid.

Nathan Perkins, a little more clear-eyed than before, was the closest to the door. He answered what he took to be an awkward knock. He expected to see the vacant face of Coye Cheevers announcing that the sheriff was back with Dean. Instead he saw – an empty hall?

And at his feet—

A human head!

Nathan began to scream, an involuntary, uncontrollable sound. A sound that brought everyone to the door, where they, too, saw the head.

Nathan was no longer screaming alone.

"TOUCH NOTHING," Jerry snapped, his voice shrill and stressed as he pulled and cocked his service revolver in one easy motion. He stepped over the head, calling for his colleague.

"Cheevers," he repeated, inching into the hallway. There in the lobby, in a spill of white light, he saw Coye sprawled on the floor. Jerry's professional eye noted he was breathing. "Piper, check Cheevers. I'm going outside."

The night air struck him with a chilly blow. An October bite pinched his nose with every breath. The street was quiet, as still as the air. Snow lit on his head, shoulders, face, and hands.

A truck bearing the Westcroft College logo slid to an awkward stop, its motor still running. The door opened. Jerry aimed his gun in a double-handed professional grip. Dean stepped out into the snow.

"Dr. Truman?" Jerry said.

The professor looked at the weapon, then raised his hands. Jerry lowered his gun. "Thank God you're here. Something's happened. Where's the sheriff?"

Dean dropped his hands and hunched his shoulders. "The sheriff? I thought he was here, with you."

A new concern clawed at the back of Jerry's mind. "No. He left to pick you up over an hour ago."

"I haven't seen him."

A new scream cleaved the air. It came from inside. Jerry ran back into the station, vaguely aware of Dean calling behind him, the sound of the truck door closing as the professor no doubt went to shut off the engine.

He didn't wait. Instead he ran back to the conference room. In the doorway Piper stood shaking and screaming. At her feet lay the human head. It had been rolled over, the face revealed.

Jerry found himself staring at the dead white face of John Evans.

29

MASON WAS PLEASED that the Timber Limb
Lodge was open and doing a brisk business despite the
weather. If he had to get to know his daughter's new
boyfriend, he preferred to do it in a place that served
beer. David Levin put his arm around Tina's shoulder.
She melted into his embrace.

Mason hated him. But he nodded and forced a grin.
This was supposed to be a meeting to make amends,
and after what John had told him, it should have been
a flat-out celebration.

The mess was over.

The stranger who had been hanging around town
turned out to be an armed lunatic and thankfully was
now in custody. As for the Polaroid, John had called to
say it was just a trick, no hallucination; Dean had
figured it out. And that meant Mason was not going
crazy.

But why Whitey Dobbs? Who knew to push that
particular button? No, it didn't matter. It was over.
Leave the mystery to John and Dean. With the pass
closed and now the bridge out, it looked like Mason

would be taking some unexpected vacation.

He looked around the Timber Limb Lodge. The restaurant was half-full despite the weather. Black Valley residents were a tough breed. They took pride in thumbing their nose at nature. He liked that.

"Isn't he the greatest, Daddy?" Tina cooed, her arms intertwined with the right arm of her young boyfriend.

Mason felt a prick of jealousy. He swallowed the pain and lied. "The greatest, dear, the greatest."

The glorious David Levin grinned. He was a good-looking kid, well dressed, well spoken. It turned out he was a business major with a real future. Good for him. But still, Tina was his little girl, and trick or no trick, his brush with losing her had only accentuated that feeling.

Tina held her hand out, inspecting the pearl ring that David had presented to her just before dinner. A ring? Jewelry was a personal gift. How long before he gave her one with a diamond? How long before Mason lost his baby girl to this jerk?

Then he reminded himself: *At least he's not Whitey Dobbs.*

DEAN CAME RUNNING DOWN the hall toward them. Piper looked at him, trying to focus through tear-veiled eyes. "Oh, God, Dean, it's so horrible." She threw herself into his arms. "Thank God you're alive."

The stunned professor stood immobile for a

moment, then returned the hug. "What's wrong?" he asked.

"We thought you were dead, too," Nathan repeated. He was sitting in a folding chair, a cold washcloth to his face.

Reluctantly, Piper released her grip, took a step back, and studied Dean's face. Relief was quickly replaced with concern. He didn't look right. "Dean? What's wrong?"

His face was ashen, his eyes anxious.

Something has happened to him, Piper realized. *Something very, very bad.*

"IT'S JOHN," Jerry said. Something had been placed on the corner of the desk and covered with a white linen towel. It was slightly oval.

"Jerry?" Dean asked.

"It's the sheriff. He killed him." The deputy took a breath and removed the towel. "He's been decapitated, Dr. Truman."

Dean could only blink and stare – looking at the severed head of his oldest, dearest friend.

"John?" he said.

As the county coroner, he had seen enough to know that this was real, no matter how hard his mind fought against it. The mouth was closed, jaw locked, but the eyes, cloudy as if preserved in a protective covering of plastic, were open and wide.

"John," Dean whispered.

"What?" asked a deep baritone voice.

They turned as one; the air suddenly gushed from the room, consumed by the group's simultaneous gasp. Jerry, Dean, Maggie, Coye, Nathan, and Piper all stared, looking in disbelief at the front entrance.

Sheriff John Evans stood in the doorway, hale and hardy, head attached.

Jerry bumped the desk.

The severed head tumbled to the floor, hitting with the thud of a ripe cantaloupe, and rolled across the carpet, coming to rest at the sheriff's size-fourteen boots. With nerves forged from iron and near superhuman emotional detachment, John reached down, grabbed a fistful of steel-gray and black hair, and lifted the head. Blood and fluids dripped in silent plunks from the neck wound. John held the head up to eye level and stared unblinkingly into his own face.

"Damn," was all he said.

A moan like a dying note on an oboe escaped as Deputy Coye Cheevers passed out again.

TINA TALKED, about school, about her sorority, but mostly about David. Wonderful, magical, walk-on-water David. They had known each other for only a short period of time, and already they were slipping away for a romantic tryst on the lake. Mason decided he would call Tina's mother as soon as he returned to Portland. Maybe she could help put the skids on this way too serious, way too early relationship.

Tina was telling some never-ending story about her history professor, who had a fondness for dressing in period clothes, and David the Great was grinning, when Mason heard it.

Click.

Flip.

It was a small sound, easily lost beneath the general clutter of utensils and conversation. Yet, a sound Mason found obscurely familiar. He didn't know *what*, but he knew *where*. It was a sound he heard often . . . in his nightmares.

ONCE AGAIN they gathered in the cluttered conference room – bleary eyed and shell-shocked. Piper crossed her arms, hugging herself, wondering if she would ever be warm again.

John explained how he had gotten sidetracked by a nasty traffic accident, then returned to the station when he didn't find Dean at the school.

"I don't like this. No, sir, not one bit," Nathan said. "This is not right. That *thing*, that maniac that attacked my Ava – it isn't human."

"Let's try to stay calm." John spoke in a firm but edgy voice. He was successfully maintaining control, though Piper couldn't help but notice how he kept clutching at his gun belt, snapping and unsnapping the security strap, fidgeting. "A lot of strange things have been going on around here—"

"That's the understatement of the year," Nathan spit.

"There is still no clear motive, but I think we have a thread of an idea—"

"Thread . . . thread . . . ," Nathan screamed. "You're talking about threads. Hell, it's more like a noose – a hangman's noose. No offense, John, but are you crazy? Your head is sitting over there in the refrigerator, and we're talking about motives?"

"I don't see panic get us anywhere."

"Nothing gets us anywhere," Nathan shouted, throwing up his hands. "We're trapped, John. Cheevers is right. No matter how you try to spin it, we are still trapped. Trapped with God knows what."

"I'll tell you what it is," said Coye, his eyes wide, and dilated. The air hung heavy with the smell of coffee and fear. "I think it's voodoo!"

"Voodoo," Jerry said. The deputy shook his head and laughed. If he was looking for supporters in his mockery, he found none. His smile faded.

Dean was silent. He sat with his head down.

Piper felt a rattlesnake of dread coil in her stomach. *Something's wrong with Dean.*

"We've got a city to keep alive, people," John said. "If we panic, then nobody stands a chance. You got that?"

John then turned to the mayor. "Nathan, I know you're worried about Ava, but we're counting on you.

We need you. Now more than ever. So tell me, what's the mood like? How are folks responding?"

Nathan still wore the face of a man in shock. "People are pretty nervous. But most just think it's a storm. I've encouraged as many businesses as possible to stay open."

John nodded and turned to his deputies. "Any sign of our mysterious Elijah?"

"None," said Jerry. "Phones are intermittent, but as best I can tell, his prints haven't triggered any alarms with the NCIC. Other than that, I've got his picture posted in every business in town. Nothing."

"Maybe we should post a picture of Whitey Dobbs." Dean's voice was little more than a whisper, but his words hushed the group.

"Dobbs?" John rubbed his chin with a callused hand.

I just saw that chin resting on the carpet, Piper thought before she could stop herself.

"Who is Whitey Dobbs?" Jerry asked for the second time that day.

"A boy we buried alive twenty-two years ago for a crime he didn't commit," Dean answered.

"M-m-mercy of God," Coye stammered.

"Buried?" Jerry repeated, as if he had somehow lost the capacity to understand English.

"It was a prank." John looked at Dean. "We thought he had raped my sister."

"Judy?" Maggie asked. Then to Dean, "Your wife?"

Dean nodded.

Piper could feel venomous fangs of fear indenting the soft muscle of her heart.

"It can't be Dobbs," Nathan said. "Despite what I heard. He's long dead. Got to be."

"It's Dobbs," Dean said. His voice flat, emotionless. "I know. I just saw him."

"What?" John asked incredulously. "When?"

"Less than an hour ago. He was at the school. John, he hasn't aged a minute. Not a minute."

"That's impossible."

"And you holding your own severed head *isn't?*" Dean challenged. "It was him. It was Whitey Dobbs."

"A look-alike," John challenged.

"His voice was the same. That laugh."

John's face was blotched red – with anger or frustration, Piper wasn't sure.

"He left this." Dean Truman held up a heart-shaped locket.

The room was quiet enough to hear John swallow. "Judy's locket?"

Dean nodded. "It disappeared from the hospital the night she died."

Coye whimpered softly.

"Bullshit!" John's riposte slashed thought the silent room "Absolute fucking bullshit! If you saw Dobbs, then you saw a guy our age with plastic surgery or someone made up to look like him."

"Not this good. No one could do plastic surgery this good."

"No one could make a Polaroid blink, but they did," Piper said, rising from her chair. "Near-science, isn't that what you called it, Dean? Technology that's here, just not common knowledge yet. If they can make a photograph wink, then I believe they can make a thirty-nine-year-old man look seventeen."

John nodded, favoring Piper with the slightest whisper of a smile. "You said it yourself, Dean. Someone is trying to push your buttons. Push you over the edge. What better way than by making you think that Whitey Dobbs is back? I know it's far-fetched, but it makes a hell of a lot more sense than the other option."

John took a deep, bracing breath and grasped his friend's shoulders. "Listen to me. I need you, Dean. I need your brain. They're trying to make you think you're crazy – and if you buy into it, then they've won. You hear me? They've won."

"Who's won?" Dean demanded. "Who the hell could do all this, would do all this just to get at me?"

"A rival technical company?" Piper asked.

"Then kill me. Don't spend billions of dollars on some elaborate ruse. It's Whitey Dobbs. He's back, unchanged, and he certainly has motive." His anger spent, Dean collapsed his shoulders like a bird folding its wings. He dropped into the nearest chair, head in his hands.

John clenched his jaw. In the dead silence of the

room Piper imagined she could hear his teeth grinding.

"Don't you get it?" Dean spoke through his hands, not bothering to look up. "I was wrong. My whole life is a sham. Everything I believe in is a joke."

Piper took the seat beside him. Her hand found his shoulder. "That's not true. I think you were right. And you *are* right."

He moved a hand to see her face. "You? You see ghosts. I thought you would be loving this. I'll tell you what Dobbs told me: 'Science is to the universe what snow is to Alaska, just a covering.' Then the bastard mumbled something about not missing a dinner date." Dean made a waving motion with his hand. "It doesn't matter."

"She's right, Dean," John said. "You're our best hope. I need you to examine that thing in the refrigerator, that head."

"I can tell you now. It's real."

"I don't doubt that, but its not *my* head. Obviously. Maybe you can find signs of plastic surgery. Whoever made that poor bastard look like me is the same person making this other guy look like Dobbs." John stopped. "Wait a second. What did this Dobbs look-alike say about dinner?"

Dean cast him a doubtful eye. "A dinner date. So?"

The sheriff checked his watch. "Jesus! Mason is having dinner with his daughter at the Timber Limb Lodge. Niles, Cheevers, you're with me."

The deputies were on their feet.

Dean stood. "You don't think—"

"I'm not taking any chances."

"I'm going with you," Dean said.

"No. You're staying here and finding some answers." He looked at Piper. "We need him. Get him back. And do it quick."

30

IT WAS TWENTY MINUTES from the sheriff's department to the Timber Limb Lodge. John was determined to make it in ten. The heavy, studded tires of the Jeep Cherokee bit deeply into the snow-padded roadway. The lodge was to the north, uphill. Even under the best conditions it was dangerous; with the accumulation of ice and snow it was downright deadly.

John didn't care. He had seen his friends slaughtered, seen his department wrecked, and held his own severed head. But what bothered him the most was that dull, flat look on Dean Truman's face. The look of defeat. Without Dean they were without hope.

John pressed the accelerator. Snow chips, revealed in the headlights, pulsed blue and white. Jerry sat beside him, his fingers gripping the dash hard enough to dimple the console and turn his fingertips white. He didn't say a word.

The car shimmied; John reigned it in like a wagon master. He didn't slow down.

John was a practical man on an impractical mission.

Was there a connection between Mason having dinner with his daughter and the man Dean thought was Whitey Dobbs making a reference to dinner plans? John honestly didn't know. But despite the insanity of the current situation, all of his instincts, all his years as a cop, screamed there was.

"AND HOW is everything tonight?"

Mason Evans looked up to see a neatly dressed young man with thick, dark hair and a thin mustache.

"I am Klaus, the maître d'," he explained. "May I get you anything?" His voice was as smooth as a freshly polished floor. And just as slippery, Mason wagered.

Mason growled under his breath but apparently loudly enough for the ever-so-wonderful David Levin to take note and smile. *He finds the maître d' as bogus as I do*, Mason realized. Maybe there was hope for the kid after all.

"My, what a beautiful ring," Klaus gushed. "May I?"

Tina giggled, just like she used to when she was five and Mason would pounce on her pretending to be the Great Tickle Monster.

She extended her hand. Klaus took it, holding her by the fingertips, closely inspecting the small pearl ring. Then, like a cheesy actor in a bad French film, he bent to kiss the back of her hand.

"For crying out loud," Mason grunted, this time making no effort to mask his distaste.

Tina giggled, enraptured by the exoticism.

Click.

Flip.

That sound? He had heard it earlier. An unexpected shudder sprinted up his body.

A glint, something shiny in the waiter's hand.

Shiny?

Klaus pressed his lips fully against the back of her hand.

Shiny, like metal. Mason's mind raced – recalling the earlier sound . . . the sound of his nightmares.

His lips still against Tina's hand, the waiter cut his eyes to Mason, the corner of his mouth drawn back in a grin.

Shiny . . . click . . . nightmares . . .

"Tinaaaa . . . ," Mason screamed, seeing the cherry-wood handle.

The world went into slow motion.

Mason watched with crystal clarity – his daughter turning a puzzled face in his direction; *the brute*, lips still pressed to her skin, eyes still on Mason, beginning to shake with laughter as the blade slid out of the palm of his left hand, its smoothness catching the light, and in one motion . . .

Blood . . .

Tina's eyes flared, too shocked to feel pain. Blood spewed from her hand like water from a fire hose. The finger completely severed.

Tina began to scream.

The bastard stood, acting as if nothing had happened at all . . . grinning . . . laughing. He held Tina's bloody digit between his thumb and forefinger, then tipped Mason a salute with the severed finger.

David Levin was slow to start but fast on his feet. He was behind Klaus. He reached out, grabbing a handful of hair. A coarse, black wig came off in his hand, revealing hair as white as bleached bones.

"Dobbs," Mason shouted, vaulting from his chair.

"Daddyyyy . . . ," Tina shrieked, holding the bloody geyser in disbelief.

Grabbing a shoulder, David spun the man around, then threw an uppercut that caught him just under the chin.

The white-haired man staggered back. David charged.

"No!" Mason shouted. The warning came too late, the knife too fast. Dobbs made a single swipe. Blood exploded from the young man's neck. His hands reflexively went to the wound, worthless against the gushing tide.

Mason could hear the gurgled gasp of an open windpipe. David's head bobbed precariously.

God Almighty, the knife had cut to the bone.

David Levin's head fell back, touching his spine, exposing a gaping hole. The boy crumpled to the floor, his life shooting out in buckets of crimson warmth.

He almost took his head off . . .

Whitey Dobbs laughed, the sound of a thousand ravens startled into flight.

THE WAITER TOOK A DEEP DRAW on the cigarette, then blew a plume of smoke directly at the NO SMOKING sign. To hell with it, it was bad enough in the restaurant on a night like this, no way he was going out in that weather for his break.

"Smoking in the boys' room," he said to his reflection.

He was only working here to make enough money to go to school, and he was only going to school to get a good job, and he only wanted a good job – well, to make enough money to pay for cigarettes. "So, there you go" – he snapped his fingers at the figure in the mirror – "the circle of life."

The bathroom door banged open.

The boss. The waiter shoved his cigarette down the drain. But the man who came in was not the boss. The man with stark white hair smiled, walked up to the mirror, and began to write.

"Hey . . . hey . . . whatcha doing?" the waiter said. "You can't do that."

The stranger only smiled as he continued to smear his message in red. "Don't worry," he said, holding up his writing instrument – a severed finger. "It's only blood."

JOHN BURST into the Timber Limb Lodge, entering a

world in chaos. Patrons were running and heaving and crying. It was a maelstrom of panic. And in the eye of the storm, Mason.

Mason was kneeling over his unconscious daughter, swaddling her hand in a bloodrich napkin. A young man, head bent backward at an impossible angle, lay next to them.

Blood was everywhere.

Mason saw John from across room; his eyes begged for help.

"Call an ambulance," John said to Jerry, then ran to his cousin's side. "How is she?"

"Alive," Mason sobbed. "Alive, for now. John, he cut off her *finger* – he sliced it off while I watched."

"Levin? His neck. What the hell can do that?"

Mason Evans shook his head, as if not believing his own memory. "A *knife*, a cherry-handled *switchblade*."

Deep, deep in his inner soul a fire ignited, roaring with unprecedented intensity. A flame that could not be extinguished by logic, by discipline, even by the law. Sheriff John Evans felt the urge, hotter, brighter, more ardent than ever before. "Whitey Dobbs," he cursed.

"He went in the men's room."

John nodded, unholstering his gun.

"He cut off her finger, John – he cut off her fucking finger. Then the bastard took it with him."

*

THE BLAZE, the fire, the fury, roared with the ferocity of a star going nova.

The perpetrator was shot and killed while resisting arrest. That was how the police report would read. No matter what, someone was going to die tonight.

John kicked open the bathroom door, knocking it askew on its hinges. He entered, gun thrust forward in a two-handed grip. He swept the room, the sound of his entrance still reverberating off the tiled walls.

Empty. Except for a man huddled in the corner.

"Where's the guy that came in here?"

The old man trembled with visible intensity as he extended a long, slim finger and pointed to the mirror.

The message was written in blood – Tina's blood. Her tiny finger left on the counter.

On the mirror the letters of the blood-written message had begun to run.

Jimmy Dean,

Tonight, midnight, Hawkins Hill! Or everyone dies.

Whitey XXXX

31

PIPER WATCHED DEAN as he sat on the piano bench. He was swaying gently, humming some song she knew but couldn't quite place. She joined him on the bench.

Their arms touched as, by reflex, Piper's fingers went to the keyboard. Five years of piano lessons and a good ear for music made the move natural. "I've been trying to identify the song you're humming."

He looked at her without seeing. Eyes as blank as a dead dog. No hope, no hope.

"Have I been humming?"

"Nonstop."

"I'm sorry."

She shrugged. "No biggie. I just can't name it, that's all."

"Hmmm. Now that you mention it, neither can I."

This surprised her. "It's familiar though, isn't it?"

"Yeah, seems like it's been on the tip of my tongue all day."

"Wait a second. Let's see if this helps." Using one

finger, she pinged out the tune he had been humming.

His brow furrowed. "What is that?"

She repeated the notes, then paused, thought about it, and played it again, this time in full, using both hands. The song echoed in the meeting room like thunder in a barrel. Heads turned.

Disgusting, the others must be thinking. *Playing the piano at a time like this.*

Let 'em think what they want, Piper decided.

"Play it again," Dean said, standing up and looking over her shoulder. She did as he asked, then paused, letting the notes run around in her memory. What was that song? Like Dean, she felt it was there, just at the tip of her consciousness.

Dean stepped back, as if struck by a sudden bolt of lightning. For a moment she thought he had been. Then she saw his eyes. His eyes, his eyes. They were alive. He looked at her and this time he saw her.

"I've got it." Then something extraordinary happened. After more than two hours of acting like an extra in a remake of *Night of the Living Dead*, Dean spoke with animation. "It's from *The Rocky Horror Picture Show*. A silly song – Judy and I used to love it. What is it called?"

Dean bit his lower lip in thought, then smacked them with satisfaction. " 'The Time Warp.' "

Piper cut loose on the piano, playing the song from memory. Dean, knowing a surprising amount of the lyrics, began to sing, supplementing "dah, dah, dah's" for unrecalled words, and both belted out the chorus. "Let's do the Time Warp again. . . ."

They finished, both of them laughing.

"I haven't heard that song in years," Piper said, flushed with relief and a tinge of embarrassment.

"I've had it in my head since . . ." He mentally chased the thought.

"Dean?"

"It's not just a song. It's a dance."

"A dance?" Piper said.

"It's the dance Elijah was doing." He straightened. Color had returned to his cheeks. The fire of certainty reignited behind tenebrous pupils. "Maggie, how many people can you scrounge up?"

The administrative assistant, who had been watching them like a teacher deciding whether to weigh in or not, hesitated for just a moment. "As many as we need. Nobody is going anywhere. Why?"

"We're going to need them."

She smiled, still tentative but optimistic.

Piper shared her emotions. "For what?"

"The answer, Piper, the answer. And do you know what the answer is?"

A cocky smile this time. "You're the professor."

"That's right, I am. And the answer is science."

"Yes!" Piper cheered, pumping her arm in victory. Impulsively she leapt into his arms.

Before either of them realized what was happening,

before doubt had a moment to be born, Dean leaned forward and kissed her.

"Thank you," he said a moment later.

She almost thanked him back, but he was deep in the burning fires of ideas. "Maggie, I need a clock. Something from the office, with hour, minute, and second hands. No digital. Digital won't work."

"A clock. They all stopped."

"Exactly. Get some people over to that farmhouse near the Willamette Bridge, Dub Pelt's place, and Nathan's. I'll go by my house, then the school. Tell everyone to look for clocks, watches – again, anything with hands, not digital. Then bring them to me at the school."

"But the sheriff wanted us to stay put," one of the part-timers said.

"No, the sheriff wanted us to solve this thing," Maggie Dane said. "And this is the man who can do it. Whatever you need, Dr. Truman, whatever you need."

"Thanks, Maggie. Piper, I'm going to need all your research papers, everything you have on the history of the city. Can you drive me?"

"To the moon."

He smiled. It was a nice smile, crooked and imperfect, exquisite in its flaws.

"That won't be necessary. At least, not yet."

THE AIR WAS ACIDIC and smelled of burning phosphate, wood, and bodies. Sirens screamed, strobe lights flashed – staccato tableaux in blue, red, and white. The scene was one of chaos and death. The wounded were being pulled from the rubble. The building, at least what remained of it, continued to burn. Screams of pain and the electronic warble of emergency sirens all mingled to produce a symphony of turmoil.

Whitey Dobbs laughed.

Here again? Well, not exactly again. He couldn't do that. But close. He had been there before and after, but never now. He judged the scene and estimated how long before his next move. Not long.

He rubbed his hands together, then held them out toward the destruction, warming his palms on the fires of disaster. He laughed, louder this time. A fireman turned his head, faceplate covered in soot. Dobbs could make out his expression of disgust and confusion. Which only made Dobbs laugh louder.

Here, always here – no, not always, just often. Which seemed like always. If he could stick around, he would see himself. But that could never happen. He searched the crowd, the faces. Somewhere out there was Dr. Dean Truman.

The thought of the doctor warmed him more than the fire.

Whitey Dobbs cackled, his voice merging with the cacophony of devastation, a high-pitched squawk like a crow on a live wire. And then he was gone.

32

THE CLASSROOM THROBBED with activity, the sound of multiple computers doing multiple calculations, the sound of idea and theory colliding, of mysteries revealed and secrets solved. They worked into the evening. Piper had been collecting, sorting, and logging information as person after person arrived with timepieces of various shapes and sizes, all frozen at specific times. She dutifully noted where each was found and when the clock had stopped. She then passed that information on to Dean, who absorbed it silently, then continued with his mantra of clacking keys.

Her own research lay beside him in various stacks and piles – individual dates circled, events underlined. Occasionally he would ask a question, always about a location, and she would respond. Outside, the snow continued to fall from a sky that seemed permanently stained black-gray.

At ten to eight John and Nathan arrived, directed to the school by Maggie. Their faces told the story. Something had happened. Something else. And while John talked, describing the events in the Timber Limb

Lodge, the death of David Levin, the amputation of Tina Evans's finger, the disappearance of the white-haired man, Dean continued to work. His mind like the machines around him, multitasking, performing dozens of calculations, evaluating and deducing even as he listened.

It was only when John repeated the message, the personal challenge leveled to Dean and written in a young girl's blood, that he stopped. Even then, as he looked at the sheriff, as he absorbed the words with his eyes, his mind was somewhere else.

He's still thinking, Piper noted, slightly alarmed by his icy detachment, but at the same time relieved at his determination.

Thirty-one minutes later, when Piper returned with a plate of sandwiches and another round of soft drinks, Dean began to explain the unexplainable.

He walked as he spoke, punctuating his thoughts with his gestures. Piper listened and felt a new coldness.

"Real?" John asked. "You're saying it's all real?"

"Yes."

It was just the four of them – Dean, John, Piper, and Nathan. Everyone else had been sent home or on an assignment.

Nathan looked to Piper. "Is he—"

"Sane?" Piper finished.

"I was going to say 'on the level,' but yes, that does cut to the chase."

Piper studied Dean, this older man who had been

both teacher and friend, this brilliant yet shy genius, who in a rare unguarded moment had brushed his lips with her own, and she smiled. He echoed the gesture with his slightly crooked grin.

"Yes, he is sane."

He thanked her with a tip of his head, then continued. "Not only am I saying it's real; I'm saying I was a fool for not realizing it sooner."

"So the ghost of Whitey Dobbs is haunting us?" John asked.

"No. There's no such thing as a ghost. At least, not in the conventional sense. Whitey Dobbs is a living being, as tangible and physical as any of us."

"But he still looks like a teenager."

"Because he is a teenager. By my calculations he is a little more than a year older than the last time we saw him."

The small fans in the nearest computers hummed. Others clicked and clucked like strange exotic birds. The mayor and the sheriff exchanged a look. Nathan nervously nibbled the crust on his ham and cheese sandwich and looked up.

Dean continued. "I believe Dobbs is encompassed in a harmonic wave distortion."

"Come again?" John said. He sat on the end of a lab table, sandwich untouched in his hand.

"He is out of phase with reality, stepping between the seconds, days, weeks, months, years. He's out of concert with time."

"Time travel," Nathan mumbled. "I think I liked it better when he was a ghost."

Piper took a bite of her sandwich, chewing without thought, swallowing without taste.

"And it's not just Dobbs," Dean continued. "I think the same thing is happening to Elijah."

"Which is how he disappeared from his cell," John finished.

"You said the same thing is happening *to* Elijah. You mean, it's not voluntary?"

"For the most part, I don't think it is. This isn't the result of a time machine. It's the result of radiation."

"Radiation? You mean plutonium or something?" Nathan asked.

Dean shook his head. "No, not radiation in the conventional sense. This is something different. Think of it as *neoradiation*. As far as I can tell, it's not overtly harmful. Actually, it acts a bit like electricity, much like an electric fence is rife with electricity, which is not a bad comparison, since it does seem to effect electromagnetic fields. If you're exposed to small amounts, there is no apparent effect. But if you're radiated with enough, you shift out of phase with normal space-time."

"Others, like Piper" – he pointed to her with his sandwich – "have just enough exposure to make them sensitive to it."

"Radiation? I'm radiated?"

Dean smiled at her. "Actually, you're radiant, but that's another story."

Piper felt herself blush.

Dean continued. "Your neorad exposure is not enough to harm you, but it is enough to allow you to sense distortions in the space-time continuum. I believe the same was true of your mother."

"How? Why me?"

Dean motioned out the window. "Hawkins Hill. Both you and your mother were born in that farmhouse at the foot of Hawkins Hill."

Mama lying on the floor in a growing shadow of red. Lightning that seemed to last forever. A stranger in the doorway.

"And this neoradiation comes from the hill?"

"It comes from that location, yes," Dean said.

"This Elijah character – he's irradiated like Dobbs?" John asked. "Is that why he dresses the way he does, like he could have stepped into the future from the past?"

Dean nodded. "Very well may have."

"Time travel." John shook his head. He waved with the still-untouched sandwich. "Is such a thing really possible?"

"Of course it is. You're doing it right now."

Dean stepped up to the new, pristine blackboard that had replaced the ruined one. "Look at it this way." He drew a straight line with an arrowhead at the end. "We are all traveling in time, as is the world around us. But only in one direction – forward. So we tend to think of time as a forward progression. But it's not."

John frowned.

"I can show you how to see into the past right now, and not just minutes, but hundreds, thousands, millions of years."

"I'd like to see that," Nathan mumbled.

"You have."

"The stars," Piper replied, suddenly understanding.

"Exactly. Even looking at the Sun is looking back in time. It takes approximately eight minutes for the light from the Sun to reach our eyes here on Earth. It takes more than three and a half years for the light from the nearest star to reach us. For others it can be billions. A star could be dead and gone for hundreds of thousands of years, but because of the distance we still see it in our night sky. We see what was, the past, even as we continue into the future."

"That's all well and good, but as you said, time only flows in one direction," Nathan rebutted.

Dean pointed with the chalk. "Or so we thought. But a tortured interpretation of a recently published theory on a relatively unconnected subject indicates otherwise."

"Your theory on quantum physics and superstring mechanics," Piper said.

"Right. On the surface it has nothing to do with time travel per se, but if you look at it from a different perspective, it not only supports time travel, but explains it. You see, under my theory a superstring of preexisting hydrocarbons—"

"Whoa, whoa, whoa," John said. "Save the fancy talk for the journals." He had finally taken a bite of his sandwich, consuming close to half of it with one chomp. "Give me the nickel version."

Dean began again. "Okay, here's the thing; I've accidentally invented time travel. I haven't worked out all the details yet, but I can see where it's going, and recent events more than support that it works. It's the only thing that makes sense."

"But time travel is impossible," Nathan said. "Every scientist says so."

"Every scientist used to say so. Then along comes quantum physics, and it all changes. Now we know that at a subatomic level the rules become counter-intuitive. The same experiment produces different results if it's being watched. And in some cases you have the effect before you have the cause."

"That's ridiculous," Nathan said emphatically.

"That's science. It's a fact. I know it sounds crazy. You might say that explaining quantum physics is like describing a rainbow to a person without eyes."

"What about the radiation?" Nathan asked. "How were Dobbs and Elijah exposed to this neoradiation, and what does any of this have to do with burning trucks, silos, glass, and severed hands?"

"And don't forget the brick," Dean said.

Dean paused. For a moment his mind appeared somewhere else. "Flash Five," he mumbled, then, "Oh, my God. That's it."

"The old gang?" Nathan asked.

Dean looked up, his eyes still unfocused. "No. The experiment. I've developed a plan, based on my string theory, to create a new energy source. I'll call the experiment Flash Five."

He paused for a moment, his eyes squinted like someone experiencing an intense headache. "At some point in the next few years I'll try it. But instead of creating an energy source, I'll create time travel. And I'll make a mistake."

"How can you know that?" Piper asked.

"Because the plant is going to blow up."

JOHN'S THOUGHTS RAN RAMPANT. *Everything is real*. If that was true . . . ? He inhaled deeply and forced himself to remain calm, at least on the outside.

If Dean was right and everything was real, then so was the severed head sitting in the morgue freezer less than two miles away. And that meant John was going to be decapitated and his head thrown into the sheriff's department like a bloodied bowling ball.

The thought of his own death was disquieting but nothing new. As a cop, he had long since come to terms with his own mortality. Still. He reached up and touched his face, his fingers tracing a thin nick created when he had shaved less then eight hours ago. John had seen the same nick on the severed head. Unhealed. Fresh. Which meant John was going to die before this day was over.

He took a bite of his sandwich and wondered if his last meal on Earth would be ham and cheese.

"BLOW UP?" Nathan repeated.

"That's it," Piper said. "That's exactly it. While experimenting on your time theory, something goes wrong and the whole place explodes. But it's not a normal explosion."

Dean sighed. "No, no it's not."

"Excuse me again," Nathan said, raising his hand like a second-grade student. "Layman in the room. Give me the bottom line."

Dean smiled. "The building will not only explode in physical space; it will explode in time. Think of it like this." He drew a circle on the board. "The blast starts here, sending shock waves and debris hurling out in an expanding fashion. But due to the nature of the blast, it doesn't just radiate outward, it radiates through time."

"The truck," Piper said.

"Was or will be parked near the plant at the time of the explosion. The truck flickered through time, which is how Cheevers saw it several days before Piper and I witnessed it crashing into the Willamette Bridge. The silo, I think that's the top of the one lost back in 1974. It wasn't a mini tornado but a shock wave that blew it off. And it was burning shards that most likely caused that elementary school fire back in 1948. Glass blown out by the explosion is what killed Meredith Gamble. The shock waves and debris are being hurled backward and forward probably, dispersing over centuries, usually in small amounts – like the brick that came through my window – but occasionally in larger doses with rather spectacular results. Using Piper's research, I've been able to isolate at least fifty-three incidents that support this theory."

"Fire and stone," Nathan whispered. "Piper's report says the first settlement here was destroyed by fire, the second by stone."

Dean nodded. "That's consistent with my theory."

"You said shock wave," John said. "Is that what hit the building? Knocked down the helicopter?"

"Exactly."

"That explains the hot wind," Piper said. "And the weather."

"I think so. I believe dozens of fissures are opening in space-time, allowing cold and hot air, from heaven knows *when*, to rush out and mix with our own air, creating these bizarre meteorological effects."

John shook his head. "So an explosion in the future is sending debris into the past. But now that we know about it, can't we just make sure the plant is never built? No plant, no explosion; no explosion, no debris."

"Doesn't work that way. It's a common mistake and part of the conundrum of time travel. It's called protected field theory." Dean tossed the chalk in his hand. "It was Einstein who first proposed that space and time were opposite sides of the same coin, like heads or tails. Different but joined – space-time. I'm sure you've heard this one before. Time passes slower for someone traveling near the speed of light than for someone standing still. So if you travel at the speed of light for ten years, five out and five back, when you return to Earth, one hundred years will have passed."

"Go on," John urged.

"Just because a hundred years pass on Earth doesn't mean you, the space traveler, will age a hundred years. That's because of protected field theory. While traveling at an accelerated speed, you are governed by your own individual laws of physics."

"That's what's happening here. Even if the plant is never built, all the debris, anything that is already in the dispersion field, remains in the field. That's why the old brainteaser about going back in time and killing your grandfather is meaningless: if you went back in time and killed your grandfather, then you would cease to exist. So how could you go back in time and kill your grandfather? And if you couldn't, then he would not be dead, meaning you would be alive to go back in time and—"

"Okay, okay, we get it," Nathan said. "The paradox. But you're saying it doesn't work that way."

"Exactly. Once you're out of phase with normal space-time, then you're operating under a different, albeit equally strict, law of physics. It's like getting into a glass ball, then jumping into a swimming pool. You're surrounded by water. If your friends jump in, they are surrounded, too. But even though they are wet and everything around them is wet, you remain dry."

"Because of the bubble," Piper said. "And the bubble is the protective field."

"So how does that affect Whitey Dobbs? How did he get in the field?"

"Ninety-nine Einstein. It was Dobbs himself who gave me the answer. As you know, NxTech does research in dozens of different sciences, with plants and factories all over the world. What you may not know is that each laboratory, every single research room, has a designation name and number. The names correspond with the field. A computer science laboratory in Colorado may be called thirty-seven Gates."

"Named after Bill Gates," Nathan said.

"Right. The name tells the discipline of science, the number means it's the thirty-seventh laboratory in the worldwide NxTech chain."

Dean reached into his desk drawer, took out a set of blueprints, and unfurled them. He anchored one side with a soft-drink can, the other with a tape dispenser. The three of them got up and walked over to the prints for a better look. "These are the plans for the proposed NxTech research center. As you see, it will be built on top of Hawkins Hill."

The blueprints revealed a sprawling, multistoried facility – each room numbered, each number matched by a corresponding legend in the bottom-right corner.

"Which lab is yours?" Piper asked.

"I will have the ninety-ninth physics research laboratory in the NxTech system: ninety-nine Einstein."

He pointed to a big room near the center of the plant. "And that is where my lab is going to be."

Nathan shrugged. "So?"

Dean took a full breath. He tapped the paper. "That is within fifteen feet of the exact spot where Whitey Dobbs was buried twenty-two years ago."

They were quiet as the reality of what Dean was saying settled in.

Piper felt the hair rise up on the back of her neck. Dean read the look.

Piper swallowed. "Something's coming."

33

HE WAS STANDING OUTSIDE. Snow up to his knees. Standing, looking, watching. The stranger, Elijah.

"Son of a bitch," John said, rising from his seat. Piper heard the snap of the safety strap, the sound of metal and leather as the sheriff drew his gun from its holster.

"No," Dean said. "Don't. He's on our side."

"How can you know that?" Nathan snapped. "How the hell can you know that? Even if everything you say is true. Even if he is a time traveler, how do you know he's not still responsible? How do you know he's not working with Dobbs? How the fuck do you know anything?"

"I don't." Dean put on his coat, held up his hands to prevent any further argument, then left the building. A few seconds later he stepped outside into the shocking white world that Black Valley, Oregon, had become.

They went to the window, all three of them. Piper noted John was holding his gun. His finger slipped inside the trigger guard – ready.

The wind was still blowing. Skiffs of snow took

flight like gossamer ghosts performing a jerking waltz. Dean walked with his head down against the wind, collar up, face hunkered in his coat.

The stranger turned to greet him. John raised the gun. Piper put a hand on his arm. "No. Not yet."

As they watched, the stranger, Elijah, began to move in a herky-jerky fashion.

"What the hell is he doing?" Nathan asked.

"Dancing the Time Warp," Piper said, her words greeted by a perplexed face. "Long story."

As they watched, Dean began to laugh. *Laugh?* Then, with the group looking on, the stranger took off his hat, turned toward the window, made a deep, elaborate bow. And then he vanished.

DEAN STOOD for a moment, staring at the place where Elijah had been a heartbeat earlier. His words still sounded in his head.

"I couldn't just tell you," Elijah had explained. "I tried that, it didn't work. In the future you are the only one who understands how it works, and even you admit that's because of an accident."

"An accident."

Elijah nodded, his hat bobbing like a bird's wing. "It happened after you watched *The Rocky Horror Picture Show*. You got that song stuck in your head. Somehow you put that with your theory, and *blam*, you figure it out. You told me, or you will tell, that you had to look at the problem sideways. If you examined it

367

straight on, you couldn't see it. So I tried to recreate those circumstances."

He began to dance. Dean laughed and danced with him.

"So, who are you?"

He smiled. "You'll figure it out."

Dean flexed his fingers, the cold working its way into his gloves. "What do you hope to get out of this?"

"A dream. I hope to fulfill my greatest dream. That's all."

They talked another minute, then he was gone and Dean was alone in the snow.

My greatest dream. That's all.

TWO OF THE THREE new computers chimed at once. Dean could hear them in the hall before entering the room. He hurried, brushing snow from his hair and clothes, slung his coat over the nearest chair, and hurried to the first computer, leaving wet tracks behind him. Piper and Nathan were studying the screen of the second machine.

"You've got something," Nathan said, then shook his head. "It's all numbers."

"Good." Dean checked the screen, then struck the appropriate keys. Across the room a laser printer hummed into action. "Send what you've got to the printer as well."

Nathan looked blankly at the computer. Piper

smiled and lightly pushed him aside. "Allow me." She tapped the keys. "Printing."

"What did he say?" John asked, showing little interest in the technology spewing from the machine.

Dean picked up the still-warm paper, the first sheet to be printed. He studied the results. Close, but not enough.

John repeated his question.

Dean sighed, picking up the second printout. "He said he wants his dreams to come true." Dean read the paper and shook his head. "Damn. Not enough."

"That's it? That's all he said?" John demanded.

"That and that I make terrible hamburgers. He said I served him one two weeks ago, his time, working as a teenager at a fast-food restaurant." Dean removed a third printout, swore beneath his breath, and crumpled the paper up. "Not enough. It's just not enough."

Across the room Piper looked up. Dean had come to recognize the look in her eyes. Sparks jumped from the doorknob.

"Incoming," she said.

Dozens of pinpricks of bluish-purple light dappled the room. Appearing out of nothing. Hanging in the air. Some throbbing. Some growing.

"What's happening?" Nathan screamed.

"Not now," Dean muttered. "Not yet." He took another sheet from the printer.

The wind began to blow. More holes, bigger now. Several the size of dinner plates, at least two as large as serving trays. Unanchored papers took flight, fluttering like thin, white, spasmodic sparrows. The wind was random, coming from a dozen different sources, at times competing with itself. The room was filled with the scent of burning rubber and ozone.

The wind grew stronger. A paper tray tipped over. A waste basket slid across the floor.

Piper, the smallest of the group, staggered as she was struck in the chest by a mallet of hot air.

"Grab hold of something," Dean shouted. "All of you!"

Piper grasped the edge of a study lab table. They were bolted to the floor and offered good anchorage.

John had holstered his weapon but now appeared conflicted. Not sure where the enemy was. What the enemy was.

"It's going to get worse before it gets better," Dean shouted. "Everybody hang on."

As if to punctuate his statement, a blue-white spear of jagged lightning erupted from one of the three computers. Sparks flew and crackled. Black smoke rose several inches, then was ripped to shreds by the conflicting winds. The air howled as if a pack of invisible, flesh-starved wolves had suddenly been set loose.

"Dean, what are these things?" Piper yelled.

"Distortions. Rips in time. We're at a conjunction point. That's why all the phenomena."

A soft-drink can tipped over. The outstretched blueprint curled back into a tube, bouncing against the tape dispenser. A rack of test tubes crashed. A computer monitor, hit by a particularly focused blast, slid six inches, stopping precariously close to the edge of the table.

"How do we make them stop?" Nathan asked.

"We can't. And I'm not sure how long it will last."

The third computer chimed, the sound almost lost in the now banshee scream of the whipping wind.

"John," Dean yelled.

"I'm on it." Holding the mounted lab table, John Evans pulled himself over to the third computer screen. "How do I print?"

"F-nine," Piper screamed.

For a long second the caterwauling wind was all they heard, then the printer beside Dean began to hum. It sucked in a blank sheet of paper and regurgitated the information from the computer.

Holding the table with one hand, Dean reached out and anxiously ripped the fresh sheet from the machine. The paper flapped in his hands like a small white flag. He tried to read the numbers. Then swore. "Not enough, damn it. It's not enough."

Suddenly three of the smaller pinpoints dried up. The wind slowed but didn't stop.

"What's happening?" Nathan asked.

"Room's pressurized," Piper told him. "The air pressure between here and wherever those holes open into is equalizing. Anything from the computers?" she asked Dean.

He shook his head. "If I had more time. I know the basics. But not the details."

"What are we looking for?" Piper screamed.

"Numbers!" Dean yelled, his voice straining to be heard over the roar of the wind. "I believe what we are seeing now is the result of what will be my earliest attempts to breach space-time. That's why the time holes are confined to this room."

"What kind of numbers are you looking for?"

"Calculations. If my theory is correct, Whitey Dobbs can't control when or where he appears. Due to the way he was exposed, his movements are random. Geographically he is pretty much limited to Black Valley, but everything else is a crapshoot. However, he's been making some rather precise appearances. I think he's using these rips to navigate between past, present, and future. I can't believe he's smart enough or lucky enough to know where the next portal will open or how to open one on his own. He must have empirical data."

"How could he get that?"

"From me, or my future self."

"Why would you do that?" Piper asked.

"Because this never happened. Like I said, anything we do now will change the future, but it won't affect Whitey Dobbs because he's in a protective field. Whatever has happened to him, in his time line, has happened – it's our future, but his past. Obviously, when he reappeared in the future, he must have snookered me, taken advantage of my guilt. His unique radioactive signature must allow him to slip through the portals without harm. I don't believe the same is true for others."

"So Dobbs becomes your own time-traveling astronaut," John said.

"Astronaut, but yes, that's about it. Perhaps he was blown into the future and may have stayed there, had it not been for these portals. He was there at least long enough to have the photograph of Mason's daughter altered and triggered to Mason's and my DNA, and he had enough time to get a new blade for his knife, one made of some futuristic metal that's sharper than anything I've ever seen or heard of."

"The computers," Piper screamed. Her words were torn from her and batted about by the persistent wind. "You're trying to re-create the time spurts. That's why you wanted all the clocks, so you could tell how much time existed between events."

"Yes. But there are two variables I hadn't counted on. I thought Dobbs's appearances were related to the rip in space-time created by the explosion. And although that certainly made the fabric more pliable, this latest phenomenon, these time holes, indicates that I am also capable of creating ruptures. And then there is Elijah. For some reason he's not as limited. I think he can sense them, like Piper. And in some cases create them."

"Without those coordinates it will be virtually impossible to stop Whitey Dobbs."

"A forty-five will stop him," John said.

Dean shook his head. "No. There's something else you should know—"

The third computer chimed again. "More," John called, striking the keys, sending the electronic information to the printer across the room.

This time Dean waited, as if superstitious that his early removal had invalidated the data on the preceding pages. The wind calmed enough to risk standing without a grip. His tie whipped behind him like a banner, but he was able to hold the sheet with two hands.

"Yes, yes."

"Got it?" Piper asked.

"Not all, but something." Dean closed his eyes. No time for computers, theories, or trial-and-error strategies. He had to process this new information himself, right here, right now.

Suddenly a spear of jagged lightning shot out of a nearby portal, striking Dean full in the chest, knocking him off his feet. He was aware of falling but not of hitting the ground. His extremities screamed as if a thousand hot knives were flaying his skin.

"Dean?"

Piper's voice was his anchor. He shook his head. His thoughts suddenly a jumble of numbers, memories, and sensory information. His ability to discern reality from fiction, to focus a clear thought, was gone.

"Dean!" she was there, somehow. Lifting him up. Cradling his head in her lap. Her face swam before him, distorted by what appeared to be a foot of churning seawater. He wanted to touch her. To play his fingers across her smooth, white skin. As if that touch alone would quell the burning that seemed to flare from his insides.

His arms wouldn't move. He tried to speak. His words were gone.

"Shhh, it's all right. Everything is all right," she whispered.

Then why was she crying? *Don't cry*, he wanted to tell her. *Don't worry about me. Just had the wind knocked out of me. That's all*. She stroked his hair. He could hear other voices. Familiar. Nathan?

Mayor Peculator. How's it going?

"Dean, can you hear me? Can you understand me?"

He tried to answer, but someone had replaced his tongue with a fat, angry salmon.

"How many fingers am I holding up?"

Dean saw more than he could count.

He could feel hands undoing his shirt, rolling up his sleeves. *Piper?*

"How is he?" Her voice was shrill.

"No visible burns," Nathan said. "Just shaken up, I think. Dean, if you can hear me, try to focus. Try to look at one thing and see that one thing. Concentrate. Let it guide you."

Dean found Piper's face. So beautiful, so fresh. A

field of virgin snow. Worried eyes embossed with tears. *Don't cry, Piper, don't cry.*

Her eyes widened. Dean felt her legs beneath his head tense. Saw the veins in her neck rise to the surface. Her eyes sparked.

He opened his mouth, tried to control the fish that had once been his tongue.

"Dean," Nathan asked. "What is it? What is it?"

They didn't know. They couldn't see her face. Distracted by her worry for him, maybe even she didn't know. Dean closed his eyes, found the word he needed, then pushed it forward with all his might.

"Incoming," he whispered.

The wind shifted once more, a cold, icy saber replacing the hot, dry air from earlier. Then from somewhere faraway and yet very close, the sound of laughter, shattered teeth on fine china.

The laughter of Whitey Dobbs.

34

THE HOLE PULSED large enough for a man to fit through. Whitey Dobbs stepped out less than three feet behind John.

Dean struggled to raise himself up. He pushed out the words. "John, behind you."

Before John could turn to face him, the white-haired demon hooked an arm around his neck. Dean caught the glint of something metallic, almost like electric silver, arch through the air, then plunge deep into the sheriff's chest.

"John!" Piper screamed.

Dean grabbed the table leg and pulled himself up. He lost his grip and fell back to the floor. Piper and Nathan stood.

The knife.

The knife.

Electric silver and blood. It struck again, sinking deep into the sheriff's massive chest. Lying on the cold linoleum, Dean used his elbows to pull himself forward. John was less than ten feet away.

As it arced in the sky the now-crimson quicksilver

blade seemed to quiver with an almost sexual delight. The knife struck again and again.

Dean was close enough to hear the faint *oomph* as it found its mark and plunged deep. John was struggling, trying to raise his arms, trying to block another blow, but the suddenness and ferocity of the attack had left the big man defenseless. Blood bubbled from between his gritted teeth.

And all the while that maniacal laughter, the sound of the devil's merry-go-round. Whitey Dobbs released his grip and big John dropped to the floor like a bloody side of beef.

"How's it hanging, Jimmy Dean?"

Dean froze in place. His face was less than two feet from that of his dying friend. John blinked. As if baffled by this new perspective, as if he were still standing and the world had somehow tilted. "It's okay, John, we're going to get you out of here. We're going to get you help."

Dean grabbed the table leg and again pulled himself up. His body tingled with the aftereffects of the electrical shock. Dobbs still held the blade, and Dean saw his original analysis was correct. It was *quivering*.

"You shouldn't be here, you know." Dobbs took a step toward him. The wind whipped his frosty white hair, tugged on his black and bloody leather jacket, but otherwise left him unscathed.

He knows how to walk through it. How to brace. Nothing magical here, just practice.

378

"Give it up, Jimmy Dean. Haven't you figured it out yet? Science – your science – is nothing. How much more proof do you need? I'm the spawn of Satan. You can't stop me. And unless you are on top of that hill tonight, everyone and everything you have ever loved will be destroyed." He looked at Piper. Her eyes seemed to shimmer with electricity. "Some slower than others."

"You're full of shit," Dean spat, hoping to keep the sheer terror out of his voice. "You're no ghost. No devil. There's nothing mystical or magical about you. You're just a poor, dumb bastard in the wrong place at the wrong time."

Dobbs's eyes widened.

Dean continued. "You were exposed to radiation up on Hawkins Hill. Radiation that lets you walk through time. Those portals. My portals. You're here because of my science, you bastard."

For the barest measurement of time a flicker of fear streaked across the face of Whitey Dobbs. Then in a flash it was gone. But not soon enough. Dean had seen it. *He's afraid of me. No. He's afraid of my mind.*

Anger contorted Dobbs's already dark and fore-boding face. "You're a fool. But you're right. This is all because of you. You and your damn experiments."

He had given up the pretense of devilment. "Do you know what happens to you eleven years from now? Do you want to know? You're the scourge of the earth. Your little time experiment goes *boom*, taking half of Hawkins Hill with it. One hundred and thirty-two men, women, and children die. Not to mention what you do to me."

Dobbs stepped over John's body, as if avoiding a puddle. "Can you imagine what it was like lying in that coffin, thinking everyone was dead? That I was trapped? Buried alive? Then something wonderful and horrible happened. Something hit me, a wave of some kind, burning me from the inside out. For a moment I truly believed I had been sent to hell. Then I woke up, falling, dropping three or four feet from the casket to a floor. A laboratory floor. Your laboratory. Ninety-nine Einstein."

Dobbs stopped and drew his head back. He smiled, an ivory crescent of pure mockery. "You were quite surprised by my arrival, quite surprised."

"That's when I learned it had all been a trick. A ruse. But the trip had not left me unscathed. I was exposed to some radiation bullshit. I would be fine, sometimes for days, then I would feel my skin tingle and find myself somewhere else – and somewhen else. You used me as a guinea pig. Oh, you said it was to figure out how to help me. But I know the truth. I know it was just to feed your morbid curiosity."

"You've screwed up, Dobbs," Dean yelled. "All of what you just said will never happen now."

"So? Changing the future doesn't change me. You told me that yourself. But it can affect the past, your past."

Dean felt the birth of a new kind of fear, something dark and sinister. A warning, deep inside his head, was screaming he didn't want to hear what Dobbs meant. He thought he could hold him off. "Look, I'm sorry for what we did, for what happened. You've got to understand, at the time John and Mason thought you had raped Judy. It wasn't until I explained that you were in the store with me that they realized their mistake. We tried to dig you up as fast as we could, but it was too late. You were already gone."

Dobbs laughed. This time Dean heard the sound of rusted bells. "Don't you get it, Jimmy Dean? I did rape Judy. I had her good. Twice."

Dean felt the world tilting. For a moment he thought he had been struck by another electrical jolt. "That's impossible. You were with me that night."

Dobbs threw his head back and cackled. "You're such a fucking idiot. Fool, I went back after the burial, after waking up in the future, I went back in time and made you my alibi. While my past self was raping Judy in the parking lot, my future self was using you as a cover story."

"So when you were in the store—"

"I had already been buried and radiated, and was flickering through time like poor reception. I raped her and you covered for me. You protected me. You're a fool, Dean Truman, an honest-to-God fool."

Dean felt his head reel. "You said twice."

Dobbs grinned. "Yeah, after making you my alibi,

381

I took another time trip. Just a jaunt, really, twelve minutes into the future and into her bedroom. I was there when she arrived home. So I raped her again. Real good this time. Real good. She must have been impressed by how soon I could get it up. What was your recoup time after doing it, Jimmy Dean? Could Jimmy Dean Jr. be raring to go just twelve minutes after popping? Yeah, I bet she thought about me a lot after that. Remembered what a real man could do to her, for her. I bet the whole time she was with you she was thinking of me, wishing it was me."

"Don't listen to him," Piper implored. "He's trying to unnerve you. He wants you rattled. He needs you alive, but he wants you mentally unstable."

Dobbs whipped his head around, his eyes locking on Piper. "You – you little bitch. You've got a bit of it in you, too, don't you, the radiation. Not as much as me but enough to see things."

The churning wind blew a sheet of paper against his cheek. He slashed it away with the bloody silver knife. "Maybe I should just go ahead and take you now."

Around them the holes began to throb like a beating heart, pulsing from plate size to man size. The wind picked up again.

"You don't have time," Dean yelled. "Your ride's about up." He was suddenly aware he had somehow finished the calculations in his head. At least partially. But he needed more. Much more.

A sheet of white paper stuck out of Dobbs's left pocket. Dean took a chance. "You can't control it without me, can you? Every couple of days the radiation builds up and you have to flicker through time to dissipate it. But without me, without my calculations, you have no control. You appear and disappear at random."

Dobbs gritted his teeth. His black eyes, twin lasers.

Dean continued. "That sheet of paper in your pocket. That's it, isn't it? That has the calculations that tell you the time and place where space-time is malleable enough for you to push through."

"Shut the fuck up!" Dobbs sneered. "Yeah, so what? Just more reason for you to feel guilty. Without you, I couldn't do anything. I guess that makes you my accomplice, my partner."

Then Dean saw it. In some respects it was as remarkable as all the other events combined, as amazing as a person walking backward through time. Astonishing because it involved no science, no tools, no special circumstances. Just a man, an extraordinary man, too tough and too mean to die. Behind Whitey Dobbs the bloody mass that was John Evans was moving.

Dean had to keep Dobbs's attention. "You don't have long this trip. I've done the math in my head, and I think the holes are about to dry up."

John pulled himself up by the table leg. His chest was a dripping red banner. Each movement the result of his massive, incredible will. Inch by inch by inch.

"You've got to leave soon, in one of these holes, or you'll wink out on your own and there is no telling where or when you will end up. And right now you want – no, you need – control."

"Shut up!" Dobbs screamed, shaking the knife at him. The quicksilver metal was less red than before, almost as if it were consuming the blood.

"What about Elijah?"

The question struck Dobbs like the lash of a whip. "Shut the fuck up."

Hit a nerve.

"You're afraid of him, aren't you? You are. I can see it in your eyes. Why? Who is he? What is he?"

The white-haired man offered a full-tooth grin. "He's history." He pulled a slip of paper from his coat pocket. "You are right about one thing, your future self did give me the information I needed to navigate these random time holes. You also gave me the means to free myself from this . . . *hell*, and you've inadvertently given me the method to destroy Elijah."

John stumbled more than walked. Falling forward. Falling on Whitey Dobbs from behind. Dobbs was startled. Reflexively the knife struck, slashing deep into John's left arm. But the big man was beyond pain. With his right hand he snatched the sheet of paper from between Dobbs's fingers, then fell toward the nearest time hole. He had no speed. The knife found his back.

"John, no. It's not large enough," Dean said. The nearest time hole was too small – pulsing, expanding and contracting from the size of a serving platter to as small as a dime, in and out, in and out.

John saw it, too. It wasn't large enough. He would never make it through. With a tremendous display of fortitude, John shoved the sheet of paper into his mouth and dove for the hole.

He disappeared up to the shoulders. The hole snapped shut. John's headless body fell to the floor, a fountain of blood pumping from a heart that didn't know it was dead.

Whitey Dobbs laughed. Thunder roared and lightning flashed through the snow, tracing Dobbs in its electric-white glow.

"Midnight. Midnight be at the top of Hawkins Hill. No guns, no tricks. Be there or be square. And oh, yeah, there's that thing about me killing everyone you love if you don't show. Just a reminder."

Dobbs turned quickly, took two steps toward Piper, then jumped into the largest of the time holes only moments before it closed. They all closed. The wind stopped. Paper fluttered to the floor like ash from Armageddon's fire.

Two hours, less than two hours.

35

PIPER SLAMMED the gas pedal to the floor. The truck's tires chewed snow. Energetic wipers vigorously slashed at the whiteness. She was driving faster than road conditions allowed, but there was no "too fast" tonight. Time was a small, precious, fleeting commodity. As she drove, her mind fought like the wipers, trying to bat away the images of John being decapitated by the very air, of the maniac with white hair, of storms inside and out.

"You can't seriously tell me you plan to meet him?" she had argued with Dean.

"I have to. It has to stop."

"He's going to kill you. No ifs, ands, or buts about it. It's a trap. There's a reason he wants to meet you at that location, at that time. It's a trap."

"I know," Dean answered, but his resolve remained unchanged. She couldn't decide if he was the bravest man she had ever known or the dumbest. But she no longer had doubts about her other feelings. She loved him. And in the end it was that love that made her capitulate.

"Listen to me," he said. "I need your help."

"Anything," she had answered, and realized that she meant it. *Anything.*

And now she was racing across the county on all-but-unpassable roads, racing to the forest department substation to pick up a very specific piece of equipment that may or may not be there.

"What's it for?" she had asked.

"No time to explain. I have to go to the hospital. I don't know if you have time to make it back before I leave."

"Then, I'll meet you on top of Hawkins Hill."

He had started to object, but she stopped him with a kiss. No brush, no peck, but rather a soul-to-soul exchange.

"On top of the hill," she had whispered.

The truck shimmied and shook but held to the road. She pushed the accelerator.

Something tingled in the back of her mind.

Incoming.

THIS WAS THE DANGER TIME. The time when Whitey Dobbs was the most vulnerable.

He had memorized the calculations carefully and knew there was no other way. To arrive where he wanted when he wanted, he would have to spend two hours in Black Valley and travel to the other side of the county. It was sort of like catching a connecting flight – only this connection opened up a world of possibilities. More options than he had ever had before.

It also made it possible for him to be at the top of Hawkins Hill at midnight. That was when the temporal anomalies would be at their peak. That was when his plan had the best chance of succeeding.

And to make matters worse, John had stolen his calculations. It didn't matter. Not even Dean could decipher the handwritten sheet in time to make a difference. Could he?

A finger of panic tentatively touched his heart. He snapped it off. *Screw that*. After being buried alive, no way out, no hope, nothing would ever truly frighten him again – nothing.

Dobbs remembered that night with a clarity that came only from having events carved in your brain with a sharp blade of terror. The coffin was small, suffocatingly small, and shrinking by the minute. Dobbs had broken his knife trying to cut his way out, and even in the dark he could feet hot, salty rivulets of blood running down his arms and splattering on his face as he beat his hands into a bloody pulp on the unyielding lid.

No way out, no way out.

Then he went to hell.

It started with a tingling, an unnerving sensation like spiders dancing on the base of his neck. Then *the wave* – that was the only way he could think to describe it, a wave of white-hot, electric fire that washed over his body from head to toe. It was a pain like nothing he had ever experienced, as if God had taken a soldering iron and was individually branding each and every atom in Dobbs's body.

A pain of pure, blinding intensity. Only he wasn't blind. He could see, and what he saw caused his already fragile sanity to shatter into jagged shards.

Light, a brilliant blue-white light, then darkness, then *fire*. And there was sound, too. Screaming voices, sirens, crying, explosions, laughter. Then fire again. Everywhere. Around him, on him, in him – fire. Yellow-orange and raw-heart red. Fire all about him, yet not touching him. He was inside an inferno – inside. But he wasn't burning.

Hell. He had gone to hell.

Only it wasn't. It would be months before he realized that for one-tenth of a second he had existed in the very heart of a raging explosion as Dean's reactor at the core of the NxTech Research Center went critical, ignited, and spewed debris and chaos throughout time and space.

But during that first moment Whitey Dobbs was sure he had died and gone to hell.

Then he was falling.

The fire was gone. The coffin was gone. Whitey Dobbs fell four feet on to a cold, tile floor. He didn't realize he was screaming until he heard his voice echoing in the large, sterile room. Others were scream-ing as well. Men and women in long, white coats, some carrying clipboards, others working with incomprehensible machinery, all staring at him, reflecting his look of shock and surprise.

He lay on the floor sucking air, breathing like a man who had just surfaced from a deep-sea dive.

Where was he?

Three, four – no, five – people, two women and three men, watched him with frightened eyes. Strangely, Dobbs took comfort from their fear. Then a face he knew but didn't know came out of the group.

Bald and wrinkled, slightly stooped, an impossibly old Dean Truman stared at Whitey Dobbs.

DOBBS SHOOK HIS HEAD, forcing the memory back into the dark closet of his mind. He had to be alert, had to be cognizant; this was the danger time. Though he had lost his notes, he still remembered the basic times and locations, if not the exact minutes and coordinates. It didn't matter. Once he was close enough, he would be able to sense the *thinning*.

The future Dean called it a conjunctive point. "A diaphanous location in time and space, distorted and vulnerable to ruptures."

Fuck that! Dobbs called it the thinning because that was the way if felt. Offering little more resistance than a heavy stage curtain, leaving his body tingling, with a slight metallic taste in his mouth. And on the other side? A different time. A different place.

Dobbs looked around the empty high school, where

he had materialized. A school he had attended twenty-two years ago, present time – but only thirteen months ago, his time. He had never graduated. Never received his diploma.

His boots beat a sharp cadence as he hurried down the hall and out the back door. Snow covered the world in a thick, pervasive blanket. There was no traffic, no sound.

A dead world as white as my hair. Cool.

He headed across the street, behind a row of modest brick homes. A serrated wind sliced across his exposed face and hands. Within minutes he was freezing. His teeth chattered. His lips thickened and quivered. Damn. He had become so accustomed to stepping from one location to another, he had forgotten the brutal harshness of the real world. Sometimes it was easy to forget he was still human.

Human. Hell, he didn't feel human.

The memory of those first days when he had escaped the coffin only to find himself in the future – forty-six years from the time he was buried alive, twenty-four years from the present – was still painfully sharp. Dean Truman was old and stooped, but he was a doctor now. Reluctantly Dobbs let himself be examined. That was when Dean concluded that Dobbs's body was glowing with something he called neorads, whatever the hell that was.

But what he couldn't explain was how Dobbs had gotten that way. Or how Dobbs had been able to survive time travel. "So far, we've only been able to transport inanimate objects," he explained.

"Wait a minute. You did this to me?" Dobbs, who could still feel the electric fire whenever he closed his eyes, felt his anger rising.

"No, no – at least, not intentionally . . ."

It got a bit nasty after that. Dobbs learned he was in a place called NxTech, and NxTech had guards, big guards. Still, it took four of them to pull him off Dr. Dean.

Less than three days later Dobbs felt his skin begin to burn and itch; sparks flashed between his fingers, his vision fuzzed, and then – he was somewhere, some*when*, else.

That was when he realized the severity of his situation. That second hop had been a bitch. He appeared somewhere in the past – far, far in the past. A time before there was a city or a settlement. No roads, no trails, no help. He had made a fire by sparking rocks – *like a fucking boy scout*. And lived off berries, crab apples, and wild onions.

The wildlife was abundant. Too abundant. He saw a bear and heard a mountain lion. This was before he had fixed his knife. He had no weapon, no way to defend himself.

By his calculations, he had been there for a little less than three days when he again felt the sparks between his fingers, the tingling of his skin. He appeared in 1948 in a service station garage, scaring the hell out of a guy working beneath the hood of a '46 Plymouth. He threatened the mechanic with a tire iron, took his money, then hurried away.

Hunger got the best of him. He was eating in the Downtown Daily Diner when a cop walked in. But Whitey was gone before a confrontation. Over the next month, his time, he appeared in fourteen different locations, never staying much more than three days, sometimes less than a minute.

It was hell. Pure, undiluted hell.

When he found himself back in the future, shortly after his initial appearance, he begged Dean Truman for help. Begged. Stupid fucker, it was his fault. But Whitey was quiet. Silently agreeing to an array of different tests.

Dean, who still didn't understand how Dobbs had gotten radiated, had devised a way of siphoning off the excess neowhatchamacallits – enough to keep Dobbs from flickering away every three days or so. But there was a catch, a big catch. He had to use the machine three times a day and he was confined to Black Valley. Anytime he tried to go more than thirty-seven miles from the NxTech building, he would disappear in time.

For eight months Dobbs played their game, pretending to be a good soldier, listening to Dean making promises of a permanent cure, feeling like the world's biggest lab rat. Eight fucking months.

And each day his urge for revenge grew a little stronger, burned a little hotter.

That was when he made the modification to Switch, his knife. It was the first of many improvements.

The wind picked up now. Whitey Dobbs felt as if his feet had been replaced with cinder blocks. *Fuck that*. He saw a pickup truck behind the grocery store. He smiled.

DEAN USED ONE GLOVED HAND to apply pressure to the jaws, while prying the mouth open with the other. Jerry stood behind him watching, grimacing.

On the stainless-steel table sat the severed head of their long-time friend. It had been stored in a refrigeration unit. Frost clung to his short-cropped hair, eyebrows, cheeks, and nose. The skin was sallow. The eyes were open but sightless.

The mouth made a slurpy pop as it opened. Congealed mucus covered the maw, as if a diligent spider had been at work spinning a particularly thick, gummy web. Dean noticed a small nick on the lower left corner of John's chin. He must have cut himself shaving. Had John noticed that? If he had, then he would have known he was going to die today. But he had said nothing. As silent in life as he now was in death.

Six feet away, draped in a hospital-green shroud, lay the corpse, dead only a quarter as long as the head.

Working with a pair of long stainless-steel tweezers, Dean reached into the open cavity and slowly pulled out a wadded sheet of paper. The mucus webbing snapped. Other strands clung to the paper and were pulled thin before breaking.

Dean placed the paper in a tray to his left.

"That what we're looking for?"

"That's it."

Dean mercifully covered the head, then turned to the paper. He straightened it with his still-gloved fingers and studied the results. It was a small slip of paper torn from a pocket-size notebook, the same kind Dean always carried with him. The same kind he had in his pocket now. It was written in ink. He recognized the handwriting as his own. But . . .

Dean felt his heart drop, an elevator without a cable. The paper was nonsensical, a series of numbers and letters arranged in algebraic fashion but meaning nothing. Even what should have been the most basic equation was meaningless.

If Dean had written this, if some future version of himself had written this, then why couldn't he read it? Was he wrong? Had someone else provided Dobbs with the calculations? Was someone else responsible for the time problem? The idea carried the faint odor of relief, release from responsibility – but it was quickly replaced by the realization that if he couldn't translate the equation, and quickly, then everything he held dear was in jeopardy. Still, regardless of who the author was, numbers were numbers, and these numbers literally did not add up.

The phone brayed, jerking him like an electrical

shock. He removed the glove from his right hand and picked up the receiver. Piper began without introduction. "He's back."

"What? He can't be back. It's too soon. Are you sure?"

"No, no, I'm not sure. I'm still trying to get a handle on it. But I just had another one of *those* feelings."

"More debris?"

He could hear the roar of the truck engine competing with the pinched stress in her voice. "I don't think so. I've been trying to quantify the sensations. This feeling has been consistent with . . . with somebody dying."

Dean checked his mental clock. "It's too soon."

"Time doesn't matter to him. Remember?"

JENKINS JONES SLICED the cardboard with a box opener, then rapidly began removing the cereal, tagging it with a price gun, and stacking it on the shelf. The store was brimming with customers, all pushing heavily laden carts, stocking up on whatever they deemed necessary for survival.

The rush had started shortly after the mayor's statement confirming that both the mountain pass and the Willamette Bridge were out, effectively stranding residents in Black Valley. Folks were preparing for the long haul. Products were being snatched from the shelves as quickly as he put them out. He had called in all of his workers. A third couldn't make it, stranded by the storm, but those that had were working at full capacity. It was like the day before Thanksgiving. A madhouse.

Business was great. Except? With no roads, supply trucks couldn't get in. Once his shelves were empty, there was no way to restock them.

"Maybe I should ration it out," he mumbled.

"Excuse me?" asked a woman with an infant. She was pushing a shopping cart filled to overflowing with boxes of hair-care products. *This is what she deems necessary to live?*

"Nothing," he said.

The woman wheeled away. He returned to his urgent task of restocking the shelves.

"Humph." It was weird how some people thought.

Jenkins was far more practical than most. When he learned the bridge was out, he had hurried back to the store, being sure to stop by the state liquor store for a bottle of Jack Daniel's, then the drugstore for a new box of condoms. Just in case.

You never knew when the storm might leave them stranded in the store. The checkers would be scared and nervous, turning to him for protection and security and probably a little reassuring loving.

"It could happen," he told the cereal boxes.

He finished the crate, then headed back to the storeroom. He was counting his supplies when out the back window he saw a white-haired stranger climbing into his pickup truck.

MASON SAT in a thinly padded faux-leather chair. He had no emotions. His nerves, like wires forced to carry a tremendous load, were burned out. Tina was in the hospital. The doctor had given her something to make her sleep. They had successfully reattached her finger but couldn't say if it would ever work again.

John was dead – his big, indestructible cousin. And Whitey Dobbs, the devil incarnate, was back. Alive. Unchanged. Unstoppable.

He sat in the sheriff's department conference room like a gargoyle on a building cornice. Watching, waiting, wondering. He had heard this was their staging area. This was where they would plan their next step. And when they did, Mason would be waiting, to help in whatever way he could. All he asked was a chance to kill the white-haired bastard.

Maggie looked across the room with questioning eyes. A phone, obviously working for the moment, was cradled on her shoulder. The room was virtually empty, save for a few office assistants and part-timers. *She's looking for a cop*, Mason guessed. The fact that she hadn't called on a part-timer meant it was important.

Mason stood. He met her gaze. "What?"

She stared at him for a half breath, then shook her head dismissively.

He took a step closer, casting her in his shadow. "I'm ready. Let me help."

Perhaps it was desperation, perhaps his similarity to his cousin John, whatever the reason, she nodded. "It's Jenkins Jones. He says someone is trying to steal his truck. A guy with white hair. If you could find a couple of regular deputies, maybe Jerry Niles, he could – Mr. Evans? Mr. Evans?"

Mason left the room at a run.

THE DOOR WAS UNLOCKED. The truck cab was as lavish as a luxury car, with real leather seats, tinted windows, and a console that looked like it belonged in a 747.

"Sweet."

Click.

Flip.

He leaned beneath the steering wheel and popped the cover off the bottom of the drive column. Whitey Dobbs found himself staring at a confusing array of wires and circuit boards. "What the fuck?"

He suddenly realized his knowledge of cars, specifically how to hot-wire them, was twenty-two years out of date and virtually useless in the age of computerization.

"Get the hell out of my truck," a gravelly voice demanded from behind him.

Dobbs raised up and found himself staring down the barrel of a wobbling .45-caliber revolver.

"Get out. Now. You drugged-up hippie freak," said the old man. His red-and-white name tag identified him as JENKINS.

"Your truck?" Dobbs asked, then smiled. "Cool."

THIS WAS IT, Jenkins realized. An honest-to-God, real-life, drugged-up hippie freak. His hair was white, freakishly white, and his eyes as black as coal shards. And when the son of a bitch smiled – Jenkins felt his testicles shrink. Jesus, that smile.

The drugged-up hippie freak blinked. Tiny blue sparks snapped between his eyelids.

"What the hell?" Jenkins drew back. The .45 waved anxiously in his hand, seeming remarkably heavy and remarkably small at the same time. He bit his lower lip and steadied his aim. "Raise your hands and get out of the truck."

"I don't think so," the white-haired man said, pointing at him with a knife. "Give me the keys."

"What?" Jenkins blinked in disbelief. "The drugs done fried your brain, boy? This here is a forty-five-caliber Smith and Wesson. Blow the nose right off your face. I got a gun. You only got a knife. I'm the guy in control here."

The drugged-up hippie freak scratched his chin and his fingers. "Think so?" He leaned forward, knife extended. He moved like a snake, moving before Jenkins could react. The knife flashed in the cold air. Striking the gun.

400

Strreenng.

It was an odd, almost musical sound.

Jenkins stared as the gun barrel fell to the asphalt.

"The keys."

Jenkins dropped the ruined weapon.

"The keys."

He unclipped his key ring from his belt and handed it over. The keys jingled like little bells.

The man fished through them till he found one that matched the truck. He stuck it in the ignition. The motor roared to life. Jenkins Jones mumbled.

"What?" asked the man with the knife. "Speak up."

Jenkins was shaking so hard, he could barely speak. He forced the words out. "I said, I – I got condoms in my desk drawer."

36

A FEELING OF IMPOTENCE. As if someone had used an ice-cream scoop to remove his brain, replacing it with a double handful of anxious spiders. The numbers, the numbers – his friends, his secret language. Now, when he needed them most, they had deserted him.

"It doesn't make sense," Dean said, shaking the small sheet of paper dappled with figures and symbols.

"It has to make sense," Nathan moaned. He had been sent to retrieve supplies they would need if forced to play Dean's desperate endgame. He had succeeded only to learn that the crucial information, the information John Evans had died for, was indecipherable. "It's based on your theory."

He was right. *Then, why can't I read it?*

Think, think. Dean ordered the spiders to behave. *Come on. Put one thought next to another.* What was the purpose of the paper? He felt sure this was a list of time fractures, sites that could be used as control points for Whitey Dobbs. A means of traveling without the random factor Dean theorized had been Dobbs's primary state. The sheet was filled with information front and back.

He was convinced there were two kinds of fractures – overt, like the visible, swirling holes in space-time that appeared in his classroom; and covert, weaknesses in the field that couldn't be seen but could be breached by someone doused in sufficient amounts of radiation. It was the latter, he felt sure, that Whitey Dobbs was using to go from one place and time to another.

Dean looked for dates, equations, codes. Nothing made any sense. Nothing.

"You can figure it out, Dr. Truman," Jerry said. His young face was taut. He looked as if he had aged ten years in the last hour.

"Sure he can. You wrote it, or at least you will." Nathan Perkins shook his head. "Time travel gives me a headache. Everything is ass-backward."

Backward?

"What did you say?" Dean asked.

Nathan rubbed his temples with the tips of his fingers. "I said time travel gives me a headache."

"After that."

He stopped his temple massage. He thought carefully. "I said everything is ass-backward," he repeated tentatively.

Dean smiled. Could it be? Could it really be that simple?

Then he remembered something he hadn't thought

of in more than twenty years. "Whitey Dobbs. He had a learning disability."

"Yeah, he was smart as a whip but dismissed as stupid early on. Wasn't until he came to Black Valley that the teachers figured it out."

Dean snatched a sheet of paper from a yellow pad and began to write. "His disability?"

"Dyslexia," Nathan said.

Jerry's eyes widened. "Is that it?"

Dean wrote frantically. "Yes, yes. Dyslexia. It means he reverses numbers."

"So if you wrote the note for Dobbs . . .," Nathan said.

"Then I would have written it backward."

Ten minutes later Dean had filled the yellow sheet with newly translated calculations. It was all there – time, place, longitude, and latitude.

Dates.

Dean recognized one of the dates now revealed. His mind bounced from point to point, each assumption of logic building on an assumption before it. No time to test, no time to question. He worked quickly, efficiently, counting on his own brainpower and intuition.

He stopped and looked up at Nathan and Jerry.

"What? What is it?"

He smiled. "Our best chance. According to these figures, to make the connection to Hawkins Hill at the time he specified, Whitey Dobbs will have to spend two hours in Black Valley and travel from one set of coordinates to another. Piper's right. He's here. Now."

"Oh, sweet Jesus."

"No. Don't you get it? He's here now. And he's vulnerable. If we move fast, we can be waiting at the conjunctive point – set up an ambush and catch him off guard."

Jerry grinned. "Can you tell me where he's going to be?"

Dean nodded. "I've got the coordinates. I need a map."

"Come on. There's a map in the squad car."

WHITEY DOBBS STARTED THE TRUCK. Old man Jenkins stood outside the cab shaking, knees knocking like castanets. Dobbs put the truck in gear, looked at Percy Street, and for the first time noticed the orange-and-white barricades.

"Damn. Fucking construction." He had planned on taking Percy to the old Beal Highway, a back road that would take him where he wanted to go with very little traffic, decreasing his chances of getting caught. "What's the quickest way to get to Beal?"

The old man blinked, mouth agape.

"Beal? Beal?" Dobbs repeated. "Talk before I cut out your fucking tongue."

Jenkins Jones pointed, his arthritic joints making his finger look like knotted pine. "Take Agate to Pearl. It's a one-way street while they expand Percy."

Dobbs slammed the door closed, thought a moment,

then powered down the window. "Why did you tell me you have condoms in your desk?"

"In case you make me do the nasty with one of my young clerks."

Whitey Dobbs cackled, his voice sharp like the crack of electricity.

"It could happen," Jenkins said. "It could happen!" he screamed as the truck pulled away.

JERRY SPREAD THE MAP on an empty desktop. Using a ruler, Dean traced the longitude and latitude.

"This is where he would have appeared after our encounter in the classroom," he said. He circled the location with a pencil.

"That's over at the high school," Jerry noted.

"And this is where he's going." He circled a second location. "Several miles away."

Nathan looked over his shoulder. "That's out in the sticks. Nothing there but trees."

Jerry tapped the map. "And the old Wherrington timber mill."

Dean became rigid. "The timber mill?"

"Yeah, but it's empty. Been abandoned for – what, two years now?"

"How close is that to the ranger substation?"

"Not far – quarter of a mile at the most. Oh, jeez."

"Piper," Dean whispered. "I sent Piper to the ranger station."

*

THE BIG CAR WAS NOT DESIGNED for severe-weather driving. Despite its weight and size, the Delta 88 slipped and slid whenever it struck a patch of ice. Mason didn't care. He pointed the automobile more or less in the direction he wanted to go and pressed the accelerator to the mat.

As a result, he pulled into the rear parking lot of the grocery store just minutes after Whitey Dobbs had left in the stolen truck. Jenkins Jones, the owner, was still standing in the snow.

Mason lowered the window and slid to a stop. "A young guy with white hair. Have you seen him?"

"He stole my truck."

"When?"

"Just now. He just left."

"Did he say where he was going?"

The old man made a face. "He's crazy. Tried to make me have sex with one of the cashiers."

"Where is he going?"

"I told him, I said, 'No way, you son of a bitch. No way am I going to put a condom on and do the naughty with those pretty young girls. You're going to have to kill me—'"

"Directions. Directions! Where the fuck did he go?"

Jenkins Jones smacked his dry lips. "Beal. He asked how to get to the old Beal Highway."

"Beal? What's out there?"

"Trees. That's all. Ranger station, couple of houses, the old sawmill, that's all."

Mason put the car in gear. "The truck? What does it look like?"

"Red-and-white GMC. A lotta chrome. Brand new. You – you tell that son of a bitch I want it back. And I still ain't going to do the wild thing with them young checkers."

Mason grimaced.

"What? It could happen!" Jenkins Jones screamed as the Delta 88 roared away.

U.S. FOREST SERVICE SUBSTATION 1240 was an old farmhouse that had been renovated. What had been a barn was now a garage used to store different equipment, depending on the time of year and the needs of the area. For the past six months an array of fire-fighting gear had been stored there. Thankfully, the need had been minimal this summer, and now, with the world mantled in unseasonable snow, it would likely remain unused for the next five months.

Fred Olmstead was alone at the station, and like the fire-fighting equipment, he didn't expect to be of much use this winter. Since his wife died a year ago, he had pretty much been living in the station. He felt safe here, far away from the constant reminders of his dearly departed bride of forty-two years. In six months he would reach the mandatory retirement age. After that – he didn't like to think about it.

He was sitting in the big armchair in the main

lobby, enjoying his *Reader's Digest*, when a young woman with bright eyes and way too much energy bounded into the room, almost giving him a heart attack.

Her request was nearly as startling as her arrival. "I don't think I can let you have that, missy. That's government property," he told her politely.

"I'm with Westcroft College. I work with Dr. Dean Truman. I can't stress to you how urgent this is."

Fred scratched his two-day-old beard and sucked in his gut, wishing he had taken the time to put on his official forest-green uniform, or at least tucked his ratty red-and-black-plaid shirt into his worn jeans. "Dr. Truman, you say?" He rolled the name around in his head. Sounded vaguely familiar, but he couldn't put a face with it. "Can't really see why a doctor would have much need for that."

The little brunette huffed and stormed past him, marching into the back room.

"Hey, hey! You can't go back there."

She began rummaging through the equipment-lined shelves. He followed her. "Authorized personnel only. I can get into serious trouble if I let you—"

She turned to face him. Her brown eyes were pooled with tears. "Please. You've got to help. You've got to."

Fred Olmstead felt his heart melt. He took a ring of keys off a peg on the wall. "Outside. In the garage. Big key gets you inside. Little key unlocks the cabinet in the back. Can't say what shape it's in or how many supplies there are."

She took the keys and kissed him on the cheek. Her lips felt like warm flower petals. "Thank you."

"Yeah, well – if I get fired, you're going to have to take care of me in my old age," he called as she rushed out the door.

WHITEY DOBBS THOUGHT of John Evans and giggled. *Damn. Always knew the dude was tough, but hell, how many times did you have to kill the man to keep him dead?*

He checked the time. He was doing well. The truck handled the snowy roads with surprising authority. It wouldn't be long now. "Not long at all, Jimmy Dean – not long at all."

He found the irony appealing. That all this was made possible thanks to calculations by Dean himself. How could someone so smart be so stupid? The future Dean Truman had theorized that something had caused fractures and weaknesses in the space-time continuum and had exposed Dobbs to high doses of what he called neoradiation. All true. But what the future Dean Truman did not know was that the weakening of the space-time was caused by him, by his experiments, by his work exploding.

Idiot.

In the few months, his time, that Whitey Dobbs had enjoyed control of his time jaunts, life had been a bit more bearable. As long as he vented the buildup of radiation with a time hop approximately every three days, he wouldn't flicker away unexpectedly. With that control, Dobbs was able to experiment.

TANDY.

His greatest desire was to save his baby sister from being murdered at the hands of their father. His chance came when a time jump put him in the past approximately two months before her death. Dobbs wasted no time. He stole a car and was on his way to Baltimore when he learned the second cruel joke life had played on him.

Approximately thirty-seven miles from the top of Hawkins Hill he flickered away, winking out and reappearing somewhere else, some*when* else, but always within that radius. He tried again and again and again. Each time the results were the same. He was tethered to Hawkins Hill.

The only thing he truly wanted to do, the only benefit to his miserable state of existence, was denied him. He couldn't save Tandy.

The closest he came was a phone call. He was surprised he remembered the number, more surprised when she answered the phone. Tandy. Her voice was small but spirited. A simple hello sent chills down his body.

Tandy alive.

"Hello?" she asked again.

She's going to hang up, he realized. His own voice

seemed to fail him. When he did speak, his words were strained and choked with emotion. "Hello, is – is this Tandy Dobbs?" he asked, knowing the answer but desperate to keep her on the line.

"Yes, it is. Who is this?" Her voice so young, so friendly, open and *alive*.

He might not be able to save her in person, but he could at least warn her, tell her to get the hell out of that house. He talked quickly, urging the young girl to leave home.

"Who are you? What do you want?"

"Just get out!" Then, desperate to impress her with the seriousness of the situation, he told her what was going to happen. He told her the future. She was quiet, deathly quiet.

When she spoke again, it was in a tiny, frightened voice. "Who is this? Melvin? Is this you? Melvin, this isn't funny."

There was a sound like the phone being dropped, and then a new voice, a horrible voice, a voice that screamed in his nightmares every night. "Who the fuck is this? You call my house again, you fucking pervert, and I'll rip off your dick and shove it down your throat. You hear, asshole? You hear me?"

His father. Dobbs physically jerked away from the phone. A cold pall settled over his mind. For a moment, the external moment that stretches between fearful breaths, he was no longer Whitey Dobbs; he was Melvin. The boy. The cowardly boy who had endured his father's beatings and witnessed his sister's murder.

Then his heart shut like a clenched fist around his rage and hatred. More than anything he wanted to go to Tandy, more than anything he wanted to kill his father *again*. There was a newspaper box next to the telephone. He read the date and smiled.

"You hear me, asshole?" his father was yelling in the phone.

Whitey Dobbs laughed. It was a sound Melvin had never made, a sound he knew could chill the bones of the dead.

His father was silent.

"Three days," Dobbs said. "Three days and then you die."

The phone went dead; the world went gray. Then Whitey Dobbs was somewhere else.

His greatest wish denied him, Dobbs had been left with nothing else but revenge – sweet, sweet revenge.

Traveling the time stream, aided by Dean's calculations, Dobbs learned other limitations as well. Although he could go up to four hundred years into the past, he could travel only ninety-eight years into the future – from the time he was buried.

Still, with control came power.

He had caught that arrogant disc jockey, Larry Pepperdine, hunting in the woods ten years before his current time period. The man about died when he saw Whitey. Dobbs knocked him out, cut off his right hand, then traveled ahead to this current time period, where he used it to choke Clyde Watkins.

Larry Pepperdine bled to death in the woods, his body not found until recently. And despite the exact nature of his wound, no one suspected the freshly severed appendage belonged to Larry.

Sweet.

Whitey Dobbs adjusted the heater vent, then started looking for signs to the Wherrington timber mill. He felt a sudden jolt, followed by a sustained shudder, as if someone were raking an electrified brush across his naked body.

What the fuck?

He pulled over. Where? An old sign, rusting and crooked, marked the entrance to the timber mill. No. Not there. He looked behind him. Another shudder. There – back there. Whitey Dobbs turned the truck around, following the impulse. He pulled into the driveway of the ranger station.

THE CABINET WAS IN THE BACK of the barn, just as the ranger had said. What he hadn't said was that there was so much other equipment that getting to it was a chore. Twice, Piper had to back up and start again. She had reached the cabinet and was beginning to search for the right key when the sensation struck her.

He's here.

The thought came to her, complete and without ambiguity. She reflexively crouched, scanning the barn

414

from waist high. The big machines sat quietly. Piper left the cabinet, working her way back to the door.

Here.

Was she imagining it? Letting her fears get the better of her?

The ranger stumbled out the door like a man who had been drinking and crossed the ranger station porch. He stopped at the steps. Turned and looked at the barn. At Piper. His eyes were like hubcaps, his skin paper-white. He tried to speak. Blood bubbled from his mouth, a crimson froth. He fell forward, bouncing down the stairs like a rag doll. A figure stepped out of the door behind him.

Whitey Dobbs.

Piper felt a shiver of electric fear arch between her mind and her heart. Dobbs looked at the fallen man. The silver-bladed knife, now red with blood, quivered. He raised his head, sniffing the air. He turned, his eyes on the barn.

Whitey Dobbs started down the stairs.

THE DEPRESSION IN THE LANDSCAPE was covered by the leveling snow. Piper hit a deep spot, sinking up to her waist. She gasped as the cold clenched her lower body.

Run, you fool, run.

She struggled through the snow, leaving an all too visible gash on the trail behind her. The land rose. She climbed out of the depression. The snow was still several feet deep. Each step was like lifting weights, each stride harder than the one before it. She had found the side door of the barn just seconds before Whitey Dobbs entered. She was sure he hadn't seen her.

It didn't matter. She raised her head. He was still coming. She could sense it. And if she could sense him, chances were he could sense her. The trail vanished into what had been the timber mill parking lot. Piper ran, picking up speed on level terrain. She stumbled.

Don't you fall, don't you dare fall, she chastised. *I'll be damned if I'll trip like some panty-wearing sorority girl in a teeny-bopper slasher movie.*

The building before her stood like the skeletal remains of a once-proud dinosaur, now fossilized in brick and broken glass. A large sign, weathered and hanging slightly askew, marked it WHERRINGTON TIMBER MILL – NUMBER 31 – OREGON DIVISION.

Piper hit the door with her shoulder. It opened half a foot, then stopped, held in place by a thick chain and padlock. Locked? No. It couldn't be locked. She looked back across the parking lot. Although he was not visible, she knew he was coming. She felt it.

The highway was close to two hundred yards away. If she made it to the road and worked her way back to the ranger station, she could get to her truck as well as the gun she kept in the glove compartment.

Whitey Dobbs came out of the woods.

No time, no time.

Piper ran down the length of the building, disappearing quickly around a corner. If he could sense her, then hiding would do no good. But there was always the chance that the sensations went only one way. She found another door. This one hung broken on its hinges. She pushed it open another foot, then slipped inside. She could hide in here. And if he could sense her? Her chances of finding a weapon of some kind were greater in the building than in the woods.

MASON EVANS TURNED TOO QUICKLY into the curve. The Delta 88 took on a life of its own. The steering wheel spun in his hands as the car pirouetted across the black highway. He had driven too fast.

He hit the brakes, locking the tires and increasing the spin.

He cursed as he tried to wrestle the steering wheel under his control. The car left the highway, tipped, and began to roll sideways. The world was a whirling dervish, the sound of screeching metal earsplitting.

The car slammed like a fist into a regal Douglas fir.

I taste blood, was Mason Evans's last thought.

THE BUILDING WAS DARK, too dark, and the air tasted of sawdust and mold. It had a thick, cloying property that made Piper feel as if she were wearing it more than breathing it. She instinctively went to the only light, where she found a flight of stairs. She climbed rapidly, her footsteps sounding like a tennis ball striking an empty building. The mill was three stories tall. The top floor was ringed with windows six feet high that ushered in the dying light of day.

The massive room was empty, save for a series of support columns. The dying sun cast the dust-laden room in ruby hues. The windows, shattered by vandals and backlit by sunlight, appeared like rows of bloody, jagged teeth. Piper realized her mistake as soon as she stepped into the open. By following the light, she had effectively trapped herself.

The sound of footsteps rose behind her. He was coming up the stairs. Piper hysterically searched the empty room for a weapon. She found a two-by-four behind one of the pillars.

A board against a time-hopping madman with a futuristic knife. What would the betting odds be in Vegas?

She had one chance and only one. Hiding behind the first support column, she hoisted the board like a baseball bat. The pillar was barely wide enough to cover her and would not mask her presence for long.

The footsteps grew louder, more deliberate – the stride of a man taking his time. She was trapped and he knew it. The glow of the knife surprised her, casting a bluish cone into the empty room. The glow grew. Her heart was a Gatling gun. She saw the tip of the knife.

Now.

Piper stepped out from behind the pillar and swung the board with all her might, aiming just behind the knife – aiming for what she hoped to be Whitey Dobbs's head. The board struck . . . nothing.

Piper had a moment of surprise before inertia dropped her to the floor. She landed hard. Numbing pain exploded from her left elbow and radiated throughout her body. Her mind seemed to slip; logic was ice, and her thoughts a clumsy skater.

The knife, the knife, the knife.

The electric-silver blade quivered as the cherry-handled knife hung suspended in midair. The sound of clapping came from the doorway. Whitey Dobbs stepped out into the dyed-crimson air.

"Bravo, bravo. Good effort, but poor execution." He nodded toward the knife, which hung magically in the air. "Pretty neat, huh? It's melded to my brain waves. Can travel up to thirty feet."

Dobbs opened his hand. The knife soared across the room, the handle slapping into his palm. "Ain't science grand?"

Piper scrambled to her feet. Pain seared her left arm, but she could move it. Nothing was broken.

Dobbs walked farther into the room. Piper began backpedaling, not daring to look behind her. Her eyes held by the ungodly grin of Whitey Dobbs and the unnatural glow of the electric-silver knife.

"Can you feel it?" Dobbs asked. "Of course you can. You just don't realize it, that's all. You were drawn here, you know? By the same force that let you sense me coming. See, this is where the thinning occurs, where the next conjunctive point will be. I don't pretend to understand it, but the laws of space and time seem to weaken here. Thin, see? For me it's like stepping through a heavy curtain. Once it's thin enough, I can cross over from anywhere within a hundred-foot radius. One step and *poof*, I'm *somewhen* else."

He laughed. The cackle reverberated through the empty room, echoing in Piper's head and heart. Melting sun dyed Dobbs's white hair a sickening pink, the color of raw flesh. "It's not nearly as much fun as it sounds. That's why I've decided to make someone else take my place."

Piper's back struck the wall. Cold air rushed in through the jagged mouth of the broken windows.

Dobbs grew closer. She imagined she could feel his hot breath on her face. An involuntary shudder raked her body.

"Just enough time for us to have some real fun," Dobbs said. He licked his lips.

"Whitey Dobbs," a voice rang out behind him.

He turned. The silhouette of a large man filled the doorway. *John*, she thought for an irrational moment. The man stepped forward. No, not John, but someone large and strong like the sheriff. An ugly cut was etched across the man's forehead, a mask of dried blood covered his face.

"You bastard."

"Mason," Dobbs said, the barest hint of surprise in his voice. "As I live and breathe – two things your cousin John can't do anymore. I knew one of these days he was going to lose his head."

"You son of a bitch."

"So, how's that daughter of yours? Will she ever be able to count to ten again?"

"You're dead. You hear me? Dead."

Dobbs waved his knife. "You really want to fight me?"

"Nothing is going to stop me from killing you. Nothing. Wrecked my fucking car getting here, knocked myself out, probably got a concussion – but that didn't stop me. You think I'm going to let a little knife get in my way?"

Mason pulled three dark red sticks from his right coat pocket and a lighter from the left. He thumbed the flint. A one-inch flame was born. He moved the fire under a trio of wicks. "This is dynamite. You know what dynamite is, don'tcha? *Hiss, snap, boom.* Three sticks is enough to take off this whole floor. Even you can't survive that."

The grin was wiped from Dobbs's face. "You're bluffing. You kill me, you kill yourself and the girl, too."

Mason looked at Piper for the first time. His vision touched hers for just a moment, then flickered away. "Better she die at my hand than yours." He moved the flame closer, a hairbreadth from the wicks. "Now, drop the knife."

A pause. Whitey Dobbs opened his hand. The knife fell.

Piper realized what was happening a moment too late. *"Nooo!"*

The knife stopped three inches from the dirty floor.

"What the hell?" Mason gasped. The knife flew, moving like an arrow. It slammed into Mason hard enough to knock him off his feet, burying itself up to the hilt in his chest. He hit the floor. The lighter and explosives fell, harmless, beside him. His mouth opened and closed as blood foamed between his lips. Then . . . nothing.

Whitey Dobbs walked over and kicked the man in the head. No response. Mason was dead. Dobbs looked back at Piper and grinned. "That was fun, wasn't it?"

Dobbs turned his head like a dog catching a scent. "Damn! It's here."

Piper felt it, too – that electric tingle that preceded something bad happening.

Dobbs opened his hand. The knife withdrew from the body with a sickening slurp. He closed the blade and put it in his pocket, resting his foot on the corpse's hip. "Oh, well. Now that he's dead, he will travel well." Dobbs pushed with his foot. The body rolled once and then was gone.

Piper detected a growing breeze. And something else: the scent of flowers. Flowers in a snowstorm? No. Flowers from another time, she realized. Air was the first thing to cross the barrier of space-time. Which would also account for the tumultuous weather.

Dobbs picked up the dynamite and lighter, flicking the flame to life. He touched the fire to the wicks. A ravenous hissing ensued as the blaze chewed the cords. Dobbs watched as the flame grew closer to the explosive. "Almost pretty, wouldn't you say?"

Piper's head was light. She was hyperventilating.

"I'm glad it's pretty, since it will be the last thing you see."

He was waiting until the last second, waiting until there was no time for Piper to run, to hide, to do anything but die. He dropped the hissing explosives, tipped his head, and disappeared into a ripple of air.

37

LIGHTS FLASHING, siren screaming, the squad car shrieked into the empty mill parking lot. At the ranger station they had found the dead Forest Service worker, Piper's truck, and the one stolen by Dobbs. The abandoned mill had seemed the most likely destination.

Dean was out of the car before it came to a complete stop.

Piper.

Was he too late?

Was she still alive?

The image of Mavis's body twisting slowly in a hangman's noose flashed through his mind. Mavis, Judy, and now – Piper.

No. Not again, not again.

He couldn't let it happen. Couldn't live if it did.

"There," Jerry yelled, pointing to the mill. "On the top floor. By the window."

Dean recognized the small silhouette. Piper. She was alive. A second shadow moved by the window.

Dobbs?

It had to be.

Dean ran to the mill. The door was locked.

"Step back!" Jerry aimed his Smith & Wesson at the lock and shot twice. He kicked off the ruined lock and pulled out the chain. Inside, the police-issued flashlight revealed an inert and empty building.

"The stairs," Dean said, sprinting in that direction.

They took the steps two by two, fueled by fear and desperation. Dean was less than six feet from the top floor when the explosion shook the building.

"Down!" Jerry screamed to Dean as a wave of orange-red flames rushed down the steps and across the ceiling.

"Piper?"

CRAWLING THE REMAINING SIX FEET, Dean found the top floor of the abandoned mill. Support beams creaked and sagged. The windows were shattered. Tiles fell from the ceiling in a rain of fire.

He had no memory of leaving the building. No recollection of stumbling down the stairs and out of the ruined structure.

Piper.

Dean sat on the Jeep's bumper, his head buried in his hands as he sobbed uncontrollably.

Piper.

Each breath seemed an insult, each heartbeat an affront – a reminder that he alone was alive, while those he loved had died. The moment clicked forward, but for once, perhaps for the first time in his life, Dean did not know what time it was.

"Shut up," Jerry snapped.

Dean looked up, staring at the deputy in disbelief. He opened his mouth to speak. Jerry shushed him with a finger. "Quiet. Listen."

A faint sound drifted in the fresh night.

"It's coming from over there." Jerry began to run. Something about the sound pulled Dean to his feet.

"Over here, over here," Jerry shouted. "She's alive."

CLICK.

Flip.

Click.

Flip.

Whitey Dobbs played with his modified switch-blade as he paced back and forth. He was in a window-less medical room beneath the NxTech Research Center, no more than thirty feet from the spot where years earlier he had been buried alive. The room was stocked with typical medical paraphernalia: a reclining examination table, blood pressure gauge, sink, and a large, oblong light extending from a long, sectioned pole, allowing it to be contorted to shine light into even the most unseeable regions of the human body.

The door opened.

Dean entered, bearing a metal clipboard and a smile. His hair was completely gray, and wrinkles webbed from the corners of his eyes and mouth, while dark semicircles hung beneath his eyes.

Dobbs turned his back and quickly retracted the blade. Dean would panic if he saw the blade.

"This is it," Dean said.

Dobbs turned around, mirroring the doctor's own smile. The professor was holding a small black box no larger than a woman's clutch purse and two blue-silver bracelets. A series of three pressure buttons colored red, yellow, and green were the only things visible on the box. There were no wires connecting the device to the bracelets.

"This is it, the prototype of the device that will ultimately save you from the time flux. It's quite a creation, if I say so myself."

Dobbs smiled broadly. "So, how's it work?"

Dean's eyes widened. He never missed an opportunity to cackle about some fucking theory or another. *Smug bastard*. Diarrhea of the mouth, his father used to call it. Dobbs bit his lip to suppress a chuckle.

"The neoradiation that permeates your body is attached not to your physical form but to your bioelectric signature," Dean explained. "Inanimate objects can be forced through the time stream, but because they lack the unique bioelectric chemistry of a living being, they don't absorb the radiation. It's that radiation that is keeping you in flux."

"Fascinating, Doc," Dobbs said with a smile. *Dickhead.*

Dean continued, "There's only one way out of the time stream. Sever the bioelectric connection by transferring the radiation to another living creature. Once we've perfected this procedure, we will find an animal of the necessary size and weight, preferably a sick one, and inject it with poison and transfer neorads to it. After absorbing the radiation, the animal will die rather than bounce around in space-time."

"Interesting," Dobbs said, playing with the device.

"We'll test it tomorrow. If it works, we may be able to use this procedure by early next year."

No fucking way I'm waiting.

"Sounds great," Dobbs lied. "How's it work again?"

Dean laughed and went through the operating procedure once more, assuring Dobbs he didn't have to worry about it, because when the time came, Dean would run the system. But he indulged him just the same. Dobbs forced himself to pay attention.

The familiar tingle began at the base of his neck. He was about to hop again. He asked Dean for a soda. Dean left.

Two minutes later Dobbs and the box disappeared into the time stream.

JERRY WAS PULLING PIPER from a snowbank when Dean arrived. Flaming debris littered the ground around them, melting deep holes in the snow. He shoved the deputy aside and swallowed the girl in a hug.

She was injured. Blood dripped from a dozen small cuts on her arms and face. But she was alive. "Alive. But how?" Dean asked.

"Elijah. It was Elijah." An uncontrollable coughing fit racked her body. Dean waited patiently.

"Elijah?" he repeated.

Piper nodded. "Mason's dead."

Dean felt a new stab of guilt. Mason. He had forgotten about his old friend. And now?

"Dobbs killed him. And he was going to kill me. He lit three sticks of dynamite and waited for the wicks to burn down before disappearing."

"Then how—?"

"Elijah. I think you're right. They can't be in the same place at the same time. But the second Dobbs disappeared, Elijah appeared. He shoved me out the window. I have to thank him." She looked around Dean. "Where is he?"

Jerry was ten feet away. He was holding a charred, floppy-brimmed hat. "I'm afraid he didn't make it." He pointed with the hat. A scorched severed arm lay in the snow.

THE SMELL WAS STRONG, strong enough to make a grown man sick. It was coming from the evidence room, a room under strict jurisdiction. Coye Cheevers wiped his face with the back of his greasy hand and made a decision. Yes, sir – he was gonna let himself in. Had to follow protocol, had to protect the chain of custody. The penalty for failing to do so was most severe.

"Most severe," he mumbled, opening the door.

But the smell. *Ye God*, it was awful. The rest of the sheriff's department might be in shambles, but that was no excuse to let something putrid remain in the evidence room.

No sirree, Bob.

The sheriff was dead. Jerry had said so. Which shouldn't have surprised Coye, since he had seen the sheriff's head roll down the hall like a jack-o'-lantern, but it did just the same. After all, hadn't he seen the sheriff just minutes later with his head still attached?

Yes sirree, Bob.

There was comfort in routine. And keeping the evidence room clean and uncontaminated was his job, given to him by the sheriff himself. It was a job he took seriously. And sticking to it was only right, a sign of respect for the headless sheriff, *God rest his soul*.

The stench was worse inside the evidence room, swelling to near unbelievable levels. *What the heck has gone bad?* he wondered as he clamped a hand over his nose and sucked air through his mouth.

Had someone been in here eating? Left trash behind? That didn't make much sense. Who would want to eat in the bleak, windowless room? A rodent, then? Rat or maybe something bigger. Came in through the rafters to escape the cold and died?

A squirrel or maybe a raccoon?

He scanned the room in quick gestures, anxious to confirm his theory and get the hell out of there. He was looking for the body of a dead animal – a raccoon, he decided. But if it was trash, if somebody had let something spoil, then the penalty would be severe, yes sir, most severe.

He moved deeper, looking behind shelves and sealed cardboard boxes, all tagged and labeled with yellow-and-red evidence markers.

Nothing.

But the stench was the worst here. Coye fought desperately not to throw up. He was determined to find the offending – albeit dead – animal.

"Aha," he cried, seeing the broom closet. It wasn't used for brooms but for weapons, hunting rifles mostly, guns seized for various violations. "Got you now, you dead, smelly varmint." In his mind he had decided it was a dog, not a raccoon – one of those big, black-muzzled, shaggy-haired dogs just like in the Walt Disney movies – except dead and smelling to high heaven and somehow stuffed in a closet.

He opened the door.

Most severe, Coye Cheevers thought as the body of Mason Evans tumbled out of the closet. Piece by piece.

Most severe.

CLICK.
Flip.
Click.

Flip.

Whitey Dobbs played with his modified switch-blade and waited. He was in the men's room, less than twenty feet from the dismantled body of Mason Evans.

Click.

Flip.

He thought of Piper Blackmoore and frowned. She was a unique one. He would have liked to have more fun with her, but that's the way it goes. Now that he thought about it, he realized he had never seen Piper even once in the future. Was he always destined to kill her in every time line? Or had something else happened?

Click.

Flip.

He thought about the plans he had made, working bit by bit whenever happenstance made him appear atop Hawkins Hill. And now it was ready. But Dobbs had decided to make a change – an interesting change.

The role of Nathan Perkins will now be played by Piper Blackmoore, he thought with a crooked smile.

Click.

Flip.

He left the blade out for a moment. The electric silver hummed, sending butterfly wing vibrations through his fingers, up his arm, and into his chest, lancing his very heart – making them one and the same, each an extension of the other. He had modified the knife himself using a new metallic material that had replaced the scalpel in medical procedures. The new metal was incredible, almost alive. The subtle, virtually inaudible hum soothed his nerves and excited his determination.

Time, age, illness – all were words without meaning to him. Yet he was impatient. Somewhere in the ache of his memory he sensed an unquenched *need*. It was a yearning more powerful, more compelling, and ultimately more satisfying than even the hunger.

His appetite was set for *revenge*.

The death of Mason Evans had been quick and unfulfilling. He peered out the small opening in the bathroom door. It was nice to know that where he would travel next was one of the few moments in time where that damnable Elijah could not go.

God, he hated that son of a bitch. Almost as much as he hated Dean Truman. *Almost*.

But even Elijah couldn't stop what would happen soon. In just a matter of minutes space-time would begin to tear, the first rips in the sequence of events that ultimately lead to the explosion of the NxTech Research Center.

To Dobbs it had been just over a year and a half since he had been buried alive on Hawkins Hill. For eight months he had endured the treatments necessary to remain in one time period. Patiently waiting until he had everything he needed to put his plan for revenge into action. Finally the future Dean had completed work on the bracelets, which Dobbs now had in his pocket.

As a safety device, Dean then gave Dobbs a series of handwritten notes, that compensated for his dyslexia and explained where and when many of the time holes would appear and their likely destinations. This gave Dobbs a means of navigating in the time stream.

Idiot.

It was the last bit of crucial information Whitey Dobbs needed to begin his plan of revenge.

Dobbs cracked open the men's room door and watched as the inept deputy entered the evidence room. There was a short scream, then silence.

He laughed out loud. Damn fool had fainted again. He reminded Dobbs of something he had seen on TV long, long ago, a herd of goats that passed out at the first sign of trouble. The deputy was like the goats.

A fainting goat.

He looked in the mirror and smiled at his still-youthful face.

Almost time, almost time. He began to giggle, then was gone.

"WE FOUND MASON'S BODY," Jerry said as Dean and Nathan frantically loaded the last of their supplies into the back of the sheriff's Jeep Cherokee. Dean heard him, the words cutting deeply into his heart, but there was no time for emotion. He continued to work.

"What's all this equipment for? Lights, generators, and what's that suitcase-looking thing?"

"Don't touch that," Nathan said.

Jerry grabbed Dean by the arm. "You don't think you're going to face that son of a bitch without me, do you?"

Dean stopped, stared at the man as if seeing him for the first time. He wiped his face with his hand. *One hour and twenty-one minutes*, his mind whispered. "Someone has to be here in case we fail."

"Then let Nathan stay."

"I need Nathan. He's had some medical training. Besides, Dobbs will tolerate him being there, but not you."

"To hell with him. Like it or not, I'm in this up to my ass. I owe it to the town, to the sheriff, to see it through."

Dean and Nathan exchanged a look. They had expected this.

"Fine, but you'll have to be prepped against radiation poisoning." Nathan opened up a medical bag and removed a vial and a syringe. "Step inside, we don't have long."

The pair disappeared. Dean continued to load the Jeep. Three minutes later Nathan returned. "I gave him an anesthetic. He'll be out for at least an hour. Damn, I hated doing that."

"It's for his own good," Dean said. "You probably just saved his life. Speaking of which, you're not going."

"I have to. You can't do this alone."

"Yes, I can," Dean said with cold determination.

"Damn it, Dean. This isn't just about you."

"You're right. It's about Piper, too. I need you to stay here and take care of her."

"I can take care of myself." Piper stepped out of the building. She had changed into borrowed clothes and was wearing the smallest sheriff's department coat available. It was still too big. She charged, arms swinging, hands lost in the coat. "Besides, I'm going with you."

"What? Like hell you are."

"You going to give me a shot, too? Knock me out?"

"I want you to stay for me. I'm being selfish. I've lost too much already. I couldn't bear to lose you. Not now. Not after all of this."

She had to stand on her tiptoes to kiss him.

"I have to go, Dean. You need me."

"I can—"

"No. You can't. I'm your wild card. I can sense things. Whatever he's got prepared, odds are he didn't figure me into the equation. You need me. And besides, if Dobbs isn't stopped, it doesn't matter whether we go or not, he'll kill us both – eventually."

Dean was quiet. Snow fell in silent feathers.

"She's right, Dean," Nathan said. "He'll kill us. Just like he did the others."

Dean inhaled slowly. He didn't want to do this, didn't think he could do this.

"How can I help?" she asked Nathan, ignoring Dean.

The mayor hazarded a short look at Dean before replying. "I need another gel pack just to be safe. Tell Nurse Atchins it's for me."

She nodded. Dark hair bounced in her eyes. She brushed it back, then saluted. Her fingers just protruded from the oversize coat, making her look like a little girl playing dress-up. But this was no little girl, Dean reminded himself. She had shown more grace under fire than any of them. In many ways, with John and Mason gone, she was the toughest member of their group.

"I'm on it. Anything else?"

"Yeah." Dean removed a small black box from the police cruiser. "Take this. It's a stun gun – police issue, five hundred thousand volts. Press the prongs against the target and pull the trigger."

"Got it," she said, reaching under her coat and clipping the device to her waistband.

"Piper," Dean sighed. "And be careful."

IT'S SWEET, *actually – but also infuriating*, Piper thought as she hurried to the hospital. She had been taking care of herself since she was a child – certainly since the night her mother died, the night Whitey Dobbs was buried alive yet lived to tell about it, lived to *kill* about it. But it was . . . well, kind of nice.

The Black Valley Hospital was busy, too busy. Patients' cries merged with bleating machinery and urgent talk to create a horrible cacophony.

Somewhere, Piper knew, Whitey Dobbs was watching and laughing.

She didn't find Nurse Atchins, but she did find the gel packs. She took two, a backup for the backup, and left the hospital quickly, anxious to be away from the pain and suffering, impatient to get on with it, to take down the monster responsible for all this.

Piper turned the corner and headed for the rear parking lot. She could see the Jeep Cherokee in the shine of the streetlight when something grabbed her from behind. A hand holding a cloth with a medicinal smell closed over her mouth, squelching her scream. She could feel hot breath on her neck as lips brushed her ear and a voice murmured, "Playtime."

38

"HOW LONG?" Nathan asked.

"We've got one hour and thirteen minutes," Dean answered without pause. "Before Whitey Dobbs appears on the Hill."

"And you think this will work?" Nathan asked.

"It'll work. It has to work."

Nathan took a slow, deep breath. "A bullet would work better."

"No, it wouldn't. I'll explain later." They labored for several minutes in silence as Nathan backed up the Jeep Cherokee and Dean attached the horse trailer. "What about the calf?"

"Old Man Peterson's got a sick one that's not going to make it. It's on the way."

Dean nodded. Despite what he had said, he was not at all confident. Too many unknowable factors remained. Whitey Dobbs would appear at precisely midnight – somewhere on the crest of Hawkins Hill, but the exact location was unclear. This meant Dobbs could just as easily appear behind them as in front of them. Using equipment pilfered from the college, Dean planned to set off a series of early detection devices that might alert them mere seconds before Dobbs fully materialized. There were twelve units in all, and each would have to be calibrated on the scene. A task that would take a minimum of twenty-one minutes.

The early warning was crucial. There was only one tranquilizer dart – one chance to take Whitey Dobbs down.

Then . . .

In the mill Dobbs had bragged to Piper he was going to have someone take his place in the time stream. That meant he had to have some way, some device, to transfer the neorads to another living creature, obviously one of them. But if they could knock Dobbs out first, then Dean should be able to transfer the radiation to the sick calf, leaving Whitey Dobbs as normal as the next guy.

In *theory*.

"Piper's been gone a long time," Dean said, locking the trailer hitch in place.

Nathan pursed his lips. "She may be having trouble finding the gel pack."

Dean frowned. Do we really need that?"

"I hope to God not, but I'll feel better if we have it. I want to take as much first-aid equipment as we can and pray we don't need it."

"We could leave without her," Dean suggested.

Nathan laughed, a strained, fragile sound. "She would just come on her own. I'll go find her."

"Hurry," Dean urged.

One hour and ten minutes.

PIPER WOKE in the dark, stirred by the sound of a baby crying. Her head seemed to swell and shrink with each beat of her heart, and there was a funny taste in her mouth. She tried to move. Her left hand struck wood, her right hit something cold and metallic.

The baby cried.

No, not a baby – a phone.

She found it lying next to her head. She pressed a button and the phone lit up. The green display was uncommonly bright in the thick darkness, revealing . . .

Her breath caught in her chest.

"Hello? Hellooo . . . ," a voice sang from the phone.

Her eyes rolled wild with terror.

"You awake?" the voice asked.

She couldn't breathe, couldn't think. Couldn't believe.

"How you doing down there?"

Piper put the phone to her ear, dousing the green light and blinding her to the horror.

"W-where . . . where . . ."

Laughter bled from the phone, merging with the oppressive darkness.

"Where are you?" Whitey Dobbs said, finishing her question. "In the ground, on the Hill. Dead and buried. Well, except for the dead part. All in good time."

Buried? Piper couldn't think.

"How do you like the accommodations? Built it myself, you know. Oh sure, it's not fancy like those funeral home coffins, just wood and nails. But it gets the job done.

Piper couldn't speak.

"Built it and dug the grave over a ten-year period – your time. For me it's been about three weeks."

Already the air was beginning to taste stale and heavy with carbon dioxide.

"There's an air tank next to you. I recommend putting on the face mask. But breathe lightly. You've only got about an hour. Oh, and only a few minutes left on that phone. I recommend you call that boyfriend of yours right away. If you can get through."

"Let me out of here, you bastard, *let me out!*" Piper screamed into the phone. She was answered with a dial tone.

WHITEY DOBBS LAUGHED. His voice echoed across the top of Hawkins Hill.

The grave was an inspired idea. If Dean had the paper describing where and when Dobbs would materialize next, then he knew he had at least an hour to prepare all sorts of nasty surprises. But now . . .

Now Dean would have to spend that hour looking for Piper. Leaving him completely unprepared for Dobbs's arrival.

Originally it was Nathan Perkins who was going to occupy the grave. But that all changed when he met

Piper and when he saw the look of affection between her and Dean. No, this was better, much better.

DEAN KNEW there was a problem the moment he saw Nathan. The fear shining in his eyes was magnified by the thick lenses of his glasses. He was trotting and carrying two gel packs.

"Where is she?" Dean screamed before Nathan reached him. "Where?"

Nathan shook his head. "I don't know. No one saw her at the hospital. But it's pretty hectic. They could have missed her."

"The packs?" Dean asked.

"I found these lying over by the alley."

The spark of fear that had been burning in the back of his mind flared into a roaring blaze.

"It doesn't mean anything," Nathan offered.

His voice seemed muffled and far away, muted by the roar of the increasing mental fire.

"Maybe she just got lost?" Nathan offered.

"In Black Valley?"

Nathan shook his head. Obviously he, too, suspected the worst. "We've got to go on. We have to stop Dobbs."

Dean's cell phone rang – "Für Elise." The sound seemed woefully out of place with the severity of their situation. For a moment he was unsure of what to do. The phones had been hit-or-miss for days. That his was now working seemed somehow suspect and ominous.

It continued to ring. Nathan met his eyes. "Answer it. It may be Piper."

Piper. That snapped Dean out of his paralysis. He hit the answer button and put the phone to his ear. He could hear crying from the other end of the line. "Piper? Is that you? Piper? Where are you?"

"Dean." Her voice was raspy and strained.

"Piper, where are you?"

"Hawkins Hill. It's Dobbs. I've been buried alive."

The fear that had been burning in his mind now rushed to his heart.

"I don't have long. The batteries are almost gone."

The stress in her voice acted as a calming influence on Dean. He had to gain control, had to clear his head. It was Piper's only chance.

Click. The sound was faint, innocuous, most likely just static on the line. But when Piper spoke again, the volume was lower.

"He knocked me out. I – I think it was chloroform. I woke up in the wooden coffin."

Wooden?

"Describe it to me."

"It's just . . . wood. He said he made it himself. Bastard seemed proud of it. I can't see much. Just from the glow of the phone. Hold on."

The snow was falling again. Flakes as large as half-dollars fluttered and danced in the shifting night air. A cry of pain from the phone.

"Piper!"

"I'm all right. Just cut my arm on a nail. He sucks as a carpenter. It's a wooden coffin. I don't see any latches. The lid must have . . . have been . . ." She choked back a sob. "It's nailed shut."

Nailed.

"Dean, I've an air tank."

Thank God, Dean thought, sagging with relief.

"Dobbs said there's only about an hour's worth of air. You've got to hurry."

An hour. "Piper, listen carefully. First of all, I think Dobbs may be listening."

"Very good," said a new voice, a male voice. "How's it hanging, Jimmy Dean?"

Dobbs.

"Let me out of here, you *bastard*!" Piper screamed.

Whitey Dobbs laughed, the sound more obscene than any swearword Dean had ever heard.

"Ignore him, Piper. Try to stay calm. I don't want you to go into shock. Understand? I think he's fishing for some kind of reaction here. He wants us to squirm. I'm going to get you out of there. I promise."

Again Dobbs laughed. The phone began to beep. The battery was going.

"Science, Piper, science. Do you understand?" Dean repeated louder this time.

The line hissed, then Piper's voice weaker now, "I – I think so. Dean, I just want to know—"

The phone went dead. Dean stood there for a

moment, the silent machine still pressed to his ear as if it, like a person, could catch a second wind.

"Dean, what are we going to do?" Nathan asked. He had heard only half the conversation but enough to know what was happening.

"Change of plans. Come on. We've got to hurry."

39

FIFTY-ONE MINUTES.

Forks of lightning jabbed the sky as the Jeep Cherokee climbed the wash-out dirt road that crawled along and up the side of Hawkins Hill. The moon was up and, finding a hole in the dome of gray clouds, doused the landscape in yellow secondary light.

The town lay to their left, an assortment of shapes and shadows sprinkled with pinpoints of light, growing smaller as they climbed. The dirt-etched trail was pocked with gullies. It stopped ten feet shy of the circle of snowless, burned earth that marked the crown of Hawkins Hill.

It's almost as if even the road is afraid to venture farther, Dean thought.

The parallel beams of the truck sprayed new light into the dead area. They stopped and shut off the engine but left the lights on. Nathan worked quickly, taking out a large black case and a medical bag and placing them on the ground beside the Jeep. He opened the bag and carefully began filling the tranquilizer dart.

"You sure about this?" he asked.

Dean stood gravestone still, though something moved behind his eyes. Nathan wasn't sure if it was fear or hatred or something much, much worse.

"I'm sure."

Nathan looked around the crest of Hawkins Hill. It was rife with chronol disruptions. Just beyond the apron of light, things seemed to move in the shadows.

The air began to whistle. "They're all over the place. Time holes." Something moaned in the darkness, as if the very night were in agony.

"Let's get these lights up," Dean said.

Nathan and Dean worked quickly, setting up two powerful battery-operated klieg lights. Bright white waves shoved back the shadows, revealing the crown in sharper detail. The ground was soggy but snow free. Something had recently burned a circle about sixty feet in circumference. At the edges snow was piled more than a foot and a half high, giving the impression of an ivory-walled arena.

And somewhere out there, under there, is Piper.

The sky cracked with thunder. Lightning flared, revealing a writhing boil of black-purple clouds. The moon was gone. The ground trembled.

"Jesus, she could be anywhere," Nathan moaned.

"No. Dobbs told her she was on the Hill."

"And you believe him?"

"On this I do. It's just the sort of thing he would like. Brings it all full circle."

Dean scanned the landscape. "And the fact that cell phone worked underground means—"

"She's not buried deep," Nathan finished. "Still, that's a lot of ground to cover in just – what?"

"Thirty-six minutes and twenty-two seconds."

PIPER HAD NO CONCEPTION of time. She felt as if she had been underground somewhere between ten seconds and ten years. *How can things be happening fast and slow at the same time?*

But she knew this was no temporal fluke, rather a matter of perception.

She could feel panic waiting at the periphery of her emotions, but she fought to keep it at bay. Dean would find her. She knew he would.

Yeah, but will I still be alive when he does?

Suck air.

The medicinal taste left by what she assumed was chloroform was not helped by the stagnant, slightly metallic taste of the bottled air. She tried to breath shallowly, sparingly, conserving oxygen.

Stay calm. Don't go into shock. Wasn't that what Dean had said? She tried to remember the exact words.

Try to stay calm. I don't want you to go into shock. Understand? I think he's fishing for some kind of reaction here. He wants us to squirm.

Piper shifted in the coffin, body contained but her mind roaming free. *Science, Piper, science. Do you understand?*

449

Do you understand?

She rolled the thought around in her mind. There was more here than was being said. Dean had known Dobbs was listening. So he couldn't come right out and tell her what he wanted her to do.

So, what did he want her to do?

Shock!

The stun gun. Piper reached beneath her jacket. Her fingers closed on the black metal box and carefully pulled it free. She felt for the controls in the dark, trying to see it in her memory. There was a power setting. She turned it to maximum. At least, she hoped she did. With her left hand she explored the surface of the homemade coffin, searching for the nail that had jabbed her earlier. She found it with her fingers. The nail had missed the coffin side, extending at least an inch and a half into the box.

Again she remembered Dean's words. Was she right? Did she understand the clue?

She had to chance it. She moved the stun gun to the nail, took away her left hand, and fired.

SIXTEEN MINUTES.

Despite the cold, Dean's flesh was covered in sweat. He wiped his eyes with the back of his hand and tried to concentrate on the area in front of him.

The clearing had been raked. Freshly turned brown earth replaced the topsoil, masking all signs of recent digging. Dobbs had covered his tracks well. Dean suspected the grave would have been dug some time ago and camouflaged. A rusted shovel with a weather-worn handle found just inside the clearing confirmed his theory.

Dobbs had been prepared – ready.

Had she gotten his message? And even so, did she still have the stun gun? And would it work? In theory, yes, but . . .

It was easy to underestimate him, to categorize Whitey Dobbs as a bully, a madman with a knife, a fool.

He might be crazy, but he's not a fool, Dean reminded himself. Dobbs had a keen mind and a gift for strategy. The fact he had convinced a future version of Dean to aid him was proof of that. And now, without the time to set up an early warning system, they were essentially blind as to where Dobbs would appear.

None of that mattered. All that counted was Piper. He had to save her, had to get her out of that grave in time. If not . . .

Twelve minutes and fifteen seconds.

He had divided the clearing into a series of grids. Nathan searched in one area, Dean in another. But it was difficult to stay focused and follow the pattern. The wind had picked up, hurling skiffs of snow into the clearing and further impeding their search. In the blaze of the powerful klieg lights his shadow stretched out before him.

Something moved on the ground. He stopped.

One, two . . . Was it a fluke, or had it worked?

Three, four . . .

"Nathan," he screamed.

Five, six . . . Dean dropped to his knees. Worms – beautiful squiggly little worms. Using the stun gun, Piper had sent an electrical charge through a nail and into the earth, causing the worms to climb to the surface.

"Here! Nathan, she's here."

Dean began to dig.

THE EARTH WAS SOFTER HERE, yielding easily to the flashing shovels. Nathan worked as fast as he had ever worked, ignoring the burning in his muscles and the jagged bolts of pain in his back. Two feet . . . three . . .

It wasn't fast enough.

Whitey Dobbs would be here soon – too soon, and they were not ready. Nathan hazarded a look to the Jeep Cherokee, where the tranquilizer gun and medical supplies waited.

One shot. They had only one shot.

Four feet . . .

"How long?" he asked.

"Five minutes and fifteen seconds," Dean answered without looking up.

Nathan's muscles were on fire. Something snapped in his back. He faltered.

"You okay?" Dean asked, his face sheathed in

sweat, his eyes wide with fear and desperation.

Nathan nodded and continued to work, ignoring the scream of pain that flashed through his body. He looked back at the Jeep.

It seemed so far away – far and woefully inadequate.

. . . four and half feet . . .

The shovel struck wood.

Both men paused, eyes meeting for the briefest of moments.

"Piper!" Dean screamed, striking the top of the homemade coffin with his shovel. "Piper, can you hear me?"

No answer. Were they too late? Was she even alive?

"Dean," Nathan said.

"Three minutes," Dean answered without being asked.

Three minutes?

"We've got to—"

Dean dropped the shovel. "Keep digging. Get her out of there."

"Where are you going?"

"To stop Dobbs."

THE RIFLE WAS NEITHER HEAVY nor light; it just was. The barrel shook as Dean took aim. He blinked away saline pebbles.

Two minutes thirty-one seconds.

He could feel the pressure of the trigger against his

finger. More sweat. He blinked again. Their air smelled of ozone. The hair on his arms and neck stood on end, registering a mild yet growing charge of electricity.

Two minutes ten seconds.

His finger jerked.

The gun fired. A puff of blue smoke. The dart! A flash of silver – then gone.

"No!" Nathan screamed as the sound of the shot reverberated in the static-thick air.

Dean dropped the now worthless weapon on the ground and ran back to the grave.

"The dart!" Nathan screamed.

Dean stepped into the grave. The lid of the coffin was fully revealed. Piper was right – the top of the box had been nailed into the wood. "Any response?"

"We've lost the dart," Nathan said, ignoring his question. "We've lost our only chance."

Dean pulled on the wood top. It cracked but didn't move. "Help me get her out."

"No hope, no hope," Nathan cried. He climbed out of the grave.

"Nathan. Nathan? Where are you going? Help me get her out. Nathan, what are you doing?"

His words flagged behind him like smoke in the wind. "Stopping Whitey Dobbs."

40

NATHAN FELT A LIGHTNING STORM FLASH beneath his skin, as if his very cells were being ignited, individually set afire at the exact same second. *My God, is this what it's like for Piper?* he wondered.

A blue-purple whirlpool opened in the center of the clearing. Whitey Dobbs rippled into existence as if reality were a still pond and he were a pebble. He stood less than twenty feet away.

For half a beat it was as if he was there and not there at the same time. *Like seeing between the seconds.* Then he blinked, becoming suddenly, completely, and dangerously real. An evil, smiling creature with dead-man's hair.

"How's it hanging, Jimmy Dean?"

Click.

Flip.

"You're not Jimmy Dean," Dobbs said, more amused than hostile.

Dean had specifically said no guns except for the tranquilizer rifle. He was convinced conventional weaponry wouldn't work. More than that, he was sure it would be used against them. It wouldn't be the first time Nathan had broken the rules. He reached behind his back.

The nine-millimeter Glock snapped free of the holster.

HE FELT HIM before he heard him. Whitey Dobbs. His presence announced in every fiber of Dean's body. The irradiated hilltop gave them all a hint of what life must be like for Piper. He took a deep breath. A new countdown was underway.

Piper.

The grave was silent. Dean's fingers throbbed from his efforts to rip the top of the coffin off by hand. The nails held firm. He tried to work the shovel beneath the lid, but the curved bowl wouldn't fit.

Laughter, as raw and electrifying as any lightning bolt ever hurled by Zeus, crackled across the clearing. The left corner of the shovel slipped beneath the lid – less than an inch, but more leverage than before. Dean pushed down. The nail squeaked and moaned in protest. The lid rose slightly as the metal was pulled from the wood.

"A gun," Dobbs said.

Dean moved to the second nail.

"I'm disappointed," Dobbs said. "Do you really think a gun can stop me?"

There was a fingernail-on-chalkboard quality to his voice, as if his words, like the knife, were made of something different from what they seemed. Both mercurial. Both deadly.

The second nail began to move.

"Whitey Dobbs!" Nathan spit out the name like a man who had just taken a hearty bite of something vile and sour.

The lid rose a half inch. Dean moved to the middle nail. Working as fast as he could, resisting the urge to look in the coffin, willing himself not to look behind him, not to watch his friend's suicidal showdown with Dobbs.

"I can't get over how old you guys are," Dobbs mocked. "Do you realize how bad you look? Though not nearly as bad as John and Mason. One lost his head and the other fell all to pieces."

Whitey Dobbs laughed again. Dean shuddered with revulsion. The third nail began to move.

"Tell me, Nathan, how's that bride of yours? Maybe after I finish you, I'll finish what I started with her."

"You bastard! I swear to God I'll kill you!"

"Naw – you've already tried that. Dead and buried, remember? Can't say as I really cared for it."

The third nail was out. Two to go. Dean blinked sweat from his eyes and moved to the next. His arms quivered with exhaustion.

The fourth nail moved. Or had Dean imagined it? He was so tired, he wasn't sure; he could no longer trust the feeling in his own limbs.

A gunshot – the sound amplified by the cold, dark air – shuddered across the hilltop.

No! Dean screamed in his mind.

The fourth nail gave. He moved to the last, working from mental programming more than conscious thought. Praying against hope he was wrong – that a bullet could do what had to be done, could stop a monster.

The last nail moved.

Nathan screamed.

A thick bolt of lightning jagged across the length of the sky.

The scream was so high pitched and raw that it rang in his bones like a bell.

Don't look, don't stop.

Dean dropped the shovel and grabbed the lid of the coffin. He had to free Piper, then . . .

What? Save his friend? Run? Face the devil!

Using his legs for leverage, Dean began raising the wooden top. The wood popped and cracked in objection. It was heavier than he thought – heavy and unwieldy. His hands slipped. The lid dropped. He caught it. It felt as if his joints were being pulled from their sockets. The move exhausted the last of his strength. He held the lid a quarter of the way open but lacked the muscle to move it higher.

The screaming had stopped. A lugubrious black wind moaned through the trees. The ozone-rich air seemed to hum with a power all its own.

"Piper," Dean whispered, begged.

Something grabbed him from behind, gripping the fabric of his coat and jerking him out of the grave. The coffin slammed shut.

On his back and beyond exhaustion, Dean looked up into the ageless face of Whitey Dobbs.

"How's it hanging, Jimmy Dean?"

41

DOBBS SMILED. Small white teeth, symmetrically even, were displayed in an oblong grin. "Not fair digging up the dead." He grabbed Dean by the shirt and yanked him to his feet. Hair as white as a bloodless face flapped in the growing wind.

"I'm impressed you found her." Dobbs looked over into the grave. "A shame you were too late."

Dean pulled away. He took a step toward the grave.

"No, no . . ." The knife was suddenly between them. The vibrant sheen of the quicksilver switchblade pulsed in the glare of the klieg lights. "We've got a lot to do. Ticktock, ticktock."

Time. How much time?

Dean turned, scanning the crest of Hawkins Hill. The air churned with whirlpools and eddies – sink-holes cut in the very fabric of space. He found the spot he was looking for, and beyond it . . .

Nathan. The mayor lay on the ground in a growing pool of blood. The gun he had used lay impotently beside him. Dean rushed to his friend.

"Oh, he's alive," Dobbs said behind him. "Just a little nick, that's all."

Nathan struggled to raise himself up. Dean dropped to the ground and helped him into a sitting position, propping him against the side of the Jeep. His leg was sheathed in red. A deep gash, just below the thigh, continued to bleed. "Hang on, buddy. You're going to be all right."

"Bastard. His knife. So fast."

Dean took off his belt and cinched it around Nathan's leg just above the cut, praying it would stop the bleeding or at least slow it.

"Piper?" Nathan asked. He saw the answer in Dean's eyes. His head dropped. He sobbed quietly into his chest. "Bastard," he whispered.

"Oh, boo-hoo, boo-hoo," Dobbs chanted. "The clock's ticking, boys, and I've a schedule to keep."

Time?

Five minutes and twenty-two seconds, answered the silent clock perpetually running in the back of Dean's mind. *Five minutes.*

"We've got to stall him," he whispered to Nathan.

"Can you guess what's next, Mr. Scientist?" Dobbs asked.

Dean stood slowly. "No. But then again, I'm not a sick monster like you."

Dobbs's right eye twitched. Just a flicker. The only sign of anger. Dean began moving toward the spot he had chosen earlier, hoping to draw Dobbs away from Nathan.

From his pocket Whitey Dobbs pulled a pair of chrome armbands connected to a small metal box. "Do you know what this is?"

Dean knew it had to be something to transfer the neorads. He played dumb, letting Dobbs talk and eat up time.

"No?" Dobbs said. "You should. You made it, or at least, you will make it."

Dean continued to move.

"This is the little device that is going to make me normal and you history – literally." Dobbs threw his head back, laughing at his own joke. Dean took another step toward the center of the clearing.

"You're the one making a trip," Nathan shouted. He had recovered the gun. Unable to stand, bracing his back against the Jeep, he aimed at Dobbs. "A trip to hell."

"No!" Dean shouted as he rushed toward his friend. He kicked, striking Nathan's outstretched arm as a shot exploded from the barrel. Flames punched the sky. The gun fell to the ground. Dean kicked it under the vehicle.

Nathan's eyes flared, his face a sculptured look of betrayal. "Why?" he choked, his breathing labored. "I could have killed him."

"You don't understand. Killing him would only make things worse. The only way to end this is to give him what he wants."

462

From behind them came the sound of hands colliding. Whitey Dobbs applauded. "Very good, very good. Now you're getting with the program. And tell me, Jimmy Dean, what is it I want?"

Dean turned, surveying the timeless man. "You want me to take your place. You want to be human again."

Dobbs opened his hands in a who-me? gesture. "How do you surmise that?"

"The radiation that's keeping you in a state of flux," Dean said. "It's attached to your bioelectrical field. I suspect that under the right circumstances the radiation, the neorads, can be transferred from one person to another."

Suddenly Nathan understood. "Then one of us would be the ghost – the man trapped between the seconds."

"And Dobbs would be just a man, albeit a dangerous one, still a killer, but human. Killable."

"Why now?" Nathan asked.

"The conditions have to be just right. Tonight, at this location, we are in the midst of one of the time rips caused by the NxTech explosion. Even as we stand here, we're all being irradiated. But not enough to affect us permanently. This increased radiation, however, should make it easier for Dobbs to transfer the neorads."

"Oh, listen to Mr. Smarty-pants. Mr. Knows Everything," Dobbs taunted. "For your information, there will be other opportunities, but I wanted this one. Do you know why?"

Dean looked across at the man with the throbbing knife. "Because in less than six months a newborn will appear, seemingly out of nowhere. His name will be Elijah."

Dobbs arched an eyebrow, clearly surprised by Dean's analysis.

"Elijah?" Nathan asked. "How does he figure into this?"

Dean looked at him. The hurt still remained, but the sense of betrayal had diminished. "Both Dobbs and Elijah are so thoroughly irradiated that they can't appear in the same place at the same time. But unlike Dobbs, Elijah was born that way. He's been off limits his whole life. But if Dobbs is human, then he can touch the infant."

"And kill him," Dobbs added.

Dean smiled. The expression was so out of place with the moment that Dobbs shook his head. "What's so funny, Jimmy Dean? Share."

"It won't work."

Now Dobbs smiled. "Oh, you're going to stop me?"

"Doesn't matter whether I do or not. Your plan won't work. You can't kill Elijah that way."

Two minutes and thirty-four seconds, Dean counted in his head, praying he was right.

"What the fuck do you mean I can't kill him? You

464

watch me, you son of a bitch. I'll make a baby-kabob out of him."

Dean laughed.

Nathan frowned, worry written on his face.

"What's so fucking funny?" Dobbs demanded.

"Dean?" Nathan asked.

"Sorry, it's just – well, our friend could use a physics lesson or two."

The knuckles on Dobbs's right hand turned white as his grip on the deadly knife tightened.

Perhaps to distract him, Nathan asked, "Why, Dobbs? Why do you hate Elijah so much?"

The night was quiet. Even the wind seemed to have taken pause to listen.

"Because Elijah is my son." He looked at Dean. His eyes were smiling. "My son – and Judy Truman's."

God parted the sky with lightning.

Two minutes.

Dean felt something break loose from his heart, a huge iceberg of pure emotion; he felt it move with cold certainty, through his veins, up his body, and into his brain, where it shattered into a thousand icy shards. Whitey Dobbs had just confirmed what Dean had come to suspect less than an hour before.

But the effect was still devastating.

When Dobbs raped Judy the second time, he was already irradiated – meaning the child was born with the same time-hopping affliction as Dobbs.

Baby bones.

Elijah.

Dean now knew with absolute certainty that there was nothing buried under the floorless basement of his home. The blood trail had been caused by Judy's search for the child, not her efforts to hide it. The infant was neither stillborn nor murdered. He had simply disappeared, warped in time to the future or the past.

"I see you're beginning to understand," Dobbs said. "Wherever he appears, I cannot, and his abilities are not as random as mine. He has greater control, blocking me from so many places I've wanted to go. But not from *now*. This three-day period is rich with time pools, making it difficult for either of us to remain for very long – making it easier for me to do what I need to fucking do to be free *and* get revenge on you and my damn child."

Judy, Mavis, Piper – all murdered because of their association with Dean. He had killed them, all of them, as surely as Dobbs himself.

Dean wore his shame in his face, his eyes.

Dobbs saw the sudden slouch of Dean's shoulders, and he smiled, lips pulled back, revealing a perfect row of ghostly white teeth embedded in pink gums. Young gums. He saw the pain he was causing and was excited by it, inspired by it. "You know what I regret, Jimmy Dean? I regret that I didn't get a chance to enjoy Piper the same way I enjoyed Judy."

"Don't listen to him, Dean," Nathan called, his voice hollow and weak. "He's afraid of you. He knows you're the only one smart enough to be a threat. He's trying to rattle you."

"You know," Dobbs said, tapping his lips with his finger, "it may not be too late. Why, I bet the body is still warm."

Piper.

Dobbs moved fast, too fast. He was at the grave before Dean could react.

The wood screeched and popped as Dobbs jerked the lid off.

"Piper!" Dean screamed, rushing to stop Dobbs no matter what it took.

But Whitey Dobbs had stopped on his own – frozen. His face suddenly as white as his hair.

Dean reached the grave and peered in.

The coffin was empty.

Piper was gone.

42

THE AIR SNAPPED with the hiss of a thousand snakes. Skiffs of snow, skimmed from the surrounding banks, wafted across Dean and Whitey Dobbs, settling in the now empty coffin.

Empty.

How? Where? Had Piper been whisked away like Dobbs? No. That didn't make sense. Then, where?

Dean's heart now began to race, energized by one thought and one thought only: Piper was alive. *Somewhere – somewhen.*

Whitey Dobbs screamed. The color returned to his face like a crashing surf. What civility he had managed to fake was now replaced by a beast, a monster, the true Dobbs that lived beneath his skin. If murder had a face, then this was it.

One minute and thirty seconds.

Dean left the grave, racing toward the center of the clearing, dangerously exposing his back to the demonic madman with the magic knife.

"Where is she?" Dobbs demanded. *"Where the fuck is she?"*

Dean found the spot he had selected earlier, and stopped. He turned, prepared to accept the full extent of Dobbs's fury. But Dobbs wasn't behind him.

Nathan screamed in pain as the white-haired man jerked him to his feet. He walked toward Dean, dragging the mayor behind him. "You've screwed up, Jimmy Dean. It's amazing, really. I mean, you got so much of it right."

He stopped less than three feet from Dean. Pulling Nathan to him, Dobbs pressed the pulsing knife to the mayor's throat, dimpling the skin. "And that's the problem."

One minute and twenty seconds.

"What was I going for here was poetic justice," Dobbs continued. "Your life for mine; you condemned to wander the time stream forever, while I take care of business here in the real world. And unlike me, you would not have the benefit of a Dr. Dean T. Science to help you sort it out, gain control, and understand it all."

One minute and ten seconds.

Dobbs continued. "That's why I tried to destroy your oh-so-smug beliefs. But you had to go and be so clever, so very damn clever. And a clever Dean Truman who can travel in time" – he shrugged – "Well, that's a state that is just unacceptable."

One minute and eight seconds.

"You've left me no choice. I've got to kill you or fuck you up pretty bad – while your old pal Nathan

469

takes my place in time. I wonder how smart you will be without your arms and legs?

"Hey, remember the joke about the science experiment and the frog? A scientist says, 'Jump, frog, jump.' The frog jumps six feet. The scientist makes a note, then cuts off the frog's front legs and says, 'Jump, frog jump.' The frog jumps three feet. Scientist makes a note, cuts off the two back legs, and says, 'Jump, frog, jump.' Frog just sits there. He says it again, 'Jump, frog, jump.' Nothing. The scientist takes his pad and writes: cutting off all its legs makes a frog deaf."

Whitey Dobbs cackled, the sound almost as sharp as the knife. "Get it? Deaf. Oh, you scientists kill me."

Somewhere in the dark periphery something growled. A tree branch snapped.

"See, you've left me no choice but to conduct my own experiment. To see if Dr. Dean Truman is still as smart after I cut off his arms and legs."

Dean's stomach muscles cramped. Fear sang in his ears.

Whitey Dobbs leaned closer. He pointed the knife at Dean. "Jump, frog, jump."

One second.

Dean jumped.

"Down, Nathan!" He grabbed the hand with the knife, jerking it with all his might, pushing the lethal blade away. Dobbs held Nathan firmly with his other hand, but he could bend.

"Get down – *down*," Dean repeated.

470

Nathan doubled over at the waist. Dean stepped aside, still holding Dobbs's knife hand.

Time.

There was whistling in the air. Then a thump, as if someone were testing a cantaloupe for ripeness.

Whitey Dobbs looked down. A long silver tranquilizer dart protruded from the center of his chest. He looked back at Dean, perplexed. He opened his mouth to speak, and his face gave birth to a grin. "A dart? A tranquilizer?"

"No. We replaced the tranquilizer with a drug to stop your heart. You know, the stuff they use for lethal injections."

Dobbs started to say something, but the words became wedged in his throat. He let go of Nathan. Dean released his grip as well. Dobbs stumbled backward, his left hand grabbing his right arm, then his chest. He clawed at the dart but couldn't remove it. His body was betraying him. He fell to his knees, his muscles in spasms. Spittle bubbled in the corners of his mouth. His eyes rolled back in his head.

Whitey Dobbs fell backward on the ground, his body twitching as if being repeatedly struck by invisible bolts of lightning.

"Look out," Dean warned. "It's going to snap."

Suddenly Dobbs's body glowed electric-white, a blue whirlpool opened up, and the white silhouette that had surrounded the young man snapped inside.

The body of Whitey Dobbs lay motionless on the ground.

Dean grabbed the gray box they had taken from the sheriff's department. He dropped the case on the ground next to Dobbs. He removed the dart, then opened Dobbs's shirt. He put his ear to Dobbs's chest.

"Nothing," he reported to Nathan. "He's dead."

"Dead?" Nathan said, as if the word were some exotic fruit that defied description. "You said he couldn't die."

"Not the way you were going to do it." Dean applied orange liquid to the man's bare chest. Nathan squatted next to him, both leaning over the body of Whitey Dobbs.

"What do you mean, not the way I was going to do it? A bullet versus what, poison?"

"Yeah, something like that." He sat back and looked at Dobbs. "How's he look?"

Nathan shrugged. "He's in perfect health, except for, you know, being dead. But where did the dart—"

"Come from?" Dean finished. "Remember when I fired prematurely? I actually shot it into one of the time holes. Once I fired the dart, I had ten minutes and thirteen seconds before it would reappear and strike its target. I had to keep Dobbs talking for that long. And in the right spot."

"So it's over?" Nathan said, his voice sagging with relief. Then his eyes widened. "Oh, no! You feel that?"

Dean nodded. "Incoming," he whispered, then looked over his shoulder as the air rippled less than ten feet away and a smiling Whitey Dobbs winked into existence.

43

HIS EMOTIONS WERE STRIPPED like the gears of an old stick-shift jerked one time too many. Panic had given way to surprise, then relief, confusion, and now fear. Just seconds before, Nathan had thought he was more afraid than he ever had been or ever could be. But as Whitey Dobbs took a step toward them he realized he had been wrong.

Dean stood up, stepping in front of Nathan and the body.

Dobbs looked at the ground, at the boots, jeans, jacket – at his own dead body – and shook his head. His face burned with anger. He closed his eyes for a moment, as if seeking control. "Don't you know it's impolite to kill someone? And for the second time?"

"How can he be here?" Nathan mumbled. "He's dead. He's dead on the ground and he's here."

"Protected field theory," Dean said.

"Screw that. Dead is dead."

Whitey Dobbs cocked his head. "Yes, I must admit I've wondered the same thing. And what happened to the mayor? How did he cut his leg?"

Nathan was confused. Dobbs was the one who had cut him.

"It's like this," Dean said, his voice falling into the relaxed, authoritative cadence of a natural teacher, as if explaining the presence of a man and his corpse were the same as explaining an algebra problem. "If I were to shoot you on Tuesday, would that affect something you had done on Monday?"

He didn't wait for an answer. "Of course not. But let's assume that what you did on Monday was go into the future to Wednesday. Since you did that on Monday, killing you on Tuesday would not affect your appearing on Wednesday."

Nathan shook his head. "If this is Dobbs from an earlier time, then why didn't the later Dobbs remember?"

"Because the loop wasn't closed. Dobbs is part of the time flux – that's his dominant state. When he drops out of flux, he has to return to the protected field for the circuit to be complete. Think about it. To begin with, Dobbs was appearing randomly. For that matter, so was Elijah as a baby. How many times do you think he appeared in the middle of a rock or partially fused with a tree? How many times did he appear and die?"

"I don't remember any of that happening," Dobbs said.

"Of course not, because the loop wasn't finished. Once you die, the neorads leave your body. You drop out of the protected field. You become normal, like the rest of us, but because the rads didn't complete the loop and because you're part of the flux, then it's as if you never appeared."

Dobbs smiled. "So I'm immortal?"

"Almost."

"Cool," he said, looking at his own body. "Damn cool."

"There is one catch, however." Dean turned, talking to Nathan now – his face showing that he desperately wanted Nathan to understand what he said next.

"Remember that radiation is attached to the body's living bioelectrical field. So when the radiation is presented with two identical bodies, it will try to attach to both. As a result, it will pull both bodies apart, cell by cell, and create a cascade effect within the protected field."

"Two bodies," Nathan whispered. That was why Dean had prevented him from blowing the son of a bitch's head off. He gave Dean a nod, then crawled over to the body and the gray case. They had brought the medical supplies for themselves. Now their greatest defensive weapon had become their greatest offensive weapon.

Nathan removed a syringe and drew a light amber liquid from a vial labeled EPINEPHRINE, a heart-stimulating drug.

"What's that?" Dobbs demanded.

Nathan plunged the needle into the chest of the newly departed Whitey Dobbs.

"What's he doing?"

Nathan removed two tan paddles, then pressed a pair of buttons on the control unit of the defibrillator. He removed one of the gel packs from the box, tore off the end, and applied the gel to the two paddles.

"I said, what is he doing?"

Whitey Dobbs was coming toward them. Dean stepped in his way. Nathan saw the flash of Dobbs's knife. The defibrillator hummed to a high pitch. A needle on a small yellow indictor bounced. "Clear," Nathan screamed, pressing the paddles against the dead man's chest.

On the ground the body jumped but remained lifeless.

The living Dobbs was still coming. Nathan pulled the knife from the dead man's hand.

"Dean."

He turned.

"Catch."

DEAN CAUGHT THE KNIFE in his left hand and quickly transferred it to his right. In his fist the blade, which had become dull, almost gray, suddenly came alive, flaring into living silver. It hummed, sending tiny reverberations up his arm and throughout his skeleton. *The knife is somehow connected to its user*, Dean noted. It was both frightening and exhilarating.

Whitey Dobbs stopped and spread his hands. "You? You're going to best me in a knife fight?"

Dean held the knife out like a crucifix, as if warding off a vampire. His hands were trembling.

"Okay, you've got a knife, my knife. Now what are you going to do with it, Jimmy Dean?"

Dobbs feinted to the right. Dean turned to follow. Dobbs moved to the left. He lashed out. His blade caught Dean's shirt, slashing through cloth and into skin.

Whitey Dobbs laughed, the sound of crackling electricity.

Behind him Dean heard Nathan cry out, "Clear!" Again the body on the ground jerked. Dean dared not look, but he saw Dobbs hazard a glance. He lunged forward, blade first. But the white-haired man, twenty years younger and far more experienced, dodged the strike with a simple turn of the body. He hit Dean with the back of his hand.

Dean stumbled. The taste of blood and bile mixed in his mouth.

"You really suck at this," Dobbs jeered.

"Clear!" Again Dean was aware of movement behind him. A jerking body? Had it worked? Would it work?

"Time to have some fun." Whitey Dobbs took a step forward. In desperation Dean did the last thing expected. He threw the knife, tossing the only weapon that stood between him and certain death. The move caught Dobbs by surprise. He tried to dodge, but the spinning blade slashed through his coat and cut a deep, red swatch across his side before tumbling harmlessly to the ground.

Dobbs reached down and touched the wound. His hand came away soaked in blood. "You son of a bitch. You cut me. You cut me."

The pain of the fresh wound was lost to anger. Dobbs's face pulsed red, accentuated by the milk-white hair.

He charged.

Behind him Dean heard the sound of someone suddenly gasping for breath. He looked over his shoulder. Nathan was holding what had been a corpse by the arms, pulling him to his feet. The revived and now radiation-free Whitey Dobbs blinked, his mouth opening and closing like fish in an aquarium, trying to orient himself.

Dean's attacker stopped, careful not to get too close. "My, my, my – he is a handsome fellow, ain't he? You know what your problem is, Jimmy Dean? You talk too much. Thanks to you, I know that the only way I can be killed is if this good-looking fellow and I come into physical contact. And that ain't going to happen."

Dobbs laughed. "You fucked up, boy, fucked up big time. Now you've got two of us to deal with."

"Think again, asshole." The voice came from behind him. Whitey Dobbs turned. "Jump, frog, jump." Piper Blackmoore struck him full in the face with the shovel.

"Piper?" Dean gasped.

She was covered in dirt and scratches, but she was alive. And pissed.

"I passed out. Snapped out of it when . . . when you cracked open the coffin." She was clearly short of breath. "Climbed out," she gasped, "while Dobbs was busy with you. Hid in the woods . . . till now."

"You!" Dobbs exhaled.

She hit him again. Dobbs stumbled backward.

"Now!" Dean screamed.

Nathan hurled the revived Whitey Dobbs into the stumbling Whitey Dobbs. Death had cleansed the first Whitey of the neorads, but the other was still radiated. In the second before they collided Dean saw a look of complete awareness and fear flash in both faces.

They struck like exploding flares. A sunburst of light and energy erupted in the spot where there had once been two. The sound of their screams echoed eerily even as the neorads tore flesh apart, cell by cell. Tiny particles like brilliant phosphorescent flares spewed into the night, arcing and winking out of existence before falling to Earth.

Then silence.

Silence.

EPILOGUE

SPRING FELL on the valley community like a shower of golden sun. The town of Black Valley consumed the warmth with a gluttonous joy. The pass was open and the U.S. Army Corps of Engineers promised to have a temporary bridge erected across the river by summer. The restoration to the sheriff's department was complete by the time Jerry Niles officially became sheriff on April 30.

The announcement that the city was rescinding its offer to NxTech had been the source of much concern. Many saw it as the death knell for the onetime timber town. But without Dr. Dean Truman's assistance, the lure of moving to the remote Northwest was considerably diminished.

This news was quickly blunted, however, with the announcement that Nathan Perkins was starting a new company, a business that would begin production, by summer's end, of a new substance, a liquid silver stronger than steel, lighter than plastic, and as sharp as a laser. Droplets of this substance had been collected from the scorched earth atop Hawkins Hill.

Dean Truman and Piper Blackmoore were officially married on June 16 during a quiet ceremony in City Hall. Two weeks later, after a honeymoon trip to the Caribbean, the couple returned to the battered house that had for so long been Dean's home and prison.

They remained there for three days, until early one morning they woke to the sound of a baby crying. The lights revealed a newborn still swathed in its mother's blood, lying at the foot of their bed. They killed the baby.

The child's death occurred under strict medical supervision and lasted exactly forty-one seconds before the baby jolted back to life. The neorads were safely transferred to a dying dog. The dog quietly disappeared.

Child in hand, completely free of neorads, the couple left the old house for good. There was no longer anything to hold them. No bones in the basement, no ghosts in the shadows.

They moved to a new home on the Washington coast, where Nobel Prize-winning physicist Dr. Dean T. Truman wrote and published what was soon heralded as the definitive work on the viability of time travel. The paper concluded, in no uncertain terms, that such a phenomenon was impossible and only a fool would waste precious seconds of real time in the worthless chase of imaginary science. Eight university studies lost funding or lost interest, abandoning the subject for loftier pursuits.

For now, time would continue one second followed by another.

And in the interim, mother and father would devote their energies to loving the amazing gift they had received.

They named the baby Elijah.

OTHER PAN BOOKS TITLES
AVAILABLE FROM PAN MACMILLAN

JIM BROWN
24/7   0 330 49098 2   £6.99

MICHAEL DAY
SLIDE   0 330 49224 1   £6.99

RAY HAMMOND
EMERGENCE   0 330 48595 4   £6.99

ERIC FULLILOVE
BLOWBACK   0 330 49099 0   £6.99